Also by Trista Russell

Going Broke
Fly on the Wall

Chocolate Covered Forbidden Fruit

Trista Russell

URBAN BOOKS LLC

Urban Books
10 Brennan Place
Deer Park, NY 11729

ISBN 978-0-7394-7406-8

Printed in the United States of America

Dedicated to . . .

**The Final Passengers' of
Chalk's Ocean Airways Flight 101
(family and friends)**

The Longest Flight March . . . 101
Lift up your head to the rising sun, Bahamaland. *
March onto glory, your bright banners waving high. *
From Alice Town to Porgy Bay the news traveled on a high sigh.
"Mommy won't be home for Christmas, a plane fell from the sky."
Rumors say, "Trees talk in Bimini," but even they stood still to mourn
this mighty act that God knew of since they were each born.
He had the plane's final flight plan fifty-eight years ago.
He knew who would arrive late and who just shouldn't go.
Who knew they had one last sunset, one last word, one last goodbye?
Who knew that a boarding pass was really sentence to die?
Faces, hugs, kisses, and talks all gone . . . only memories remain.
But even the memories won't last longer than this shocking pain.
National news shows the video back to back to back.
Along with the NTSB ruling out a terrorist attack.
But at least then we'd have someone to blame,
We'd have some hateful criminal to name.
Someone to hunt, capture, and brutally maim . . . no kill.

Instead, the list of names just grows longer up on Spook Hill.

Sure, on Bimini we have our share of drama,

but we treat every older lady as though she's our mama.

This is why Mrs. Genevieve and Mrs. Salome will be missed,

Bimini offered Sabrina, Barto, and Sabrea a love they couldn't resist.

It used to be nice to hear Chalks spanking the blue waters,

until it took away two sets of mothers and daughters.

Sophie and Betthany, Jackie, and Nyesha gone too soon,

The plane should've been here earlier this afternoon.

Mr. Don and his grandson, Jervis, also went up that day,

Their earthly bodies came down, but their souls continued upward.

Pressing onward, marching together, steady sunward.

Channel ten news reported no survivors that day,

But on the island of Bimini we all survived to say,

Lift up your head to the rising sun Bahamaland,

Til the road you've trod leads unto your God,*

March onto glory, your bright banners waving high.*

From Alice Town to Porgy Bay the news traveled on a sigh.

"Mommy won't be home for Christmas, a plane fell from the sky."

Written by Trista Russell (a girl from Bimini, Bahamas before anything else).

---

*From the National Anthem of The Bahamas, written by Mr. Timothy Gibson

Acknowledgements

What you are about to read is actually the first book that I ever wrote. It just so happens to be the third one to be published. However, it had to be that way. Why? I'll tell you. With two books published prior to this one, I now have somewhat of a following, and within that group beats one heart that the message within these pages will change. There is one life that would've missed God's voice had this book been published before the others. God uses the least of His servants to spread the Word, and yes, even in a work of fiction such as this. As with anything that shines a tad bit of inspirational light, this book has stirred up the enemy, but I thank God for a praying family.

I was able to keep the main male character of this book holy simply by observing the way certain men of God live their lives day to day. Because they love the Lord and put Him before anything else on this earth, I must honor them: Reverend Everett Russell (my father), Pastor Larry Ferguson (my pastor), Minister Phillip Russell (my brother), Reverend Rupert Rolle (my uncle), Reverend Olsworth Russell (my uncle), Reverend Carlise Russell (my uncle), the late Reverend Hosea Moss (my uncle), Minister James Lee, and Minister Sherman Moss. Because I have lived under the same roof with at least six of these men (at various times in my life), I can attest that they are who they proclaim to be—men of God.

I thank you, God, again, for your undeserved grace and mercies in my life. I would also like to thank and acknowledge my immediate family: my other and better half, Steve Burris—God gave me you and I love you; my parents, Reverend Everett & Mrs. Zerlean Russell; my siblings, Roslyn (and Mike), Phillip (and Stefanie), my nieces, nephews, and other relatives near and far. Because of what I have chosen to do with my life, and because of what I write about, you have all been subjected to a certain amount of cruelty. But what some people don't know is that no weapon formed against us shall prosper.

Thanks to my publisher, Carl Weber, authors LaTonya Williams and Joy King, my editor, Lisa D'Angelo, and my agent Sha-Shana Crichton. Thanks also to my friends who guided me and this story during the time I was originally writing it: Pastor Robin Johnson-Green, Ms. Hermione Forde, Erica Calderon, and Roshunda Slaton. We all fell in love with Isaac together and grew closer to each other through this book. Ken Hadley, Lori Sanchez, and Angela Redmon, thanks for reading it in adavance and giving your honest opinions.

To my readers: my books *Chocoalte-Covered Forbidden Fruit, Fly On The Wall,* and *Going Broke* were among many that you could've selected from, but you chose me, and I am grateful to you for your support. If you are that one person that is spoken to through these pages, please go to *www.TristaRussell.com* to write to me.

Chapter 1

My Favorite Sins

"It doesn't matter how the surface got slick, or if it's shaven at all. Men will take it nappy, braided, dreaded-up, or parted to the side as long as it's good," was my answer to Madison's question of why I had chosen to use a $4.99 bottle of hair removal cream instead of joining her for a $45 bikini wax. First off, at twenty-two years old, and a recent college graduate, my spring break days should've been over, but she and Yvette convinced me that one last wild hooray was what we needed. So we were Daytona Beach bound for Black College Reunion Weekend.

Madison made the hotel arrangements, I secured the rental of an Escalade, and Yvette was *supposed* to find out the who, what, where, and when of all the events that weekend. Instead, all she did was extend invitations to everybody and their mamas. I still can't believe that she talked me into letting Kantrell tag along. The "Kantrell" idea didn't sit too well with Madi, but funds were tight and she realized that rental car and hotel expenses were cheaper divided into four.

"Neat, break me out," Madison said after putting her bags in the back and hopping in the front seat. "This is a kick ass truck." She looked around at the black leather interior.

She was more of a sister to me than my older and biological sister, Tyann. Sometimes she felt more like family than my two brothers too. Madi and I had been best friends since the sixth grade. I met her on the first day of middle school. And although she was always the one to get the cutest guys, I managed not to strangle her. It was no secret why men flocked to her, her smooth dark brown complexion and slightly slanted eyes were just the beginnings of her unique beauty. Madi's mother was a Blackfoot Indian, which blessed her with the type of long wavy dark hair we black women pay tons for. Her father, Reverend Isaac M. Flack, Pastor/Teacher at Mt. Pleasant Missionary Baptist Church, was very protective of her, his only daughter.

People based what Madi should act like on who her father was, but she was just the opposite. In middle school she talked Yvette and I into skipping classes by hiding in the restroom and standing on top of the toilets. She schooled us on not showing our report cards until *after* the weekend. We all tried the smoking thing, but gave it up when we realized that buying weed cost more than buying school lunch. Plus, the more we smoked, the more we wanted to eat; we just simply couldn't afford both.

After having our hearts broken in the eighth grade, we made a vow that love was a game we weren't grown enough to play. In high school we broke the vow but learned that we *still* weren't sufficient to or for love.

Love got us grounded, put on daily progress reports, and on the special prayer requests list at church. Shit, love even got one of us crabs, and with us sharing the same clothing so often, gave it to the other. We still don't know who caught it first and where from.

Yep! We were Daytona Beach bound. It was 5:29 P.M. and as I pulled out of her driveway, the front door eased open and Reverend Flack stepped out wearing a tight fitting black tank top and a loose pair of black slacks. Saying that he was sexy, fine, hot or cute was like describing a Jaguar as just another four-door car. He was 6'3 and 215 pounds of firm chocolate tenderness. If I had three wishes, the first would be to make him not be Madi's father; my second wish would be for just one night alone with him without a Bible in sight; and last I'd ask for forgiveness. The fact that he was single just made him more delicious.

Eight years prior, in 1995, Reverend and Sister Flack were to attend the National Baptist Convention in Charlotte, North Carolina. The night before their flight, one of the church deacons had a car tire blowout, and while walking to the next exit to get help, he was struck by an eighteen-wheeler and killed. Mr. and Mrs. Flack decided that she'd go to Charlotte alone, and Reverend Flack would stay to comfort the family and help them make arrangements. If the funeral wasn't right away, he'd join her later that week for the end of the convention.

Bianca Flack, along with 103 other passengers, perished on Northeastern Air flight number 672 when it crashed six minutes after leaving Fort Lauderdale Executive Airport. Reverend Flack was devastated by the loss of his wife. His faith dangled between him questioning God and finding a reason for why he had to suffer this way. It took him almost a year to get back into the pulpit.

After battling the tragedy within, Reverend Flack got back on his feet and delivered the Word with a new meaning and with more vigor than anyone else in the community. To my knowledge, and as far as Madison knew, he hadn't been with a woman since the loss of her mother. He dedicated all of his time and effort into spreading the Word, bettering the neighborhood, and making sure his children found everything they needed in him.

"This man really thinks I'm still twelve. Why did I ever come back here after college? I have to move out real soon," Madi said, rolling her eyes as he walked toward the truck. "I thought he was asleep."

Mr. Flack approached and I quickly asked the Lord to help me not stare at his bulging biceps or his beautiful brown eyes. This man could quickly become one of my favorite sins. He could easily pass for a thicker and slightly lighter complexion version of Denzel Washington. It may sound farfetched, but the man was all that.

Though he was forty-two, he didn't look a day over thirty. He maintained his youthful appearance working out at the local gym five days a week. He smiled as he got closer to the vehicle and his pearly white teeth gleamed like piano keys playing behind his dark brown lips. Each step he made toward us made his dress slacks fall against his thick thighs and the print of his masculinity was in 3D.

He folded his arms and partially leaned into the vehicle. "So, you were just going to leave, huh?" He smiled at Madi and pushed her playfully.

"Daddy," she leaned over and kissed his forehead. "I thought you were sleeping. I didn't want to bother you."

"I was reading up on tonight's Bible study scriptures."

"Umm," she continued sarcastically, "with your eyes closed?"

"There was an interesting verse . . ." he mumbled, "on the inside of my eyelids."

She touched his head and I wished I were one of her fingertips. "I thought I'd let you rest."

"Thanks for being considerate, but you know that I like to see you off." He looked over in my direction with a smile. "Hey there, Miss Thalia Tyree." I tried hard not to blush, but it was too late. He always called me by my first and last name. Saying it had a nice ring to it. He reached over Madi to shake my hand. "What's up? How are you doing?"

"I'm fine, Reverend Flack," I delivered without drooling.

"What did I tell you about that Reverend and Mr. Flack stuff?" He laughed. "Isaac is fine with me."

"Sorry, I always forget." I smiled.

"I haven't seen you at church in quite sometime." It had been about four or five months since I visited Mount Pleasant.

"I find myself grading papers all weekend long these days." As I responded he seemed to be staring at my lips, or maybe he was just watching my lies form. "You'll be seeing me within the next few Sundays."

"I'll be looking forward to it." He let go of my hand. "Well, I won't hold you two up any longer. You girls have fun at the family reunion." Isaac reached into his pocket, pulled out a phone card, and placed it in

Madi's hand. "I know that your cell phone only goes as far as West Palm, so use this." He smiled. "Call me when you get there." He took a step away from the vehicle. "Drive safely."

I slowly reversed the truck and let up the windows. "Family reunion?"

"I've got to move out." She shook her head.

I looked over at Madi. "You told him that we're going to a family reunion?"

"It's Black College *Reunion* weekend." She buckled up. "We're all black and like family, we went to college and we're reuniting."

"Whose family reunion are you *supposed* to be going to?"

"Vette's." She laughed.

"You're twenty-two. I don't understand why you're lying to him." I was a little confused. "He's so down to earth, you can tell him anything."

"Lia, c'mon, he gave me a damn phone card."

"Because he cares," I continued in a mumble. "I wished my dad gave a shit." My father married a woman he barely knew five months after my youngest brother, his fourth child with my mom, was born. "Be glad that your dad is even around."

"I know." She thought about it. "I guess he's cute sometimes."

"Sometimes?" I said. "Let's try every goddamn day of the week and every hour of every day." I raised my voice. "That man is off the chain."

"Yuck, I don't mean like that you pervert." She turned the volume up on Sean Paul's cute ass singing about how he gon' stick to some chick like glue. If I were glue I would be all over Mr. Flack.

* * *

For a while we drove in silence and enjoyed the glow of the streetlights, and then the question pierced the peace. "You think Trell and I will finally have our long awaited fistfight this weekend?" Before I could laugh she continued. "I think it would give me closure."

Years ago, in our high school days, Madi and Trell were friends until they fell for the same guy, Derek Cowan, in the tenth grade. As if turning them against each other wasn't enough, he asked them both to the senior prom. Derek, a senior, and a star football player, was truly a demon seed. He fueled a tremendous fire, telling them both that the other was saying nasty things about her. Madi and Trell ended up two words away from a fistfight.

In the meantime, Derek turned the other way and went to the prom with Jennifer Kolinsky. Sounds childish? It was, but Madison still wanted to shake up a can of whoop ass and open it in Kantrell's face.

I couldn't believe that she was still dealing with this issue after seven years. "Are you serious?" I glanced over at her. "High school days are done. Shit, college days are even done. I thought you were over that."

"I thought I was too, but hearing her name for the first time after all of these years just woke up something inside of me." She was angry.

"That was seven years ago, in nineteen ninety-six. We were fifteen and in the tenth grade, Madi."

"Nineteen ninety-six," she chuckled. "Those were the days."

"Yes, but without that bastard."

"Yeah, but I really liked Derek. I feel that Trell ruined what could've been a great thing."

"A great thing?" I was shocked. "Obviously you haven't been keeping up with the Derek Cowan story." I laughed. "He works at the Wal-Mart in Florida City."

Her mouth flew open. "You're lying!"

"No, ma'am," I went on. "Saw him stocking meat the other night."

"I thought he went to NYU?"

I smirked. "That brotha went to WHATSAMATTA U."

"Wal-Mart?" Her hands flew to her mouth. "Stop lying!"

"Ask Yvette."

"Derek?" She was in disbelief. "That's all well and good, but I still feel like I need to say something to her. She's not about to think that she can . . ."

"C'mon, Madi, she's over it and she's moved on, otherwise she wouldn't want to be traveling with us this weekend." I didn't want this drama to ruin our trip. "Please let this outdated foolishness go."

"Okay, Ms. Sense and Sensibility." She's been calling me that ever since I went to the theater three weekends in a row to see that movie. "I'll let it go."

"That's my girl," I said as we pulled up to Vette's apartment.

Madi reached over and blew the horn. "They better be ready."

"Madi, stop!" I grabbed her hand. "That old lady might call the cops again like that night I was knocking on Vette's window." Before I could grab my cell phone, the door to Vette's place swung open.

"When do I get to drive?" Vette asked before even saying hello. "Why are you guys so late?"

I winked at Yvette before I spoke. "Reverend Sexy held us up."

"The Holy Ghost can fall on me anytime if it looks anything like him." She did the sign of the cross. As she walked back toward the back of the truck she added, "I might just join Mount Pleasant if he promises to be *pleasant*." We loved to gang up on Madi about her dad.

Madi had had enough. "My dad can spot demons five miles away, so you both would be cast out."

"Yeah," I joked, "but would he have to lay his hands on me to cast out the demons?"

"Fuck you." Madi rolled her eyes. "Both of you sluts need Jesus." In laughter, Madi helped Vette load her luggage into the truck.

While lifting a bag that was heavier than Vette herself, I asked, "Did you forget that we're only going for four days?"

"I went to college in Daytona Beach," she defended herself. "I know what I'm doing. I've been to BCR before."

"You have to be kidding me." I threw the suitcases in the back of the Escalade.

A voice crept up behind me. "I have one suitcase and I guarantee you that I'll look just as good or better than you will with your three bags of clothes." I turned around to see the honey brown chick that could be Trina's stunt double, Kantrell Jackson.

"Trell!" I said loud enough to get Madi's attention while she organized Vette's bags. "How are you?" I gave her a hug.

"Girl, I'm good." She looked me over. "How are you?"

"I can't complain," I answered and then paused, but as Madison peeked out of the window I added, "You look great." She really did; the years had been on her side. Still slender and her make-up was model perfect.

Finally Madi hopped out of the backseat and stared at Trell with a look of disgust. I held my breath until mean ass Madi cracked a smile and walked toward Trell. "Hey, girl."

As they entered a short embrace I exhaled and couldn't help but usher in the thought that this was the beginning of a great weekend.

Chapter 2

A Moment of Silent 'Sexual Fantasy' Meditation

Our journey began a few minutes before six P.M. with a mug of café con leche at my side. During our five-hour drive we reminisced on our high school days and relived our lovable college years. Vette graduated from Bethune Cookman. Kantrell stayed in Miami, at U.M. Madison went to Florida State, and I was also in Tallahassee, but at FAMU. Madi and I never bothered going to Freaknik, Black College Reunion, Kappa Beach Fest, or Black Bike Weekend while in college. And for the life of me I didn't know why we were deciding to go now.

All the talk about college forced me to think about Three, the last man I was bold enough to claim or call my boyfriend. His nickname was Three because he had his father's name but wasn't a Junior, he was 'the third,' and he used to get ragged on so much about it that he flipped it into a catchy nickname and also sported the number on his football jersey. We dated almost three years ago, for nine months during my sophomore year in college until he found greener grass on the lawn of an address he had no business knowing. Madi was the only person privy to my relationship with Three . . . and she knows not to mention that bastard's nickname, real name, last name, shoe size, or his car year, make or model in my presence.

Since Three, I've dated many men, had booty calls, and even tried my hand at relationships, but in the back of my mind I couldn't relax enough to completely trust a man. However, I'm ready to settle down. I want a serious relationship. And here I am going to Black College Reunion Weekend where the playas of the world unite to fuck women over. What a bright fuckin' idea!

The moment I steered the truck onto the exit ramp of I-95 in Daytona Vette yelled, "We're here!" The way she was acting you'd think we were on a pilgrimage to the Holy City. "Black College Reunion two thousand and three, baby," Vette said. It was 11 P.M. and traffic stood still two seconds down the off ramp. It didn't creep or seem delayed; the road was a parking lot. People were sitting on the hoods of their cars, and many used the opportunity to walk about and socialize with others who had nowhere to go. I had to blink my eyes three times to believe that there really was a man with a barbecue grill earning a profit in the accident lane, and he had a line.

"No way." Madi looked around in disbelief. "There's that many people up here? This is going to be crazy."

Cars were bouncing, paint jobs sparkling, and chrome was shining so bright it hurt to look at, and white and beige leather interiors were immaculate. Though our ride was rented and we weren't rolling on twenty-inch rims, we all had one thing in common, we weren't going anywhere anytime soon.

Yvette took the wheel and I escaped to the back seat. The showoff of the group, she nixed the AC, rolled the windows down, and let music rush in from every direction. On the right we heard the Ying Yang Twins, *To the windows, to the wall. Till the sweat drop down my balls.* On the left was, *Hey Ya!* by Andre 3000. But homeboy in the metallic Titanium Silver BMW M3 in the front of us brought funk to the game when he opened his speaker-filled trunk and penetrated the air with Beenie Man's *Dude.* We all sang our anthem, *"I want a dude with the wickedest slam, I need a one, two, three hour man. I want a dude who will tie me to the bed, a thug that can handle his biz like a man."* It was every girl's dream. Who ever prayed to God for a small dick, two minute, sorry fuck, can't stay hard or eat pussy right man? I didn't, but I sure had my share of them.

Every other brotha was naked from the waist up, and all of the females seemed to have shared one yard of fabric. There was enough brown skin showing to cover the entire white population of Daytona Beach. Looking at some of the racy outfits made me feel like I had packed for a church convention.

I had nothing in my suitcase that could compare to the outfits walking by. I'm an elementary school teacher for crying out loud, though it's not warranted I wear suits to work Monday through Thursday. I wasn't bad on the eyes by far, but I *could* afford to do some sit-ups, run a lap or two, and lay off of chocolate cake. At five feet eight and 150 pounds, I considered myself hot stuff, but I was never one to parade around half-naked. I was scandalous in other ways, and no one needed to know it at first glance. I couldn't help but to say it. "I am going to be so out of place up here."

Vette chimed in. "Lia, you only live once. I say unleash your inner freak, she's human too." She went on and on and on until a piece of dark chocolate eye-candy walked by and we all paused for a moment of silent 'sexual fantasy' meditation.

"Check out Mr. Red FUBU cap," Madi whispered and we all searched until we found him. His shirt was draped around his neck and his exposed chest reached out to us as though we had on 3D glasses. "I wonder if he needs a massage." Madi was always handing out her business cards. "Excuse me," she got his attention, he was all smiles as he walked over.

He showed all his gold teeth. "What's up, ma?"

"You." There was never any shame in her game. She touched his chest. "You feel a little tense." She giggled. "Can I work that out for you?"

He blushed. "F'sho." He leaned into the window. "Where y'all from?"

"Miami."

"Word?" He got excited. "I'm from Fort Liquordale."

"Good." Madi popped out her business cards and slid one between his lips as he smiled. "Call me and let me iron out the kinks for you."

He read over the card. "Bet, so I get a free massage?"

"Free? Hell no." All the sexiness left her voice; she didn't play when it came to making money. "My rates are on the back."

He flipped the card over. "Damn, what else can I have for these rates?"

"You can have a Coke and a damn smile," Madi snuck in as he walked away. "With your broke ass."

Kantrell interrupted. "Look at the guy on the passenger side of the blue Benz on the left."

Vette started singing, "*Sitting on the passenger's side of his best friend's ride* tryin' . . ." She stopped herself in mid-verse. "Whoa, he's cute."

Cute? The brother would've confused Michelangelo. He was a work of art, and after feeling four sets of eyes on him, he quickly turned in our direction and rolled his window down. "How's it going, ladies?"

"It'll be going great once we clear this traffic," Vette said with a smile so big it could probably be seen from space.

"I hear you." He leaned a little out of the window. "Where are you girls from?"

Thinking selfishly, Vette spoke only for herself. "I'm from Miami."

He continued with a smile. "Nice."

"He's mine," she whispered back at us. "Madi, if you pass your card to him I will snap your neck. No joke."

"High yellow brothas went out of style back in junior high," Madi laughed. "Plus he's on the passenger side, honey."

"So I guess it's true," Mr. Passenger Side said.

"What's that?" Vette asked.

"Miami women eat sunshine for breakfast because they all have a sexy glow." That was corny, but I'd give him two points for effort. "It must be true because you certainly do."

"Thank you. Where are you from?" She was still blushing from the compliment.

"Atlanta."

"I love Atlanta," Vette said. Now, last I checked she said that she would commit suicide if she ever had to drive through Atlanta again.

The Benz's rear window went down and out popped a head that looked exactly like the guy in the front seat. It was obvious that they were twins or went to the same plastic surgeon. "Hmm, all of a sudden high yellow is my favorite color," Madison said with a smile and rolled her window down. In a second he was out of the car and leaning into ours. His twin felt a little upstaged and stepped out and began a private conversation with Vette.

"So, what hotel are you all staying at?" the backseat twin asked.

"The Hilton," Trell was eager to let him know.

"By the way," he said. "I'm Jordan and he's my twin brother Jervis." Suddenly their Benz was like a clown car; two other men popped out. Jordan pointed at the dark-skinned guy with the nice build. "That's Anthony." Then he directed his attention to the thin caramel complexioned guy emerging from the driver's seat. "And that's Leon." We all greeted each other and before long everyone was yapping right in the middle of the International Speedway Blvd.

Normally when you see four men together one of them is always labeled "Mr. Why Are You The One Trying To Talk To Me?" by women, but all four of these guys were all well kempt, seeming intelligent, above average on the handsome scale, and they were staying at a hotel only two blocks from ours.

We talked for fifteen minutes before traffic finally started moving. But not wanting to completely lose our newfound friends, we arranged to meet them at the bar across the street from our hotel in an hour.

We arrived at our seventh floor hotel room around midnight. The two-bedroom suite was plush; it had everything: two full baths, small scale kitchen, living room, and a Jacuzzi by the window. The suite was more like a really nice two-bedroom apartment. After a walk-through, we crashed on the sofa.

"If dude wasn't so fine I wouldn't leave this room for Jesus tonight," Yvette joked.

"Maybe we don't have to leave." Madi picked up the phone playfully. "They may have men on the menu."

Trell slapped fives with Madi. "Then I say we order the biggest blackest motherfucka up here right now."

I butted in with the most important question. "How are we sleeping?"

"You and I will take the room down the hall." Vette winked at me to see what Madi's reaction would be.

Madi made us all proud. "Sounds good to me."

Ten minutes later I was walking out of the shower and slipping on my dark blue boot cut jeans and a fitted black low cut shirt. After doing my makeup, I blew my-self a kiss and said, "Bring on the weekend." I wanted my mind to be as far away from grading third grade spelling words as possible. Vette was right, I needed to change gears. I would try hard to kick into risqué for the weekend.

In the living room I met Trell and Madi laughing as though there was never a break in their friendship. "Party over here," Vette said as she entered the living room. I almost needed a magnifying glass to see her shorts and tweezers to pull them out of her ass. Vette's shirt was so skimpy that Lil' Kim would call her a tramp. She looked terrific, but I wouldn't be caught dead in that getup.

"What?" Vette saw the deadpan look on our faces.

"I've been working out for the past seven months just so I could get in these shorts."

"And you'll be working another month just to take them off," I said, giving her another look.

"Amen," Madi imitated her father. "I gotta second that motion."

As Madi stood up, she revealed a red strapless dress that hinted at all of her curves. She had an awesome physique and that dress showed it off more than anything I'd ever seen her in. People always told her how much she resembled TLC's Chili. I'm sure that no one would be *Too Proud To Beg* her tonight.

"Sexy, sexy," I teased her. "If the Reverend could see you now."

"Shut up." She rolled her eyes with a smile.

"He said to call when you got here. Did you?" I asked.

"No, would you like to call him?" She was being a smart-ass.

"Oh, don't think I won't," I smiled and grabbed the key to the room. "Let's go."

The bar was across the road, so we wandered through the crowded street to meet up with the boys from the blue Benz. They were watching a basketball game, but quickly converted their attention to us once we walked in.

After the initial greeting we all fell into place with the semi-stranger we talked with earlier. Madi linked up with Anthony, a comedian that had been featured on BET's Comicview, but none of us had ever heard of him. Jervis and Jordan, the twins that had Trell and Vette about to do cartwheels, owned and operated a nightclub called Hurricane in Atlanta. And Leon, the electrical engineer, was intriguing earlier, so I wanted to see if he could still hold my attention late into the night.

"Hey, Thalia." He remembered my name. Good sign.

Leon stood up and gave me a once over and smiled his approval. I assumed that he especially liked the amount of cleavage I had on display. Though he was a little hyperactive, he was very handsome: brown-skinned, six two, 195 pounds, strong masculine facial features, and through his perfectly aligned teeth and succulent lips he asked, "What are you drinking?"

"I'm not sure." I never knew what to drink when it was on someone else's tab. If I was paying, it would be the cheapest two-for-one drink going. "What are you drinking?" I asked.

"Whiskey." Then he added, "Johnnie Walker, black label." I knew nothing about whiskey except that older white men talked about it on television a lot. "I don't think I can handle that."

"What can you handle?" The way he touched my hand caused my panties to moisten a tad. Whoa... pump your brakes, sir.

"What would you suggest? I'm daring to be a little risqué." I winked at him.

"Is that right?" he asked. "Then how about a Blowjob?"

"Excuse me?" I backed away. "What did you say?"

"Slow your roll," he laughed, "it's a drink."

I still wasn't smiling. "*Blowjob* is the name of a drink?"

"Yeah." He snickered. "It's a Black Russian with whipped cream on top in a shot glass."

I sighed. "Oh, okay." If only he knew how close he came to getting slapped.

"You up for it?" he asked.

"Yeah." I was a little reluctant. "I'll give it a try."

"Cool!" Then he added, "Now here are the rules."

"Rules?" I interrupted. "What rules?"

"You can't pick up the shot glass with your hand, you have to pick it up with your mouth and turn it up with your head."

"Wow." It was awkward just thinking about doing it.

"You said you wanted to be risqué, right?"

"Yeah, I did say that, huh?" What did I have to lose? "Bring it on."

Chapter 3

Thank God for Magnums

Leon ordered two rounds of Blowjobs for my friends and me. I rested the first small glass on the bar and picked it up with my mouth. I turned the glass up and let the thick liquid drain into my throat. When it was all said and done I had whipped cream all around my mouth; thus explains the name of the delectable drink.

"You did that really well." He wiped the corners of my mouth with a napkin. "Almost too well."

"I always do." My statement was followed by a few seconds of uncomfortable silence. "Well, I didn't mean it like that."

"No need to explain. Here's number two!" He placed the second one in front of me and I handled it like a pro. "Damn, no whipped cream around the edges this time, I'm impressed."

Just when I thought I had common sense I looked him in the face and said, "Get me another one." He was too happy to tell the bartender to keep them coming.

When we were talking on the highway our conversation was more of a communal one, so I didn't know all that much about Leon, but here we were, strangers, with nothing but sexual innuendos now. I had to break the tension. "So, you're an electrical engineer?"

"Yeah." He looked around the room. "What do you do in Miami?"

"I'm an elementary school teacher."

"No shit?" He sounded impressed. "What grade?"

I spoke proudly. "Third."

"Those kids should be around eight or nine, right?"

Wow he knew math. "Yes."

Leon made it known that he was checking out a younger girl across the room in a green dress. "How long have you been teaching?" I'm sure he only asked to stop from drooling.

"This is my first year."

He turned his attention back to me. "You like it?"

"Yeah," I smiled. "It's better than I thought it would be."

"Do you have kids?"

"No," but added, "and until I'm married, that's the way I'd like it to stay."

"Why?"

I thought his question was odd. "Why?" Doesn't America have enough single mothers? Was he serious? "I'd like to offer my children a two-parent home."

"Marriage is overrated." He eyed the chick in green.

"Well, it's worth a try." Where were the men with morals? "Do you have children?" I asked.

His head moved up and down. "Yeah, a five-year-old daughter."

Code Red! He was sharing an intense bond with a woman for at least the next thirteen years. I glanced down at his left hand; he wasn't wearing a ring, but on his ring finger there was a thin strip of skin that was slightly lighter than the surrounding area, exposing the truth. "How long have you been married?" Yeah, I was Detective Colombo.

"Seven years, my daughter's mother." He looked down at his hand and gulped the rest of his whiskey in one big swallow. "We're going through a divorce, but it's been over for more than two years. I stayed around longer than I probably should have for the sake of my daughter." He looked away. "I just moved out."

I tried to be comforting. "I'm sorry to here that."

"I'm sorrier." He laughed away the frown. "I hope to get custody of my daughter."

It was none of my business, but since he was talking about it I wanted to know more. "So what happened?"

"Well," he took a deep breath, "her lover got the best of her."

"Wow." I was speechless. "She was cheating?"

"She slipped up." I wanted to tell him that he didn't have to share the story, but what the hell . . . I wanted to know. "She forgot to lock the bathroom door."

My eyes popped open. "You walked in on her with another man?"

"I walked in on her snorting cocaine off of the bathroom sink."

It was one of the most awkward moments in my life. What do you say to someone after they say something like that? Nothing!

"She said that she would get help so I stayed. I believed her, until I found a nickel bag of that shit hidden in the baking powder container."

"Oh man," was the only thing I could say.

"All I want is my little girl. I can't stand the thought

of my daughter catching her using or running into that stuff." He called out to the bartender, "A double please." Amazingly he was still glancing at the other woman and without even trying to whisper he added to his drink order. "And give that young lady in the green anything she wants on me." What the . . . Was he stupid? That was just wrong and rude.

I felt like shit. "I'll be back." He strolled away in the direction of the restroom but who was to say that he didn't go and give her his sad song?

I took advantage of his tab and ordered two more shots while he was gone. When he returned I tried to seem upbeat, but truthfully the alcohol was getting to me. "Now I get to interrogate you," he said.

"I have nothing to hide."

"What brings you to BCR?"

"I needed a break." The bartender brought over his drinks and yet another shot for me.

"Another one?" I kissed the whipped cream and licked my lips as he watched me down another Blowjob.

"Mmm," he moaned. "Was it good?"

I winked at him and in no time that sexual tension was back in the house. He looked at the bartender. "I don't want to see this young lady without a drink for the rest of the night."

"In a generous mood tonight, huh?" I asked sarcastically.

"Always." He sipped his Whiskey.

I'd shoot myself later, but I had to ask. "What is the lady in green drinking?"

"I don't know." He looked at me strangely. "I noticed that she walked in alone and I just wanted her to have a good time." He got the bartender's attention again and handed over a credit card. "Run it for everybody's drinks."

After a little more conversation and my sixth or seventh Blowjob, he couldn't control his words. "Looking at you with all of this whipped cream on your mouth brings one question to mind."

"What's that?"

"Do you have a boyfriend?" It took me two seconds to bridge the connection, his dirty mind was something.

Meeting the guys for drinks was expected to be the beginning of our night. Afterward we were supposed to go to a club where we'd let our hair down and dance the night away, but my drunkenness was already in full effect. I had added two Long Island Iced Teas to the mix. There was no way I was going anywhere. I looked over and Madi was laughing at something Anthony was whispering in her ear. Trell and Jervis also seemed to be engaged in an interesting conversation, and Vette and Jordan were in a dark corner dancing to a slow song along with a few other couples.

"So what are you girls doing tonight?" Leon asked.

I was buzzin'. I worked hard to organize my thoughts before speaking. "We're supposed to be going to a club, but I don't think I'll be going." I could barely see straight. This was far from the relaxed jazzy feeling I was going for. Was this what risqué felt like? "I'm ready for bed."

"Then let's go." He enjoyed being bad. "Are you sleepy?"

"Not really, but I'm tired and not in the mood for a big crowd." Right then the music in the lounge took a turn for the better. It was Kemistry's, AKA Kem, *Love Calls*. "*I'm sittin' here thinkin' about you tonight.*" I closed

my eyes and sang softly. Leon grabbed my hand. "Would
you like to dance?"

"Sure." I hopped off of the stool.

Still standing near the bar he drew me into his arms.
Each time I inhaled, his seductive cologne rushed up to
my brain. He was looking into my eyes like he had just
heard the saying about the eyes being the window to
the soul. If he was looking for my soul he needed to
come back tomorrow because right then my soul was
out to lunch. "You feel real good."

"Thanks." We were uncomfortably close. "What are
you and your boys doing tonight?"

He playfully corrected me. "I think you mean what
are *they* doing tonight?" He paused. "You know what I'm
doing."

"Actually, I don't know." I was sorry to inform him.

"Well, I'll be with you." He smiled. "Holding you if
you let me." If only he knew that one more drink meant
he'd be holding me up and over a toilet.

At the end of the song was an oldie but goodie,
Lauryn Hill's *Can't Take My Eyes Off You* came on, and
Lauren was right. I couldn't take my eyes off of Leon.
When the song was done, he handed me a freshly
mixed Long Island Iced Tea. "Here's to the new memo-
ries."

Was he serious? "This is the last one," I told him giddily.

Vette walked over. "Are we still going out?"

"Y'all can," I heard myself say.

"Are you all right?" She observed the way I was leaning on the bar.

I felt my head move up and down. "Yeah, drunk
though."

She flashed a devilish smile. "Trell, Madi, and the guys are still going to the club, but I think Jordan and I will chill in his room."

"That's right, don't stop being a slut tonight. Go for what you know." We both laughed at my intoxication.

She walked over to Leon thinking that I couldn't hear her. "Will you keep her company until I get back to the room?"

"Vette!" I jumped in. "I'm all right."

She looked at me and then back at Leon. "Like I said, will you please keep an eye on her?"

"I'll watch out for her," he said smiling. "That's no problem at all."

"Great, I'll see you in a few hours." She ran off and then Madi and Trell came over to say goodnight.

I tried to get out of him accompanying me. "Trust me; you don't have to do this."

"Shh," he hushed me. "I won't touch you." He held up his right hand. "Scouts honor." He continued. "When you're ready to go let me know."

I was nervous about being left alone with Leon, not because I was a "goody-goody," but because I was *no* "goody-goody." I was drunk, he was handsome. "Are you sure you don't want to go with your friends?"

"Look, if you'd rather I leave then I will."

"Don't get me wrong. I've enjoyed your company, but I am very tired."

"If you're tired then I'll see you to your room and leave you alone." While Leon waited on the bartender to return his credit card, I jumped down off of the stool, wobbling. "Are you okay to walk?" he asked. I couldn't answer, I had to concentrate. It felt as though I should raise my feet two feet higher in order to take a step. So

I did. I lifted my foot and came down so hard on it that I had to have shattered my kneecap.

"Give me your hand." He came to my aid. "You're in bad shape."

I held his hand and followed his steps out of the dimly lit lounge. "Just get me across the street, I'll take it from there," I said once outside and I could see, but he didn't just leave me. We reached the lobby. "I'm on the seventeenth floor. If you can just point me to the elevator I can handle it from there."

He looked at me strangely. "This hotel has no seventeenth floor."

I was embarrassed. "I meant the seventh floor."

"Thalia, you can't even walk straight. I'm not just going to put you on an elevator." He rubbed my hand. "That's not my style."

I wondered why I didn't want his company. My body was telling me yes, but something deep inside said, "Hell no." There I was, trying to make a logical decision piss ass drunk. When the elevator jerked, the only way that I could stand was by leaning on him. When we stepped off he urged me, "Let me see you to your room."

"Thank you," I said as we made it to the door. "Do you wanna go home?" I asked him.

He grinned. "It's not the first thing on my list."

"What is?"

He looked me up and down sensually and bent down so that his face was right in mine. "Whatever you want is the first thing on my list tonight." Our lips were a half inch apart.

I pushed the key into the lock and opened the door. Leon made a beeline to the Jacuzzi. "This is great." He soon joined me on the couch where we sat in silence for a complete minute. "Will you get into the hot tub with me?"

"Will you be naked?"

"Nope." He held his hand over his heart to swear.

"Then I can't get into the hot tub." I laughed. "Actually, that sounds like a good idea." I hopped up. "Give me a minute to change." I wobbled into the room. "Start running the water," I yelled back.

I wasn't wasting a swimsuit for this, so I found a pair of short shorts that I sometimes slept in and a tank top. They'd have to work. A few minutes later I made my way back into the living room. It was surprisingly dark, but the moonlight was shining in. Leon stared out of the window as the water plummeted into the Jacuzzi. I watched him remove his shirt; his back was so chiseled that I was afraid to see his chest.

"Hey," I said, startling him. He turned toward me and his pants fell to his ankles. He was wearing black cotton briefs, the tight ones that stop at mid-thigh.

I stood in awe of his body. "Wow," I whispered.

"Make sure the water isn't too hot for you."

"I seriously doubt that. When I shower, I like the water so hot that it's stinging my skin."

He laughed and said, "So you're one of those girls that like pain?"

"No, I'm not into pain, but if *you* are let me know, I'll spank you." He did deserve a whooping for that stunt he pulled earlier, buying that chick a drink.

We got in, and once settled, our conversation grew more interesting. We started out talking about him being an electrical engineer and before I knew it we were yapping about football. We exchanged recipes for our favorite dishes and even briefly discussed religion.

After an hour of the babbling, bubbles, and steam, I

could barely move. I think we stayed in too long. "You ready to get out?" he asked.

I was drained. "I can't move."

"You don't have to." He scooped me up and stepped out of the hot tub. With me in his arms he made his way to my room.

"You wanna lie down in these wet clothes?" he asked.

"I don't care," I managed to say as I felt my back hit the mattress.

"You might get sick."

"I don't care." I just wanted to sleep.

"Are you sure you're all right?"

The alcohol and the tub sucked all of my energy from under me. "Yeah." He pulled my shirt up and began towel drying me.

"Thanks," I said as he moved the towel over my legs. I was out of my mind tired, but it didn't keep me from being ignorant. I sat up and removed my shirt, exposing my breasts. Though the room was dark, the moonlight's glow allowed me to see his smile and as he moved the towel over my chest, his breathing intensified.

I laid back and closed my eyes. Then I felt him tugging on my shorts and I allowed him to remove them. He began to dry me below, but the more he patted me dry down there, the more wetness he created. Before long I was grinding into the towel and he was rubbing instead of tapping. I began to moan and he threw the towel aside and massaged me with his fingers.

I don't know when the transition took place, but his tongue replaced his finger and I was clutching the back of his head between my thighs. His head directed my pleasure. Left, right, left, left, right, up down, down, up, in, out, in, in, in. My body trembled, my hands clenched my nipples, and my toes clawed into the sheets. If someone could bottle this feeling, Bill Gates and Oprah would be moved down on the billionaires list because that would be one rich motherfucka.

With a loud groan I felt warmness dripping down toward the crack of my butt, but he didn't let it go to waste. He wanted it and took it all in.

My chest rose and fell like I had just finished running a marathon. When he moved his body over me, I thought sure he was in search of the main event, but instead he fell next to me and pulled the covers over us. That was supposed to be it, but as though I was possessed with a horny demon, I flung the covers off of us and I ran my hands over his body, from his chest right down to his bone. His compass pointed the way to the stars and was as solid as a ball of steel. I stroked him and felt his veins protruding. His dick was fat, long, and pulsating. I asked, "You want all of this to go to waste?" He didn't answer, he couldn't answer. Leon just squirmed at my touch and pushed up repeatedly into my hand. "It feels too good."

His movements beneath my hand coupled with the dimensions of his tool drove me wild. I wanted him, a complete stranger, inside of me. It was insane to me how his wife could choose cocaine over a man with a dick like this. I'm a sucker for a big dick! I believe that the most powerful men probably had penises the size of my clit. Why? Because a big dick motherfucka didn't have to do a damn thing . . . pussy and power just fell into his lap . . . preferably onto his dick. Therefore, Laura Bush is probably truly a *Desperate Housewife*.

Leon spoke in a whisper. "You think you can handle all of that?"

"If I can't, then you just give me the rest tomorrow." I kissed his chest and my hands surfaced with a condom from the nightstand. Thank God for magnums because nothing else would hold that fat boy.

"Sit on it." He coached me, but as I hovered over him, my brain started functioning; I didn't know this man from a pothole in the street. This was just my first night in Daytona Beach. Is this what I came to do? "Ride it." Before I could answer my question, Leon pushed upward and suddenly it didn't matter what I thought I had come for, there was at least eight inches of dick in me.

Chapter 4

Waiting to Inhale

The sun had no mercy the next morning, boldly shining through the curtains like it was partly paying for the room. I had a headache, but it was nothing that a little peace and quiet couldn't cure. I sprawled out in bed and had more space than I started out with. Leon wasn't there, but when I turned to the right, Vette was kneeling next to the bed and all in my face; I nearly jumped out of my skin. "Good morning, care to open up the Magnum File so that we can go over the details?" The Magnum Files were the stories we shared about any man that was blessed enough to fit into that size condom.

I turned my head. "What are you talking about?" My voice dragged and my body shivered as I thought about the way Leon put me to sleep. I pulled the sheet over my head.

"When I got here Leon's clothes were on the sofa."

She pulled the cover off of me. "And there wasn't just one, but two magnum wrappers on the nightstand."

"Two?" I must've been dead the second time.

"Yeah, two." She giggled. "And you call me a slut?"

"Shut up, we got in the hot tub, we were tired, and went to bed. I took those wrappers out before we even left here last night. They were in my jeans pocket from months ago."

"Tell that to someone who wasn't there when you bought those jeans *last week*," she reminded me. "Black College Reunion Weekend is not exactly the place to find a baby daddy."

"Time out, Vette." I turned the tables. "Where did you sleep?"

She blushed. "See what had happened was . . . "

"Please tell nothing but the truth, so help you God." I had her under oath.

"I showed Jervis around Cookman's campus then we went back to his room and ordered a late night snack." She paused. "His cell phone rings too damn much for me." She added, "And he answers it every damn time."

"Did you sleep with him?"

"Did I sleep with him?" She repeated the question in an overly dramatic southern accent. "Just what kind of girl do you take me for?"

"Yep, you did it." I threw my hands up.

She tossed a pillow at me. "I didn't sleep with him, but I did think about it." Just then Madi and Trell walked in. Madi sat at the foot of Yvette's bed and Trell lay next to me.

"Leon's clothes were in the living room this morning." Madi smiled.

I was sick of the questions already. "We got into the Jacuzzi."

"Is that the story?" Madi asked Vette.

"That's the one she's telling," Vette said. "But the evidence," she pointed at the condom wrappers, "says otherwise."

I wanted to go back to bed, but it didn't seem possible now that the Let's Talk about Sex Committee had assembled. "Why is everyone up so early?" I asked.

"It's a quarter to nine and we didn't come to Daytona Beach to sleep." Madi seemed well-rested and ready to go. "If you were at the club and saw the type of men we saw, you would've been out of this hotel room two hours ago."

"So how was your night with Anthony?" I asked.

"Anthony is cute, no he's fine," she corrected herself, "but his breath smelled like he drank a shit shake. I can't inhale around him. Forget Terry McMillan's book, I can write a book, *Waiting to Inhale.*" We were dying laughing as she finished up. "I was losing oxygen to the brain, about to slip into a coma. I really couldn't breathe. I saw that bright light folks say you see right before you die." Madison was hilarious. "He's a nice guy but there are not enough mints in the fuckin' world."

"So what are we doing today?" I asked.

"Let's just get out there. We'll run into something." Trell had a valid point, we just needed to get up and out, and we did just that.

On every corner there was loud music, a crowd of people, food, and alcohol. We checked out a few of the block parties, but the scene was the same everywhere: overly eager men wanting names, numbers, and pictures with as many girls as possible. Black College Reunion was turning out to be a little freakier than I expected. Chicks were walking through the streets in thongs. And the rest of them were showing their breasts while posing for pictures with strangers. One chick posed for a picture with a guy while bending over the hood of a car. The guy, in broad daylight, pulled aside her thong and parted her "lips" with his fingers as she smiled for the camera. Still, that was tame compared to the other things we had seen.

We collected a lot of beer and wine coolers during our ride through the party zones. After two hours of drinking, laughing, and taking pictures, we were out of our minds and Madi proved it. "I have a challenge."

"What is it?" I was curious.

"Who's paying for drinks tonight?" Nobody answered so she continued. "I say the person who pays for drinks tonight is the girl who doesn't lift up her shirt and show her goods for the next picture."

"Deal." Yvette's speech was slurred.

"Deal?" I asked her. "Are you guys high?"

"The only thing that's going to be high is your bill if you don't do it," Trell said.

"You're doing it, too, Trell?" I couldn't believe this. "Come on, Madi, pick something else. I'm not ending up on the Internet. My students could see that shit someday." In the midst of my whining, two nice looking older men walked up and started a decent conversation. They were from Valdosta, Georgia and seemed like two lonely country bumpkins. As they were about to leave, the shorter one asked if he could take a picture with us.

"Lia, I hope you brought your checkbook," Vette teased.

The gentleman stood in the middle of the four of us and his friend held the camera ten feet away counting down, "Three, two . . ." My hands reached for the bottom of my shirt, and by the time he said 'one', my 36C's were in full view.

"Damn," the guy posing in the picture said, looking at me. My friends all dropped to the ground in laughter. "You dirty fuckin' bastards." They set me up. I was the only one to lift up my shirt.

The guys walked away quickly. "I'm sorry." Madison came over and hugged me. "We didn't think you'd actually do it." I was livid and pushed her away.

"That was wrong." I looked around at them. "I can't believe you did that to me."

"Have a beer." Vette handed me a Corona. "You've got balls. Your drinks are on us for the rest of the weekend."

I grabbed the beer. "For the rest of your damn lives."

"I'm sorry." Trell smiled.

About a minute of silence went by before I was able to laugh at it too. "So . . ." I paused, "did they at least look good?"

"It looks like you've been drinking your milk, girl." Madi started giggling again. We joked about it a little more and then decided to load up. Thirty minutes down the road we heard a horn blowing. It was Leon and the boys in the Benz trying to get our attention.

Madi sighed. "I can't deal with Anthony's stank breath right now." She reluctantly pulled over into the parking lot of a convenient store and they followed.

"What's up?" Leon approached my door.

"Hey." I blushed. "What are you guys up to?"

"Nothing much. I was hoping to run into you."

"Oh yeah?" I was relieved.

"Yeah." He shaded his eyes from the sun. "What have y'all done today?"

"We've jumped around." Thinking of the joke my friends played on me, I said, "This place is wild."

"I wanted to wake you before I left this morning, but since I kept you up late . . ."

I flirted and interrupted. "You didn't keep me up, you put me to sleep."

"Too much information," Madi yelled, laughing. "Please step out of the truck and stop torturing those who have no tale to tell."

We walked toward the back of the truck. "Where y'all headed?"

"Back to the hotel," I answered. "Why? What are y'all doing?"

"Nothing really, we just about emptied a liquor store, so we're about to get our drink on." He added, "You ladies want company?"

"That would be nice." I barely let him finish his sentence. "Let me see if everybody is up for that."

I talked it over with the girls and everybody, even Madi, was cool with it. It's amazing what free alcohol would make a girl agree to. We headed to the KFC and bought enough chicken to feed a small military base.

Once in the room, Tony and Jordan lined the countertop with a large bottle of Hennessy, a bottle of Absolut, two bottles of Harvey's Bristol Crème, and a small bottle of Wild Spirit, which no one had ever heard of, two six packs of Coca-Cola, pineapple juice, grapefruit juice, and three bags of ice.

"I'll mix the first round!" Vette yelled, "Say what ya want, people."

Madi walked toward the kitchen where Anthony was starting to put the food together. "You didn't buy any mint schnapps?" She joked about his breath loudly and he didn't even get it.

We sat around in the living room area drinking and eating chicken, macaroni and cheese, mashed potatoes, baked beans, and biscuits for about an hour before Madi came up with the worst idea possible . . . again. "Let's play truth or dare," she blurted out.

Anthony responded, "How about strip poker?"

"No. Truth or dare should be fun," Trell said.

"I'm down," Jervis said.

"Count me in," Jordan joined in while taking a sip of his Bristol Crème and pineapple juice.

I had played that game enough in college to know that it could get carried away quickly. Someone always revealed something they later wished they hadn't. "Can't we play something else?"

Leon said, "Come on, it's just to kill some time." I couldn't believe that *he* actually wanted to play this silly game.

"There are other ways to kill time." I winked at him. "But fine, I'll play."

"Let me add a special rule," Anthony said. "Everybody has to take double shots of Wild Spirit before we begin." He smiled. "And if you're chosen and you pick truth, you have to take a shot of vodka before you answer the question."

We each took two shots of Wild Spirit each, which completed the bottle. It tasted like chocolate and would probably be very good in hot cocoa.

"Madi, truth or dare?" Vette asked.

She grabbed a vodka shot. "Truth! The whole truth and nothing but that shit." She was already buzzing.

Vette asked, "Is it better to give or receive oral sex?"

"It depends on the person, but I must say that giving stimulates me more." She blushed. "The fact that someone is being pleased by my mouth really turns me on."

"The gates of heaven just opened." Anthony passed Madi his cellular phone. "Program your number in there, I got plans for you."

Then it was Jervis' turn. "Trell, truth or dare, my dear?"

"Truth," she said and took her shot.

He asked, "Did you enjoy tossing my salad last night?" We all burst into laughter. "I'm just kidding." It took him no time to come up with the question. "Do you masturbate?"

She didn't hesitate. "Yes. Who doesn't?" She didn't crack a smile. "Who's next?"

We rolled again and this time Madi won. "Anthony, truth or dare?"

"Truth," he answered.

And with a straight face Madi asked, "Do you toss salad?"

Yvette, Kantrell, and I fell out of our chairs laughing. Madison was taking yet another cheap shot at his bad breath.

"Not before dinner." He chuckled, but the joke was on him. We moved on with the game.

"Jordan, truth or dare?" Vette asked.

"Dare, damn it!" He stood up, ready for the challenge. "What you want me to do?"

"Show me some skin," she said. "Take off your shirt."

"That's nothing." Jordan proudly removed his shirt exposing a washboard stomach and a nipple ring. Vette seemed shocked. I guess they really hadn't fooled around . . . yet.

"Let the church say amen." That was her way of asking our opinion.

"Amen," all of the girls agreed.

It was Tony's turn again. "Madison, truth or dare?"

"If Jordan was brave then I can be too, dare," Madi answered.

"Kiss somebody in the room." Then Anthony threw in a curve ball. "The person can't be a man."

"What?" Madi was shocked. "You're kidding, right?"

Anthony said with a straight face, "Nope, you have three beautiful friends, just kiss one of them."

"C'mon, man." She looked at him. "I can't believe this."

Before she could even look my way I blurted out, "Don't even play."

Madi stumbled around the room. "Pucker up, Trell."

"Me?" Trell asked in total shock.

"You," Madi confirmed.

"Oh no." She seemed embarrassed, but apparently not enough. "Just do it quickly," Trell said and then closed her eyes.

Madi looked back at us. "I'll only be doing this once, so please pay attention."

She gave Trell a few innocent pecks on the lips and then a tongue slipped out. It happened so quickly that I couldn't tell which one of them it belonged to. But it didn't matter because soon two tongues were lashing back and forth. For about fifteen seconds the room was completely silent. No one expected such a performance.

When they finally parted, the guys were on their feet clapping. "That was off the motherfuckin' hook!" Anthony said.

"Encore!" Jervis yelled. "Encore, let's see that again."

"You're pretty good, Madison." Trell winked as she wiped her lips. "What are you doing later?" We all laughed.

I was speechless! Yes, I wanted Madi and Trell to be friends but damn . . . that was outrageous.

We rolled the dice and Leon got the highest number . . . he won. "Thalia, truth or dare?"

"Truth." I took my vodka shot. "I'm not kissing anybody."

"Not even me?" He was sitting on the floor with his back against the sofa. I leaned into him and we both forgot about our viewing audience until his cell phone started ringing and he pulled away. "Damn," he mumbled as he looked at the number. Agitated he said, "I have to get this." He disappeared into the bathroom. We carried on a conversation until Leon emerged with a look of disgust on his face.

"Is everything okay?" I asked.

He whispered in my ear like it was confidential. "My daughter has a fever of one hundred and two. I may have to fly back tonight if it doesn't break." He brought his hands to his face and pushed upward on his temples.

"I am so sorry to hear that."

"Yeah, I just hope that this isn't another one of Diane's ways to get me back in Atlanta," he mumbled. "She's gonna call me back to tell me what's going on."

"Well, I'll understand if I don't see you later."

He stared at me. "I can be in Miami next weekend."

"Really?" I blushed. "Then be there."

The game kept going for another hour. During that time everyone showed some skin. Anthony had to walk to the ice machine naked and Madi had to call the front desk and talk dirty until the clerk hung up. On the telephone Jordan asked another hotel guest to order him food from the kitchen because he was staying at the hotel illegally. We had a ball.

As the guys prepared to leave, we made arrangements to meet at a club later. Then Leon pulled me
aside. "If things get worse I'll have to fly out, but if she is
feeling better I'll see you tonight. If there is no change,
I'll have to wait by the phone and I probably still won't
be out, but I'll meet you back here tonight." He kissed
my right cheek. "Is that all right with you?"

"Right here is the place to be," I said as I walked him
to the door.

Chapter 5

Ghosts of Ghetto-Past

Straight out of the shower, I moistened my body with my Estée Lauder *Pleasures* body lotion and looked into the mirror. I frowned as I noticed the differences in my body since my college days. The flab, the stretch marks, the new forming cellulite. "I'm too young for this." I always had hopes of aging gracefully because to me my mother was still a fox . . . but I wasn't sure anymore.

I grabbed my cellular phone and called Mama. "Hello?" she answered.

"Hi, Mama."

"Hey, Lia, how are you?" Not giving me a chance to respond, she asked, "Are you okay?"

"Yes, I'm fine. How are you doing?"

"I couldn't be better." I could hear her smile through the phone. "How's Daytona Beach?"

"A little crazy, but fun." She wouldn't approve of 99.9 percent of the things going on. "It's hot too."

"Hot? Honey, it was so hot down here that today the

devil moved from Homestead back to hell," she joked. "How are my girls?"

"We're all doing great. We're having fun, eating, meeting people . . ."

"Men?" she interrupted. She wanted a husband for me more than I wanted one for myself. She always told me that I deserved the best man God ever created. However, she was concerned about the bad apples I would encounter before meeting the golden one God had ordained for me. Those were her words exactly.

I blushed. "Yes, there are men in Daytona Beach, Mama."

"You just be careful." She wasn't finished yet. "And remember that your body is the temple of the Holy Ghost."

I didn't want one of her hour-long Sunday Morning Good News talks. "Speaking of my body, I have another one."

"Another what?"

"Stretch mark."

She giggled. "What did I tell you?" She always had a way to bring God into any problem I was having. "That body isn't yours, it's God's body, and if He wants to write on it then let Him. When you get older those lines are going to come together and spell out thanks."

"Thanks?" I asked.

"Yes. Thanks," she said. "He'll be thanking you for following what He asked. Thanking you for not doing as you please with the body He has blessed you with, but for doing His will." She knew how much of His will I wasn't doing, but she kept me in her prayers anyways. "He's going to say thank you." Suddenly my insecurities melted away like week-old snow.

"Thanks, Mama."

She was so humble. "You don't have to thank me."

"I know, but you always brighten my day with the things you say. If I don't go to church for five months just one conversation with you will bring me up to date."

"Speaking of church . . ." Why did I go and mention church? "You need to start coming again."

"Wow, look at the time. Mama, I need to get dressed."

"Yeah, right!" She wasn't buying it. "Pastor Flack is always asking about you."

"I know, I know . . . I saw him the other day when I picked up Madi." My mind quickly reminisced on how amazing he looked. "I promise I'll go with you next Sunday."

"All right."

"Mama, I have to get dressed."

"Be safe, sweetheart."

"I will, Mama. Love you."

"I love you too." If no one else ever loved me it wouldn't matter because the love I received from my mother was more precious than gold.

Speaking of love, I loved my new navy blue spaghetti strap dress. It was a perfect fit, and the low v-neck enhanced my cleavage, and it hugged me in all the right places, stopping just a few inches above my knee.

"That dress was made for you," Vette said as she walked in.

I had to say it. "Say that again."

She looked at me strangely. "I said that that dress was made for you."

"Thank you." I smiled. "Then I shouldn't catch you in my closet?"

"Shut up." She powdered her nose. "So, Leon's daughter is sick?"

"Yeah." I applied my foundation. "His wife was calling because . . ."

"Wife?" Vette was appalled.

"Let me finish," I interrupted her rude disruption. "He's getting a divorce, she's a damn fiend. She called to say that his daughter has a fever and he might have to fly out tonight if it gets worse."

"Rewind," Vette said. "What do you mean she's a damn fiend?"

"She's on powder."

"Get out!" she yelled. "No way."

"Yes way." I laughed. "So where are we going tonight?"

"They're supposed to meet us at a club called The Volt."

I slipped on my high-heeled sandals. "The Volt?"

"Yep." Vette checked herself out in the mirror, then grabbed my hand and the keys to the truck. "Let's go."

The Volt was circular and had two open levels above the first; folks on the second and third floors could look down onto the first level, which housed the main dance floor in the center.

The first floor had three bars and lounging area with huge loveseat-type sectionals lining the walls with small tables in front. The second level offered the same furniture setting, but more privacy, with one bar and an open balcony area where you could look down onto the first floor and still enjoy the party. The third level was VIP and invitation only, and the balcony area was encased in glass, so they had their own party going on up there.

Fifty Cent's *In Da Club* was playing as we made our way to the bar. *"You can find me in the club, bottle full of Bud."*

We were at the bar for forty minutes and went through two drinks each before I jumped down from my barstool and yelled, "Let's dance!" None of us could win the spotlight on soul train, but we looked good doing what we could.

"May we cut in?" I heard Anthony's voice behind me. I turned around and saw Anthony with Jordan and Jervis behind him, but no Leon.

"Hey, we've been looking for you guys." I had to yell to compete with 50's *P.I.M.P.* "Leon isn't coming?"

"That fool has drama, man," Anthony said. "Didn't he tell you?"

"About his wife and stuff?"

"Yeah." He shook his head. "Maybe he'll come down."

"Down?" I asked, but some Eminem song came on and the crowd went wild. As the guys danced with my friends I sashayed myself over to the bar and asked politely, "May I have a Screwdriver, please?"

The bartender quickly returned, "Actually, I was asked to give you this by a gentleman upstairs on the VIP level." She handed me a little card. On the outside were the words, You've been invited to VIP. When I opened it, it had a handwritten note in blue ink. "I'll foot the bill for your heart's desires tonight if I can have you my way tomorrow."

I smiled so big that my wisdom teeth were probably exposed. Was this what Anthony meant by Leon might come down? Ah . . . he meant down from VIP. I liked Leon's style. For once in my life after sleeping with a guy too soon he wasn't giving me his ass to kiss, he was coming after me. I looked up at the VIP section, but there were so many tall brothas looking down I didn't know where to begin.

I called the bartender over. "Where is he?" I asked.

"I have no clue, sweetie. The doorman from upstairs brought it to me along with enough money to pay you and your girls' tab. He said that it was courtesy of a guy upstairs." She shrugged her shoulders. "Somebody up there wants you. Those invitations are one hundred dollars a pop."

"Whoa!" Why didn't Leon just come down and talk to me? He could've put that money in my pocket. "So what do I do?" I asked.

"Take that card to the elevator and it'll get you up there free of charge."

She didn't have to tell me twice, so I sprung up into action. When the elevator doors slid open the ambiance in VIP reminded me of a popular French restaurant on South Beach. A spectacular live floral arrangement of white hydrangeas was on a table adjacent the elevator. Strangely the dim lighting didn't hide anything, but it accentuated the mahogany furniture and the beige marbled floor.

I walked over to the balcony and prayed that Leon would spot me and come over instead of me having to walk too deep into the room. The sistas up there were a force to be reckoned with. You could smell the expensive perfume like it was flowing from a fountain. And their jewelry! Lord, I needed protective eyewear up here, these ladies were iced out. They were gawking at me, the new competition, and I hated every second of it. Some chick dressed in Prada from her fake eyelashes to her corns stared at me, the JC Penney Queen, so long and hard that she willed me away. Yes, I flipped my tight weave in defeat and began walking back toward the elevator.

"Where are you going?" A guy the shade of coffee after adding three tiny drops of milk grabbed my arm. He was about six foot four, 220 pounds, sporting a fresh haircut, beige Armani suit, and wouldn't let go of my hand. "I was worried that you weren't coming."

"Excuse me?" I smiled him off. "I think you have the wrong girl."

"I have the *right* girl," the words slipped out of his bright white smile. His face was slender with a freshly trimmed goatee. His nose was sharper than most black men I've seen, and his slightly slanted eyes were hypnotic. "I was wondering if I may talk to you for a moment."

"Well, that depends on what you have to say," I said.

"Okay, well, for starters," he began, "how are you today?"

"I'm good, how about yourself?"

"I'm fine." He glanced at my chest hoping I didn't notice. "Are you here with someone?"

"Yes." I smiled as he took a step back. "I'm here with my girlfriends."

"Are you from here?" he asked, taking a sip of whatever was in his glass.

"I don't think that anyone here this weekend is really from here. I'm from Miami," I answered. "I'm just here for the weekend. What about you?"

"Philly, I'm here until Monday." He smiled.

He looked familiar. "Did you go to FAM?"

"U Dub." He cleared things up. "The University of Washington."

For the two seconds we were silent a rude overweight guy came over and struck up a conversation with him. I glanced over the room quickly and just as I suspected Leon was talking to a gentleman by the bar.

"Barry, may I catch up with you later?" Mr. Armani asked his pudgy friend. "I was getting to know this intriguing young lady." Barry immediately apologized and excused himself. He grabbed my hand rather suggestively. "Sorry about the interruption, where were we?"

"Actually," I frowned, "maybe we can talk later." Leon had paid big bucks for me to be in VIP. "There's someone that I came up here to see."

"Huh?"

"Yeah, I'm sorry." Showing him the invitation, I turned the hold he had on my hand into a handshake. "It was very nice talking to you."

I headed in Leon's direction, but before I could reach him a tall slender and good-looking sista did. She tossed her long hair to one side, extended her arms, and he fell between them. Imagine my shock when he kissed the heifer on the lips. By the end of their smooch I was right behind her. Lo and behold, his wedding band was back on and shining bright. Ain't that a bitch?

"Hello, Leon." All signs said that he peed on himself when I spoke. The woman turned to face me with a what-the-fuck expression.

"Thalia." No hug, handshake or even a head nod, just a glued on smile. "What brings you here?"

"Well," I giggled nervously, "you."

"Me?" he said, giving me a chance to retract my answer.

"Yes, you." I then turned toward the woman. "Hi." I politely reached for her hand and surprisingly she shook it.

Her thin hand trembled as she asked, "Do I know you?"

"No." I looked at Leon. "Should I know her?"

"This is my wife," he stated. "Diane."

"Oh." I pretended to get his drift. "Your wife!"

"Yes," she snickered. "His wife."

I continued to smile. "Nice to meet you, Diane."

"Want a drink?" he asked, but before I could open my mouth he motioned the bartender over. "Give the lady whatever she wants on me." He couldn't think that a ten dollar glass of anything would buy my silence.

The bartender asked, "What can I get you, ma'am?"

When I couldn't answer, Leon, with eyes that were pleading for peace, had the nerve to ask, "What do you normally drink?"

"Oh," I smiled at him and flipped the script, "you know what I like."

"What?" His eyes bugged out and he stuttered, "I . . . I don't know." He looked at his wife then looked back at me. "Wine?"

"No," I corrected him. "I guess watching me down Blowjobs tonight won't be as fun in front of company, huh?"

"What?" He looked at me like I had lost my mind.

"A Screwdriver would be nice," I said to the still waiting bartender. Five seconds of silence was so uncomfortable that Leon was sweating, and I could tell that she couldn't wait until I left to question him. And for two minutes neither of us said a word, not I to him, not him to me, not her to him, not her to me . . . you get the picture.

When the bartender brought my drink I grabbed it and said, "I'd love to sit and chat," I converted my attention to his wife, "but the fact that I had sex with your husband last night, who said that you two were no longer together, makes for a very uncomfortable gathering, ya know?"

"What?" She looked at him and I began walking away until I heard her say, "How could you sleep with that nasty bitch?"

Screech! I made a u-turn, rested my drink on the bar, and called upon the spirits of all of my ghetto acting ancestors that had gone on before. "Excuse me, what did you say?"

She did the talk-to-the-hand thing. "Bitch, I'm talking to my husband, not you."

The Florida ghosts of ghetto past came rushing from Liberty City, Opa Locka, Homestead, Florida City, and Goulds. "Who the fuck are you calling a bitch?"

"You." Oh no she didn't.

"I got your bitch, you don't even know me." I was a foot away from her. "I will whoop your ass in here."

She was ignoring me. "This is the one you met in rehab isn't it?" She grabbed Leon's hand. "I spent ten thousand fucking dollars for you to go to a rehab and you fuck around on me?" She added, "You drove my damn Benz here for you to meet up with your crack whore?"

"Crack whore?" I was in her face. "You're the damn powder head."

She glared at me. "Did you meet him at Wishing Well Rehab last month?"

"No." I was confused. "I met him last night." I looked at him. "*You* were in rehab?"

She didn't allow him to answer. "Yes. My husband is a functional coke addict. Didn't you tell her?" She stared at him like a mother would at a rude child. "Are you using again?"

"He said that he caught *you* doing coke."

"Oh, I'm the one with the problem you sorry son of a bitch?"

A few people gathered to stare. "He said that you had a cocaine problem and that you two were getting a divorce and he was seeking custody of his daughter."

"Custody of our daughter?" She grabbed her purse and slapped him with it. "We don't even have a fucking daughter." She pranced off and he was on her tail.

I walked away from the scene of the argument like I wasn't a part of it. He must've been trying to surprise me, but she surprised him by showing up after he sent the invitation to me. A functional addict, wow! Well, for what it's worth, he was the best looking addict I had ever seen and the first one I had had sex with . . . that I know of.

Chapter 6

Too Much HBO

I leaned on another section of the bar, finished my Screwdriver, and walked toward the elevator. "Where do you think you're going?" the familiar voice asked as the elevator doors opened. I turned to see the welcoming smile of Mr. Armani Suit. "Leaving?"

"It seems," I said.

He reached toward me and pointed at the invitation. "So you're turning me down?"

"Huh?" I was confused. "It was you who invited me here?"

"Yeah, and here you are trying to get away from me."

"No, I saw someone that I knew and assumed that it was from him." I was embarrassed. "Why didn't you say something earlier?"

"I thought you knew." He held his hand out to me. "I'm Andre."

"Thalia," I said as we shook.

We nestled in at a small corner table. "I saw you down at the other bar earlier."

"You should've came over and talked to me," I continued jokingly. "It would've been more economical."

"Economical isn't my style." He smiled. "What would you like to drink?"

I needed a liquor break. "Water."

"Water?" he repeated. "I'm impressed."

"Don't be, I've been drinking all day. I just need a break."

"What do you normally drink?"

I was not about to say Blowjobs, Smirnoff Ice or Coronas which my weekend was already full of. "Well, this weekend my friends and I have been trying a little of everything, but I'm normally a wine drinker."

"Really, what kind?"

"Syrah." I thought about the first time someone asked me that and I answered red.

"Which?" he asked.

A while back my answer to this question would've also been, red, but I was somewhat a mini-connoisseur now. "Napa Valley."

After a few minutes of talking and the ice chipped away I could feel Andre's eyes on my skin. "So when are you leaving Daytona Beach?"

"Monday," I answered. "I have to be at work on Tuesday."

"Oh yeah." He got comfortable in his chair. "What do you do?"

"I'm an elementary school teacher."

"Is that right?" He smiled. "What grade?"

"Third." I then asked, "What do you do in Philly?"

After sipping his cognac he responded, "I'm a detective."

"Wow, a real live detective," I teased him. "How old are you?"

"Twenty-seven." He licked his lips. "What about you?"

"I'm twenty-two," I mumbled out, still pondering his age. "Aren't you a little young to be a detective?"

"Criminology major, as well as two years in the Marines," he spoke proudly. "This is my first year as a detective though."

"Is that always what you wanted to do?" Our drinks arrived in the middle of my question.

He answered, "Football is my first love."

"Did you pursue it?"

"Yeah, I received an athletic scholarship to the University Of Washington. I would've been an NFL first round draft pick about six years ago." He swallowed hard. "But I got hurt, and my major was criminology."

Remembering the Leon situation I quickly asked, "Are you married?"

"Nope." He joked, "I wouldn't be here if I was."

Relieved, I asked, "Children?"

"Not yet."

I had to get all three questions out. "Girlfriend?"

"When women realize that I *used* to play ball, they're more interested in my friends that still do." He continued. "I have a question for you."

"Shoot."

"Are we on for dinner tomorrow?"

I blushed. "I don't see why not."

The club's photographer came over. "Mr. Teasdale, may I have a picture of you and the young lady?"

He turned to me. "Would you like to?"

"Sure." When we stood and he held me around the

waist I wasted no time feeling like in his arms was where I wanted to be. I was such a sucker for love.

"Let's dance," he said as the DJ switched to Reggae. You can't be from Miami and not have a Jamaican friend show you some Dancehall moves. I shook everything I had to Elephant Man, Buju Banton, and Bounty Killer. The DJ must've seen when my knees almost gave and slowed it down with Ginuwine's *In Those Jeans*. I held Andre tight around the neck, and by the way he stroked, rubbed, and caressed my body, I knew it would be hard to turn him loose. Something told me that I would leave Daytona Beach with a man . . . and he just felt like the one. Yeah, I know . . . I'm trippin'. I thought Leon was too . . . but a girl has to dream. At the end of the song his lips touched my ear. "How does a glass of Syrah sound now?"

"Sounds like music to my ears."

I excused myself to the ladies' room as he strolled over to the bar to let my request be known. From the restroom I made a call to Madi just so that they would know that I was all right. On my way back to the table I noticed a young lady occupying my seat . . . not again! Why tonight? She was all smiles while talking to Andre, but he was smiling at me as I continued toward him. "Welcome back!" Obviously, whatever she was saying wasn't important. He stood and handed me the glass. "Here's your wine."

"Thank you," I said and cleared my throat. I was trying to be polite, but she wasn't getting up.

"I'm sorry." He looked down at her. "What did you say your name was?"

"Samantha," she said with a half-smile.

"Samantha, this is Thalia," he pointed to the chair, "and that is her seat. I tried telling you that before you sat down." She gave him the fuck-you look, stood up, and sauntered her narrow ass away.

I joked, "I said to keep my seat warm, but damn."

"She just came out of nowhere and offered me her hotel room key."

"Wow." I sipped my wine. "You have it like that?"

"I don't want it like that though." He stared at me intensely before he asked, "So, you don't have a man?"

"No."

"Husband?"

"Nope." I copied his earlier answer, "If I did I wouldn't be here."

"Children?"

"They'll come along with the husband."

"No husband, no boyfriend, and no kids." He paused. "You must have a booty call then."

"Yes, but only on Tuesday nights," I said with a straight face.

"Tuesdays, huh?" He lifted an eyebrow.

"Nah, I have no booty buddy." I laughed. "What about you, do you have midnight booty calls, or as you men say, a girl that comes over and the two of you just," I used my fingers as quotation marks, "hang out?"

"Midnight is too late. My calls come in around nine thirty-ish." He smiled. "Nah, man, it's just me."

"You mean you're not going to take Samantha up on her offer?" I asked.

"No way." He shook his head. "I've had enough of those types of women." He added, "They always find me. Most of them remember my face; they still think that I'm playing."

"Most men would die to have it like that."

"Don't get me wrong. Those days were hot for a while. But I'm growing up. I want a respectable woman that I can come home to after a long day at work." He was serious. "A woman who'll have sex with me after only knowing me a few hours would have sex with anyone." He paused. "That's trashy."

Images of my night with Leon, less than twenty-four hours ago, were haunting me. I *was* the trash that he spoke of. "Well, you've found me out," I confessed. "I was a groupie once."

He stared at me in disbelief. "Huh?"

"I was willing to beg, steal, cheat, and kill for Tony Thompson from Hi-Five back in the day," I spoke proudly.

"Oh yeah, I remember that group. He was the lead singer from *I Like the Way*." He laughed. "So what happened?"

"Tony Terry," I said.

"Dude that sung *Everlasting Love* with the red high-top fade?"

"Yep. He was supposed to marry me, give me five red-headed kids, and life was supposed to be good."

"Isn't he gay now or something?"

"Beats me, when he didn't answer one of the seventeen letters I sent to him I dumped that brotha."

For the next two hours we talked, danced, and drank more and more. Andre was a gentleman, my type of guy. I was smitten and certain that there was something special about him. As we returned from the dance floor he took me by surprise. "Let's get out of here."

Did I here him right? "Huh?"

"It's getting louder in here by the minute. Would you mind leaving with me?"

Why did I keep doing this to myself? "Sounds like a plan, but I'll need to tell my friends." This was the second night . . . a second stranger. Was I desperate?

On the dark elevator he pulled me into a slight embrace. The door opened and to my surprise Vette was stepping out of the restroom adjacent the elevator. "Hey." I was shocked to see her. "I was just coming to let you all know that I'm leaving."

"Okay." Vette checked out Andre and tried to whisper, "Who is this?"

"This is Andre," I pointed to him. "And Andre, this is my girl Yvette."

"It's nice to meet you." He shook her hand.

"It's very nice to meet *you*, Andre." It was obvious that she approved of him.

"I'll see you later," I said and couldn't help smiling.

"Really?" Vette asked. "Wanna watch Magnum P.I. later?"

I giggled at the magnum comment. "Nah, don't wait up."

I cut the conversation short before she said something else to embarrass me.

Andre opened the door of his rented Jaguar for me and once inside I reached over and opened his. "My dad told me that if a woman was considerate enough to open the door for a man, she was indeed a good woman," he said.

I was just doing the right thing. "It's an instant reaction."

"Well, actions speak louder than words," he said. "Keep impressing me, Thalia Tyree."

I laughed. "Now why are you calling me by my full name?"

"I think it's pretty."

"Thank you." I blushed. "There's only one other person that does that."

"It has a nice ring to it," he said.

"That's exactly what he says."

"Who," he put the car in drive, "an ex-boyfriend?"

"No," I stared out of the window, "my best friend's father."

During the drive we learned that we were both staying at the same hotel. Our rooms were just three floors apart. Being alone with him was a lot different than being in a crowded nightclub; I clammed up, we didn't talk much at all. We pulled into a vacant spot in the hotel's parking area. He looked over at me. "May I steal a little more of your time?"

"How are you going to use it?"

He reached over and grabbed my hand, pulling it to his lips to kiss. "Do you drink coffee?"

I was speechless minus these two words. "I *will.*"

I was glad that he didn't suggest more alcohol. My consumption in two days doubled my annual intake of the previous year. Thinking of having another glass of anything was making me queasy, but maybe coffee would do some good.

The elevator doors opened on the fourth floor and he led me down the hall. "Have you ever been to Philly?" He pushed the key into the lock and turned the handle.

"No, but I've always wanted to go."

He was sly. "Why haven't you?"

I wanted my answer to spark a little something. "I don't know anyone there."

As I walked past him to enter the room the jet-black hair of his goatee was an inch away from my mouth. "Now you know me." He removed his jacket and draped it over a chair by the room table. "Do you mind if I change?" he asked.

"Not at all, you do your thing and I'll get the coffee going." I made my way into the kitchen and got things percolating. Afterward, I took off my shoes and made myself at home on the sofa.

"Good God," I mumbled to myself as Andre walked back into the room wearing only gray sweatpants. He still had the body of a football player. His chest was firm, abs tight, arms stacked, and that picture perfect face. My mouth was opened so long that I felt a drop of drool sliding down. I looked away humiliated. "The coffee should be finished."

"How do you like yours?"

To be certain that we meant the same thing, "Coffee?" I asked.

"Yeah." He smiled.

"The way I like my men." Yes, I used that age-old line. "Dark!" I continued. "A drop of cream, two sugars."

"You are so attractive," he said as he returned with the mugs. "When I say attractive, don't feel as though I'm speaking only of your physical attributes. I'm saying that you have a way of attracting people to you." He sat next to me and propped his feet up on the coffee table. "It's the way you talk, the things you say, and the things you do."

After an hour in his room I asked, "Where does the last name Teasdale originate?"

"Well, I don't know how true it is, but my family tree is said to be connected to the family of the late Sara

Teasdale, the poet. My great, great, great-grandmother was rumored to have been married secretly to Sara's uncle." He chuckled. "At least that's what my grandmother told me. But we've never been invited to any family reunions."

"Wow." I paused. "That's pretty interesting. Are you familiar with any of her work?"

"When I first heard the story about my kinship to Sara, I went to the library to familiarize myself with her. But as time passed and I got older I stopped being so enthused about it," he said. "I only remember the one she was most popular for, it's called *Moonlight*." He smiled. "What about your first name; does it mean anything?"

"No," I lied because normally when I started telling people they leave me babbling to myself.

"Wasn't Thalia in Greek Mythology?" He raised an eyebrow.

"Yeah, wow, it's amazing that you know that." I was impressed.

Andre asked, "She was the muse of good cheer or something like that, right?"

"Yeah, you're absolutely right." Finally, someone that was familiar with the story. "Thalia was the daughter of Zeus and Mnemosyne; she was the goddess who presided over the arts and sciences."

"There are a lot of similarities between you two." He offered me a smile.

"Like what?" I tested him.

"For starters, she was in charge of the arts and sciences, and you're a school teacher." He held up one finger. "Two, she loved beautiful things, look in the mirror." He was quite a character. "And three, she awarded people with good cheer. I must say that you've made me feel good all night long."

It was after four in the morning when the room fell silent and I caught his eyes the way I'd been meaning not to all night long. "What is it about you?" he asked as his hand gripped mine, pulling me closer to him on the sofa. His hands slid around my waist and his touch started a fire deep within me and I wanted him to not throw fuel on it; I was trying to behave.

I whispered, "Don't let me do anything stupid." I was dead serious.

"I won't." He introduced his lips to mine and as I wrapped my hands around his neck his hands climbed up my back and pressed my body even closer to his. Our tongues communicated in a language we had never heard, but we understood, and we understood for fifteen minutes. His breathing elevated and his hands dropped from holding my waist to softly caressing my butt.

Then it hit me, the worst decision of my entire life. I don't know what attributed to it more: the alcohol, the coffee, or too much HBO, but I pulled away from Andre's kiss and found myself kneeling down in front of him. He was just as surprised as I was when I began grabbing for the waist of his pants. Something in his eyes told me to stop but his lips never moved. Once his pants were pulled to his thighs his fully erect eight-inch chocolate bar sprung into view. With veins protruding from the sides, the pulsating domed-tip let out a droplet that I caught with my finger and licked off. Why couldn't I just leave well enough alone?

I kissed it gently and with more saliva than needed. I licked him leaving him glistening, and then folded my lips back over my teeth and went down for the count. I bobbed up and down and felt his hips slightly rising up and down to maximize his pleasure. "Oh yeah," he moaned. "Shit." His words scratched the itch of encouragement within me and I struggled to take all of him in. "Damn girl." He was very excited; his thrusts became more and more aggressive, but our rhythm was a bit off, he was pulling too far out as I moved away and was pushing in too far while I was coming down. I corrected it a few times but as the feeling intensified we were thrown off track again.

He thrust upward as I was moving downward on him and seemed to hit the back of my brain. Suddenly my mouth was filled with coffee, wine, and a mixture of other liquids and chunks of food. It was vomit, and it gushed down his pole and then onto his lap. "Oh shit!" he yelled and jumped up. At that very moment the door to the room opened and two men walked in. He was so engrossed in the nasty slime draining down his thighs that he didn't notice them. He pushed me away and walked off. "Damn it!" I heard the bathroom door close and the water shooting out at full force.

With puke still spewing from my mouth and nose the men stared at me like a rotten piece of meat. I stood up as tears rolled down my cheeks. I just grabbed my shoes, ran out, and thanked God that the elevator was already on the fourth floor.

I made it to my room under perfect conditions; no one else was there yet. Therefore, I had no explaining, no story to tell, and no questions to answer. I took a shower, downed two Tylenols, and then hopped into bed and fell into deep thought. The tears found me again; the pain wasn't so much from the embarrassment of the vomiting or his friends walking in. It was the fact that I had reached a new level of desperation. How could I have gotten on my knees in front of another stranger? I remembered our conversation at the club and what he said about women who were willing to sleep with him on the first night. He called them trashy. I rolled over and cried my trashy ass to sleep.

Chapter 7

Naughty Girl

The Let's Talk about Sex committee met again, waking me up for the second morning in a row. Vette slammed herself on my bed and said, "How did you manage to snag that fine brotha and still make it home before everyone else?"

"Good morning to you, too," I said sarcastically with my eyes half-closed.

"Good morning," Madi laughed, joining in. "Now, how did you make it home before us?"

"Forget all of that." Trell was the only one who had some type of sense. "Please give us the details on Leon and his wife." For some reason hearing that fool's name brought a smile to my face. I sat up and told the whole story, from me receiving the invitation to VIP, to Andre bringing me to the hotel. However, I created a more reputable ending: Andre walked me to the room, was a perfect gentleman, and told me that he'd call me when he woke up. "So how was your night with Anthony?"

"You mean plunger tongue?" Madi joked. "We didn't gel too well; Trell and I stuck together most of the time."

"What happened to Jervis, Trell?" I asked.

"He's a little too fast paced for me," she said. "You know that Negro had the nerve to show me his dick the first night," she complained. "I'm going to send out a worldwide e-mail. Men need to know that as good as their dicks might look or as big as it may be, showing it off to a stranger makes you a loser." Trell rolled her eyes. "I am sick of men."

"Amen to that," Madi agreed.

"Well, Jordan is nothing like Jervis," Vette vouched for him.

"So what are we doing today?" Madi asked.

It was 11:22 A.M. I lied back down. "I'm not doing anything." I couldn't remember what Andre's friends looked like and I wasn't about to take the chance of them recognizing me.

"Oh that's right you have a date with Mr. Detective," Trell teased.

"That's right." I forced a smiled. They'd never hear the real story. In less than twenty-four hours Andre and I would be almost as far away as you can get from someone and still be on the East Coast, so I just had to get through the day.

In two hours I had the entire hotel room to myself. I thought of just wallowing in depression, self-pity, and embarrassment but that wouldn't change anything. Everyone is entitled to one mistake in life, right? I needed to talk to someone. It was Sunday; the time was now 2:15 P.M., and if a Baptist church was still in service that meant somebody was showing off. I called my mother.

"Girl, Pastor Flack threw it down today." She was still excited.

"Really?" I knew she was going to tell me but I decided to ask, "What did he preach on?"

"The topic was: Where is Your Armor? And he let folks have it. The church was on fire." She added, "Sister Goodman's son got saved today."

"Who, Craig?" I asked.

"Yes."

"Craig got saved *again*?" I couldn't believe it. That had to be the third time this year. "He gets saved more than drowning people."

"The Lord doesn't care about that foolishness." She got serious. "That's why *some* people can't get saved now. They're too worried about who else is getting saved." She was hinting at me.

"It's more like who else is backsliding," I giggled and quickly changed the subject. "So which choir sung today?"

"The youth choir, with those crazy rap sounding songs."

"Mama, that's what is needed to bring young people in."

"It sure hasn't brought you in."

"I told you that I'm busy grading papers on most Sundays . . . Jesus."

"Stop taking the Lord's name in vain." She continued. "I told Pastor Flack that you'll be there next Sunday."

"All right. I just wanted to say hello."

"Okay, I love you." My mother, Nadia Tyree, wasn't always saved, sanctified, Holy Ghost filled, and fire baptized. During the ten-year merry-go-round that my father stayed on with her, my mom turned to alcohol, marijuana, and dabbled in cocaine to heal her emotional scars. She was a functional addict. She wasn't a scary or abusive addict. She paid the bills, cared for her kids, kept a job. She looked like a regular educated black woman. She kept herself together and remained nothing but Mama to Devon, Tyann, and me. I didn't know that she had a problem until we had to live with our aunt for a few months while she was in rehab. She worked as a loan officer at a bank, and being a faithful employee, her boss didn't question her three-month leave. She is now the Senior Executive Loan Officer.

Later she confessed to us that she got high enough to forget that our father didn't respect her, but not high enough to forget her love for him. Though she kicked the habits she still couldn't kick him. So whenever he called, she was still available and whenever she was available he took advantage of her. My mother was only sober for eleven months when we learned that Daddy married a white woman he had recently met. Mama hit rock bottom and knew that if she started to use again she'd never recover. At thirty-two years old she ran to the nearest church, Mount Pleasant Missionary Baptist. At the time, Pastor Flack was fresh out of college with his master's degree in Theology.

Six years after joining the church my mother was one of the ladies of the church that saw to it that Pastor Flack wanted for nothing after he lost his wife. Whenever I went to visit Madi, Mama had me carrying a pot of something or other, a loaf of bread, a gallon of milk, and if we didn't have enough food to share with his family, she'd send me with a few dollars. Fourteen years later she still loves the church, loves her Pastor, but most of all she's still in love with the Lord. "I love you, too, Mama." I added, "I'll call you later on."

As I hung up my cellular, the hotel room phone rang. "Hello," I said when I picked it up.

"Good day, Miss Tyree," a sexy deep voice came across.

"Hi."

"How's your day going?" His cheerful tone led me to believe that he forgot last night.

"It's been fine thus far." I blushed. "Yours?"

"Great, it's beautiful here in Miami." Oh crap, I thought it was Andre. "Is my daughter there?" Reverend Flack asked.

"Mr. Flack? I mean Isaac?" My eyes widened. "No, I'm sorry, Madison isn't here."

"I missed her call last night so I figured I'd try her back after church," he said.

"I'll tell her that you called." I was nervous. "I assure you that she's in one piece, still breathing, and un-harmed."

"Great. Well, make sure you're not a stranger when you get back." He paused. "Your mother said that you'll be there next Sunday." A few months back I found my-self spending two hundred dollars on a dress, shoes, purse, and accessories hoping that he'd notice me at church.

I hadn't spoke a word of this to a soul, but honestly, I couldn't tell if I was going to church to hear the Word or just to hear words coming out of his mouth. Now if that wasn't a sin then I don't know what is. How could I ever get saved with the preacher being as fine as him? There were too many ungodly thoughts associated with just looking at him. All the joking Vette and I did about Madi's father turned into constant fantasizing about him in positions that were far from holy. "Yes, I'll be there with her."

"Good," he said. "I look forward to seeing you and your mother."

With the mention of my mother I straightened up because if she ever learned my thoughts about *her* Reverend Flack I'd be drinking holy water and quoting scriptures backward. "All right, I'll tell Madi that you called."

"Well, Thalia, you have a blessed day."

"Thank you, Isaac, you do the same." I hung up the phone so fast you'd think it was a stalker on the other line. "Damn." I was seriously crushing on him. He wasn't just Mr. Flack, Reverend Flack, or Madi's daddy in my eyes, he was 'da bomb', excuse me God, but he is sexy as hell.

This will more than likely send me to hell, no lines, no waiting, but at the end of his sermons, which Baptist folk call the climax, it seems like we're climaxing sexually. He's screaming out of control, drenched in sweat, and breathing heavily. The vibrations from the speakers run throughout the walls of the church straight to my panties, leaving me scared to stand up during alter call. Whenever I hear him preach I climax during his "climax." Oh, Happy Day.

There were even a few desperate nights where lying in bed alone I imagined going into his office in tears for counseling. At the end of our meeting, while on my knees in front of him listening to his powerful prayer for my repentance, I unbuckle his pants and seek out his oldest member. To my surprise it's hard. Through the unzipped peephole I baptize him with my saliva and then he begins to pray for himself, asking for strength to walk away, but deliverance doesn't come in time and he begins thrusting powerfully yet innocently into my mouth . . . then in walks Sister "Sanctified" Stride, president of the mission board and every other damn board in the church, with five gallons of blessed olive oil to slip slide the demons out of us.

I sat around the room for another fifteen minutes contemplating ordering room service. When I finally called, the guy in the kitchen said that they were backed up and I'd probably have a better chance just eating at the restaurant. I was too hungry for the hour and a half wait that he was talking about so I got dressed and made my way downstairs. I sat down at a table against the wall and was waited on immediately. My salad arrived and I tore into it like a hungry sailor. The vinaigrette dressing was creamy and tangy yet sweet and the romaine lettuce seemed fresh from the farm. "Make sure you leave room for dinner," Andre said as he approached my table with a large bouquet of sunflowers. "We are still on for dinner, right?" He rested the flowers on the table and sat across from me.

"Hi." I didn't want to look at him.

"Hello."

"Look," we both said at the same time and then laughed.

"Go ahead," I said.

"I'm sorry about last night," he apologized. "I'm sorry for overreacting and for my friends walking in, and I'm sorry that I didn't stop you."

"I don't know what got into me." My eyes never left my salad.

He lightened the mood. "I know what came out of you though." We laughed. "I was just in disbelief when I realized what happened. I wasn't a happy camper, but I didn't know that you would up and leave me."

"Your friends walked in and I freaked out."

"They said that you were crying."

"Crying?" Men always focused on drama when it came to women. "I was embarrassed. Plus I thought of the conversation we had in the club about women . . . on the first night." I paused. "I got overwhelmed."

He stared at me. "Forget the whole night." He held out his hand to me and said, "Hi, I'm Andre."

"Nice to meet you." I looked over at him for the first time and took his hand. "I'm Thalia."

"So, what's with the flowers?" I asked. "You're just walking around the hotel looking for a pretty girl to give them to?"

"Yes, that's exactly what I was doing." He smiled. "I was walking around the hotel looking for a pretty girl to give them to." He placed them in my hand. "I didn't know your room number so I've been in the lobby hoping to run into you, pretty girl."

"Thanks," I blushed.

We shared the food that I had already ordered and decided to get out and see Daytona together. I appreciated the fact that Andre wasn't trying to get me up to his room to finish the job. But first I needed to put the flowers in water. I ran up to the room as Andre waited out in the car for me.

When I left the room earlier the girls were still out. So when I walked in and heard Beyonce's *Naughty Girl* playing in Madi and Trell's room I was surprised. I put the sunflowers in a Big Gulp cup until I could do better. Wanting Madi to know my whereabouts I turned the knob to her room. The knob was locked, but because the door wasn't pushed all the way in I was able to open it. Beyonce wasn't the only naughty girl in the room. What I saw nearly sent me into full cardiac arrest.

Trell, with her eyes squeezed shut, was naked and lying on her back with her head to the foot of the bed and Madi, also naked, was atop of her with a strap on dildo. As Madi rose and fell, the jet-black veined delight disappeared into Trell over and over again. Madi kissed her more passionately than she did during the truth or dare game. In syncopation with the song Madi gave and Trell received, their breasts wiggled and jiggled, and from below Trell clutched Madi's butt as a plea for as much dick as she could possible spare. Madi rose up onto the palm of her hands, the way a man would, and gave Trell what she wanted . . . more.

I stood in the cracked doorway and watched Madison handle Trell like a man. Watching wasn't my intention; I tried to walk away but I forgot how. I didn't know how long I was actually standing there, but I saw Trell's body go into convulsions. Her screams sounded over the music, and when her buck wild body fell life-less to the sheets, Madison's eyes found mine. The look she got from me said, "Straight women don't walk around with a strap on in their purses." She quickly looked away and I walked out without even bothering to close the door.

On the elevator to the lobby my mind was working overtime. Madison didn't seem like an amateur, but very well skilled and passionate about what she was doing. I questioned myself, but couldn't supply an-swers. *Was she bisexual or gay? Was I the type of friend that she couldn't tell that to? And how long has this been going on?*

I made it to Andre's car. "Are you all right?" he asked, probably referring to the dazed look on my face.

"Um." I couldn't tell him that my best friend was a

carpet muncher. "I'm fine; I just got a little dizzy on the elevator."

"No pun intended," Andre smiled, "but it looks like you want to throw up."

"Oh yeah, and you of all people should know what I look like when I want to throw up." I took the opportunity to laugh.

"Where to?" He pulled onto the road.

"Just take me away," I said. "Far away."

After a bit of riding around he looked over at me and asked, "Can you shoot pool?"

"I love shooting pool," I lied. I was terrible.

"Think you can take me?" he asked.

I was the number one shit-talker. "Not only will I take you, I'll completely embarrass you."

"Two out of three games cool with you?" He pulled into a parking spot quickly. "Two out of three will give you a chance to not lose completely."

"Whatever! We can shoot one game, but if you're unsure of your game we can shoot three." My bark was thirty times the size of my bite.

"It's like that?" He smiled.

"Yep." I knew that I was about to get my ass torn out of the frame, but took another cheap shot anyway. "Let's see if Philly is good for anything other than cheese steaks."

We entered the pool hall, paid, selected sticks, and found a table. By now I was wishing I hadn't talked so much crap.

"Would you like to break?"

I stepped over to the table and chalked up my stick, said a little prayer, bent down, glanced over at the balls, pulled my stick back, and begged at least one ball to fall in . . . that didn't happen.

He took his shot, then a cheap shot at me. "Do you need glasses?"

"Nope," I said as I sent the yellow solid ball flying into the corner pocket; I was shocked but I couldn't let him know.

"Whoa." He seemed a tad impressed. "Nice."

"I know," I said, smiling.

Just my luck, my next shot landed one of his balls in. He didn't say a word, but he didn't have to, the ear-to-ear smile said it all. During that game I never got to shoot again, he ran the table on me all the way down to him blasting the eight ball in the side pocket. I wanted to laugh at myself but he was doing it for me.

He looked around the bar. "I wonder if they have people to rack the balls after each game." He then pointed upward and read an imaginary sign. "Losers must rack the balls after each game. I think that would be you."

I rolled my eyes. "That was just practice."

"Was it?" He moved close to my face. "Then how about a little wager on the next game?"

"What kind of wager?" I asked

"I'll leave it up to you." He looked away smiling.

I couldn't think of anything original and snappy so I said, "Loser buys dinner tonight."

"Cool." He laughed.

I racked the balls up and he made the break, landing nothing in, so I was up to shoot. I stuffed a striped ball in the side pocket then turned around and put one in the corner pocket. On my third shot I sunk nothing. He made two in at once but also scratched, so it was on me again. The game went on for another fifteen minutes and came down to only the eight ball. He aimed at it, pulled back, but didn't hit it hard enough, so it dangled on the edge of the corner pocket. I grabbed my stick and sent the ball to sleep quietly in the corner. I won!

I looked up at the imaginary sign and said, "What does that sign say? Loser racks balls and buys dinner later."

"Well, I was treating you to dinner anyway, so I didn't lose." Then as he set the balls up he asked, "You want to bet on this last game?"

"Sure! What?" I couldn't think of anything.

He already knew what he wanted. "If I win you fly me to Miami, if you win I'll fly you to Philly."

"Okay." I laughed. "Bet."

He meant business. "I'm serious."

"Sure," I agreed and we shook on it.

"It's your turn to break." He handed me the white ball, I aimed, and hoped that I would sink a striped ball because I seemed to do better with them, but I sunk nothing. When it was his turn Andre walked over to the table leaving his cue stick behind. He grabbed the eight ball and dropped it into the corner pocket.

"I lost." He grabbed my hand and pulled me to him. "When can you come to Philly?"

I asked, "Are you serious?"

"When is your next school break or long weekend?"

I couldn't think straight. "I don't know off-hand."

"Well, I want to see you again," he whispered. "I'm not big on phone calls." His face moved closer until our lips touched and his hands wrapped themselves around my waist.

Chapter 8

Planes, Trains, and Automobiles

After the pool hall we rode around some before his phone rang. "Hello." He smiled and answered and then continued guardedly. "Hey, sweetie, how are you?" Did he say sweetie? "That's good, I'm doing just great." I wasn't trying to be nosey, but what else could I do? "Nothing much, just driving." He continued. "Listen, about what we discussed, how did it go?" He was choosing his words carefully. "Really? Karen, that sounds great. I can't wait." He added fuel to the fire. "Did you get the roses?" He was still smiling. "So you didn't think that I could be a romantic guy?"

She got roses and I got sunflowers? By this time I had the "oh-no-he-didn't" look all over me. I wanted to do the jealous woman thing, you know . . . the fake sneeze, yawn, or nonchalantly ask him a question so that Miss Karen would know that he was with someone else. "Talk to you later." He ended the call. That sure didn't sound like detective work. As he put the phone away he asked, "You hungry?"

"No." I didn't even know what an appetite was at that point. He was just talking to a woman that he sent flowers to and right after giving me flowers and inviting me to visit him in Philly.

"It's after seven." He looked at the clock. "Are you sure?"

"We can go somewhere, but I'll probably just have a salad." I didn't have an attitude, I was disappointed. However, I didn't know this man from Adam and was dumb for allowing my naïve ass to think that he was about to be somebody in my life.

We pulled into the parking lot of a park. We got out and followed the trail between the perfectly manicured bright-green grass. The sound of birds chirping under the glow of the orange sky was awesome. There were small lantern-type lights hanging from fifteen-foot poles every twenty-five feet. The dim lighting gave the park a foreign yet romantic appeal.

There was music coming from somewhere in the darkness. I recognized the popular Italian song. *"When the moon hits your eye like a big pizza pie."* I couldn't help but think who would be listening to that at a park. He wrapped his hands around my waist and swayed me from side-to-side slowly with the beat. With every step we took the mandolins cried out more. "Are you hungry?" he asked.

"Yes."

"Then let's eat." He pointed in the direction of the music and as we got closer I noticed candlelight on a wooden picnic table adorned in a beige linen tablecloth, a bottle of red wine, a pair of wine glasses, matching china with gold trimmings, folded gold linen napkins, silverware, and a bouquet of white roses in a frosted vase sitting between the candles. A small CD player was sitting on the end of the table. "Dinner is served." He led the way over to the table.

"Are you serious?" I was in disbelief.

"You do like Italian, right?" He smiled. "I guess I'm up the creek if you don't."

"I love Italian."

He pointed at the bench. "Then have a seat."

"When did you do this?" I was puzzled.

"Ahem." A woman's voice came from behind me. "*He* didn't do anything."

"Karen Porter," he said.

"Andre Teasdale." She looked in his face and smiled. "You haven't changed a bit."

"It's been a long time." He wrapped his arms around her and kissed her on the cheek.

"Too long." He laughed. "It's so good to see you." Karen was a short, bright skinned, heavyset sista. "Karen, this is Thalia." Then he pointed to her. "Thalia, this is Karen. Karen owns an Italian restaurant here in Daytona Beach. We went to college together. I called her this morning to set this whole thing up."

"Hi, it's nice to meet you." I shook her hand and glanced back at the table and looked back at her. "It's incredible."

"When he called me early this morning with instructions, at first I said no because this was the first I'd heard from him in a year." A man in a chef's hat brought the food to the table and opened the bottle of wine. Karen asked Andre to page her when we were leaving so that she'd send someone to pick up the equipment, then she went away.

"Wow," I said as I looked at the seafood lasagna.

Andre sat across from me and grabbed the wine. He filled both glasses and handed one to me. He softly toasted, "To the planes, trains, and automobiles that we'll be using to keep in touch with each other." At that moment I knew that as soon as I possibly could, I'd be in Philadelphia.

We ate then danced, talked, and kissed the night away at the park until close to eleven. Once in the hotel and in front of the elevators, he jokingly asked, "Coffee?"

"I don't know about that," I said timidly. "I can't handle seeing your friends again right now."

"I got another room." He placed a hotel key in my hand, it read 634. "We'll be alone."

In his room I crashed on the couch and he nestled in next to me. I was beat. "When can you come to Philly?"

"I don't know, but I will." I yawned.

He rubbed my arm. "Tired, huh?"

"Exhausted."

He asked, "Are you sleeping with me tonight?"

"Huh?" Did I hear him right?

He clarified. "Are you spending the night here?" He ran his fingers through my hair.

"Yeah." Before the word was completely out of my mouth, his lips touched mine. We decided that in eighteen days I would be on a plane to Philly, but until it was time to say goodbye I wanted to be in his arms. I closed my eyes and prayed that the sun would find another place to rise, and when it did, I would still be clothed.

The next morning he accompanied me to my room

to watch me pack and then to see me off. My things were scattered under the beds, on the table, on the dresser, and on the chairs. But with Andre's help I managed to do my packing in thirty minutes flat. I wanted to create a cause to be there with him a little longer, but there was none.

When he walked me downstairs to the truck, he kissed me on the cheek and whispered, "Planes, trains, and automobiles," in my ear. I didn't know or care how I would get time off or if the eighteenth day would fall on a Tuesday or a Friday, but I was going to be in Philadelphia rain, snow, sleet or shine.

"Eighteen days." I blew a kiss out of the moving vehicle and watched him as he watched me disappear.

Black College Reunion was history. During the long ride home, Madi avoided conversation with me, but no one could talk if they wanted to. Vette was so hyped about Jordan coming to Miami the next weekend that she talked about it for four out of the five-hour drive. I didn't know when Madison and I would talk, but I certainly couldn't wait.

Ten minutes back into my apartment I started to wonder if what Andre and I had was the beginning of something legitimate or the end of a fling. I definitely wasn't calling him first. Who was I fooling? Within an hour I was searching for his cellular number and felt my heart beat out of control as I dialed it. My question was answered . . . it was just the beginning. We talked every day for hours at a time. Just as promised, eighteen days after leaving Daytona Beach, I boarded a plane for Philadelphia.

Andre greeted me with a dozen red roses and a tight

embrace. Holding him again made me realize just how much of a fling we didn't have, it was so much more. We drove through Philadelphia to Jersey, where he had already made plans for us to spend the weekend in Atlantic City at the Borgata Hotel Casino and Spa.

For a girl that tried to go down on him on the very first day, he was a total gentleman to me. All weekend he never touched me in a sexual manner and I couldn't believe it; you only found men like that in movies. For example: Wesley Snipes' character in *Waiting to Exhale* to be exact. At night he held me, rubbed my shoulders, and ran his fingers through my hair, but his hands never slid down to my breasts or into my panties. We spent the entire weekend eating and gambling. Andre was amazing at the blackjack table and walked away with over $5,000 after a three-hour sitting. When I left Atlantic City the only thing I regretted was losing $75 at the roulette table.

A month later I was on another nonstop flight to Philadelphia. This time there was no plan for a weekend escapade in another city. We would be staying at his house. When he pulled in front of the large cream-colored house I was in awe. The four bedrooms, two and a half bathrooms, living room, kitchen, and dining room areas were immaculate. The step down living room with its elegant furnishing, plush carpeting, expensive paintings, custom built entertainment center, and vaulted ceiling made me feel as though I had entered royal territory. Complete with waxed hardwood flooring, the gigantic den was Andre's home office, library, and cognac and martini lounge.

We spent my first night cooking, listening to slow songs, and the next day he showed me all around Philly. We even visited Market Street, where I had the biggest

Philly cheese steak sub I'd ever seen. We still weren't having sex and by now I was frustrated. This brotha had to want some of me.

On my last night in Philly I spread a blanket on Andre's living room floor. I had planned a romantic in-house picnic. I popped the cork on a bottle of Veuve Clicquot champagne and fixed a small platter of finger foods. I also strategically placed candles all around the room, lit them, turned on a jazz CD, and then I lay out on the blanket and waited on him to come out of the shower. He exited the restroom with a huge smile. However, all we did was kiss!

Later as I closed my eyes under the warm waterfall of the shower, I wondered what Andre's angle was. And when I opened my eyes, I found myself in darkness. I quickly backed away to reach for a towel, but bumped into something that shouldn't have been there. "Are you trying to knock me over?" Andre asked.

I was startled. "What are you doing?" As my eyes adjusted I noticed the flickering on the ceiling and on the shower curtain. He had brought candles with him.

"I hope that I've been good long enough." My back was now against his chest. "I just can't wait anymore, I want to feel you." His hands moved slowly around my wet waist and trailed over my stomach.

"You scared me," I said, still trying to get over the shock.

"Shh." He gently pushed me under the water as he kissed my shoulders and then my back. "You have nothing to be scared of, I'll never hurt you." One of his hands crept up and began caressing my breast. "You know that don't you?"

"Yes." It came out more like a groan.

He grabbed the soap and rubbed it between the

palms of his hands and used them to lather my body. The soft, sexy, subtleness of his goatee touched my back as his hands slid over my frame. My back was against his chest when he parted my legs. I felt his warm hand glide between my lower lips, and after a few strokes, I found myself trembling. Moments later he turned me around to face him. His hands grabbed my buttocks firmly. "I want you." While kissing me he gently thumped my clitoris and then tauntingly rubbed it.

He knew that the wetness between my thighs had nothing to do with the shower water. "I see that you want me too," he said.

He bent down and started kissing my stomach so I reached down and parted my drenched vaginal lips so that he'd without a doubt know to continue on down. He leaned me onto the wall and raked his hard tongue over my lips, then through my slit and sucked on my clit. If I gripped the shower curtain any harder it would have tumbled down on us. I was screaming out things that didn't sound like English. Then when I thought it couldn't get any better, two of his fingers glided in between my lower lips.

He brought his fingers down slowly and raced them back into me, but he kept his tongue on my knob; the entangled pleasure was amazing. The vibrations from his groaning sent wicked sensations through my body and I exploded like waves crashing against the shoreline. My body began to jerk wildly. He showered me with kisses until he was back at my upper lips. Our tongues became hard and fiercely intertwined. And once again, our passion mounted up and we were ready to soar.

He pressed my backside against the tiled wall again and I threw my hands up as a sign of sweet surrender and welcomed him to take me. He scooped me up so that my legs wrapped around his waist and I held him around the neck. He lined his plane up with the runway and I cleared him for takeoff. He entered me with such force that I was concerned about the tiles behind me. I savored every thrust, every in and every out. I growled, screamed, purred, and moaned for almost thirty minutes before our sweaty bodies collapsed into the large tub. I lay in his arms as though we were in bed. The hot water was now ice cold but it didn't matter because when it hit our steamy bodies it just melted away.

Three weeks after I left Philadelphia, Andre was in Miami. I hadn't planned on him meeting my family during his trip. However, Mama insisted that my behavior was strange, and our phone conversations were too short. So she stopped by without calling one night as Andre and I were preparing dinner. My romantic table setting for two turned into a gathering for three.

The next day she called me with rave reviews about Andre. She loved him and wanted to know when she'd see him again, which surprised me. The first question she usually asked about any man that I was dating was, "Is he saved?" Andre wasn't saved but he quoted a few scriptures, knew the words to her favorite hymn, *Draw Me Nearer,* and that was enough for her. I didn't even know that the boy could sing. She took an immediate liking to him, just as I had.

On my third trip to Philadelphia, Andre and I spent the weekend at his parents' house in Pittsburgh. He was the spitting image of his father, so Mr. Anthony Teasdale had to be a wanted man back in the day, because at age fifty-nine he was still a sight to see. His mother,

Norma, bright-skinned, medium-built, and long hair, reminded me of Coretta Scott King. She was as sweet as honey.

In October during Andre's visit, my sister, Tyann, an entertainment lawyer, and her husband, Colin, invited us to dinner. Because my 'well-off' sister can't do anything small scaled, it turned into a dinner party. Tyann and Colin Ingraham III found any excuse to show off their seven-bedroom house in Coral Gables. I walked in and there were servers, a saxophone player, and tables and chairs draped in linen. To my surprise, she was expecting thirty-eight guests. The guest list included our other family members and my closest friends.

Up until that night, Madison and I had only seen each other a few times, and this was odd. She avoided me like the plague and our phone conversations were short, and she never brought up what I walked in on that day in Daytona Beach. I loved her too much to let it ruin our friendship, so I agreed to the unsaid agreement, and it went unsaid.

Andre walked into the party and the music stopped. The brotha got down on one knee and asked me to be his wife, presenting me with an 18k white gold three-stone diamond ring. And I said yes. However, once back at my apartment I expressed my concerns about us still being in the beginning of our relationship and not knowing each other well. Andre suggested that one of us relocate. Lo and behold, the next morning he was on the phone getting estimates on moving trucks from Miami to Philadelphia.

During a visit I interviewed with the Philadelphia County school board and a few weeks later landed the job as a fourth grade teacher at New Liberty Elementary School. The school was a fifteen-minute drive from

Andre's house in Northern Liberties, so I would be leaving Florida.

When I told my mom that I was leaving before getting married, she didn't like it. She cried like a baby. She said that living with a man before marriage was not a good sign. She also told me that it was always her prayer that I found a better man than she did and hoped that Andre would do right. She wished me well.

Out of common courtesy I went to my father's house before I moved. He was recently divorced; I wouldn't have gone if he were still married to Francesca. My sister and I hated his wife; not because she was white, but because she had two kids when he married her, and he opted to take care of them instead of us . . . his own flesh and blood. A few months after he married Fran they moved to California where he pursued an acting career. He never landed a big role, just many small ones and a few commercials. After ten years of being passed up for major roles, he got the message and moved back to Miami where he opened a used car lot.

I arrived in Philly one week before the Christmas break and didn't have to report to work until after. It was my first real winter and I can count on one hand how many times I went outside without it being mandatory. Andre took vacation time and was off for my first two weeks there. We spent every waking moment sexing each other, sleeping all over the house.

When school started, Andre and I arrived at home around the same time each day. Things were lively and lovely. We'd greet each other with smiles, hugs, and kisses. Afterward he'd retire to his office to put together pieces to the puzzle of a case while I prepared my lesson plans and graded papers to take back the next day. Around nine he'd stand in the doorway of the living room and watch me with a smile. I knew what he meant!

Child, please! After a little over a year of living together I had to remind Andre that my reason for moving to Philly was because he had asked me to marry him. So in November 2004 he gave me the okay to begin planning a New Year's Eve night wedding in Miami. His parents were excited. Mrs. Teasdale even flew to Miami to finally meet my mom, the caterers, and view reception halls. Things between Andre and I weren't perfect anymore, they were about average. Andre's hours at work were longer, and our sexual appetites were on a bit of a diet, but I still created a guest list of two hundred and twenty-six people and we had chosen the members of the bridal party.

Though the event would double as a New Year's Eve formal, our colors were set to be sage and lavender. My mother volunteered to pay for my dress, and my father, not wanting to be upstaged, insisted on covering the entire cost of the reception and honeymoon to France. I couldn't argue with that.

I hired a wedding planner and in August the invitations were waiting in sealed and addressed envelopes. But three days before I was to take them to the post office, Andre and I got too happy in our morning love making and only had forty minutes to get dressed and be at work. We sprinted around the house eating, ironing, searching for keys, asking for money, and grabbing cell phones.

After walking my class to the music room, I received a call.

"Hey, baby," I heard my wedding planner, Erica, in my ear before I could say hello.

"Erica?" I asked.

"Thalia?" she gasped and seemed a little perplexed. "Oh my goodness, I must've hit your number by mistake." Her enthusiasm grew. "Since I got you on the phone I guess I should tell you the good news." She paused. "The florist can match the flowers on the cake the exact same color as the girls' dresses." She was really worked up. "Oh, and by the way, that clerk at David's Bridal was fired after I spoke to corporate about how rude she was to us."

We spoke for a few more minutes before hanging up and that's where everything went haywire. As I hung up the phone I realized that though it was the same make and model, it wasn't my phone at all, it was Andre's. I didn't even know that she had Andre's number. And why did he have her listed as Eric? He had three unplayed voice mail messages and I'd be damned if I wasn't checking them. They were *all* from Erica. *"Hi, baby. I miss you. I can't stop thinking about you since you left last night. Sorry that I missed your calls yesterday. Call me."* Then there was, *"Hi, Dre. I was talking to another client when you called."* She giggled. *"Wedding planning keeps me busy. Call me; I can't wait to see you again. Oh, and thank you for the flowers. They were beautiful."* It was the last message that opened the floodgate to my tear ducts. *"Hi, baby. You left something at my place last night. What is it? A hole in my goddamn mattress."* She laughed. *"Holy shit, you were awesome, baby. You can't hit and run on me like that again. Damn, I can't wait until next month when we're in Vegas to do it whenever and wherever we like."* She took a deep breath. *"Bye, bye, Mr. Good Dick."*

Andre told me that he was meeting his frat brothers in Vegas the next month. With tears drenching my face and clothing for the next twenty minutes, I continuously listened to her messages. I took a half-day, went home, and started packing my belongings.

Surprisingly, Mr. Good Dick showed up a few minutes later looking for his phone.

"What are you doing home?" he asked, then he noticed the suitcases on the bed. "What are you doing?" He approached me and I threw his phone at him, barely missing his face. "Whoa! What in the hell . . . "

"Get away from me!" I yelled, still crying.

"Talk to me." He took a step toward me. "What's wrong with you?"

I tossed some pants in the suitcase. "Ask Erica what the fuck is wrong with me."

His eyes grew wide. "What are you talking about?"

"She called you today." I picked up a shoe and threw it in his direction, missing again. "She calls you every goddamn mothafuckin' day."

"She calls about the wedding," he stuttered. "She calls both of us about the wedding."

"Oh yeah, well she doesn't call me Mr. Good Dick." I pitched another shoe and he caught it. "You're going to Vegas with that bitch next month, huh?"

"What are you talking about?" He pretended to look lost. "I'm going to a frat convention."

"Fuck you and your frat convention! I heard all of the fuckin' messages." I stuffed more clothing into the suitcase. "How long have you been doing this, Andre?"

"Doing what?" He shrugged his shoulders. "What am I doing?"

"Fuckin' the damn wedding planner, how long?" I yelled. "Erica, how long have you been fuckin' her?"

"Fine." His body language changed. "Stuff happened." He couldn't look at me. "But I don't want her."

I had to ask. "What do you mean stuff happened?"

"Thalia." He fell onto our bed and put his head in his hands. "I'm sorry."

I moved across the room like I was a cast member in the Matrix. I punched him in the face, and before I knew it, he was on his stomach covering his head and I was pounding his back with my fists. "How could you do this?" He tried to push me off, but I had the strength of ten thousand men. "Why would you do this to me?" When he turned over I slapped him in the face. "I'll kill you." I ripped his shirt and wailed my hands like a mad-woman. Surprisingly, his partner was in the living room and heard the whole thing and ran in to rescue him.

For the next two weeks I stayed at a hotel and didn't answer even one of his daily calls. He sent flowers to my job and I disbursed them to my students at the end of the day. Thank God the wedding invitations weren't out yet. I called my immediate family members and the bridal party to tell them that the wedding was off. When they asked why, I made up the story that Andre and I decided to save the money because we were thinking of buying another house.

One evening I went back to the house to pick up some papers I needed for school and found Andre looking a hot mess. He had grown a full beard, reeked of vodka, and looked as though he hadn't slept in days. I truly believed that I could just walk in, tell him to kiss my ass, get my papers, and walk back out. This crazy man handcuffed me to the ladder attached to the book-shelf in the den and begged me to listen to him.

His tearful story was that Erica started calling him two weeks after she was hired. He said that she came on strong and in a moment of weakness he fell into her trap. He wanted to tell me, but she convinced him not to ruin our special day over a few nights of sex. Soon she grew possessive, and when she learned of his trip with his frat brothers, she bought a ticket too, just to be alone with him.

After an hour of hearing him beg, he loosed the handcuffs and instead of opening another can of karate on him, I, like an idiot, fell into his arms. I didn't believe Andre. I knew that I could call Erica and find out the truth, but something within me didn't really want to know the whole truth.

I forgave him because what he didn't know was that I had come within an inch of being unfaithful. I had flirted and eventually kissed the assistant principal at my school. And though I didn't succumb sexually, I knew just how easy it was to get caught up in something wrong. Plus, something within me just wanted a warm body to lie next to that night. We agreed that the wedding was still on, but would be pushed back, way back.

For the next few weeks I couldn't keep Andre away from me, but even that was a façade. I guess Andre felt that since I was stupid enough to stay with him after the Erica incident, he'd just try my patience until his luck ran out. In early October his cell phone started ringing late at night and he'd get up to answer it. Before I knew it, he would be dressed and leaving for what he called a stakeout. Then it became overtime because a few colleagues were on vacation, then the overtime became mandatory. After that, the excuses stopped and he came home later and later without explanation.

Soon he approached me about pushing the wedding date back even more. He said that it was due to the promotion he was sure to get if he handled a few big cases

right. He said that he needed to dedicate all of his time
to work. Mama was disappointed, for the second time,
and wasn't praising him like she used to. However, she
tried to cheer me up by saying, "So we have more time
to plan." But I knew that she wanted to ask me to come
back home. My father didn't know my personality well
enough to know the pain in my voice, so he asked me to
wish Andre the best with the promotion.

I was convinced that he didn't want to get married or
he was on crack, because Andre transformed into a
complete stranger on me. I saw him only on the nights
he crawled on top of me, and on the mornings when he
was half-human enough to say goodbye. I felt as though
Andre's only reason for returning home every day was
because the house we lived in belonged to him. The less
time he spent at home, the better mood he'd be in
when he returned.

He was saying, out of the blue, anything he thought
would send me packing. His topic of choice became the
weight that I had gained since moving in. He constantly
brought to my attention what his friends' wives and girlfriends looked like in comparison to me. He enrolled
me into a local gym, and one night as I prepared
shrimp stir-fry, he rushed into the kitchen and slammed
the membership card on the countertop saying, "Have
you looked in the mirror lately?"

One morning, as I prepared some of our suits to go
to the dry cleaners, I found a receipt for a tuxedo rental
in one of his jacket pockets, which was dated two weeks
prior. I placed it under a magnet on the refrigerator
and waited for him to notice it that evening. Through
him I learned that the precinct had the annual
Policeman's Ball and he went without me. He said that
he didn't ask me because it was during the same week

of rigorous standardized testing for elementary students, and he just assumed that I was busy.

The tuxedo never entered our home, so where did he take a shower and get dressed the night of the Ball? It was obvious that he was, again, seeing another woman. I started planning my escape. I wasn't going to be a prisoner of lack-of-love any longer.

Chapter 9

Emancipation of .T.T.

"See you when I get back."

Those words rang in my head for a complete fifteen minutes after Andre closed the door and walked away. Little did he know, if all went well, those would be the last words he'd ever say to me. His voice continued to play in my brain like a song I wished I didn't know the words to. "See you when I get home." My plan was to be 2,000 miles away when Andre returned from work.

It was the first week of 2006 and I had played the role of a fool for far too long. Philadelphia had its share of crime, but for Andre to leave home at 5:30 in the morning and return close to midnight, he'd have to be the only detective in the entire city. Maybe if I saw his face on the eleven o'clock news reporting on how some stakeout finally paid off, I'd believe him. Yet, I saw to it that he came home to a hot meal, a clean house, a semi-smiling face, and a warm bed. Enough was enough. I'd been planning my departure for weeks and only death would keep me from it. Not a day longer, I was leaving today.

Looking around I saw nothing that I'd miss. The funny thing was that I didn't think he would miss me at all. I walked over to the shelf that housed our photographs and shuttered as I saw the picture of Andre and me at the club where we first met. It brought back many memories, but none of them gave me a reason to stay. On the picture my smile was almost three years younger; I was feeling every kind of happiness a girl feels when she ran into a fine brother that promised the moon, stars, and good sex. Something told me that dealing with Leon with a wife and a drug problem would've been simpler than the road I had chosen.

I made my way around the house with a few garbage bags to remove my existence from his life. I filled the bags with everything that I never wanted to use again because of him, and everything I couldn't stand the thought of him using without me. Call me crazy, but it was house-cleaning time. Candles, wine, bubble bath, books, pots, pans, bed sheets, suits, shirts, ties, shoes, and many other items all had to go. Next in the bags were our pictures, his colognes, his underwear, and the favorites from his CD collection. If it made him smile and was small enough to fit into the bag, it had to go. He'd better thank his lucky stars that his angelfish died last week because that sucker would be in jeopardy today.

I heard the rumbling of the garbage truck a few streets away and couldn't get my slippers on fast enough. I dragged the first two bags to the roadside and ran back to get the last one. Halfway down the walk I started feeling incredibly stupid. What would throwing this stuff away solve? All it meant was that the next woman would get the pleasure of purchasing these items just as I did. "Hmph." I shrugged and smiled, that was good enough of a reason for me, but I wasn't completely convinced that I wasn't deranged.

Something fell from the bag. I reached down and it was the same picture I looked at inside. It was taken almost three years ago in Daytona Beach the day Andre and I met. He stood next to me and was holding me like he never wanted to let go. A tear ran down my cheek as the garbage truck roared just two houses away. "This is what I have to get away from." I sniffed. "Away from waiting for the man I met to come home from work." The stranger that walked through the door these days didn't move me here from Miami.

Andre could kiss my butt with the lips of his first born, *if* he is ever so blessed to conceive. I am nobody's verbal punching bag. I could not allow him to continue to push me down with hurtful words. I didn't give a barbequed hot damn what his friends' wives looked like. Though it wasn't doing much at 790 W. McDonald Street, my 170 pounds at five foot eight was still turning heads everywhere else in Philadelphia.

"Ma'am." I didn't even notice the trash collector standing in front of me. "Is that trash?"

I smiled. "Yes, it's trash."

As he walked to the truck he peeked inside and seemed impressed with its contents. He turned to look at me. "*This* is trash?" I knew then that the suits, shoes, and CD's would never make it to the dump. It didn't matter, maybe they could really serve their purpose in lives far away from the one I lived. "Are you sure you want to throw this stuff away?"

"I just don't want it here."

"Wow." He threw the bag in the front seat of the

truck. "Thank you." His eyes lit up. "See you on Monday." I'd be very far away on Monday morning. I stood there and watched some of my memories become one with what others considered junk, and suddenly I realized that my memories with Andre were just that . . . useless junk.

Once back inside, I grabbed my suitcases and began packing. It didn't take long at all. By eleven o'clock there wasn't a trace of Thalia Tyree in the place. I had managed to pack everything that was in my drawers the night before. My shoes were in a big box for weeks; he thought I was trying to save space. He also thought that all of my suits were at the cleaners, but they, along with a shoebox filled with goodbye letters from my students, were sent to my sister, in Miami, through FedEx.

Over the past few months, I started attending church more often. I've even entertained the thought of getting my life right with God. It was amazing what a no good man would make you think about. I've been taking one day at a time, praying, and reading the Bible. I've even lost weight by using scriptures as comfort food. I'm not perfectly inline with the Word by far, but I'm not what I used to be that's for sure. The only things still on my list of sins are sex, which after today will be history, drinking, but I have it down to just a few glasses of wine a week, hatred, which only Andre was a victim of, and cursing, but how in the hell else would I express myself?

I was dressed and waiting for the airport shuttle to take me away like Calgon. I studied the king-sized bed that used to fill my nights with passion; it had lately become my worst enemy. If the mattress could talk it would've comforted me on the many nights I cried there alone.

I sat on it one final time and Andre's cologne raced upward and attacked my nostrils. His fragrance took me back to the previous night. He entered the bedroom and made a beeline to the bathroom without saying a word to me. During his shower I put away Terry McMillan's *The Interruption of Everything,* turned off the lights, and pretended to be asleep. I didn't want him to feel the need to talk to me. Seconds after the water stopped, the door opened and Andre climbed into bed, turned me onto my back, straddled and penetrated me without ever saying hello. I guess he felt that the soapy water on the tip of his dick was enough moisture to get the job done.

It was cheap, cold, and quick, much like being molested. No, I was being molested. He pushed and tore his way into my dryness and never looked into my eyes. Had he tried kissing me during the process, maybe I could have forced myself to please him, but our lips had become fourth cousins. I knew that they were out there, but accepted the fact that we'd never meet again.

Last night I couldn't sleep, as a matter-of-fact, I never wanted to close my eyes in Philadelphia again. Knowing that sanity and freedom would come with the sunlight, I waited up for it all night.

"It's quitting time," I said to the bed. My bags were packed and waiting by the door. My car, which he thought was being repaired, was put on an Amtrak train to Miami two days prior. Because Andre paid the majority of the bills, I had saved a lot of money. My new apartment was waiting for me; I called my former landlady two months ago. She had a vacancy and was happy to know that Senorita Tyree was returning to the Sunshine State. Tyann also knew of my plan, but I asked her not to mention it to Mama or any of my friends, I said that it was because I wanted it to be a surprise, but something deep within told me not to tell too many people because I may not be strong enough to pull it off.

I fell to my knees in front of the bed. "God, I thank You for giving me the strength to leave. I thank You for the wisdom You've given me in this situation. I thank You for the peace You've allowed me to have during all that I've been through here. I know that this is not Your will for me. I need You to walk me out of that front door. Walk me out of these tears, out of a broken heart, out of depression, and out of this pain. Walk me into the new life You've promised me. Let Your will be done in my life. Today is the first day of the new life You promised me." I paused. "Thank You for blessing me in spite of the way I've been living my life. Now that I'm out of this situation I can try even harder to live my life the way You've intended me to. Lord, I beg You to remain merciful and stay by my side. Guide me through the rough times I know are ahead. I thank You for the strength to walk away today. In Jesus' name I pray. Amen."

I sprung to my feet and wiped my eyes. Andre held me an emotional slave from the day we met, so today would be marked as my emancipation. I was free! The emancipation of T.T., *Thalia Tyree.*

A horn blew outside; it was the airport shuttle. I jumped up from the bed and made my way to the front door to see a tall skinny man making his way up the walk. "Hi." He looked at the papers in his hand. "Miss Tyree?"

"Yep."

"Are you ready?" He was ten minutes early and that was fine by me.

"Ready is not the word." I waved him in. "I need your help."

He was awestricken when he entered the house. He complimented the architectural work, the vaulted ceiling, and the paintings on the wall. I graciously accepted his kind words, but told him that I was just a visitor; the owner of the residence wasn't home. We loaded my things into the shuttle in two trips.

My last time inside I took a deep breath. My departure was long overdue. I wished I had never come back after the Erica situation. I'd do anything to be a fly on the wall when he got home today so that I could see his reaction. No more Thalia, but a five sentence farewell note instead.

Tears made their way down my cheeks again as I placed the house key atop the note lying on the kitchen counter. He'd have nothing to ask me to return. I set the house alarm, locked the door from the inside, and slammed it shut. I was giving up a house to move back into an apartment, but felt that much more was waiting for me.

I reached the shuttle crying, "Let's go."

"Are you okay?" he asked and handed me a Kleenex and looked at me through the rearview mirror. "How long have you been visiting?"

"Way too long." I looked at the house. "Way too long."

My flight left Philadelphia International at 1:35 P.M., arrived at Chicago O'Hare at 2:59 P.M., and thanks to Expedia.com, I had a three-hour layover in Chicago, leaving to Miami at 6 P.M. What a great day.

The shuttle arrived at the airport a few minutes before noon. I checked in curbside to avoid the lines at the counter. Then I was on to TSA. Never in the history of the world has a job gone from nothing to something like that of the TSA's on September 11. I know that we need security, but flight attendants packed more weight than ninety percent of those correctional officer rejects. Since 9/11, you couldn't tell TSA anything. They got off on pulling people to the side like they were the law. I want to say, "Excuse me, do you realize that you don't have a gun, a night stick or a flashlight?" I also want to say, "If someone had a bomb they could easily kill more people in the ticketing line and in the parking lot than on a plane. So calm yourself down." However, I just took my laptop out of its case, removed my shoes and belt, and waited until they granted me permission to walk through.

It seemed like my gate assignment was always the one furthest away. If there were gates H1—H62 I was almost guaranteed to be going to at least H-57. Today was no exception. After walking to Jerusalem and back, I reached my gate. I looked around to find an empty seat by the window and dashed toward it. As I made my way over, I saw why no one bothered sitting there; there was thick yellowish liquid on the seat. Oh, what a great day!

Once on the plane I stuffed my carry-on into the overhead compartment and took my window seat hoping that no one was going to sit right next to me, but as people kept loading onto the plane, I knew that the chances were slim. A tall Arabic looking man sat in the aisle seat and I nearly peed. I quickly looked around to see if anyone who could be an air marshal was close by. Then an elderly woman that came along with a big smile said, "Howdy partners, I think we're traveling together today."

I offered her a smile and helped her into the seat. Takeoff was delayed a bit, but while taxiing the runway all I heard about was her granddaughter's pregnancy. She even showed me pictures and read me the poem her youngest grandchild, Emily, wrote for her on Mother's Day. She asked me to hold her hand during the takeoff. She admired my watch, asked to see it . . . actually played with it, and five minutes later, she pulled out a Ziploc bag full of homemade chocolate chip cookies and put one in my hand. It was pretty good.

I said goodbye to Mrs. Wilkinson, whom I secretly nicknamed Adelaide, because of her resemblance of the maid from Diff'rent Strokes, and I walked around the gigantic airport as though it was a mall. I made my way to a Starbucks coffee shop. The new coffee craze never hit me. Whatever happened to just plain ol' coffee and tea? Looking at the menu was confusing. I didn't want to say the wrong thing. Latte, Tall, Frappé, Mocha, Tazo, Cappuccino, Frappuccino. "May I help you?" the young man asked.

I couldn't be the only person that felt like ordering from Starbucks was like ordering from a French menu. "A cappuccino please?" It came out as a question.

"Sure." He smiled. "Short, tall, grande or venti?"

"Short?" I answered in a question again.

It was like he was taunting me. "Single or double shot?"

Damn it! Was he serious? "Never mind. Let me have a slice of lemon cake." What a wonderful day . . . I still tried to convince myself.

I paid him then quickly strolled to the table farthest

from the entrance. Along the way, I grabbed a newspaper that was neatly folded on a vacant table.

Looking at my watch it was only 4:47 P.M., and then I remembered that Chicago was on Central Time so I set my watch to read 3:47 P.M. I still had a long time to wait. After thirty minutes of skimming through the newspaper, a story caught my eye. I read it and was close to tears as I realized that a young mother lost her three daughters in an apartment fire two nights before. She left them alone and went downstairs to the mailbox. On her way back she heard an explosion and saw flames shooting out of her apartment door. She ran to try to get them out but the smoke was thick and flames too hot. The Chicago Tribune quoted her as saying, "I wish I would've died with my babies, they were all I had."

I closed my eyes to avoid crying. I couldn't even begin to understand her pain, but I could imagine what she went through as the bodies of her flesh and blood were brought out one by one. With my eyes shut, I thought I heard someone say my name, but it couldn't be; I was in Chicago. Then it happened again, but this time the voice seemed closer.

"Thalia Tyree, is that you?"

I opened my eyes and started from the ground up. First I saw a pair of black Spanish leather shoes. Slowly lifting my head, pinstriped charcoal slacks that seemed to flow from thick thighs came into view. Then my eyes ran into a charcoal pinstriped jacket that hung open from wide muscular shoulders revealing a matching vest. Underneath it all was a burgundy tie sitting on a plain white shirt. I couldn't get to his face fast enough. "Is that you?" he asked. I threw up a harsh glance and met the soft, soothing, sexy brown eyes of Reverend Isaac Flack, my best friend's father.

Chapter 10

Logged on to Yahoo

"Mr. Flack!" I jumped up from my seat and my arms found their way around his neck. "What are you doing in Chicago?" It was nice to see him, not just a familiar face, but him.

His lips pressed against my forehead just like he used to when Madi and I did junior high homework at his house. "The question is what are you doing here?" He pulled me away with a smile.

"I'm on my way home." I was all smiles.

"Back to the city the of brotherly love, huh?" He didn't pause long enough for me to correct him. "How are you? I heard that you were in Miami a few months ago."

"Yeah I was," I said. "Sorry I didn't visit, Mama kept me pretty busy."

"No problem." He looked at me strangely. "So, what are you doing in Chicago?"

"Oh, I actually just have a layover here." I looked at

my watch; it was now 4:00 P.M. Chicago time. "I still have two hours to wait."

"Okay." His eyes widened. "My flight got in about thirty minutes ago."

"What brings *you* here?" I asked.

"The National Baptist Convention." As he spoke I was enamored by how he seemed to look better after all these years. At forty-five he still had enough going for him to make twenty-five-year-old men re-evaluate their own style.

I smiled. "Wait until I tell Mama that I ran into you, Mr. Flack."

"Thalia, c'mon, call me Isaac. Mr. Flack is my father." He laughed and then looked around the coffee shop. "Are you traveling alone?"

"Yeah, I'm flying solo." In more ways than one, I thought to say, but changed the subject. "How is Madison?" Madi and I still talked, but it was down to about once or twice a month, which was nothing compared to talking for hours a day, but I knew why and when things changed.

"Madi's doing great. I helped her lease space in a new plaza that she turned into a day spa." I could see that he was still sticking to his four day a week workout regimen. The way that suit wrapped around his brown skin made that burgundy tie look like a bow. Whew! He was truly a gift. Were men of the cloth allowed to look this good? His lips were moving but my ears were temporarily out of order. "Thalia?" he said with a blank stare. "Would you rather me stay out of your business?"

"Huh?" I came out of my daydream and dropped into embarrassment headfirst. "I'm sorry, please repeat that?"

"I asked about your fiancé," he repeated. "I don't remember his name."

He wanted to know a name that I was working very hard to forget. "Well," I threw him a smile, "now that I'm moving back to Miami, you don't have to worry about remembering his name."

"What?" He looked surprised and regretful of asking. "I'm sorry. When you said you were going home, I thought you meant Philadelphia."

"No, it's back to Miami for me." I tried to sound upbeat about it. "I can't wait to get home." My voice cracked in mid-sentence and he seemingly saw right through my grown-up act, like he knew that I was just a hurt little girl.

"We all have to go through something in order to get to somewhere else." He smiled. "Everything is going to be just fine."

"I know." I paused to catch my breath. "I believe I've done the right thing." I faked a smile and changed the subject once again. "I can't believe that you're here, this is such a coincidence."

The pastor in him spoke up. "Nothing is a coincidence. Everything is God." Isaac smiled. "I was about to go check into my hotel and make a few phone calls. But I have to come back here to pick up Sister Stride."

"Oh, I won't hold you then." I was a little disappointed that he had to leave.

"You're not getting rid of me that easily, but excuse me for a moment." He pulled out his cellular phone and dialed a number informing the person on the other line that he wouldn't be ready for pickup until seven thirty. "Sister Stride's plane will probably be here shortly after you leave. So I might as well just stay and keep you company." I was already lost in his treacherous brown eyes. "So what are you drinking?"

"Nothing," I said. "I just had a slice of cake."

"Would you like something to drink?"

"Yes, thank you." I wasn't about to go through the Starbuck menu shuffle again. "What do you normally have?"

"I love the Caramel Macchiato."

I couldn't repeat it. "I'll have one of those." Why was I blushing? Was I crazy? When he walked away, to avoid the temptation of admiring his broad shoulders, I sat down and tried to focus on the newspaper again. However, I found only sales advertisements. There was nothing that was able to divert my attention from him. Shortly he returned with two large cups. "One Caramel Macchiato for you, Miss Tyree."

"Thank you, but only my students call me Miss Tyree, so unless you want me to be your teacher, you can call me Thalia." I took one sip and fell in love. "This is great." Was this what I had been missing in life . . . Starbucks?

Uncomfortable silence crept up. "Does the convention start tonight?" I asked.

"No." He put his cup down. "It begins tomorrow at noon."

I didn't know what else to say. Mama always said when all else fails, talk about the Lord. "So how's everything at the church?"

"Oh, things are marvelous. Mount Pleasant is truly being blessed. The youth ministry is flourishing." He seemed excited. "As a matter-of-fact, I have twenty-three young people and six youth leaders here already, they traveled yesterday."

"Wow! That's great."

Then out of left field came, "So, did he ask you to leave?"

I nearly choked on my caramel whatchamacallit. "Huh?"

"Your fiancé," he repeated the question. "Did he ask you to leave?"

"No, but it was understood," I said.

"Understood?" he asked. "What do you mean by that?"

Holy shhh . . . I said I would work on the cursing. Did he think I was seeking spiritual guidance? "It was understood, meaning I could tell that my presence was no longer desired."

"How much talking did you two do about it before deciding to call it quits?"

I chuckled out of frustration or something. "We didn't talk about it." I was getting annoyed by the topic. "In fact, we never talked about anything anymore. That's why I packed up and shipped out."

"What did he say?"

"I'll let you know when I find out." It was still early and my farewell note was still undiscovered. "He doesn't know yet."

"Whoa!" Isaac looked at me like they may've spiked my drink, but ended with a joke. "You'll be getting an interesting phone call tonight."

"Maybe." I didn't know what to expect. "Maybe not."

"Why didn't you just tell him that you weren't happy and wanted out of the relationship?"

"I did." I continued. "I left him a note."

"A Dear John letter?" He smirked.

"Yep."

A look of concern fell on his face. "Was there physical abuse?"

I said, "The brotha is dumb, but not stupid."

He cleared his throat. "I don't believe that the relationship was meant to be, but I think that you've just opened up to the first chapter of a book that you won't want to read." He continued his counseling. "Had you talked to him about leaving then today would be the final chapter, your flight would've been the end of the book. But because you didn't, I can almost guarantee you that there is more drama to come."

"Well, he never thought I needed to know where he was most of the time, so I didn't think he deserved to know about me moving."

"So what church were you going to up there?"

"Ebenezer Baptist," I said like I was a member. "Pastor Tyler Moore."

"Okay." Isaac smiled. "I'm noticing something different about you."

"What?" I blushed. "I'm all grown-up now?"

"Yes." He looked me over innocently. "But there is something else."

I was curious. "Something like what?"

"In the midst of this turmoil," he spoke, "I feel the spirit of peace in your presence." He smiled. "Like the Lord is doing a great work on you."

The only person I told about me *trying*, and I stress the word trying, to turn over a new leaf was my mother. I called her crying late one night and said, "Mama, I'm tired of everything going wrong in my life. I'm tired of being hurt and being kept back by craziness. It's as though every good relationship or friendship I've had has gone wrong. Things are hard and I have no one, and nothing to turn to, so I think that I'm going to get serious about knowing who Jesus really is."

If you would've heard my mother screaming and crying you'd think that I just told her that an angel came to me and said that I would give birth to The Messiah. I didn't tell anyone else because I was still in the beginning stages and was unsure of how strong I was and how long it would last. I couldn't tell whether or not I was serious or just wounded and afraid and trying to find something else to cling to. I looked over at Isaac. "I've made some changes in life."

"What kind of changes?" he asked.

I was skeptical about telling him, or anyone, because I didn't want them watching me like a hawk and screaming bloody murder at every ungodly thing I did. "I've been going to church a lot more and trying to really understand who God is and step into being a better person."

"That was a great decision." Of course he would think that.

"Thank you," I said and I hope he understood that I wasn't running down the aisle or speaking in tongues or anything. I didn't even go up to the altar at church during the call to discipleship. I just made up my mind that I wanted to apply God into my living.

"When was the last time you spoke to Madison?" he asked and I was glad he wasn't going to talk me to death about the church thing.

I was ashamed that I actually had to think about it. "It's been about a month," I said and then thought about our last conversation, it was about Nick, someone she was spending a lot of time with. I was glad to hear that she was back on the other side of the sexual bridge. "I've been meaning to call her."

He asked, "She told you about her new place?"

"No, *you* just told me about the spa."

"No," he paused shortly, "I meant her apartment."

"Apartment?" I was surprised. "No, she never mentioned that."

"Yeah, she moved out," he said. "A friend of hers was looking for a roommate."

Oh, suckie suckie, don't tell me that Madi moved in with this Nick guy already . . . I had to know. "Who is her friend?"

"Nekia. Well, she was or is actually a client of Madison's."

So Nick was really Nekia who was a client of Madison's. Yeah right! The only massaging going on there was likely Madi's tongue between this chick's legs. When will she finally come out and tell me the truth? Well, since I won't be 1,500 miles away anymore . . . maybe now would be the time.

Isaac went on. "She's a really nice girl." He was no doubt at ease, if only he knew. But you know they say that the preacher's kids are always the worst.

I smiled and said, "I can't wait to meet her." Oh man, I couldn't wait to meet her.

"Does she know that you're coming?"

"No. The only person I told was Tyann, and I made her swear not to mention it to anyone." If my sister leaked it I had a few things that I could leak about her too.

"I'm grateful that I only have to keep your secret for an hour." He reached over and touched my hand in a friendly way. I exhaled, inhaled, sighed . . . I was doing all sorts of crazy things inside.

When he spoke I wanted to listen but my mind disobediently took me back to one of the last times I had seen him before moving to Philadelphia. It was in the parking lot of the Southland Mall. He was walking behind my car and I nearly reversed into him. "Whoa!" he yelled and then walked over and jokingly said, "You look like one of those hit and run types."

"I am so sorry." I looked out of the window to make sure that he was okay. "I didn't see you."

"Not a problem." He leaned into the open driver's side window. "How are you?"

"I'm good." I tried not to be ashamed about nearly killing him. "Just hot," and it had nothing to do with the outside temperature. "How are you?" I asked.

"I'm blessed." He placed his hand on mine. "I haven't seen you at church in quite some time." This was the statement he always made when he saw me.

"I'm sorry, I've just been busy," I lied.

"Is that right?"

"No," I conceded with a smile. "You'll be seeing me before I leave to Philly." I held my hand to my heart signifying that I'd be true to my word.

"Don't make me wait too long." He flashed that smile. "Drive safely." For the rest of that day I, a then engaged woman, pacified my fantasies about him with the thought of him saying, "Don't make me wait too long," and about other sinful things I had planned. Now here I am in Starbucks looking into his eyes and wanting to say to him, "Don't make *me* wait too long."

We talked for over an hour on various subjects, but the main topic in my mind was "Is he for real?" Meaning, I've known him for years and he has never done anything out-of-line. Was he one of those freaks behind closed doors pastors? Was he one of those holy men of the altar that at night logged on to Yahoo and would say that his name was Walter? Or e-mail women dick shots taken on his camera phone? Or show his piece in front of a webcam? With so many corrupt ministers, pastors, reverends or whatever else they're called around, I had to wonder what his fault was. What was he hiding? Especially being single for so long . . . he was up to something. And sinfully I wished it was me.

In the midst of me telling him about an e-mail I received about a conspiracy theorist claimed that the levees in New Orleans were blown up as part of a government plot against blacks, he interrupted me. "Excuse me for a second, but what time is your flight?"

"Six o'clock." I looked at my watch and it was 5:23. "Wow, it's almost five thirty. I should be boarding." I jumped up and began throwing my belongings into my bag.

"Sit down." He smiled and calmly said, "You have the wrong time."

"Thank God," I sighed. "I thought I was running late. I set this stupid watch earlier." I sat down and fumbled with it. "So what is it, four twenty-three?"

"Not quite." He was confusing me.

"What time do you have?"

He said, "Six twenty-four."

"What?" My heart dropped. "Are you serious?"

"You missed your flight."

I fell back into the chair. "This could only happen to me."

"I am so sorry," he said. "I'm partially to blame. I should've been watching the time."

"But I thought I set my watch to Central Time." All I could think about was the fee I was going to have to pay to get on another flight. "Oh my goodness." My head fell into my hands.

"Don't beat yourself up." He was so calm. "We all make mistakes."

I tried to seem upbeat. "Yeah, but this mistake wasn't in my budget." I continued to gather my things and said, "Well, I guess I'll be seeing you in Miami once you get back."

"We need to make sure you get on a flight first, or maybe you won't be in Miami when I get back." He stood up and grabbed his coat. "Let's go and see what they can do."

Fifteen minutes later we approached the ticket counter. Behind it was a tall blonde woman typing something into a computer.

"Hello." I was anxious.

She never looked up. "What can I do for you?"

I took a deep breath and read her nametag. "Lily, I think I just missed my . . ."

"And how can I help you?" she interrupted me.

"I was supposed to be on flight one nine seven six to Miami, it just left."

She glanced at her watch and corrected me. "It left almost forty-five minutes ago."

"Okay," I said with my best Christian smile.

"So what are you going to do?" she asked. Her non-chalant behavior said it all. It was my problem and not hers.

"I need to get on another flight." I handed her my ticket.

"Another flight?" She smiled while looking at Isaac and then looked back at me.

"Is that impossible?" I asked sarcastically.

She spoke to me as though she was a kindergarten teacher in another life. "We have a flight to Miami in two hours, and another one two hours after that." I felt relieved, but Lily burst my bubble. "But they're both full."

"Do you have anything else?" I was now at her mercy.

"Yes, at two in the morning, and it has a connection in Orlando."

"Nothing nonstop?" I decided to get picky.

"Beggars can't be choosers, hon," she said tauntingly.

"I'm not begging, I'm paying and because I am paying I can choose whatever I want." Like I said before, since 9/11 airport workers are high on authority, Lily had about two minutes before she'd be high on the heel of my size eight shoe. "Do you have any nonstop flights?"

Looking up from the computer screen Lily said, "Well, tomorrow there's one at seven, noon, and six." She sighed. "There are seats available on all three, but either one will cost you," she paused to use the calculator, "one hundred and five dollars." Lily went on. "But I can put you on at two A.M., with the Orlando layover, free of charge."

I wanted to roll my eyes so badly. "I'll take that one then." Free was my favorite word.

"Hold on," Isaac interjected. "You want to fly at that time of night?"

"Not really," I frowned, "but it's no charge."

"Never settle." Isaac placed his American Express card on the counter. "What time do you really want to fly out?"

"Put that away." I tried to move his card. I didn't need a love offering from Mount Pleasant. "I'll leave tonight, don't worry about it."

"Thalia, this is the least I could do. I feel a bit responsible for you missing your flight." He handed Lily the card again.

"No, it's okay." Staying the night in Chicago would entail a whole lot more than just an amended plane ticket. I would need a taxi to a hotel, a hotel room, food, and a taxi back to the airport. "I'll leave tonight," I said to Lily.

"Thalia, you're stopping a blessing."

I was dumbfounded. "Are you serious?"

"Very," he said.

I conceded. "Thank you." I looked at Lily and said, "Will you please repeat tomorrow's flight times for me?"

"Gladly." She was chipper now that she saw that I didn't have to beg. "One is at seven, the other at noon, and the last one at six."

"I'll go at six." This was my first time in Chicago; I might as well enjoy it. Hopefully I had enough stuff in my carry-on to make it through the night. I turned to face Isaac. "Thank you so very much."

"Don't mention it."

But of course I did by saying, "I have the money. If you like I can repay you as soon as I'm settled in Miami."

"This has nothing to do with you having the money or not." His eyes met mine. "But if you feel that you must repay me then I have something in mind."

"What's that?"

"Seeing your face in the congregation next Sunday will be the perfect payback."

"Deal." I smiled. "I heard that your membership is skyrocketing so you won't know if I'm there or not."

"I always know when you're there." He winked at me playfully.

Lily cut in, "Would you like a window seat, Miss Tyree?"

"Yes, please," I answered then asked, "Can you suggest a nice but economical hotel near the airport?"

"Yes, ma'am." She handed me a brochure. "Take a look at this."

Isaac seemed disappointed. "You didn't think I would volunteer to keep you here and not find you a place to sleep tonight did you?"

"I couldn't ask you to do that."

"You *didn't* ask me," he reminded me.

Lily was all smiles. It's amazing what an American Express card can do. "Here you go, sir." Lily handed him his credit card and a receipt to sign.

We left the counter with Isaac pulling my carry-on behind him. "Oh," he looked at his watch, "Sister Stride's plane is in."

Sister Rosie Stride, president of the mission board. She also served on the Usher Board, and sang in the senior choir. She was just over seventy, but never missed a beat in the community. When I was younger, I along with other kids in the neighborhood called her "Holy Rosie" because she was famous for catching the Holy Ghost almost anywhere. At the supermarket, elementary schools, Christmas plays, the doctor's office, choir rehearsal, weddings, children's birthday parties, even high school football games. As children we used to bet our Sunday school offering on how long Sister Stride would sit still. She wasn't someone that I wanted to see at the moment, but I didn't have a choice.

"What time is her plane landing?" I asked.

"About thirty minutes ago. She's probably thirty-eight hot by now." His use of slang caught me off-guard. "You're about to clown me now, aren't you?" he asked.

"Wow, you didn't even bite your tongue," I joked.

He chuckled. "Being around the kids at church all

the time, I am well versed on the latest words in the street."

"Okay." I then added, "The next time you're going to spring slang on me, give me a two minute warning." We both cracked up as we raced to the luggage carousel. There she was. Each time I saw Sister Stride she looked more and more like Martin Lawrence playing his mother on the *Martin Lawrence Show*. Her wig, Lord that wig, needed to be served an eviction notice, but if you told her that, you might hear a word, and it wouldn't be from the Lord.

As we approached, her smile got bigger. "Pastor Flack." She threw her arms around him.

"Hello, Sister Stride." I was surprised that he could speak. She had a strong hold around his neck. "How are you?"

"Oh, Pastor, I'm blessed." She threw her hands up. "Jesus dun' brought me from a mighty long way." Suddenly she yelled, "Hallelujah, Glory to God! Oh, I give him thanks today." She waved her hands above her head. "That plane could've gone down, but my God saw fit for me to see another day, another time zone, another city. Oh, I thank Him for being God today."

Where were my Sunday school buddies today with their change and crumbled up dollar bills? What did I tell you? I can now add airport to the list of Sister Stride's conquests. Saved or not, I believe that she was a great actress; she didn't look real to me. Of course Mama wanted me on my knees for even suggesting that Sister Stride was faking the spirit. Just as fast as it came, her *spirit* was gone. "Those are my bags right there." She pointed at two large suitcases then stared at me in confusion. "Who is this?"

Isaac explained, "This is Sister Tyree's daughter."

She thought a while. "Tyann?" she asked.

"No, ma'am, I'm Thalia." I extended my hand for a shake because there were rumors that she wouldn't hug an unsaved person, especially not an unmarried woman with a child, or a woman living with a man outside of wedlock. "Tyann is my sister," I stated.

"You two look so much alike." She barely shook my hand.

I pretended to care. "How was your flight?"

"Like all flights," she smiled, "too long."

After a few seconds of small talk I walked over and paid for a luggage cart and returned to see Sister Stride looking at me strangely. "I didn't know that you were coming to the convention." However, what she really meant was, "You haven't been to church since Jesus turned water into wine, so I hope that our bake sale money ain't paying for your heathenish ass to be here."

"Oh, no, ma'am, I'm not here for the convention. I'm on my way back to Miami from Philadelphia. I had a connecting flight here in Chicago but I missed it." We started walking.

"How did you manage to miss your plane?" she asked.

Isaac, who was walking a step ahead of us, looked back and smiled. "It was my fault."

"Where are your bags, Pastor?" Sister Stride asked.

"I sent my things with the youth group yesterday. I had a bad experience at the last convention, so if it came one day late this time it'd be here right on time." Pushing the luggage cart made his muscles bulge beneath his suit; the strength in his thighs reminded me of the horse that played Sea Biscuit in the movie. His strength both physically and mentally was so attractive. He could easily become my favorite sin.

There was a chauffer holding a sign that read Reverend Flack. Isaac greeted him with a handshake, exchanged a few words, and then turned to us. "The car is right outside."

The electronic doors flew open and that Chicago hawk flew straight through my flesh and into my bones. Isaac, seeing my obvious almost frozen state, snatched opened the door to the pearl stretched Jaguar limousine. "You ladies wait inside."

Sister Stride made herself at home on the limo's long seat facing sideways. There was no way I could muster up enough energy to crawl in and sit next to her or make it to the front seat behind the driver. I just slid from the right side of the backseat to the left.

The interior was beige leather with wooden side finishing and complete with TV, VCR/DVD, CD player, sunroof, and bar. "Wow, Isaac is sure riding in style."

"Isaac?" Sister Stride's neck nearly cracked to look at me. "Isaac?" she repeated like I had just said the Lord's name in vain. "He is a man of God."

"Yes." I shook my head. "I know."

"Do you call me Rosie?" she asked.

"No, ma'am, I don't," I paused, "but if you asked me to I would."

"So when he asks you to then you can." She thought she was about to stomp me. "Until then you should . . ."

"Sister Stride," I smiled while interrupting her, "as a matter-of-fact, he has already asked me to refer to him by his first name."

"Oh?" She was humbled. "Well, excuse me."

We sat in silence for a few minutes before Isaac stuck his head in and asked, "Are you all comfortable?"

"Very!" I lied.

"All right, let's roll," Isaac said as he got in and sat opposite me on the right side of the backseat.

As the car began to move, Sister Stride started her fifteen minute prayer for our safe arrival to the hotel. And as though there was a possibility of the Lord not hearing her cry, she broke out into the old negro spiritual slash ninety-eight-year-old Deacon Jones version of *Guide Me Oh Thou Great Jehovah* . . . all three verses.

After the rolling mini-church was done, Isaac reached over and picked up a soda from the bar. "Would either of you ladies like something to drink?"

"No, thank you," Sister Stride said then finished her sentence louder, "Pastor Flack."

"I'm not thirsty." I looked in his direction. "But thanks."

Moments later he pierced the darkness with another offer. "Would either of you like to join me for dinner?"

Neither one of us answered. Honestly, I was waiting on Sister Do No Wrong to answer before I did. If she was going then he could count me out; no doubt she was waiting on my answer. If I said yes then she probably would too, just to protect her pastor against all evil . . . me. "Whoa, don't answer all at once," Isaac joked.

"I'll take you up on that offer, Pastor," her old voice creaked. "Where are we going?"

"There is a restaurant at the hotel." He then turned to face me. "What about you, Thalia?"

I was starving, but I couldn't be around Holy Rosie anymore than I needed to be. I'm sure she'd see me as an ungodly interruption. "No, thank you."

As Sister Stride started up about last Sunday's Sunday school lesson, I rested my head against the window. It was 8:50 P.M. in Philadelphia and Andre was just two hours away from coming home and finding empty shackles; his slave had escaped. He'd walk into the house, first looking in the microwave, then refrigerator to see what wonderful meal awaited him. He'd search relentlessly before storming into the bedroom to ask me about his dinner. The empty bed in the master bedroom would surely puzzle and stun him. Scurrying through the house he'd angrily notice that I'm nowhere to be found.

Storming back into the kitchen he'd grab the cordless phone to attempt communication with me on my cellular. Right around the time that my "I'm not available to take your call at the moment" message comes on, he'd see the note on the countertop. After reading it a few times he'd make a beeline to the room to check my drawers and the closet. After calling me names and yelling obscenities while searching the house for items he considered treasures, he would find many of them MIA.

Chapter 11

The Same Room, Bed, and Sweat

The limousine came to a slow stop then the back door flew open. "We're here," Isaac said as he stepped out and reached his caramel hand inside for mine. However, Sister Stride railroaded me and reached for it before I had a chance to sit up. But he reached in again as I slid over and then he pulled me to my feet. I loudly humored Sister Stride. "Thank you, Pastor Flack."

Isaac playfully squeezed my hand. "What did I tell you about that?"

"Some may consider it disrespectful," I said for you know who to hear.

"It's not the title that makes the man; it's a man that makes the title. I'm just a servant," Isaac said. "As long as people respect me for who I am they can call me whatever they're comfortable with, and I'm comfortable with you calling me Isaac."

"Are you sure?" My hand was still in his.

"Thalia," he must've noticed it at the same time I did, and let my hand go slowly, "I'm positive."

We were in front of the Renaissance Chicago Hotel in downtown Chicago. The twenty-seven story hotel was five blocks away from Lake Michigan. It was in the center of everything that was anything.

Isaac fished thirty dollars from his wallet and presented it to Hank, the limousine driver. Hank refused. "Don't worry about it. Bishop Ducreay took care of everything."

"It's a tip, for you," Isaac insisted.

Hank was grateful but still turned it down. "I'm your driver for the rest of your stay. The Bishop gave me your schedule. I will be here thirty minutes before each of your engagements." He dug a card from his pocket. "Here is my cell phone number, please call me if you need anything."

Isaac asked, "Not even a tip, huh?" Hank shook his head as Isaac continued. "Well, thank you very much for your services." Isaac was very appreciative.

"If you need me tonight, just call," Hank said like he had nothing better to do.

"Well," Isaac looked at his watch, "I think I'm in for the night."

Shaking hands Hank said, "Have a great evening, sir," then he walked away.

I turned to Isaac. "This Bishop really takes care of you, huh?"

"Well," he winked at me playfully, "somebody has to."

We followed the bellhop. Complete with marble floors, large live floral arrangements, and a sophisticated chandelier hanging from the very high ceiling, the lobby was enormous and very elegant. There was a large cocktail lounge with live piano music and a magnificent spiral staircase leading to two chic restaurants.

The bellhop reached the front desk before we did and briefed the middle-aged front desk clerk on who we were. "Hello, Reverend Flack." He smiled.

"Hello," Isaac responded.

"Mount Pleasant of Miami, Florida, correct?" he asked.

"Correct."

The clerk cleared his throat. "There were a total of sixteen rooms reserved for your church; the group yesterday and the day before used thirteen of them."

"Great, we'd like to check into the last three tonight."

I took a few minutes to silently thank God that Isaac wasn't putting me in the room with Sister Stride.

"Okay, ladies." He turned to Holy Rosie and me while dropping a key in his pocket. "I'm in room two-oh-two-eight." Then he placed a key in her hand. "You're in room two-oh-oh-two." Turning toward me he extended his hand. "Thalia, you're in two-oh-three-one."

Sister Stride walked away toward an older lady exiting the cocktail lounge. They hugged and kissed. I assumed that it was someone she knew from one of the other churches.

While making our way to the elevators I said, "Thank you, I truly appreciate this." I couldn't see any other man doing this without expecting to sleep in the same room, same bed, and same sweat as me. I don't know if he did what he did as a minister of the gospel caring for a charity case, or because he was genuinely sincere. Whatever the reason I was truly appreciative. "Thanks a million."

He smiled. "I told you how you could repay me."

"I'll be there next Sunday at eleven sharp." I had planned on keeping up my end of the bargain.

"Don't forget Sunday school."

"Wait a minute," I giggled. "You never mentioned Sunday school."

"So let's throw it in."

"Come on, eleven o'clock worship service is enough," I whined.

"Not a chance." He wasn't buying it. "Sunday school too."

"I cannot wake up that early on Sundays."

"I'll have Deacon Martin give you a wake-up call." He smiled. "We have many members that can't get out of bed. So Deacon Martin does wake-up calls between seven and eight." He chuckled. "So what's your number?"

"You're determined, huh?" I looked up at him.

"Yes, ma'am." I swear he looked me up and down as he continued. "I never give up."

Sister Stride and the Napoleon Dynamite look-a-like bellhop approached the elevators. "You guys are with the Mount Pleasant group on the twentieth floor, right?" the bellhop asked.

"Yes," Isaac and I answered in unison.

"Jinx," I called out and pinched his hand.

He stared at me. "You really don't want to come to Sunday school, huh?"

I couldn't believe that I had just pinched him. Being an elementary teacher had its disadvantages, and this was one of them. The children in my class played so many games that I at times joined them jokingly and it somehow, like now, leaked into my personal life and I looked like a fool. "I am so sorry."

"Don't be sorry." He lightened the mood. "Just explain the reason why you just tried to take the skin off of my hand."

"It's a game that my students play," I explained. "When two people say the same thing at the same time, the first person to hit or pinch the other person and say jinx wins the rights to whatever was said." I never realized just how dimwitted it was until I had to give details on it. I guess that's why eight- and nine-year-olds played it.

As we continued to walk he stared at me seriously. "Is that the whole game?"

"Yep."

He joked, "So you're not going to wrestle me down to the floor or anything?"

"Nope, that's it." I could wrestle him to the ground, but it would have nothing to do with the game.

As the elevator door opened a young waiter carrying a serving tray exited. I stopped him as he brushed past me. "Excuse me." I needed something to celebrate my newfound freedom. I told him secretively, "May I have a bottle of Syrah delivered to room two-oh-two-eight?"

"Yes, just allow me about thirty minutes."

"Thank you," I said, getting on the elevator.

As we moved up, Sister Stride looked at the bellhop, who looked like he needed to travel with an oxygen tank, and said, "If there is a fire on the fifteenth floor, how do we get down from the twentieth floor? The ladders on the fire trucks only reach to the fourth or fifth floors."

"You don't have to worry about something like that, ma'am," he assured her.

"Yes, I do, anything can happen."

"Would you like a room on another floor?"

"No," she snapped. "I'd like to be with my church group."

"Okay, then just call down to the front desk if there's a problem." The bellhop seemed annoyed.

"What can they do?" Sister Stride complained. "They won't be the one suffering from smoke inhalation."

"Ma'am, if the alarm goes off just run like hell, jeez." The bellhop's comment was inappropriate, but funny. I had to jar my giggle for later. What happened to all of that faith she had? Didn't she know what Matthew Chapter 17 Verse 20 said? *If you have faith the size of a mustard seed, you can move mountains, nothing is impossible.*

As we exited the elevator the bellhop informed us, "Both of your rooms are to the left and around the corner. Her room is to the right." He looked at Isaac and me. "If you two can wait here, I'll take her luggage down the hall and I'll be right back."

"Actually, all we have are these." Isaac grabbed his laptop carrying case and my carry-on tote bag from the cart. "I can take these." He handed the youngster a tip. "Sister Stride, are you still having dinner with me?"

"Oh my goodness. I'm sorry, Pastor, I forgot. I'm going down to the fourteenth floor to visit with the New Hope office staff for a little bit. Sister Stella was filling me in on some information." Information was the church word for gossip.

"All right, well, I'll see you in the morning." He added, "If you need anything, feel free to call my room."

I waved to her as she walked away. "Goodnight, Sister Stride."

"Goodnight." She turned to look at me. "What time does your plane leave in the morning?"

"Actually, I'm not leaving until six in the evening."

She sounded disappointed. "Oh, I'll see you tomorrow then." *Not if I could help it,* I thought, as she and the bellhop started their trek down the hallway.

Isaac's eyes met mine. "I'll see you to your room."

"Thank you." I couldn't wait to take a shower.

We walked in complete silence. I was kicking myself about not taking him up on his dinner offer earlier since Holy Rosie cancelled. I was hoping that he'd ask again before the walk was through.

He briefly stopped one door down from mine to rest his laptop bag on the ground and removed his coat and tie, hanging them on the doorknob to his room. His white dress shirt pressed against his chest was a sight to behold.

"What?" He caught me staring.

"Nothing." I couldn't believe that I was cheesing.

"What are you all smiles about?" he asked.

"I was thinking about Sister Stride's questions on the elevator," I lied.

He laughed. "I wanted to fall to the floor."

"I think she even wanted to laugh," I said.

After a few minutes of small talk he asked, "Are you going to bed?"

"Eventually, but right now I think I'll take a shower and then watch TV." Ask me to dinner, ask me to dinner, ask me to dinner, I willed. "You?"

"I can't wait to get out of this suit," he said, looking down the hallway. "But I have to find out which one of these rooms my luggage is in. Then I'll be taking a shower and having dinner." He unbuttoned the first two buttons of his shirt.

"Well, have a nice evening." I was desperate for him to invite me to dinner so I slowly inserted my key into the lock and then slowly I pushed the door, creating a sense of urgency.

Handing me my bag, he said, "Umm, it was really good seeing you." He extended his right hand toward me.

I shook his hand quickly. Why were we shaking hands after such a warm embrace earlier? "It was great seeing you again as well." I think I blushed . . . Lord, I hope I didn't blush.

"Can we talk more tomorrow?" he asked.

"Of course, if you have time, but I know that you'll be busy. So if you don't . . ."

"I will . . ." Just as he interrupted me a room door down the hall opened and a little girl came out with an ice bucket. "Pastor Flack," she screamed and dropped the bucket while running toward him.

"Hi, Tanya." He smiled at her.

"When did *you* get here?" She was no older than five.

He picked her up. "I'm just getting here." He kissed her forehead. Her tiny legs wrapped around his waist as she hugged him around the neck.

"Did you ride on the airplane?" she asked anxiously.

"I sure did."

"Did you get cookies and soda?"

"Yep." He pinched her cheek. "Do you know where I can find my suitcases?"

"Yes, they're in my room."

"Really?"

"Yep."

"Where were you going?" He put her down.

"I was just going to get some ice for my soda."

"I need to have a word with your mom; you shouldn't be out here alone. I'll go with you," he said, pointing down the hall. "Go get the bucket and wait right there." Tanya skipped off.

"Well, it looks like I've found my bags." Isaac smiled. "You have a good night."

"You do the same, Isaac." His name felt good when it passed my tongue.

He stared at me and I shockingly challenged his gaze. There was no way to tell exactly how long we were negotiating what to say to each other. He gave me his hand once again and I took it. But this time we didn't shake hands, squeeze or rub, we just touched. The heat from his body connected with mine and right away I knew that it wasn't just me, I wasn't just making it up in my head, he was suppressing the very same attraction that I was.

"Come on, Pastor Flack." Tanya had made her way back to us and pulled his hand away.

"Goodnight, Thalia."

I felt like I had just gotten up from a dream. "Goodnight, Isaac." I looked at his little friend. "Goodnight, Tanya."

"Goodnight," she said while she held onto his hand and pulled him down the hallway.

Chapter 12

On an Empty Stomach

Once in my room I quickly undressed and took a long hot shower. With a towel wrapped around my waist and my hair combed into a shabby ponytail, I called my sister. The phone rang once. "Hello?" Tyann sounded as though she was in a rush.

"Hi, Ty."

"Thalia, oh my God, I was just about to leave." She must've looked at the Caller ID. "Wait! Where are you?"

"I'm so sorry . . . "

"You sure are." Her tone totally changed as she cut me off. "I knew you couldn't leave him. Thalia, when are you going to open your eyes?"

"Tyann, let me explain."

"No, Thalia!" she spoke firmly. "Are you going to wait until that asshole starts hitting on you?"

"Will you shut up?" I yelled. "I'm in Chicago."

"What!" She was confused. "What are you doing in Chicago?"

"I missed my flight."

"What do you mean?"

"I had a connecting flight in Chicago and I missed it."

"So when are you leaving?"

"Tomorrow evening," I answered. "So you owe me an apology."

"I'm sorry," she said quickly. "How did you miss your flight?"

"I let an old lady I met on the plane look at my watch and she must've changed the time."

She was amused. "So your watch was set to European time?"

"Probably." I laughed.

"So you're out of Philadelphia for real, huh?"

"Yes, I see that you have no faith in me."

"Wow!" She sighed. "I'm so happy for you." I could hear her smiling. "What do you think he's going to say?"

"I don't even care," I said with a smirk.

I heard rapid movement of the telephone. "Hey, Miss Tyree." It was Colin, my sister's husband. We could hold our own over the phone, but we couldn't get a conversation going face-to-face. "Hi, Colin."

"How are you?"

"I'm away from Philadelphia so I'm great."

"That's good. So when will you be in Miami?" he asked.

"Tomorrow night, are you coming with Ty?" I was hoping that he wouldn't be.

"I'm working on something this week, so I might be at the firm a little late tomorrow." He sighed. "I was coming with her tonight, what happened?"

"I missed my flight, I'm in Chicago."

He laughed. "So what are you going to do?"

"I decided to just come tomorrow evening."

"There were no flights before that?" he asked.

"Yeah, but this is my first time here so I figured I might as well run with the opportunity."

"Are you staying downtown?" he asked.

"Yes, I'm at the Renaissance." I remembered by looking at the phone.

"If you have a chance, take a cab to Rush Street and visit The Backroom." He continued. "They have great live jazz."

"Thanks." I couldn't wait for him to give the phone back to Ty.

His last words were, "Well, have fun."

"I will."

Two seconds later Tyann asked, "All right, what's tomorrow's flight information?"

I was chillin', lying down with just a towel thrown over my naked body; there was no way I was about to get up. "Ty, I'll call you tomorrow with that stuff."

"Fine," she said. "So you're on Wacker Drive?" My sister did enough traveling to have her own daily show on The Travel Channel.

"I think so."

"How did you get all the way out there?" She was asking too many questions. "There are tons of hotels closer to the airport."

"It was recommended." I didn't want to bring Isaac into this equation. "I need to rest; it's been a crazy day, I'll talk to you tomorrow."

"Bye, Lia."

I sprawled out on the king-sized bed and grabbed the remote control from the nightstand. Flipping through channels, I decided to stop on a repeat of an episode of MTV's Real World/Road Rules Challenge, the Gauntlet one, two, or something. Man, Alton from Real World Las Vegas has grown up and into a hunka hunka burning love. I don't know about anyone else, but I am waiting on someone to beat the slut out and off of Veronica. There was a knock on the door.

I forgot all about my wine. "One minute, please," I said as I grabbed the thick terrycloth bathrobe and wrapped it around me. I ran toward the door, snatched the ponytail holder from my hair, and opened it. Isaac was leaning against the corner of the outside of the door holding a bottle of Syrah. "What am I supposed to do with this?"

"Huh?" I was in shock. "What do you mean?"

"Room service delivered this to my room," he said. "Two-oh-two-eight."

I looked at the numbers on my door, they read 2031. "I am so sorry. I made a mistake and told him to take it to two-oh-two-eight." I had to ask. "How did you know that it was mine?"

"I didn't," he answered. "I just thought I would take a chance on you."

My picture should be in the dictionary next to the word embarrassed. "Sorry for the inconvenience."

"No problem." Before handing it over he pointed at the bottle of wine. I assumed he was about to preach to me on the wickedness of alcohol and how I shouldn't partake in such sinful pleasure. "You shouldn't drink this on an empty stomach." He put the bottle in my hand. "So how about joining me for dinner?"

As I took the bottle I was in shock, my mouth dropped open, and then it dawned on me that I was only wearing a robe. "I'm not dressed." I quickly reached for the upper middle portion of the robe, making sure my extremities were covered.

He looked at the robe. "Is that all you had in your suitcase?" he asked.

I smiled. "No."

"Great, get dressed." He smiled and walked away confidently in his khaki slacks and navy Polo shirt. "I'll meet you in the lobby."

The elevator doors opened to the lobby and every step I took in my high-heeled sandals sent the hem of my black dress hitting the bottom of my knees. The dress was rather provocative, but it was the only decent thing in my carry-on.

I saw Isaac conversing with an older gentleman so I nervously stopped and read the menu showcased in glass adjacent to the elevators. The sixteen ounce New York Strip, steamed broccoli, and rice pilaf sounded good. Though I had my dinner selection out of the way, I pretended to study the menu and hoped Isaac wouldn't notice me until his company was gone. Then it happened, his deep voice pierced my pretend concentration. "Thalia." He was still standing next to the older gentleman but waved me over. As I approached, Isaac introduced me. "Thalia, this is Bishop Edward A. Ducreay, the President of the National Baptist Convention." He paused. "Bishop, this is Miss Thalia Tyree." We shook hands.

"It's very nice to meet you, Miss Tyree." Bishop Ducreay offered a very pleasant smile.

"Nice to meet you as well, Bishop. I've heard . . ." I had only heard two sentences about him, but I was so nervous I said anything. "I've heard a lot of great things about you."

He laughed and looked at Isaac. "How much is this going to cost me?" They both burst into laughter.

"A blank check will do just fine," Isaac teased. "I'll decide the amount when I get to the bank. But if your checks are like your golf game, then you can keep it, brother."

"Oh, there you go with golf again," Bishop said.

Isaac's face lit up. "You should've learned your lesson after the first three years of that spanking I put on you."

"You call it spanking, I call it coming in second."

"I call it last place, since it was just us two," Isaac went on. "The next time you pray ask, no, beg for a new game." Isaac clutched his hands and moved them in a swinging motion. "You need to fast about your game, man."

Bishop Ducreay then swung his hands, mocking Isaac. "What about that time at the Doral Country Club?"

"Oh." Isaac's enthusiasm died. "I had the flu."

"Yeah, I *flew* right through you." Bishop Ducreay then turned his attention toward me. "Is this your first time at the convention?"

I didn't know what to say. If I said that I wasn't with the convention but was with Isaac, that wouldn't sound *righteous*. If I said that I was with the convention but couldn't tell him squat about it, he'd think I was an idiot. "Actually, Isaac and I ran into each other at the airport." Did I just call him Isaac in front of one of the top officials of the Baptist Church? "I'm off to Miami tomorrow."

Bishop looked at Isaac. "I'll be in Miami at the beginning of next month."

"I didn't forget you, man," Isaac reassured him.

"How is Madison?" he asked.

"She's doing great."

Bishop went on. "How about the boys?"

"Junior just finished medical school and Julian's at FAMU, changing his major every time he meets a new girl." He laughed.

"So Tyler is the only one at home now?" Bishop questioned.

"Yes, but he's off to Morehouse in a few days." He was proud. He had all the rights to be. Many black parents can't say that all of their children made it to college.

"Good." Bishop smiled. "I was worried about Tyler."

"Me too, but he picked up his grades when he dropped a few of those knuckleheaded friends." Isaac looked down at his watch. "Bishop, would you like to join us for dinner?"

"I wish I could, but Omari is down at McCormick Place seeing that everything is set up properly for the opening ceremony and seminars tomorrow." He chuckled. "I was supposed to pick her up ten minutes ago."

"That is one extraordinary cook right there." Extending his right hand toward Bishop Ducreay, Isaac reminisced. "I can still taste those greens. You are truly blessed, Bishop."

"I thank God every day for Omari, she's my right hand. When I'm asleep she's working, and when she's asleep, I'm asleep." All three of us laughed. "Let me get down there and get her or she'll have my head."

"It was very nice to meet you, Bishop Ducreay." I shook his hand again.

"Likewise, Miss Tyree. Maybe I'll see you in Miami." He shook my hand while looking at Isaac for confirmation of a Miami reunion. Thankfully Isaac said nothing, but Bishop had words for him. "The Lord has spoken to me regarding you, son. 'Eye has not seen and ear has not heard'." He paused. "The Lord has a blessing for you. Be encouraged and be blessed."

"I can't be anything else, Bishop." He smiled and embraced Bishop Ducreay. "I can't be anything else." Bishop turned and walked toward the main doors.

What Bishop Ducreay said to Isaac bewildered me. Just three weeks prior, a guest speaker at my church in Philadelphia said the same thing to me. The speaker, Evangelist Rose White, pounced on me in the parking lot after service. She said that the Lord pointed me out to her during her message and told her to say to me, *"Things which eye has not seen and ear has not heard, and which have not entered the heart of a man, all that God has prepared for those who love Him."*

I didn't know what it meant but I cried all the way home. Up until then I thought God had forgotten about me. I was thrilled to hear that I still meant something to Him. I was elated to know that He was reaching out to me in spite of the mess I had created with my life. I used the words given to me that day as final confirmation. "Eye has not seen," meant whatever God had for me wasn't where I was so I had to get out of Philadelphia to get it.

As we walked toward the restaurant I was a half a step in front of Isaac and out of the corner of my eye I thought I saw him staring at me, and like an idiot, I snickered.

"You saw me, huh?" He laughed and continued without my answer. "You look very nice."

"Thank you." I blushed.

"No need to thank me," he said as we walked up the fancy stairs from the lobby and into the Great Street Restaurant.

"Hello." A tall and very feminine pale-white man in a gray suit approached us. "Table for two?" We were so overwhelmed by his girly voice that we didn't answer. "Table for two?" he asked again while looking at us strangely.

"Yes," Isaac spoke up. "Non-smoking, please."

"Right this way." He snuck a peek at his watch while leading us to a table at the far end of the restaurant.

As Isaac pulled out my chair I tried hard to remember the last time that was done for me. "Thank you."

Isaac took his seat and the man politely rested two menus in front of us. "Jacqueline will be right with you."

Thick white jarred candles flickered on every table, which were covered in beige linen, and soft jazz filled the air. The vacant shadowy restaurant looked like a place for angels at rest. White roses were in full bloom everywhere. The smell in the air wasn't food but a charming soft perfume. Everything was so snug, dreamy, and romantic that it made me uneasy. I couldn't help but wonder if Isaac was regretting Bishop Ducreay or Sister Stride not coming along.

"This place is beautiful." I turned my attention to him.

"Yes, it is." He ran his hand over the top of the flickering candle. "I love the lighting."

"I do too." I gave the place a second glance.

"Good evening, my name is Jacqueline." A petite lady with dark hair came out of nowhere. "Are you two ready to order?"

I knew what I wanted from studying the menu earlier, but I opted to wait for him. "Not yet," we said in perfect harmony. Isaac reached across the table with a smile and gently pinched my hand. "Jinx."

Jacqueline was puzzled, but wasn't trying to get into our business. "May I get you anything to drink?"

Isaac, like a true gentlemen, allowed me to order first. "I'll have a Sprite, please, no ice."

"Apple juice for me," he responded.

"Okay, I'll return with your drinks in just a moment," Jacqueline said before walking away.

"You got me," I said, referring to his soft pinch.

"Yeah, I caught you off-guard." He smiled.

"Don't worry, now that I see that you're on your P's and Q's I'll be paying attention." I slightly brushed his hand. "And my pinches won't be spongy."

"You've got a deal." He seemed comfortable.

"I hope you're ready for me." As the words left my mouth my stomach churned into a big knot. What was I thinking? "So what are you having?" I brought the conversation back to a place were I could breathe.

He opened his menu, and after a few minutes, he announced his selection. "New York Strip Steak sounds good."

When Jacqueline returned with dinner rolls and our drinks in stylish tall cylinder-like glasses and set them before us she asked, "Are you ready to order?" We ordered our salads and entrées.

As the waitress left, Isaac began telling me of his many visits to Chicago. Two days ago, had I thought of Isaac in Chicago, all I would've pictured him doing was eating, sleeping, praying, and preaching. But he told me of his visits to Navy Pier, the various museums, the Buckingham fountain, he even enjoyed a few plays. He did these things by himself.

Right as our salads arrived, his cellular phone rang.

"Would you mind me taking this call?" He was so polite. "I'd like to make sure that everything is all right."

"Go ahead," I said.

"Thank you." He then spoke into his phone. "Hello." A huge smile graced his lips. "Hi, how are you?" He paused. "I'm fine."

Here we go with this phone thing again; Leon, Andre, and now Isaac. Who could be calling him so late? I wasn't trying to listen to the conversation, but his voice was the closest thing to me. Okay, yes I was trying to listen. I felt like a nosey operator, wanting to release the line but desiring more. "How did everything work out?" He waited in silence for a minute. "Sweetheart, I'm so happy for you. I knew you'd make the right decision." This was getting interesting to say the least.

"The flight was fine." He sipped his apple juice. "I'm having dinner with a friend." Resting the cup down, he continued. "In the hotel restaurant, why?" He blushed. "Aren't *you* inquisitive?" He looked away shyly. "Come on, give me a break." He changed the subject. "I'm going to need a neck massage when I get home." I was about to faint. "Did you go to the house today?" he asked. "C'mon, Madison, you know how Tyler can be. I do want to have a house to come back to." Oh, it was just Madi. I exhaled. Oh snap . . . it was Madi!

Hearing Madison's name was like cold water thrown in my face; it woke me up from the fantasy that I was on an actual date. "Check on him tomorrow." He sat silent for a minute, listening to whatever Madi had to say. Jacqueline appeared with the main course. "All right, I'll call you tomorrow," he said joyfully. "That was Madison."

"Is everything all right?" I asked.

"Yes, she's fine." He looked at his plate and curtailed the talk of reality. "This looks great."

I picked up my fork and then Isaac began to pray. What a sinner, I had totally forgotten all about saying grace. I joined him at the end. "Amen."

During dinner I tried to make small talk, but we ran out of comfortable topics. A few times I found his eyes piercing me and was flushed with nervousness. The temptation of responding to Isaac as a man I found attractive was all too real. So out of all things to talk about we ended up discussing animal rights. I could give one damn about animals, I was scared of all of them, but it was a safe topic; we couldn't afford a moment of silence.

Out of nowhere Isaac asked, "Do you think he knows now?"

"Excuse me?"

"Your guy in Philadelphia." He waved his fork around, trying to remember Andre's name once again.

I had a hard time swallowing my last piece of broccoli. "If you don't mind, I would rather not discuss him." Though my smiling expression said one thing there was sassiness in my voice.

"I'm sorry. I just thought I would ask." He was apologetic. "I'm not trying to upset you, but you have to begin to think about it before you can stop thinking about it."

I lowered my head. "I just don't want to deal with it right now." I was too weak to defend myself.

Isaac placed his hand on mine. "Don't go getting all fragile on me." He rubbed my hand gently. "I understand what you're dealing with, but there are certain steps you have to go through before you can get to where you want to be. Deal with what you're dealing with now so that in the future you'll truly be free and not a prisoner of the past."

"I know." I truly did. "I just didn't prepare myself for this feeling."

"What are you feeling?" he asked.

"I'm just wondering about what he'll do when he gets home tonight," I admitted.

"So you're in a tizzy about his reaction?"

"I don't know if I'd call it a tizzy." I stopped him in his tracks. "I just wish I knew what he'll think when he finds out."

"What if he never calls to look for you or to ask you why you left?" he asked. "How will you feel?"

"That might be a relief," I lied. If Andre never tried to contact me I would be devastated. I would feel like I played right into his plan. I continued to pretend to be strong. "I would like to see the look on his face when he finds the note, but if I never hear from him again it won't make a difference."

"Thalia, I would love it if all of your ties were completely cut."

"I'd love it too." I finally looked up at him.

"I'm sorry I brought it up." He seemed genuine.

"Thank God I was done eating because that would've taken my appetite away quickly." I tried hard to lighten the mood. With his hand still on mine I tried to act like I didn't notice but it went on too long. "What?" I met his glare.

"You are amazing." He stunned me with his words. "I wouldn't have wanted to run into anyone else today."

"Thank you." I struggled with a response. "I enjoy seeing this side of you."

"Really?" he said. "What side is that?"

I had to choose my words wisely. "I guess it's a friend-lier side."

"I thought we were always friends." It sounded like he was flirting. "But I must say that I am enjoying this opportunity to get friendlier."

Now that the walls were coming down I was ready to run. "Thank you."

He took a deep breath. "Is it possible that I can continue seeing this part of you?"

I tried not to take his words to heart. "Well, the night is still young."

"I know," he said nervously, "but I meant even when we're both back in Miami."

I played the stupid role in an effort to make him say what he truly wanted to say. "If you're talking about me coming to church I'll be there, I promise."

"I was actually hoping for another dinner opportunity."

"Dinner?" I was giddy.

"Yes." He seemed shy. "I'm sorry, if you don't . . ."

"No, no! Dinner would be fine," I interrupted him. "But haven't I bored you enough?"

"Boring would've been me sitting here all alone, which I'm very much accustomed to." Isaac reached into his wallet and placed cash on the table. "I've really enjoyed your company."

Chapter 13

The Sudden Jerks of His Body

We smiled all the way to the twentieth floor. While inserting my key into the lock he was so close that I could feel the heat from his body. "I guess this is where we say goodnight," I said to him.

"Is it?" he asked.

I didn't know. "Isn't it?"

He moved closer and my heart was beating like somebody who had stolen something. "Maybe you'd like to invite me in."

"Ya think?" I pressed myself against the door and played hard to get. "You think I would do a thing like that?"

"I'm sorry." He took a step back and paused. "I wasn't trying to . . ."

I interrupted him. "Would you like to come in?" I had no fancy words, just a yearning to be near him. He looked stunned. "Come in." I turned the knob and walked into the room. While switching the television channels I happened upon TV Land, which was showing an episode of *The Odd Couple.* "I used to love this show," Isaac said as he made himself comfortable on the sofa. I plopped stomach down on the king-sized bed facing him. "This is how I gave Madison her name."

"Are you serious?" I giggled and wondered if she knew.

"Yes, ma'am, from good ol' Oscar."

Isaac was really into the show; I was relieved when it went off, but just when I thought I had his attention the theme song played again, it was a double feature. After the second episode he grabbed the remote and pressed the power button, bringing his attention to me. "You had me worried," I joked. "For a moment I thought you were using me for cable."

"No, ma'am." He changed his position on the couch to better face me. "I'm here for more than cable." He paused and left my imagination running into a brick wall. "I'm here to make a new friend." He stood up and I examined him. He reminded me of how the midnight sky could be intimidating, yet in its ebony magnificence it was amazingly soothing. He was midnight to me, and though he was daunting I knew that if I reached out to him he'd help assemble my broken pieces.

On his handsome face I could still see the same pain that was often a part of his daughter's pretty facade. The death of his wife years ago was still very much a part of him today. "May I ask you a question?" I heard myself say.

"Go ahead."

I couldn't believe what I was about to ask. "Do you ever get lonely?"

"Lonely?" His facial expression, or the lack thereof, was confusing. He dragged a chair over to the bed. "Yeah, I get lonely."

"So how do you deal with it?" I hoped I wasn't asking too many of the wrong questions.

"I've learned to live with it."

I was the new Barbara Walters, I wanted answers. "But just living with it, are you happy?"

"Happy?" He scratched his head. "Happy the man, and happy he alone, he who can call today his own. He, who secure within, can say, tomorrow do thy worst, for I have lived today. Be fair or foul or rain or shine, the joys I have possessed, in spite of fate, are mine. Not Heaven itself the past has power, but what has been, has been, and I have had my hour." He never looked away from me.

"Wow," I said, but thought, *What* was that?

"That's John Dryden's *Happy the Man.* I learned it years ago." He swallowed hard. "It was on the inside of a sympathy card."

"I'm sorry." I felt guilty.

"There is nothing for you to apologize about. It's just a poem."

"I know. But I'm sure it makes you think of . . ."

"Those times are gone, God got me through them. When I received that card I was so angry with Him I couldn't even open my Bible. Because I knew that if I did He'd make sense of the situation with a scripture. I didn't want it to make sense; I wanted it to hurt because if it didn't then it wouldn't seem real." He paused. "The card came from nowhere, no name, no address, no nothing, but when I read it I got the message. God wanted me to know that yesterday couldn't be changed, tomorrow wasn't promised, and in spite of adversities I had to give everything to today."

I tried to smile. "That's powerful."

"To answer your question, yes, I get lonely. I would love to come home to warm hugs. Someone to laugh at my jokes, help me clean, cook, and join me at different functions." He wasn't finished. "I wish I had a guaranteed amen or hallelujah in the congregation." He smiled. "I miss having the small things that most people take for granted."

"Like what?" I wouldn't be one hundred percent woman if I didn't ask.

He stated, "Like having to readjust the seat in the car after she got out of it, phone calls in the middle of the day, flowers, movies, praying together, just having a best friend." He wiped his eyes as though he thought a tear could possibly be there. "People don't bother asking me anything that might lead to talking about Bianca."

I felt bad for asking. "I'm sorry, Isaac."

"No, it's okay. Every once in a while I need to remember."

"I hope that my next question isn't out of line."

"Another one?" He clutched his chest playfully. "You're like Barbara Walters. You don't stop until you see tears." We both laughed.

"Have you dated?" I was curious.

"How much is my daughter paying you to ask me these questions?" he joked.

"Not enough." Though Madison and I wondered if Isaac ever had a girlfriend after her mother's death, I never thought I'd ever have a forum to ask him candidly.

"Yeah, I've dated, but nothing too serious. On one occasion I thought that this one woman was the one, but, man, nothing could've been further from the truth." He continued. "As it stands I'm waiting on God."

"So for eleven years you haven't . . ." There was no way I could finish. "Never mind." I wanted to ask him about his sex life.

Sex was another reason why leaving Andre was important. When I did go to church I tried hard to worship, but I felt guilty because that night I'd be fornicating for sure with Andre. I looked forward to being free from the bondage of a sexual relationship. It would allow me to purify myself physically, spiritually, emotionally, mentally, and sexually.

During Bible study at Ebenezer I learned that each time a person has sex with someone, out of the realm of marriage, there is a demonic spirit transfer that takes place between the two of them. Now I've spun my own Thalia Tyree logic from that. This evil spiritual exchange can be attributed to the reason why most people walk away from sex feeling like they've just fought a battle. It's because they have, the body is under attack by enemy forces. Also, if you think about the times you've given yourself to someone and then started having unusual thoughts like suicide, homicide, stealing, hurting someone, etc., those things may have entered your mind through the gateway of the spirit that you attained through sex with someone who was having those thoughts or dealing with those issues. And this exchange happens each time you have sex. Can you imagine how many demons I must've had? Whew! I have enough things going wrong! All I needed was to add on somebody else's craziness to mine. Therefore, I had made up my mind to wait until a man, not just any man though, until the appointed man, asked me to be his wife.

"I've been abstaining." Isaac answered my unasked question. "No sex."

"Hasn't it been hard?" I asked with no pun intended.

"Yes, it has been, but I'm on a mission. My faith is an anointing, and my capacity to operate in the spirit is stronger than anything of this world. Loving the Lord is my life, not a convenience."

I was questioning a man of God about his sex life. "Please forgive me." I was uncomfortable and ashamed that I didn't use better judgment. I sighed. "I'm sorry, I shouldn't have gotten so personal with you."

"No, that's cool." He moved next to me on the bed. "I have nothing to hide." He tried to reassure me. "I got personal with *you* about *your* relationship." With him being so close to me, and of all things on a bed, my brain went into panic mode.

"I wasn't sure if I had crossed the line or not," I admitted.

"I don't want there to be a line, Thalia," he said as though he was trying to convince himself. "If we're trying to get to know each other there are some questions that must be asked." He smiled. "For example, are you ticklish?"

Before I could answer I was laughing hysterically. Just thinking of someone tickling me was funny. "Yes." He began to laugh too. "Stop, stop, stop." I was trying to contain myself. It took a full minute for me to get a serious face together.

"So I take it that you're ticklish?" he asked.

"Very much so, don't get any ideas."

"I won't tickle you." Then he added, "At least not tonight."

I sat up on the bed. "Good because tonight is your night." I quickly reached out to his abdomen and began moving my fingers around fast, tickling him.

"Wait, no, stop, stop, stop, no, wait." He laughed and tried to stand but couldn't. I enjoyed the feel of his skin beneath my fingertips, the jovialness in his voice, and the sudden jerks of his body at my command.

Chapter 14

Churchwomen Aren't Blind

After three minutes of me tickling him, Isaac exhaustedly collapsed on my bed. When he was finally able to keep a straight face I challenged him to a round of thumb wrestling. He accepted my offer, not knowing that it was just a desperate ploy to hold his hand.

"What can your little fingers do to me?" he asked.

I gave him a flirtatious smile. "Wouldn't you like to know?"

What he didn't know was at New Liberty Elementary, my fourth grade class spent their recess time enhancing my thumb wrestling skills. The bout between Isaac and I started with the best of three, but quickly turned into the best of five, then ten, then twenty. Isaac couldn't believe that my little fingers were overpowering his.

Sprawled out over the bed, we sparked an interesting conversation about simple things we wish we could slow down enough to fully enjoy. I shared that I wanted to make time to watch the sunrise at least once a month.

He stated that because of his busy schedule he didn't get to study the sky at night like he did as a young boy.

It was nighttime and we had nothing to do, so I saw no sense in making him wait when opportunity and all the available amenities were at hand. When he excused himself to the bathroom I quickly snatched the bed covering and two pillows from the bed. I spread the quilt on the floor in front of the picture window and turned off all of the lights. When the bathroom door opened I stood in the darkness before him and said, "Your wish is my command."

I led him to the blanket and slid the long earth toned curtain to the side, revealing the onyx Heavens. The moonlight skimmed the side of his sweet handsome face as he took my hand to his lips. If a doctor were in the room he or she could've confirmed that my heart stopped for at least fifteen seconds. Isaac didn't kiss me like a man hoping to impress me. His kiss was just what a kiss should always be, innocent, mysterious and brand new, but I wished that he were kissing my lips instead. We sat back and watched the moon and stars in silence. "Thank you." He wasn't talking about the sky.

The next few hours were spent exchanging endearing stories of our past, and sharing future ambitions until our bodies grew tired. The stars came to us as his head fell back onto a pillow and mine landed on his shoulder. The safety I felt in his presence was like that of the president's, with twenty-five secret service officers willing to die to keep me protected. The feeling I experienced lying in his arms was like a newborn baby. I cooed, we cuddled, and he cradled me.

*   *   *

The clock read 9:12 in the morning but the darkness told another story. I wiggled my fingers in front of me and panicked when I couldn't see them. I scrambled around on my hands and knees until I found a lamp. The light illuminated the room, bringing comfort back to my unfamiliar state. Isaac was gone and the curtains were closed.

With the exception of my shoes, I was fully dressed from the night before. I made my way into the shower and thought about the previous night. Somewhere, somehow, we innocently connected, yet it was so powerful and I knew that it would be impossible for us to ever be the same again. As the water beat down on my body, I recalled the entire night with a huge smile.

Toward the end of my shower I heard a noise inside the room and turned the water off. "Hello!" I yelled. "Isaac?" I smiled. "Is that you?" When no one answered I wrapped myself in a big towel. "Is someone out there?" Scared to death I cracked the door. "Who's there?" The room was silent. I stepped out and saw that everything was just as I had left it, but as I looked around for the remote control there was not only a copy of the Chicago Sun Times on the desk, but also a small arrangement of fresh flowers, a fancy covered tray, and a large glass of orange juice. A tiny bit of steam escaped as I removed the cover from the two pancakes, scrambled eggs, bacon, and toast. I carried the tray to the bed and noticed a folded piece of hotel stationary next to the orange juice.

Thalia,
Sorry about leaving early. I contemplated waking you to watch the sunrise. Instead, I took the opportunity

*to watch you, which was far more exciting. If possible I
would've added a few more hours to our night. But since
I couldn't I thought I'd add a smile to your day. Thank
you for placing the moon and stars at my feet. ~Isaac*

I felt like a queen and Isaac's note was my diadem,
my throne, my perfectly polished pearl. I opened the
curtains and smiled at the sun. I put on a pair of sweat
pants and a T-shirt, ate my breakfast, and watched Regis
interview Susan Lucci for what had to be the fiftieth
time in his career. Susan went on and on about a made
for TV movie that she was starring in. During a com-
mercial break the room's phone rang.

"Hello," I smiled and answered.

"Bitch, where the fuck is my shit?"

"What?" Oh my goodness, it was Andre. I didn't
know what to say. "What?"

"Did I forget to say good morning?" he said in an
angry and sarcastic tone. "Let's cut to the damn chase,
Lia. Where is all my shit?"

Scared thoughtless I panicked. "How did you get this
number?"

"Let's not forget who the hell I am." He'd never let
anyone forget. "I'm a detective and I'll find you wherever you go."

I said in disgust, "Who gives a damn about who you
are?"

"You'll care when I have the Chicago P.D. knocking
on your fuckin' hotel room door." He added, "Or
should I let them drag your sorry ass off of your
Continental Airlines flight at six o'clock?"

How did I think that I could hide from him? "Do
whatever makes you happy, Andre." I tried not to sound
intimidated.

"I'll be happy when you bring back my shit, bitch." I had never heard him so angry with anyone that was not a criminal.

"Hold up." I gathered my strength. "You will not call me anything outside of my name."

"Get the fuck over yourself," he yelled. "Until I get my things I will call you whatever I damn well desire." For the next sixty seconds he did just that. Andre called me everything that I wasn't.

I waited for him to pause to ask, "Are you done yet?"

"No, I'm not done," he huffed. "You better never set foot in Philly again."

I said, "I hadn't planned on it, but thanks for reminding me."

"Shut the fuck up." He laughed. "What are you doing, moving back to your stupid ass crapped up apartment?" He continued. "You women trip me the fuck out with all of that independent bullshit. If you wanted to be independent then why did you move here in the first place? You weren't shit until you moved here and you ain't shit now."

"I moved there because I thought I was in love. I thought I was getting married." I took a deep breath. I couldn't believe that he still wasn't getting it. "I didn't know that my fiancé would end up . . ." I couldn't find a better word, Lord forgive me . . . "fuckin' the wedding planner." I snickered. "Thanks for the ring brotha; the money should tide me over for a while."

"Oh yeah? I swear I'll take you to court." He was angry. "You don't want to piss me off, trust me."

"Oh now you want me to trust you?"

"You know what the fuck I mean." He breathed heavily. "I spent a lot of money on that ring."

"I know. It'll pay first and last month's rent plus the deposit on my stupid ass crapped up apartment."

"That ring cost me over five grand. You'll be hearing from my lawyer."

"Your lawyer?" I giggled. "Who Tiffany? Aren't you fucking her too? That's a conflict of interest. Buy Tiffany her own damn ring."

"I should've beaten the shit out of you while I had the chance."

"That was very manly." He caught me off-guard. "Say it again and I'll have your badge for threatening bodily harm to me you bastard." I was proud of myself for using only three or four curse words during the whole ordeal.

"You'll regret this tantrum."

"It's not a tantrum, it's called a lifestyle change," I stated. "And if you don't mind, please e-mail me this sad story of yours, I have things to do."

"Lia, kiss my . . ." Before he was through I returned the receiver to its cradle.

I couldn't sit in the hotel room any longer. After calling Tyann with my flight information I visited The Magnificent Mile. At noon I knew that the members of The National Baptist Convention should've already been assembled and ready for worship. Like a girl with a crush, I wondered if Isaac was thinking of me. I couldn't help but imagine what he looked like among all of the other dignitaries, reverends, pastors, bishops, elders, and doctors. He had to have been approached by women at every church he visited. Lord only knows how many women made their way to the altar to see if they qualified for special prayers from him. The moment they found out that he was single they'd almost certainly be willing to give him more than just a love offering.

Churchwomen aren't blind; they recognize a fine man when they see one, and if he's also a good man you might hear them speaking in tongues. Some women make it clear that they're only in church to catch a man. Everyone has been to church at least once and couldn't tell whether they're at a fashion show or eleven o'clock worship. Women walk up and down the aisles like they're on the catwalk and hope that a heavenly-looking brotha with an eternal bankbook will envy their audacious presence. You know these women . . . the ones wearing four hundred dollar suits, umbrella hats, and Payless shoes asking the deacons for three dollars back from the five they dropped in the offering plate.

I wasted an entire sightseeing day daydreaming of Isaac. During my cab ride back to the hotel I willed the message light on the phone to be on, but I had no such luck. I stuffed my new tote bag with my new purchases, and decided to wear a new hunter green sleeveless top and a short fluted bottom skirt to the airport.

Before leaving I sat on the bed and picked up the phone. "Front desk, how may I assist you, Ms. Tyree?" the chipper female voice on the other end asked. Now I see why it was so easy for Andre to locate me, the room was in my name.

"Hi, I need a cab to the O'Hare Airport."

"I'd be glad to help you with that."

"Thank you."

"When will you be downstairs?"

"In about five minutes."

"Will you need assistance with your bags from the room to the lobby?"

"No, thank you."

"Okay." She was very professional. "Is there anything else I can do for you today?"

I thought for a few seconds. "Yes, would you please transfer me to room two oh two eight?"

"Sure, please hold." The next thing I heard was a recorded message. *"The Renaissance guest you've attempted to reach is unavailable. Please leave a message after the tone. Thank you."*

"Hi, Isaac." I hated talking to answering machines. "I just wanted to say thanks for everything. Breakfast was quite a delicious surprise, but I wish that we could've eaten it together." Was I out of my mind? "I've read your note five times and it just keeps getting better. I had a wonderful time last night and wish we could do it all over again tonight." I giggled. "This is all so strange. I never in a million years thought . . ." The automated voice interrupted me. *"To send as an urgent message, press one. To send with normal delivery, press two."*

"I wasn't finished," I said into the phone as though she cared.

The automated voice reminded me, *"To send as an urgent message, press one. To send with normal delivery, press two."* I pressed one and hung up. I couldn't believe that the beep went off on me. It was just Wednesday and he wasn't returning to Miami until Monday. We had exchanged cellular numbers, so only time will tell what will happen.

I gathered my things and headed downstairs; the cab was already waiting. I slid my tote bag onto the backseat. I made it to the airport twelve minutes to five, which assured me that Lily wouldn't throw her evil smile at me.

When it was time for coach passengers to board I was almost last in line. There was a woman and her husband behind me arguing over the amount of frequent flyer miles he had. Apparently he said that he was off on business a lot, but the frequent flyer information said something different, he had almost none.

Then I started thinking about what Andre said. What if hanging up on him angered him enough to have the Chicago Police Department haul me off of the plane before takeoff? Were air marshals already waiting on the plane for me? Was what I did to his belongings illegal? I was scared and started having second thoughts about boarding. "Miss Tyree, I need you to come with me." A hand grabbed me from the back.

Chapter 15

The Enchantment

I turned around ready to explain to the police why I did what I did, but instead it was Isaac's welcoming smile. He was dressed in a black Calvin Klein single-breasted suit with a royal blue woven silk tie. Now I truly saw the resemblance he had to the actor most people compared him to. For a split second I didn't know if I was looking at Isaac or Denzel straight off of the set of *Out Of Time.* Just any ol brotha cannot pull off looking as good as Denzel, so to look just like him was earth shattering. Well, he shattered my earth.

"What are you doing here?" I asked.

"You didn't think I was going to let you leave just like that?"

"Thanks for coming." I wished he'd shown up earlier because it was time for me to go. "I can't believe you came all this way to say goodbye."

"Goodbye?" he said seriously. "That would be insane."

I was confused. "I don't get it."

"I didn't come to say goodbye." He smiled. "I came to ask you to stay." His eyes said please.

"Are you serious?"

"Yes."

"But I already checked out of my room." I didn't know what else to say.

"We didn't use two rooms last night," he joked.

Then I heard Lily's voice on the speaker again. I asked, "But my ticket . . ."

"That means you'll stay?" He sounded excited.

"Yes." I couldn't believe my mouth, my heart, and *him.*

He grabbed my bag and we approached the counter. He did all of the talking, and before I knew it he was pulling out his credit card again. "Is ten in the morning fine with you?" I shook my head to agree and smiled. When the transaction was complete we began walking and I couldn't believe that I was still in Chicago. "How did you get past security?"

"I have friends in high places." He looked up. "But I have a few lowdown dirty ones too."

Tonight we traveled in a black Town Car. It wasn't the limo but it was still very nice and Hank was once again the driver. Sitting side-by-side he broke the silence. "I guess you want to know why I asked you to stay, huh?" He smiled then began his explanation. "After the chemistry we had last night I couldn't imagine being alone tonight, not if all I had to do was ask you to stay."

"Oh, Isaac." No words I knew could amount to his statement, no embrace was strong enough, and nothing in the world was worth its value, but suddenly I remembered that my sister was once again unaware of my change of venue. "My phone is in the trunk in my carry-on and I need to call my sister, she was supposed to pick me up. May I use yours?"

"Go ahead."

I was glad to hear her voicemail; if she were there I knew for a fact she'd begin questioning my reasons for staying in Chicago. "Hello, Ty. I've decided to stay in Chicago another night." I looked over at Isaac. "I'll be in tomorrow, but you'll be at work when my flight arrives, so I'll take a cab." I hung up. "She is going to kill me."

During the remainder of the ride we discussed the first day of the convention. He was greatly fascinated by the combined choir because the director had only two days to assemble the youngsters, but they performed as though they were rehearsing together for weeks. The workshops were very informative and the youth ministers did an excellent job making sure that all of the young people were learning on the correct level. Isaac seemed enthused; I could hear it in his voice.

The car stopped fifty feet away from the biggest Ferris wheel I had ever seen. We stepped out and I took in the beauty of my surroundings as Isaac instructed Hank to pick us up at eleven.

"So this is Navy Pier?" I looked around at all of the flashing lights and people.

"Yes, it is." Isaac took my hand, my hand . . . I still couldn't believe any of this, and we began to walk. In passing I saw the gigantic Ferris wheel; up close it was even more spectacular. It seemed twenty stories high and it would take Jesus himself to come down and make me get on it. The merry-go-round carousel was brilliant; the music began to take me back to my childhood years. We skipped over a leapfrog fountain without getting wet and walked alongside a beautiful garden. "There she is."

"Who?" I didn't know we were there to meet someone.

He pointed at the luxurious two hundred foot, four story yacht. "The Enchantment." He pulled two tickets from his pocket. "A dinner cruise."

"Thank you." Standing in awe of the ship I said, "This is beautiful."

"Thank *you* for staying," he said as we walked up the ramp of the vessel.

"Welcome to The Enchantment," a young lady greeted us as we approached the entrance of the ship.

"Dinner for two," Isaac said, handing her the tickets.

She reviewed her list and said, "Mr. Flack and Miss Tyree, you two will be dining on the fourth level. The top floor is semi-private, with only five other couples." A gentleman walked over and then she continued. "Jason will gladly see you to your table."

"Right this way." I followed Jason and Isaac was close behind. We entered the dining area where the light fixtures gave off an emerald glow leaving everything a sexy shade of green. The waiters and waitresses all wore emerald green cummerbunds and ties. A small arrangement of fresh white flowers sat on every table in tall crystal vases.

The other floors had so many people on them that all you could hear was chatter. However, on our level soft piano music streamed out before Jason could even open the door. He led us toward a table set up for two next to the piano. There was a couple already seated at another table six or seven feet away. Looking down at a card in his hand Jason said, "Mr. and Mrs. Herrington."

Jason then looked over at Isaac and me. "Mr. Isaac Flack and Ms. Thalia Tyree will be joining you for dinner tonight."

"Hello." We all smiled at each other.

Isaac pulled out my chair and joked, "You blend right in here," he pointed at my outfit.

We sat down. "So is this what you had on the agenda today for yourself tonight?"

"No." He frowned. "There is no way I would be on here alone."

"How did you know that I would stay?"

"I didn't know." He smiled. "It's crazy that all of this would happen on this day, but I spent all day contemplating what to do and how to do it, or if I should even do it. Finally I just prayed that you were feeling what I was feeling." He paused and asked, "Well, are you?"

I didn't know what he was feeling and I was confused about what the last twenty-four hours had done to my life, but somehow I believed that we were on the same page. "Yes." No other words had to be spoken, we had said a mouthful.

There was a soft jerk as the boat moved away from the dock and suddenly Jason appeared. "Have you all decided on beverages or appetizers?" I hadn't even looked at the menu but apparently Isaac did. He asked me to try the roasted zucchini stuffed with spiced vegetables along with him, and I agreed. Of course I agreed. At that point Isaac could ask me to bite his toenails and I would not only bite them but swallow them whole, take Ex-lax, pluck them out, and do it again if it meant impressing him.

Jason left and Isaac's cell phone rang. He looked at the number strangely. "Do you mind?"

"Not at all," I lied.

"Hello!" He lowered his voice. "Ah yes, hold a moment please." He held the phone out toward me. "It's for you."

"For *me*?" I asked, as he placed the phone in my trembling hand. I was filing a restraining order against Andre as soon as my feet hit soil. "Hello?"

"*Who* is that man?"

"Excuse me?" I tried to remain cool.

"Who is that man?" Tyann asked again. "The man who answered the phone, who is he?" she inquired. "Where are you?"

"In Chicago." I should've known that the Star-69 queen would do something like this. "Didn't you get my message?"

"I did, but the number that showed up on my Caller ID with your message had a three oh five area code," she explained. "So who was that guy?"

"That's fabulous." I didn't want to unfold the drama at the table. "Hold a moment, please."

Isaac asked, "Is everything all right?"

"Yes, it's Tyann. Would you mind me taking this conversation away from the table?"

"Only if you promise to come back," he flirted.

"That's a definite." I smiled.

Isaac stood up like a true gentleman would when a lady was leaving the table. "By all means then."

I stood. "Thank you." I rushed toward the restroom sign. "Why did you call me at this number?"

"This is the number you called *me* from. It's a Miami number. I thought you were here and playing some kind of joke, so I called you back."

"No, trust me," I belted, "I'm still in Chicago."

"I called your hotel, you checked out, but yet you're staying an extra night? You're calling me from a man's phone that has a Miami number yet you refuse to tell me who he is." She was relentless. "Something isn't adding up."

"I just decided to stay." I knew that'd make no sense to her.

"Yeah, with some guy." She continued. "Yesterday you missed the flight, or at least that's the story you're telling. Tonight you just decided to stay, without a hotel room, and calling me from a Miami cellular phone?"

"Yep," I said sarcastically.

Tyann had had enough. "Who is the guy you're traveling with?"

"I'm not traveling with anybody."

"You know what?" She pulled out the big gun. "I'm gonna tell Mama."

"What the? Are you out of your mind?" I asked her then continued. "Tell Mama; have her call the number too." I couldn't believe that she went there. "I am grown, Tyann. If I decide to stay in Chicago, New York, Vegas or anywhere with someone then so be it."

"Lia, all I'm trying to say is that you're just getting out of a screwed up relationship. You need time to breathe." She sighed. "How long have you known this guy, a few hours? That's how you ended up with Andre at BCR, you need to . . ."

"For your information he's not a stranger." I knew that I could trust her down the line but not right then. "He's someone from back home that I ran into here."

"Who, Craig?"

"Yuck." I made a face. "Why would I be anywhere with Craig?"

"He moved to Chicago last year," Ty informed me, but moved on quickly. "So, who is it?"

"Ty, all you need to know is that I'll be there tomorrow." I rushed, "Bye, I need to go." I hung up on her and as I fixed my hair the phone was ringing again, it was her number. "Tyann, what in the hell are you doing?"

"I'm going to keep calling this number until I get answers." She giggled.

"Tyann, I won't speak to you ever in my life if you call this number again." I was dead serious.

"Fine, but you better tell me tomorrow." She'd do anything to hear my business.

"I'll think about it." I knew that I wouldn't. "I have to go, Ty." My eyeliner was smeared so I grabbed a Kleenex from the countertop to tidy up, and the phone rang again. I couldn't believe that my big sister was about to play these games. I was very agitated. "I cannot believe you." A ghostly silence followed my voice and sent chills up my spine. "Hello?" I said.

"Hello." Madison's voice came across the line of her father's cell phone. "Who's this?" My eyes nearly jumped out of their sockets. I couldn't answer her question. "Hello," she said again.

I quickly closed the flip phone and told myself that this had to be a bad dream. In twenty-four hours Isaac had become so much more to me than Madison's father. He was the author of the heartfelt note sitting next to my breakfast. He was the man that rushed to the airport with intentions of begging me to stay, only he didn't have to, I was willing. It was as though I was an actor in a Lifetime's movie of the week.

I left the restroom and headed for the table. I handed him the phone and saw that the appetizer was there, but untouched. "I've been waiting so that you can try it."

I smiled nervously. "You didn't have to."

"There's a lot that I don't have to do, but when it's done for, to, or with the right person there is almost nothing I wouldn't do."

"How sweet," I said. I couldn't say more, not while my sister had hound dogs following his scent and his daughter possibly recognizing my voice on his phone.

As Isaac reached over the table and touched my hand his phone rang again. "It's Madi, you mind if I take this? I promise it'll be quick. She was supposed to go to the bank and handle something for me today."

"Go ahead." I should've said something.

"Hello," he said with a smile that slowly faded away. "What? What is that supposed to mean?" His eyebrows moved toward each other then he looked over at me. "Excuse me." He stood up with his hand covering the phone.

Mrs. Herrington noticed my discomfort and while her husband was also away from the table said, "Girl, it looks like you've seen a ghost." She walked over and sat in Isaac's seat. "Are you okay?"

"Just a pinch of drama." I sighed.

Her eyes grew wide with anxiety. "Is he married or something?"

"No." I smiled. "Not that kind of drama."

In less than five minutes I told Terah, that was her first name, my entire story. I briefed her on Isaac not only being a minister, but also my best friend's father. I informed her of our chance meeting at the airport, our dinner and night together. She was in awe when I told her how he swept me away from the airport and brought me straight to the yacht. The tale was unbelievable. Even my heart had to catch up with my mouth as I spoke.

"You have one life to live and you're not doing anything wrong," Terah lectured, looking at me in adoration. "Seize the moment." Those three little words from a stranger brought me loads of comfort, but that only lasted until I saw Isaac stomping back toward the table. It was like the Michael Jackson case, the trial was over but no one truly wanted to hear the verdict.

His face was emotionless. "May I have a word with you on the deck, please?" Isaac asked to be polite, but it really wasn't a question.

"Sure." I was almost afraid to trail him. We climbed up a flight of stairs and passed through a door that took us onto the deck. He stretched his hands over the white railing and stared at the water before he turned to look at me. The wind wrestled through my hair and pulled my clothes in every which way.

"I'm sorry." His words surprised me.

"Huh?" I asked. "About what?"

"About all of this." His eyes moved away. "I don't know what I was doing, or even thinking for that matter."

"Doing or thinking what?" It sounded like he was breaking up with me before even asking me out. "I don't understand."

"I allowed myself, for the first time in years, to be selfish and . . . " he paused, "I had forgotten all about her."

"Forgotten about her?" He was trippin'. What did Madi say to him? She needed to come off of that shit about her father being with women. "Look, I care about a lot of people too, but in life sometimes you have to do things for you, it's not selfish, it's called being you." I tried to make sense of what my crazy heart was doing. "These last twenty-four hours have lifted my spirits." I felt vulnerable and changed my tune quickly. "But if you feel like being here with me is doing something wrong then . . ."

"I just feel like," he interrupted me shaking his head, "like I crossed the line."

I got sassy. "I thought you didn't want there to be a line?" He couldn't be trying to put a cap on a feeling that toppled over within me hours ago. "Did she recognize . . ." His intense stare stopped me in mid-sentence. "What?" I asked.

Isaac held a single finger up to his lips, asking me not to speak . . . my mouth fell silent at his request. "No, she didn't recognize your voice, but the fact that I'm with a woman, any woman, on this day is hard on her."

What day? I thought. "What do you mean?"

"Today is the anniversary of her mother's death."

My hands rushed to my mouth. "I am so sorry."

"She was upset at the fact that I forgot." He turned his back to the railing. "I was actually glad that I had forgotten, that means that I am human again." He chuckled. "People want me to grieve for my entire life and I . . . I . . ." he stumbled over his words, "I just can't." He raised his head and his eyes met mine. "My vows with Bianca were, till death do we part." He was close to tears. "Death has come and gone. What am I supposed to do, bury myself too?" He slammed his right fist into his left hand. "Everybody wants me to be happy, but it's only their version of happiness for me that matters to them."

He started quoting the very popular Bible verse. "*To everything there is a season, a time for every purpose under heaven.*" He took my hand in his. "*A time to be born, and a time to die. A time to plant, and a time to pluck what was planted. A time to kill, and a time to heal. A time to break down, and a time to build up. A time to weep, and a time to laugh.*" He pulled me into him. "*A time to mourn, and a time to dance. A time to cast away stones, and a time to gather stones. A time to embrace, and a time to refrain from embracing.*" He went on. "*A time to gain, and a time to lose. A time to keep, and a time to throw away. A time to tear, and a time to sew. A time to keep silent, and a time to speak. A time to love, and a time to hate. A time of war, and a time of peace.*"

I remembered him preaching a sermon three years ago from Ecclesiastes Chapter Three. His topic was *What Time is it in Your Life?* Thinking aloud I asked, "What time is it in your life?"

He smiled, knowing that I had to have been in church that Sunday. "It's time for me." He pulled me into him. "It's time for me to be happy."

His hands caught me around my waist then moved up to my back and stroked me softly. I smiled at his touch. "I think your happiness is long overdue."

"Yours is too," he whispered in my ear. "Yours is too." He looked at me closely, his face moved in on mine. I closed my eyes awaiting his soft lips but a smothered rumble disturbed the silence. "That was my stomach," he said, "it's the way to a man's heart," he joked.

"Let's eat then," I said, and with my hand still in his, we made our way back to the emerald dining room.

Chapter 16

Still a Sperm

"I thought you two had sailed back to shore," Karani Kerrington joked from the next table.

Isaac laughed. "We're not going anywhere as long as food is onboard." He was right, because the food turned out to be awesome, and by the end of dinner Terah and Karani were sitting with us. In an effort to curtail the conversation with them, Isaac gave Karani a card and said, "Let's stay in touch."

"What?" Karani yelled. "I thought I knew you." He studied Isaac carefully. "You were on the church channel a few weeks ago."

"Yes I was," Isaac answered all smiles. My mom mentioned something about cameras in the church but she didn't elaborate. I guess partly because she didn't agree with them being there. "TBN broadcasts live from my church every third Sunday morning."

When it came to preaching Reverend Dr. Isaac M. Flack was just as powerful as Bishop Eddie Long,

Bishop Clarence E. McClendon, and Dr. Creflo A. Dollar. But the two bishops and the doctor had nothing on Isaac. Bishop Long had the body, Bishop McClendon was fine but a bit too pretty, and Dr. Dollar, well he looked as good as one could look after being given a first name like Creflo. Other than trying to win souls I could see TBN's reasons for broadcasting from Mount Pleasant; look at the pastor, he had to pull up their ratings.

Karani stretched his hand out and shook Isaac's. "Man, you tore it up, almost had me on my knees," he said with a smile. "Just don't start wearing those gowns like McClendon. I think there is something funny about that." We all laughed. "How long have you been a pastor?"

"Fifteen years."

"Wow." Karani did some mental math and when it didn't add up he said, "What a minute, how old are you?"

"Forty-five," Isaac said proudly.

"Man, you don't look a day older than me." Karani was loud. "God really has your back."

"Yes, He does, and I hope He always will," Isaac said thankfully.

The topic slowly focused on something most church-goers tried to avoid talking to each other about, tithing. Karani mentioned that he doesn't tithe at his church because he doesn't think that the money is being used in the right way.

"What the money is being used for has absolutely nothing to do with you, Karani." Isaac was taking him to school. "You must make wise decisions concerning the money God is blessing you with." Isaac seemed to glow when he talked about God. He spoke with a smile and his eagerness was very impressive. "The first ten percent of any financial income you receive is holy. If you don't tithe, I guarantee that you won't enjoy that portion of your income because it's being misused. You'll spend it fixing something that suddenly broke around the house. You might have to use it to pay a traffic ticket, pay a mechanic to fix your car or even at the doctor's office."

"Will a man rob God?" Karani jokingly quoted a portion of Malachi 3:8. "*Can* a man rob God?"

"Yes, you can rob God. To rob is to take knowing that someone is looking at you; you are being watched. God is omnipresent, He sees everything you do." Isaac was on a roll.

"What about people that really can't afford to give?" Karani asked.

"Everyone can give, but lack of faith makes people think that they won't have enough. The ten percent that they rob from God will never bring them joy. You've got to believe God when He says He will pour out blessings that you won't have room to receive." He paused. "Tithing is your measure of love for Christ by obedience in your giving. Just step out on faith and He'll do the rest."

"Thanks for shedding light on that." Terah smiled. "We've been having many talks about that these days, but I was explaining it all wrong."

Karani said, "Plus a lot of times during the offering we hear preachers screaming, 'Bring ye all the tithes into the storehouse!' But what it really sounds like is, 'My wife and I need a bigger house!'" We all chuckled.

"Regardless to what the devil makes you think God's money is being used for, just remember that God won't do anything for you unless you're doing something for

Him, that goes for everyone in the congregation and double for the officers, those in the pulpit, and me."

"I believe that, but what about when deacons and pastors aren't satisfied with the offering and beg for members to give more?" Karani was starting to get on my nerves. "Sometimes they won't sit down until they can get what they want out of the members. It's almost like an auction, it kills the spirit."

Isaac had even more answers. "I agree with you on that. That's something that I don't allow at my church. God loves a cheerful giver. He would rather you give Him five dollars with a smile, than for someone to force you to give twenty with a grumbling heart."

"This stuff is complicated." Karani looked at Terah. "Thank God I don't have to worry about fornication." We all laughed.

The piano player took a break and a slow but upbeat song played over the speakers. "Remember what I said earlier about there being a time to mourn and a time to dance?" Isaac asked.

"Yeah," I replied.

"It's time to dance." He stood up and reached for my hand. "Do you know how to step?"

"Step?" I blushed. "No."

"I think it's mandatory in this city. You can't leave Chicago without knowing how to step." He pulled me to my feet. "It would be a shame."

On the dance floor he held both my hands and taught me the essential moves of a basic step. "Step right, step left, cross right, cross left." Then he twirled me once and pulled me in. I pushed back and started the process again. It was so much fun. No, we didn't look like the folks dressed in white on the boat on R. Kelly's

Step in the Name of Love video, but we were steppin' and I loved it. "May I trouble you for another walk on the deck?" he asked.

Before long we found ourselves back on the deck. The lights of downtown Chicago glistened far away; it was a beautiful sight. I looked down into the water of Lake Michigan with my hands spread over the railing on both sides of me and surprisingly his hands wrapped around my waist and his chest was against my back. Not only was I trapped between him and the rail, I was trapped between him and the heat he stirred within me.

He spoke directly into my ear. "Can we do this in Miami?"

"I don't know." We'd have to travel far and wide to not run into someone who knew either one of us in Miami, especially with the way the membership at Mount Pleasant was skyrocketing. "We probably couldn't do anything like *this.*"

"Why couldn't we?" he questioned me.

"Someone might know you." I continued. "Members of your church or your family. They might see us or hear something."

"Something like what?" he asked.

"Something about us being together, I don't know." Though I felt he already knew I told him anyway. "You know how people talk." C'mon, Baptist folks will find and spread gossip about Jesus if it was juicy enough. Sister Celery picks up the hella phone and tells Sister Onion and Brother Broccoli where she saw Sister Tomato's husband. But early on Sunday morning when the news is well spread, she's the first to break down and scream out, "Lettuce pray."

He turned me to face him. "What did I say earlier?"

The bass in his voice made my knees weak. "I'm through with living my life by others' definition of happiness." He went on. "I'm a single man."

Now it was me trippin'. "What about Madison?" I asked. "She won't appreciate us hanging out."

"Who said anything about hanging out?" He gently pushed my head up to look directly at him. "Thalia, I'm talking about dating you." He wasn't done. "I'm not trying to hang out with you just for hanging out sake. I'm going to try and hope that I succeed in showing you a woman's worth." The silence that followed his voice was the kind that follows rain on a stormy day. "It's not like we're strangers, I've known you since your first Algebra test in junior high." He moved closer. "I know that this is all happening unexpectedly, Thalia, but after me, there will be no question of what a real man is. You deserve the best of everything there is on earth, and I want to try to give it to you."

He was wrong. There was nothing in my life I had done to deserve a man like him or anything that he had to give. I wasn't a girl about town, but I definitely wasn't an angel when I lived in Miami. I had slept with more men than he had suits . . . and shoes. If people saw Isaac and me together they'd think one of two things. One, he backslid to be with me or two, I'm playing with God just to be with him. I hadn't changed my life enough to share it with him. He knows the Bible inside and out, while I can only recite the names of the books of the Bible up to Deuteronomy, and even then I find myself mixing in January, February, and March.

He was a full-grown man of God and I was just a fetus, no, I was still a sperm. I didn't even know if I could fertilize an egg. Why would God put such a man in *my* life?

As though Isaac could read my mind he said, "Don't worry about a thing." It should be no surprise that by now he was leaning into me. His face slowly moved closer to mine and it seemed like an out of body experience. Our unhurried journey toward one another continued to progress, but once his mouth was close enough that I could feel his breath, we both froze up. Our kiss was now in the cool Chicago breeze. He removed his jacket and draped it over my shivering body.

Sixty minutes went by in sixty seconds and before I could even think about trying to find the kiss that got away, we were back at the dock. We left the ship together and strolled through the gardens along the promenade hand in hand.

As I exited the Town Car at the hotel a church van pulled up behind us, and of all the people in the world, Sister Stride was being helped out of it by a younger woman. Isaac was talking to Hank about what time to be at the hotel the next morning because of my flight. I was trying hard to pretend that I didn't see Sister Stride, but when she clutched her Bible and glared at me I knew it was over.

"Pastor Flack?" she yelled. I thought his neck would snap the way he turned to look at her. "Where are you coming from?" She walked toward us and the woman followed her.

"Good evening, Sister Stride." He smiled. "How are you?"

"Where are you coming from?" She questioned him like he was her son.

Isaac cleared his throat softly. "Dinner."

* * *

She looked at her watch; it was almost eleven thirty. "Dinner at this time of night?"

"Yes, dinner." He then asked her, "Where are *you* coming from?"

"I went to the hospital to see Minister Green with the Mount Tabor members." With her crooked old finger she beckoned the woman who was standing behind her. "Deborah, have you met Reverend Doctor Isaac Flack?"

"I don't believe I have." Deborah, a light-skinned sister, thin, with wavy hair pulled into a tight bun, and couldn't be a day over thirty-five, was all smiles as she shook Isaac's hand. "It's very nice to meet you, Reverend Flack."

"It's nice to meet you as well," Isaac said then looked over at me. "This is Th . . . "

"Deborah is Reverend Albert Baker's daughter." Sister Stride bum rushed him with information. "She is the Praise Dance Instructor." Then she added, "She's not married either and no kids yet." Deborah blushed.

"Great." Isaac smiled and said, "Deborah, this is Thalia."

Never once acknowledging Sister Stride, I reached over to Deborah and offered her my hand. "It's a pleasure to make your acquaintance, Miss Baker."

"I thought you would be gone by now," Sister Stride said to me.

"Well, it turns out that my work here just wasn't done yet," I said in a sophisticated tone that could never be mistaken for rude. "I'll be leaving tomorrow."

"Tomorrow is not promised," she reminded me with scorn. "Never put off for tomorrow what could be done today." As Deborah walked away Sister Stride turned to Isaac. "You'll have another chance to see Deborah tomorrow night at the service, she's a really nice girl, powerful woman of God, and can sing. Lord have mercy that gal can sang." She winked at him. "She's a good girl, Pastor." She yawned. "Well, it's bedtime for me."

"You have a good night," he said as she walked away.

Sister Stride was officially on my list. I didn't want to comment on what she said and I didn't want him to feel like he had to either so I quickly changed the subject. "Thanks again for a wonderful evening."

"Thank you for joining me." He pulled my suitcase behind him. Before we could make it to the elevator a man in his mid-twenties ran up to him with eyes as red as an apple. "Pastor, I need to speak with you."

"Okay, Jimmy." He touched the young man's shoulder. "What's up?"

Jimmy looked at me and then back at Isaac. "Alone."

"Sure, sure, no problem." He handed me his room key and my suitcase and whispered, "Make yourself at home."

I made it to his room, dragged my luggage into the bathroom, and paced the tiled floor for at least ten minutes trying to decide if staying the night with him was a good idea. The night before wasn't planned, but tonight we were knowingly sleeping in the same bed. I took a shower to clear my head and for a while it helped, but then came the decision of what to wear. Whatever! I put on a pair of shorts and a tank top.

Stepping out of the bathroom I saw that he still wasn't there. What was there was a king-sized bed seemingly taunting me, his laptop on the desk along with pens, sheets of paper, and beneath it three pairs of shoes lined up in a row. In the mirror I practiced the look of innocence I planned on giving him when he

walked in, but after thirty minutes I didn't look so innocent anymore; it was well after midnight. I crawled into
bed and then practiced the sleep look I would have
when I would pretend he woke me up. At one A.M. I
didn't have to practice anymore . . . I fell asleep.

At 1:36 I heard him creep into the room and into the
bathroom. The shower was on for about ten minutes
and when it stopped my heart nearly did the same.
He's naked, he's naked, he's naked. My mind kept screaming at my brain. In five minutes he was out of the bathroom and extinguishing lights throughout the room.
When he switched off the one next to the bed I was the
best stunned actress I could be. After a heavy shocking
sigh I said, "Oh, it's you," through barely opened eyes.

"I didn't mean to wake you."

"It's okay." I forced my voice to be more tired than it
was. "Is everything all right?"

"Yeah. Sorry it took so long." He sat on the bed. "The
young man was dealing with something serious, and
then after that, one of the chairmen was having computer problems and called me to help out with that
too."

"You're a jack of all trades, huh?" I joked.

"Yes, but a master of one." Without being able to first
fantasize about what it'd be like, he bent down and our
lips met, they slightly parted, and our tongues gently
touched; it was very sensual. His eagerness was that of a
curious boy wanting to know what it would be like, but
he was well experienced and mysteriously strong. I
found myself aroused by his taste and reluctantly pulled
away. But right away I regretted it. Isaac was a forbidden
fruit, nevertheless things that were off limits were always said to be the sweetest. The Bible said, 'taste and

see.' Well, I tasted and now I can see. We stared at each other hoping that one of us had the courage to initiate another kiss, but we didn't.

"Well, I'll let you get back to sleep," he said. "I'm going to study my notes for a class I have to teach tomorrow."

"Okay." I would agree to anything to avoid us being awake and in bed together at the same time. "Good night."

The next morning I woke up to find Isaac asleep on the sofa. After my shower I woke him up. Though we were up at our scheduled time we were still thirty minutes behind schedule by moving too slow and didn't make it to the car until 8:00. Thanks to traffic we reached the airport at 9:25. I checked in curbside, but it wouldn't make sense for him to get out of the car, I needed to run.

Leaning on the car Isaac said, "I hope to hear from you later." He looked as pitiful as I knew I'd feel once I buckled my seatbelt on the plane.

"I hope to hear from you too." I squeezed his hand.

He wrapped his arms around me. "I've never wanted to get back to Miami so bad before."

I blushed. "I've never wanted to stay in Chicago so bad before."

Hank interrupted. "Ma'am, you need to get going if you're going to make the flight."

He quickly kissed me on the cheek. "I'll be seeing you." He let go of my hand and I knew I had to walk away or I'd be staying for one more night. I couldn't wait to see him again and right as I thought about turning to look at him, I heard him say, "Jinx, I was thinking the same thing." I continued walking because looking back meant having to say something, and I couldn't . . . not without staying.

My flight to Miami started out quiet and relaxing. I didn't bother paying for headsets to watch the in-flight movie, my thoughts of Isaac was enough entertainment. An hour after takeoff the lady to my right and the man to my left decided that they'd flirt around me, in Spanish. It had to be one of the most annoying conversations ever.

He was suave and reminded me of a character from one of those Spanish novellas. The lady was pretty, but a lot older than he was. He must've had some serious game for her to be halfway bent over me amusing him. For two hours all I heard was "Que," "Y tu," "Porque," and "Ay Dios mio." The flight attendant passed me a few times with an empathic welcome to Miami smile.

When the plane was at the gate of the Miami International Airport I unbuckled my seatbelt, sprinted from my seat, and jumped into the aisle, giving them a straight line of Hispanic communication. As I exited the plane the first sign in view read, "Beinveindo A Miami." Welcome to Miami in Spanish! Ain't that a *you know what?*

Chapter 17

Giving up the Booty

I visited the Continental Airline's Special Help Desk about my luggage that arrived two days prior. The girl behind the desk was on top of things and was done with me in less than ten minutes. When I exited I saw a Budget Rent-A-Car shuttle pulling off and waved it down. There were no lines and no waiting, and I left in a silver 2006 Mitsubishi Eclipse convertible. I dropped the top, hopped onto 826 southbound and thanked God that I wasn't wearing a weave that day. Bonding glue would never survive the drive.

Within thirty minutes I was in Kendall and in front of Serenity Fortress, my apartment complex. My old landlady was so happy to have me back, she sent my paperwork to Philly and I signed and express mailed it back with a check to cover the security deposit, and first and last month's rent.

As I entered the office Mrs. Diaz ran to me and embraced me. I sat down and talked to her about why I never sent an invitation to the wedding. She kept looking at me and saying, "Pobrecita." I knew that I was going to have to tell this story many times, but saying it to a sixty-five-year-old Cuban woman, who first started learning English at the age of sixty-three, was hard.

After an hour in the office she walked me to my new residence. It was perfect! It was just what I needed; I loved the place.

"You like?" Mrs. Diaz asked.

"I love it." I did, but up until then I had forgotten all about furniture. Damn! She handed me two sets of keys, and after a few minutes of scoping out the place I locked up and hit the road to Homestead.

Homestead and Florida City are neighboring cities, the last cities you drive through before you get to the Florida Keys. Both cities were destroyed by Hurricane Andrew back in August 1992. Now it didn't do us like Katrina did New Orleans, but we lost everything including homes, schools, businesses, and lives.

No one expected the storm to pack such a punch; Andrew came like a thief in the night . . . with more than 215 mile per hour winds, our shudders flew away from the windows leaving Chance, Mama, and me to battle hurricane force winds locked in the bathroom holding onto one another. The next morning people walked around their own block to survey the damage and got lost. Paint had been stripped from houses, all the trees had disappeared, and street signs and traffic signals were a thing of the past.

*   *   *

When I turned on the street I noticed Mama had painted the house peach since my last visit. Her aging Toyota Camry was parked in front of a brand new Nissan Maxima, and I couldn't help but wonder who was inside with her.

I quietly turned my key and opened the door. "Who is that?" she said from the kitchen. I didn't answer. "Hello," she said. A smile rushed to my face as the familiar smell of home greeted me. "Tyann, is that you?" When she turned the corner and pushed her glasses up on her nose tears ran down my cheeks.

"Thalia!" she screamed. "What are you doing here?" She rushed over and her arms were around me.

"Hi, Mama," I cried. "I'm home."

She kissed my cheek. "What's wrong?" She hit the light switch. "Are you okay?"

"Yeah, I'm fine." I was so happy to see her.

She was genuinely a loving person. "Is Andre okay?"

"No." I managed to roll my eyes.

"What happened to him?" She grabbed my hand. "What happened?"

"I'm back home, Mama," I said. "That's all that matters."

Mama panicked. "Thalia, tell me what's wrong." She handed me a paper towel.

I wasn't up for a long story. "Andre was cheating on me and I left him. I'm back to stay."

She escorted me to the sofa and held me. "Oh, baby, I'm so sorry." She rubbed my back. "Look at me." She touched my chin. "God works all things together for good for those that love Him."

"I know." She had said that very thing to me for years. "I know, Mama."

"So wipe those tears up, this is a blessing." She

smiled. "If your tears can't create a river then God doesn't need them." She always knew how to heal my wounds without Band-aids, rubbing alcohol, or hydrogen peroxide. "You know my doors are always opened for you. You can stay here as long as you want."

"Thank you, Mama," I paused, "but you know that you're just too neat for me." I giggled. "I have an apartment, but until I get new furniture and work some other things out I will be shacking up with you." I remembered the strange car I saw outside. "Whose car is that outside?"

"Mine." She blushed.

"Yours?" She never mentioned that. "You never said anything about a new car. When did you get it?"

She stood up and glared at it through the window. "About two weeks ago."

At age fifty-two my mom was glowing like a thirty-year-old and her bronze skin was still hugging her frame. At five foot seven and 178 pounds she was very shapely and wasn't sagging a bit. Nadia Tyree still had it going on. Her thin face was always decorated with her favorite pair of gold loop earrings and she had traded in her wire-framed glasses for soft contacts and sported jet-black micro braids that fell onto her back. You go, girl! I didn't realize that I was staring at her until she said, "What?"

"Huh?" I caught myself.

"Why are you looking at me like that?"

"You just look real nice." I smiled. "Come on and show me your new car."

She had an extra bounce in her step as she described the car's features to me. Then she popped the hood and went on and on. ". . . and Nissan improved the performance of the new Maxima, by increasing the horsepower of the engine . . ." What did she know about an engine?

"How much did you pay?" I asked.

"I didn't pay." There she was blushing again. "It was a gift."

I looked at the car then looked back at her. "What?"

"It was a gift," she said louder in case I missed it the first time.

"Gift?" A car as a gift meant that some man was tapping that ass and it made me sick to my stomach. "Why would someone give you a car, Mama?"

"It's the least he could do," she mumbled.

I hoped for the best. "Mama, are you talking about God?"

"No," she said. "But He had to be in the plan."

"So who is *he?*" It was a thirty thousand dollar gift. "And what made him buy you a car?"

"Well, we've been talking a lot over the past year." She whispered, "We decided that we make great friends."

"Well, are you giving up the booty to this friend?" I truly didn't want to know, but I had to ask.

"I can't believe you just asked me that." She smacked me on the hand.

"It's a car, Mama, how friendly are you with this man?" I asked, but she never answered.

"Let's get back in the house."

Later we cooked together and sat down to dinner the way we did when I was younger. For two hours we talked and laughed about things that happened over the years, but the minute the phone rang she disappeared into the den and I couldn't hear her conversation. She resurfaced briefly to say, "I have to go to work in the morning." She patted the top of my head like a puppy. "Turn off the lights before you go in."

"I'll be out here a while, I need to make a few phone calls."

"Who are *you* calling?" She was nosey.

"I'm going to star sixty-nine your boyfriend and see if I can get a new ride." We both laughed and she disappeared down the hallway. When I heard her bedroom door close I picked up the phone and dialed Tyann's number. The Caller ID queen answered. "Hi, Mama."

I pretended to be a man. "This ain't your mama, trick."

"Excuse me?" She sounded frightened. "Who is this?"

I burst into laughter. "You scare too easily, Tyann."

She teased, "You finally made it to Miami I see."

"Yep." I curled up on the sofa. "How are you?"

"I'm great." Taking the phone away from her mouth a little she said, "Colin, Lia's at Momma's house." She continued in a matter-of-fact tone. "You and I need to have a long talk, baby girl"

I ignored her. "How's my favorite brother-in-law?"

"Funny," she said. "He's your only brother-in-law and he's great."

"Who bought Mama that car?"

I could hear the smile in her voice. "Who is Mr. Chicago?"

"What is this Jeopardy?" I asked. "Answering a question with a question? Where did she get that car from?"

"Who is Mr. Chicago?" she asked again.

When I hung up from Ty it was 9:15 P.M. Isaac had been on my mind all day, but I was waiting on him to call me first. You know how women are, I didn't want it to seem as though I had nothing to do but call him as soon as I was two feet away from a phone. I wanted to hold out until at least eleven so I picked up the phone and dialed the next best person.

"Hello?"

"Hi." I was shocked that someone other than Madi would answer her cell phone. "May I speak to Madison?"

"Yes, you may." She sounded very sophisticated. "Who's calling?"

"This is Thalia."

"Hi, how are you?" I guess she knew of me.

"I'm fine." I faked it. "You must be Nekia, how are you?"

"I'm great. Hold on a moment, here she is." Shortly after I heard the same voice I had heard the night before on Isaac's phone. "Hello."

"Hey, loser," I teased.

"Thalia?" She was excited. "Where are you?"

"Homestead at my mother's house."

"Oh my God!" she yelled. "When are you leaving?"

"I'm not."

"What?" She was confused.

"I'm not leaving," I informed her.

"Yeah, right," she said in disbelief.

"I'm serious."

She laughed. "Are you really?"

"Yep." I was so happy to talk to her. "You're making me feel like you really missed me."

"I did." She paused. "Wait a minute, what about Andre?"

"I'm spitting him out like a hot French fry." I laughed.

"Oh my goodness." She giggled. "No, no, no, we have to sit and talk. We have to meet for lunch or something tomorrow."

"That'll be great, but after I'm done shopping for my cheap furniture." I added, "Mrs. Diaz is letting me move back into Serenity."

"You're back at the old folk's fortress again?"

"Yes, and I love it." I reminisced on all the good times we had together. I missed having a best friend. "Where and what time would you like to meet?" I asked.

"Two o'clock at the Red Lobster on Kendall Drive?"

"Perfect."

Madi and I talked about how well her business, Island Pleasures Spa, was doing. She owned and operated the salon and worked as a massage therapist. Her clientele was mostly middle and upper class African-American women that were also members of her father's church. Island Pleasures' current special was $200, and you'd receive a facial, manicure, pedicure, a total body conditioning, a full body massage, and your last thirty minutes were spent in a state of the art steam room.

Island Pleasures had a Caribbean theme; it even housed a small Tiki bar that offered complimentary virgin Pina Coladas and Strawberry Daiquiris to clients with reservations in the waiting area. She joked about how the church folks wouldn't ask if it was a virgin drink until they had one more sip left. There was calypso music playing throughout the spa, and though fake, tropical trees and flowers around every corner. The walls were covered with bamboo sticks, the steam room had a sand floor, and the wall that separated the two massage rooms was a large aquarium filled with tropical fish.

I was pathetic, it was 10:47 and there was no way I could sit for thirteen minutes and not pull my hair out. "Forget it." I dialed the number and felt my heart racing.

"Hello, beautiful."

I was glad I was already sitting down. "Hi."

"Hi," he said back.

"Busy?" Not that I cared because I wanted to talk to him regardless.

"No, I was just sitting here reading the paper hoping you would call, because I lost the sheet I wrote your number on."

"Wasn't that the same sheet you had your notes for today's class on?" I asked.

"Yes," he joked, "so today's lesson changed a bit, to say the least." He paused. "Are you getting settled in?"

"Yeah, I got the keys to my apartment. I'm at my mom's until I get furniture." There was silence and then I said, "I can't believe that I'm talking to you."

"I thought about you all day." His words almost made me run to the airport to get back to Chicago.

"I can't wait to see you." There was more silence, but not the kind where there was nothing to say . . . the silence said everything we couldn't say. "I was starting to wish that I had missed my flight."

"Me too," he joked. "But since you didn't where would you like to have dinner on Monday night after you pick me up from the airport?" Talk about initiative, Isaac had it by the pound.

My favorite fondue spot came to mind. "How about The Melting Pot?"

"I'll make reservations." He was smooth. "How about seven?"

"Seven's a great time." I turned out all of the lights and made my way to my old room, wrapped myself up in bed, and used his voice as a teddy bear to cuddle with.

Chapter 18

Reminisce

I was at Cultured Furniture Store ten minutes before they opened their doors, and within two hours I walked out with a receipt and delivery information for my bedroom and living room set and two twenty-seven inch color televisions.

I arrived at Red Lobster before Madi and sat in the waiting area studying the various pictures on the walls. "Do you think this is a museum or something?" I quickly turned around and looked into Isaac's eyes on Madison's face.

"Hey," I said as I hugged her tightly.

"I can't believe you're back," she said.

I took a step away back to look at her. "Look at you all dolled up." Madison was always naturally beautiful and makeup intensified her attractiveness. Fitting close to her body was a professional navy blue skirt suit.

"Sorry I'm late. I had a meeting today about the building I want to lease on South Beach." So that explained her attire and sexy four-inch heels. Over the years every pound she gained fell right where she needed it. Her shoulder length jet-black hair was neatly layered and framing her face.

"You look great," I complimented.

"Thank you. You look marvelous yourself. If I didn't know better I'd say somebody was treating you right." We both laughed.

We were seated at a table next to a window. We ordered appetizers and beverages and then she listened to the story of how my blue heaven turned into a hot red hell. I told her everything from our happy engagement party at Tyann's house to the bastard sleeping with the wedding planner, then onto the policeman's ball, and finally to me trying to change my life and walking away. "Enough about me, what's going on in your life?"

"Well, you know that there is something we never really got to talk about." Her pretty face showed nervousness. "For years I was in denial," she said. "I'm bisexual. I don't deny myself anymore, but I don't fully share this information with many people."

"Wow." The word slipped out, I didn't expect that to be the first thing she said.

"Nothing to say?" she asked.

"So, you're not a lesbian?" Oh God, what was I saying?

"I don't think so." She laughed. "I'm still into men at times, but there is a woman in my life right now."

"Okie dokie then." I unfolded my arms. "So who is she?"

"Nekia, my roommate." She didn't seem half as uncomfortable about the topic as I was. "This is the first time I've been with a woman and it's more than just sex." She continued. "I feel for her, it's something about her that makes me . . ."

"Love her?" I finished her sentence.

"Yeah." She blushed. "I love her." For the first time since I've known her, Madison was humbling herself in pursuit of her definition of happiness. "It's just so hard. There's so much explaining I always have to do to. People don't understand that it's the spirit within the person. Nekia just happens to be a woman. I guess that's why I haven't completely come out in the open with it yet." She looked at me. "I tried to distance myself from you because I didn't know what you'd say or what you thought of me after what you walked in on."

"I had a lot of questions, of course, and I still do, but I love you no less, Madi." I touched her hand and smiled.

"I love you, too."

We ate and caught up on our lives. The more she asked me about meeting someone new, dating, and loving again, the more uneasy I grew and couldn't look her in the eyes.

If she ever learned of my friendship with her dad, she would probably imagine him touching me the way he did her mother. This would never sit well with her and I wasn't prepared to persuade her. What would I do if Madison were dating my father? I honestly couldn't see our friendship surviving such a tragedy. Though he hadn't been much of a father, just thinking of him having sex with her made me woozy.

Madison was talking but my mind was back in the Windy City. "So have you called your dad since you've been here?" Madison's question brought me back to Miami on a one second flight.

All I heard was the word dad. "What?"

"Have you called your dad?" she asked.

I giggled. "No, but I will this evening."

"Good."

I was curious. "Why?"

"Well, since he's on good terms with your mom again I was hoping you'd at least give him a chance."

"On good terms?" I thought twice. "Who?"

"C'mon," Madi rolled her eyes, "men don't go around buying brand new cars for just anybody."

My blood boiled. "He bought her that car?"

"Oops." She covered her mouth. "You didn't know?"

"No." I was upset, yet strangely gratified that he was finally leaving her with something other than a kid. "What else?" I knew there was more.

Madi didn't know if she should smile or not . . . she didn't. "Well, rumor has it that they're back together."

"Back together like how?"

"Like Nadia and Devon sitting in the tree, K-I-S-S-I-N-G." She laughed.

I couldn't believe it. "I knew something was up."

"I think he finally wants to do right." She went on. "I think he sees the errors he made in the past."

"What are you his campaign manager?" I joked angrily. "I see it as though he's trying to buy his way into our lives again. Just like him offering me to pay for my now cancelled honeymoon and reception."

Madi did what she was supposed to do as a friend, talk sense into me. "Look, you'll never forget that he wasn't around for a great portion of your life, but just appreciate the fact that he's around today and trying to make things right." A light bulb must've gone off in her head. "Oh, and speaking of fathers, let me tell you about mine." She leaned closer to me. "He's in Chicago at a church convention. I called his cell phone two nights ago and some chick answered it."

"What?" I tried to sound astonished. "What did she say?"

"First she answered the phone by saying, 'I cannot believe you.' So I was like, 'Who are you?' But she never said anything else," Madi huffed.

"Madi, you have to get off of that though." I was almost begging. "He's been single for a long time."

"I know, it wasn't the fact that he was with someone, but it was the anniversary of Mom's passing. I was sitting home looking at her pictures like I do every year and he's out partying."

I giggled. "I'm sure he wasn't partying, you drama queen." *I would know!*

"I'm a daddy's girl," she confessed. "It'll just be hard for me to see him with anyone after only seeing him with Mom or alone."

I had to speak my mind. "If he decides to be with someone, that doesn't mean that he didn't love your mother. Wedding vows are until death, and unfortunately that happened."

"What are *you* his campaign manager?" She mimicked my words earlier, but didn't know just how much there was to what she said.

"It's time for you to be more understanding about him dating. What if he meets someone and doesn't feel as though he can tell you about it so he keeps it from you?"

"Well, that's essentially what I'm doing with Nekia," she said.

"Exactly, everybody wants to be able to share good

news with family. Don't let that happen between the two of you."

"I know, but who is this chick to be answering his phone?" She paused. "My thing is that I don't want him involved with someone who is using him. My dad is such a genuinely loving person; he'll give anyone the shirt off of his back." She sighed. "He's been out of the dating scene for so long that I don't think he can tell the difference between a loving woman and a money hungry diva."

"Oh my God, Madi," I snickered. "I think Isaac would know how to select a woman." Did I just call him Isaac in front of her? Holy crap . . . I grabbed my purse and searched for my credit card so that I wouldn't have to look at her. "Who did he say the woman was?"

"He said that he was on a dinner cruise with a woman, no excuse me, he called her a young lady, and that *she* was using his phone and my call must've somehow come through because she wouldn't just answer his phone." She rolled her eyes. "He apologized on her behalf."

I joked, "So he's cheating on me, huh?" Bad joke.

"You're so silly, Lia." She dismissed it. "No, but for real, he called her a young lady. What if she's like our age?"

"Oh my goodness, you're obsessing, can we stop talking about this, please." I laughed knowing good and well that the woman *was* our age . . . the woman was in the restaurant . . . at our table.

"Yeah, you're right," she agreed. "So knowing that you're all saved and walking in the light and stuff, you can't go to the club with me, huh?"

"Shut up, Madi." I pushed her. "I don't know what I

am; I'm just trying to make some changes and establish a better relationship with God."

"Please don't tell my dad this because then he'll be all on me about doing the right thing," she begged playfully.

We paid the check and carried our conversation into the parking lot for another couple of minutes before we parted. We promised to get together on Saturday and this time we'd invite Yvette. I was anxious about all three of us being back together. I jumped in the rental and headed north to my sister's house.

"Hello!" I yelled as I knocked on the oversized door for the third time. They were the only blacks in the area and they owned the most extravagant house on the block. "Is anyone here?" I knocked a little harder and finally heard movement within the house.

I heard the latch move and watched the door spring open and there he stood. At six foot three, 170 pounds, his bald head and chest glistened as the sunlight crept through the door on him. He was the color of a brown paper bag and the army green sweat pants he was wearing made him look like a fully armed soldier.

Looking at him made the words to Mary J. Blige's *Reminisce* come to mind. *I don't remember how we fell apart.*

There stood the man that filled my nights with passion during my sophomore year in college. Three . . . Mr. Colin Ingraham III, attorney at law, and my sister's husband. Colin was in law school in Tallahassee when I was at FAMU; we dated for four months before we were sexually involved. I fell hard for him . . . I mean hard, but once we started having sex it took over our innocent and meaningful friendship and relationship and ruined what I thought would be something memorable.

All of the little things that should've come first didn't. So for the last five months, as our relationship fizzled, we were Friday and Saturday night booty calls.

I returned to Miami for the summer and didn't bother keeping in contact with Three. Upon my return to FAMU for the next semester his apartment was empty and already up for rent. Shortly after, I received an e-mail saying that he had moved to Miami to finish his law studies at the University of Miami. During my Christmas visit to Miami my sister showed up for Christmas dinner with Colin Ingraham III . . . Three. We pretended not to know each other and up until this very moment we've never spoken a word about our past. My sister gave him something that I couldn't, and he gave to her what he couldn't give to me . . . love.

When he opened the door he was tying the drawstring on his pants before he looked up. "Thalia?" He was shocked.

I struggled with words each time I saw him. "What's up, Three?"

"I haven't been called that in quite some time." He grinned, still standing in the doorway. "Brings back memories."

"Yeah," I said, trying not to stare at his chest.

He said, "Come in." I entered, sliding right by his pecks. "You look great," he uttered while closing the door. "It's so good to see you."

"It's nice to see you too." Our conversations were always awkward; I could never even look him in the face.

"Ah, give me a hug, girl." His arms were wide open. I walked over and put my arms around him innocently, while he tried to do the same. But moments like this made forgetting his touch almost impossible. Seeing him always brought back those nights as though I was still receiving late night calls from him begging to come over.

Especially the night I've since dubbed "the forgotten night," the night he talked me into trying ecstasy. Until this day I'm going by what *he* said we did, which was a hell of a lot, but I have no recollection of it.

"I was working out," he said as we ended our embrace. "I got sweat all over you."

It wouldn't be the first time. "Oh, it's no big deal."

"Tyann isn't here." I knew that he had to remember our intense oral sex, or the way he loved to have me on top. I knew that he was uncomfortable because I was almost ashamed to be in his presence.

"Do you expect her soon?" I asked. I couldn't wait long.

"Yeah, she forgot her key so I was waiting around for her; she should be here any minute." He chuckled. "I actually thought you were her."

"Wouldn't be the first time . . ." I caught myself, "that someone mixed us up."

"Yeah." He always dragged his words when he was nervous. "Give me a minute and let me get cleaned up." He pointed to the living room area. "Turn on the television, make yourself at home, then we can catch up." As soon as he disappeared up the stairs my mind was in Chicago again. I dialed Isaac's cell phone number.

"Hello," he answered in a whisper.

"Hi, there." I couldn't help but have a chipper voice. "Are you busy?"

"I'm teaching a class and forgot to put my phone on vibrate," he carefully informed me. "One of the ministers had to leave because of an emergency, so I took over for him."

"I'm sorry." I was embarrassed for him, but I still had to let him know. "I was just thinking about you."

"Jinx," he spoke softly, but I could tell that he was smiling. "Talk to you later."

I flipped from channel to channel hoping that something would stick. *Gothika* was on Showtime so I decided to check it out. Twenty minutes into watching it I nearly pooped when someone knocked on the door. "Who is it?" I yelled.

"Who are *you?*" my sister joked from the other side. "You're in *my* house so you better be family." When I opened the door she pushed herself on me and into my arms. "Lia!" she shrieked.

Colin made his way downstairs seemingly relieved that he and I wouldn't be alone together, and I was too. The three of us talked for hours and of course the famous Andre the Jerk story had to be told. However, there was something else I wanted to discuss... Mama's brand new car. Tyann told me that Mama had only had the car a few weeks and she just assumed to let me be surprised when I got there.

"Lia, just let them be." Tyann was now thirty, five years older than me. Therefore, when daddy finally stopped coming around she was old enough to hurt more than I did, but she had a bigger heart. Since Daddy moved back to Miami she has started a relationship with him, and even gone as far to say that she has forgiven him. Ty was all for Mama and Daddy giving their love another try and begged me not to interfere. How could she forget the pain he caused and all the tears we cried?

"Baby, my shoulders are killing me," Tyann whined to Colin. "Can you give them a little rub, please?"

He looked at me and hung his head. "That may agitate it." He never said that to me when I asked.

"C'mon, Colin," she begged, "five minutes."

"Ty, how about a warm towel?"

She frowned. "I didn't give you any excuses last night did I?"

"Wow, too much information," I said half-joking as I stood up. "Why don't I just leave so that you too can feel each other up?"

"No, Lia, I was just about to cook," she said. "Stay for dinner."

"Nah." I declined. "There's something that I need to do." Mama and I needed to have a long talk.

Chapter 19

Walking off of a Ledge

I opened the door to Mama's house and heard two sets of laughter coming from the kitchen. The high-pitched squeaky giggle belonged to my mother, and the husky baritone chuckles were that of my father. I rounded the corner and saw the both of them by the stove. She was peeking into the oven and he was stirring something on the stovetop. I wasn't used to seeing them together without her being an emotional wreck.

"Hi, sweetheart!" She greeted me with a hug and a nonchalant whisper of, "Please be nice," into my ear.

My Daddy stood frozen. He was still tall with the same thin face, dark brown skin, wavy hair, and trimmed mustache. Daddy was fifty-seven years old, still in shape, spoke English better than most professors, and could win a woman over with just two dollars in his pocket, as long as he had that smile. "Hey, baby girl," he said as he walked toward me to embrace me warmly.

I tried to seize the moment. "How are you, Dad?"

"Fabulous now that I'm standing in the company of two beautiful ladies," he said.

Mama cut in. "Thalia, I was hoping that the three of us could sit and talk tonight."

"Okay." I wished she had told me this earlier. "Just let me wash my hands and I'll help." I turned away. "I'll be right back."

As I made my way to the bathroom I heard her giggling playfully again. I didn't like it. For so long there were only four people that made her smile and she had given birth to the four of us. Did she forget the nights she couldn't sleep, and the habits she took on to block his memories? How could she just forgive him? She never told us to hate him, but what was I supposed to do now that she was starry eyed again? Do I pretend that he was there all these years? I didn't want to disrespect him because he was my father, but on the other hand I wanted to disrespect him because he wasn't my father when I needed him.

"Lord, help me," I said under my breath and suddenly a Bible verse that I learned when I was just eight rushed into my head. Ephesians 4:32, *"And be ye kind to one another, tenderhearted, forgiving one another, even as God for Christ's sake hath forgiven you."* How could I expect God to come through for me and forgive me when I wasn't willing to forgive others?

As soon as my thumb pressed the button on the lock on the inside of the bathroom door I fell to my knees in front of the toilet and began to pray. "Lord, I know that You will give me the strength to forgive and I thank You. Wash my heart and mind today, restore the right spirit in me, Lord. You and You only are my Lord and Savior and I truly want to forgive my father. Forgive me for hat-ing him. I was angry. I want to walk out of that anger today and into Your wisdom instead. I want to forgive him for lack of love, caring, support, interest, and for never marrying my mother. Father, cleanse me of the stored up negative feelings in me toward him. Lord, help me take back the ground that I gave up when I held onto things of the past regarding my father. I ask that You take back this ground and no longer allow Satan to operate. Give me wisdom to deal with this situation in the future. Heal now the wounded places in my soul. Heal my memories so that I can look back on them and know that You have healed me. Lord, I ask that You bless my relationship with my father with Your abundant mercy. In Jesus' name I pray. Amen."

I prayed that God's perfect purpose presented itself in my life right away and suddenly I felt a change. My heart got full as I remembered that even though I wasn't perfect, He was still Jehovah Jirah, my provider. It was He that kept me and supplied for me all of these years and not my mother, father, or even myself. God had been good to me, and I never thanked Him enough. I was always too busy complaining about the things that didn't go right. As I got up off of my knees my physical eyes were closed, but my spiritual eyes were wide open. God would restore a flourishing relationship between my father and me.

Each teardrop I cried was like a pound of hatred leaving my system. If someone would've told me that in a matter of ten minutes I could erase over twenty years of hurt by just praying, I would've asked them if they were smoking an advance version of crack. I felt like a new person.

*   *   *

I headed back toward the kitchen. "Did you take a shower?" Mama asked.

"No." I smiled. "Why?"

"You were in there a while." She licked chocolate icing from her fingertips. "I need help."

"Well, use me," I joked. "I'm here now."

"Would you mind helping me with the table?" Dad asked and Mama held her breath not knowing what to expect from me.

"Not at all," I replied. "What would you like me to do?"

I helped him set the table and made small talk with him until Mama yelled, "Lia, I want you to grease my scalp later."

That was always my chore. "Yuck!" I yelled as Dad laughed.

"What?" She stood with her hands akimbo. "What are you saying?"

"I'm saying we're about to eat."

"Please," she laughed. "Dandruff has never killed a soul."

"Dandruff?" I joked. "You have snowflakes?"

"Speaking of snowflakes." She walked to me. "Tyann called me. Who was that guy from Chicago?"

I avoided looking at her. "There is no guy *from* Chicago."

"Okay, since you're spinning words," she said, "who is the guy *in* Chicago then?" She went on. "Who is Mister Chicago?"

"There is no Mister Chicago," I said.

"That's true because Tyann said that he has a Miami number." She looked at me and winked. "I have all the information."

"He's just someone that I ran into there that I know from here, that's all." I smiled. "I would be glad to grease your scalp, Mama, but no more talk of Chicago."

"Deal." She laughed.

My dad was already at the table so Mama and I brought over the seasoned yellow rice, baked chicken, mixed vegetables, salad, and chocolate cake. As we ate I saw him giving her flirtatious looks in between conversation. She was giggling nonstop, even when nothing was funny. She was giddily in love with him, again. I won't question his motives any longer because happiness for just one day is still happiness. And happy she was.

If memory served me right, this was the first time my father and I had dinner together, but all of the years I secretly wanted him beside me were wiped away by him being there now. I turned to him and I hoped that I wasn't stepping too high in the clouds. "Dad, maybe we can have lunch one day."

"I would love that." His smile said it all. "Nadia, did you get around to telling Thalia about . . ."

"No, not yet, Dev," she interrupted him. "That can wait." She shot him the same look she used to give me when she turned to see me talking in church . . . it meant 'don't you say another word.'

"You mean about the car?" I asked and they brought their attention to me. "Madi told me."

"I'm not talking about the car." He reached across the table and grabbed both of our hands. "I'm talking about the wedding." He paused. "I asked your mom to marry me."

"What?" My emotions were a hybrid of sad and glad, but not truly either. However, I looked into her eyes and I saw more than just my mama, I saw an older woman that had never married. This was all she had ever wanted and I was happy for her.

Dad went on. "I have made tons of mistakes in my life, but she is the mistake I regret the most. Your mother is the only woman I've ever loved." He sighed. "I know that I put all of you through a lot, but she has forgiven me, and my gift to her is happiness until death."

"Oh my goodness." I sprung from the table and threw my arms around him and tears paraded down my cheeks. By then Mama was crying too. "I'm happy for the both of you." I hugged Mama. "Congratulations."

It was such a revelation, the three of us together, smiling, talking, and discussing wedding plans of all things. Apparently he asked her three weeks prior and she said yes and was even wearing the ring when I first arrived the night before, but I didn't notice.

I was the first of the four kids to know. She wanted to wait until we were all together, but he just couldn't help it. I think it was something he felt that he had to do to show me that he wasn't just hanging around.

Later that night she walked him out and returned to see me washing dishes. Mama crept up behind me and put the backside of her hand on my forehead. "Are you feeling well?"

I chuckled. "No, I have a fever of two hundred and eight." I already knew why she was asking.

"I'm so proud of you." She hugged me from behind. "Thank you."

"Thanks for what?"

"For letting Dev have his moment without coming down on him." She was calling him Dev again; this *was* serious.

"Mama, I'm really happy for you." I shifted in her arms and turned to look at her. "I can't hold pent up anger for him any longer, especially if he's making you happy." I continued. "Look at you, you're glowing, I've never seen you like this."

"Oh, stop." She blushed.

"Plus, I know that the spirit of God can't reside in an unforgiving heart." I smiled.

"So I see that you're still on the right track with the Lord." She covered her mouth with her hands. "I can't believe that my baby is saved."

"Mama, I don't call it saved." I paused. "I don't really know what to call it; I've just made some changes in my life."

"It's called saved." Her right hand went up into the air. "Hallelujah." Tears ran down her cheeks. "Thank you, Jesus." She lifted her other hand. "You are worthy of all the praise, Lord." She looked at me. "Don't you let the devil hear you say that you don't know what to call it," she said. "You are a child of God."

"Yeah, I know, Mama," I whined. "But sometimes I don't know where my head is."

"Baby, keep your head lifted up toward the hills." She touched my chin. "No matter what comes your way never lose sight of God. Don't get wrapped up in worldly foolishness. God has something for you that you don't even have room to receive, just keep trusting Him." She spoke with such conviction. "You have to learn how to step out on faith. That means walking off of a ledge knowing that He'll create another stone for you to step on. Thalia, God is going to use you, He has mighty works for you, but you're still holding onto some things. You must let them go for Him to take you to where you're going."

"I love you, Mama." I wept.

She held me. "I love you, too."

"I'll be all right," I cried. "It's not as easy as I thought it would be."

"You know why?" she asked and then answered herself. "Because the first thing you have to do when you get saved is tell people." She wiped my tears away. "You've been running around telling people that you're changing this and you're changing that, but you won't say that you got saved."

I interrupted, "Because I don't know if I'm saved or not."

"Do you believe that Jesus died for your sins?"

I knew that as a child. "Of course."

"Do you accept Him as your personal Savior?"

"Yes."

She went on. "Romans tenth chapter verses nine and ten says: '*If you confess with your mouth the Lord Jesus and believe in your heart that God has raised Him from the dead, you will be saved. For with the heart one believes unto righteousness, and with the mouth confession is made unto salvation.*'" She smiled at me. "That means that you're saved, baby, but you can't be ashamed to own Him because then He'll be ashamed of you. Tell folks that you got saved and stop walking around talking about that you've made some changes. Be proud to be a part of the army of the Lord. You have to believe in your heart and confess it with your mouth."

"Thank you, Mama." I hugged her. "I'm saved."

"Yes, baby." She smiled. "Hearing you say those words makes me so happy. That's all I've ever wanted for all of my children, one out of four ain't bad." She threw her hands up again. "The angels in heaven are rejoicing over that soul which was lost." She giggled.

We rejoiced a little together while cleaning the kitchen. We sung her favorite hymn, *Draw Me Nearer,* but of course she didn't appreciate me adding a little soul to it. "Stop playing with my song, girl," she joked.

Chapter 20

Chocolate Covered Forbidden Fruit

After my shower Mama met me in the living room with her rattail comb and Royal Crown grease. "Here you go." She handed them to me, threw a pillow on my legs, and lay across the couch with her head on my lap.

"I thought you were kidding." I parted her braids . . . it would be a long journey to the back of her head. Fifteen minutes in, my cell phone rang and she snatched it up like she was paying Cingular. "Hello," she answered. "Good evening to you as well." She paused. "I'm doing just fine." She giggled. "You sure can, hold on." She put the phone in my greasy palm; I sat it on my shoulder and bent my head to it.

"Hello."

"Good evening, beautiful." Butterflies danced in my stomach.

"I was just thinking about you." I tried to limit my words. "Can't wait until you get back." Though the TV was on Mama probably found the live entertainment more interesting.

"That's the way I want you to feel whenever I'm away from you." His words were from a place he didn't know still existed and I could hear it. "So how did everything go with your shopping?" he asked.

"Ah." I was still lost for words. "Um, my furniture will be delivered next week." I changed the subject. "So what did you do tonight?"

"Well, Sister Stride asked me to join her downstairs in the restaurant for dinner."

"That was nice of her." I fought to be polite. "How was it?"

"Well," he sighed, "she brought Deborah with her."

"Oh." Steam spewed from my ears. "That should've been nice."

"Sister Stride left before they even brought the appetizers, something about a pill she forgot to take and had to go up to her room, but she never came back."

"Well, Deborah seemed like a great person so dinner was probably very enjoyable." I felt like I would choke.

"Every other Sunday there is a deaconess or older sister trying to fix me up with their daughter, niece, neighbor, or some single woman." He laughed it off. "I'm used to it. I knew that Sister Stride was trying to play cupid, but just like everybody else, her arrow missed the target." He paused. "Deborah isn't what I'm looking for." He snickered. "The moment Sister Stride left the table she asked the waiter to fix our food to go." I forgot all about my mother's hair as Isaac went on. "When they brought the food out she winked at me and started talking about how much better dinner would be in her room."

"Yeah?" I felt my eyes twitching. "So how did it go?"

"It didn't go," he said. "I told her me having dinner with her in her room wasn't going to happen." Issac added, "Thalia, as long as you remain interested in getting to know me you will have me to yourself."

Though nothing happened I was still bitter. "Well, I'm sure that everyone will say that she's a better candidate." I tried to smile. "I hope that you didn't turn her down because of me." Why would I say that?

Isaac hit me with, "Excuse me?" He cleared his throat. "Thalia, what took place between you and me didn't happen by chance. Do you think that I make a practice of frequenting women in their hotel rooms?"

"Well, I," I stuttered, "I was just saying . . ."

"If that is what you think of me I would appreciate knowing it." He hogged the conversation. "I am a true man of God. I'm not one of those pastors in the ministry for money, women, clothes, and cars." He took a breath. "I love the Lord with everything that I have and even all that I don't have. There is nothing that comes before His will for me." He continued. "Me inviting myself into your room that night I felt like I had to, after years of avoiding that very type of intimate situation it was something that, believe it or not, God not only allowed, but instructed me to do." He spoke with so much of an anointing that everyone on his floor of the hotel should've felt it, and he wasn't done yet. "I serve a God that talks to me and he spoke to me about you. I'm not coming back to Miami to play Playstation or Xbox with you. I don't have time for games. When I come I'm coming for real."

My grin spanned 1,500 miles. "What am I going to do with you?"

"Whatever it is just do it without thinking about what

people will think or say." He sounded serious. "Regardless to where we are it's just you and me."

"Just you and me." I hoped Mama wasn't paying attention. "You make me wonder, Mister Chicago."

"You make me smile, Miss Miami," he said. "Tomorrow is Friday; before you know it it'll be Monday."

"I might need to see you before then," I joked.

"If you need," he interrupted himself before he went on, "and the keyword is need. If you *need* me before Monday then I'll be there."

"Then where you at, brother?" I asked.

"For now when you want me, just call." He yawned. "But when you need me, I'll be there."

I blushed. "You tired?"

"Yeah," he responded. "It's been a long day."

I hated to see him go. "Well, have a good night."

"I'll call you in the morning." He promised.

"Bye." I closed the phone and rested it beside me.

I leaned over and looked in Mama's face. Her eyes were closed, but before I breathed a sigh of relief I waved my hand in front of her lids to confirm, that's when I heard her say, "Every shut eye ain't sleep." Her voice startled me. She turned to lie on her back to face me. "You can't be like that."

"Like what?" I was praying that if she knew what I was talking about she didn't know who I was talking to.

"Stop being concerned about what people will say about you. That's why you stayed in Philadelphia so long. Do what makes you happy, stop living for what folks say, live for God and you."

"What are you talking about, Mama?" I dove back into her braids.

"He's not like the others, Thalia."

"Huh?" She couldn't know.

"He's gonna blow your mind."

I laughed. "Mama, you always think you know some-body."

"I *know* his voice." She waited until our eyes met. "Every shut eye ain't sleep, and every goodbye ain't gone."

I nearly plucked a braid clean off of her head. "Mama, what are you talking about?"

"This is the will of God," she said. "He's been alone a long time." She was serious. "Please be good to him, he's a good man."

"What?" I laughed nervously. "I can't pick a good man if he had a sign on his chest, remember? I'm just like Eve; I'm always ending up with bad apples." I continued. "Or some other kind of forbidden fruit."

"There is nothing forbidden about him," Mama said. "I thank God that you've run out of awful apples, bottomed-out bananas, and crummy cantaloupes." She smiled. "You call him a forbidden fruit, but he's really God's will for your life. So stop being afraid of what you may feel and what people may think and welcome your destiny." She touched my face softly. "In your mind he may seem off limits because of who he is, his age, and what he does, but he's really the golden apple and the sky is the limit with him." She continued. "Every once in a while our hearts try to run away from something real because it's afraid that the feeling may soon go away and it'll all be just a memory. Don't be afraid of what *may* happen, but embrace what *is* happening." She finished with a flourish. "If for some reason you can't shake the thought and your foolish heart tricks you into thinking of him as forbidden fruit, then think of him as *chocolate covered* forbidden fruit, because forbidden love is twice the treat when dipped into something chocolaty sweet."

I was in awe of her, but didn't dare show it. "Mama, you've flipped your lid." I made one last attempt to make it seem as though she wasn't on the right track.

She looked at me sternly. "I see that you want me to be blunt with you." She paused. "A mother could never want a better man for her daughter." She looked up at me. "Pastor Flack is truly a move of God in your life."

Chapter 21

You'd Die For Me

She knew! I should've known that she'd recognize his voice. She loved her pastor, and crossed hell and high water seeing to it that he was respected and getting the best of treatment from everyone.

For the next thirty minutes the only voice that could be heard was that of Lucy Ricardo as we watched *I Love Lucy*. Mama said nothing else of Isaac, she didn't have to, and I didn't want her to. I was done with her hair but she continued to lie in my lap. I enjoyed her body heat. It made me think of the way she must've felt when I was growing within her. I loved her for everything she was and even for things she wasn't.

"I have a surprise for you." She bounced up and disappeared down the hall. When I heard her footsteps coming back she yelled, "Close your eyes." Then I heard plastic rustling and her moving around. "Open 'em."

I unfastened my eyes and Mama, Nadia Tyree, soon

to be Nadia Banks, was wearing an eloquent white suit with white fur adorning the bottom of the sleeves and lapels, four striking crystallized buttons lining the center, and the skirt stopping at her knees. She looked like a model. "Whoa, Mama, that is hot."

"Isn't it?"

"What's the occasion?" I asked.

She cooed, "The wedding reception, dinner with the Lord."

"Excellent choice, Mrs. Banks." I called her by her future last name.

She laughed. "I got it in white to blend in with the angels that have kept me from killing your daddy over the years." She spun around.

"I love it." I stood up and ran my hand over the fabric.

"We'll start shopping for the wedding gown right after we tell Tyann, so that all three of us can pick it out together." She looked at the clock. "Ooh, it's after eleven, I need to be in bed."

"You're always sleepy." I kidded her. "Sometimes I think you took a lifetime dosage of Nytol."

She winked. "I'm sleeping now because after the wedding I won't get any sleep."

"Gross." I turned up my nose like a ten-year-old. "That's just nasty."

"It's natural." She came over and gave me a good-night hug. "How about us meeting for lunch tomorrow?"

"Sounds good to me," then I quickly remembered, "but I have to turn in the rental and pick up my car from the Amtrak station."

"What time?" she asked.

"The train will be in at eight but I have to give them

time to unload the cars. I'll probably leave down here at about ten."

"I'll tell you what, call me at the bank when you have your car and are headed back in this direction."

"Sounds like a plan." I missed our mother/daughter lunches. "Have a good night." She turned to walk away but as I sat back down she returned to the living room staring at me. "What happened?"

"Do you know how much I love you?" Though she asked this question many times before, there was something odd about it this time, she wasn't smiling. She asked again, "Do you know how much I love you?"

"Yes, Mama," I answered. "You'd die for me." I said it just as I had many times before, but this time I added, "I couldn't ever let you die for me, because I can't imagine my life without you."

She bent down and kissed me softly on my lips. "I love you, Thalia."

"I love you, too, Mama." I stood and gave her a hug. "Goodnight."

"Goodnight." She was already halfway down the dark hallway.

The next morning I took my last ride in the stylish Mitsubishi Eclipse; it was time to return it to its rightful owner. Traffic to Miami from Homestead wasn't bad. I made it to the Budget Rent-A-Car by the airport in thirty-five minutes. I closed the rental agreement and boarded the Budget van to the Amtrak station nearly twenty minutes away.

Everything was fine, except for the amount of dust on my black Altima. I visited a gas station about a block away, filled up, and got a premium wash and wax job.

My black beauty was shining again. I hopped on I-95 south and heard my cell phone ringing in my purse, which was on the floor on the passenger side. I couldn't bend that far and still see the traffic ahead of me. It was probably Mama inquiring about lunch so I stepped on the gas and tried to make it to Homestead in a hurry.

Thirty minutes later I was at the toll in Cutler Ridge, just ten minutes from the bank where Mama worked. I was then able to grab my purse and reached in for the phone to call her but there was a message, it was from her. "Thalia, I forgot my glasses, they're on my nightstand, please bring them with you. I'm starving so as soon as you get here we'll leave to go to Applebees." She paused. "By the way, do you know how much I love you?" I smiled and then she said, "I'd die for you."

It was a beautiful South Florida day; I turned off the air conditioner and rolled down the windows. I rushed to her house, ran inside, and found her glasses right where she said they'd be. I jumped back into my car and the sun was still shining forcefully but that Miami sea breeze kicked in. My phone rang again, "Hello?"

"Good day, gorgeous." It was Isaac. At the sound of his voice frozen lakes melted down to small puddles.

"Hi." I was on cloud eleven.

He asked, "How are you?"

"I'm doing great." I patted my steering wheel along with the music. "I got my car back."

"Good." His tone was upbeat. "What are you up to?"

"I'm meeting Mama for lunch."

He joked, "Tell her that I said hello."

"Why did you have to go and be so polite on the phone last night?" I asked. "She recognized your voice."

"I'm sorry," he apologized. "I guess I have one of those voices."

"Nothing to be sorry about, she actually said that she thinks it was the work of God."

"Really?" he asked. "So you and I definitely have something to talk about tonight."

"We do." I continued. "She acts like you're the best thing since sliced bread."

I could tell that he was blushing. "Mama knows best."

When I pulled into the bank's parking lot my heart nearly left my chest. "What in the world happened here?"

"What?" I vaguely remember him asking.

"Oh my God." I pulled into a parking space sideways. "Oh my God."

"Thalia, what happened?"

"Something is wrong at the bank." There were about fifteen police cars, three ambulances, and a helicopter flying over." I panicked as people crowded the parking lot. Everyone looked filled with shock, and was holding onto someone else. Yellow police tape was already roping off the front of the bank and police officers were running back and forth. "Something happened at the bank." My chest got tight and my head began to swing. I hopped out of the car with Mama's glasses, forgetting the key and anything else. Sweating, I stood still imagining the worst possible outcome.

"Thalia, are you there?" Isaac was concerned.

"Yeah, but I, I . . ." I was scared to move toward the crowd. "I, I have to go."

"Wait a minute," he pleaded. "Tell me what's going on."

Tears filled my eyes. "There are police, ambulances, and a helicopter. Something is wrong. I have to find Mama." I felt faint as I scanned all the women wearing business suits. "I don't see her."

"Calm down, Thalia." He paused. "I'm going to stay on the line until you find out what's going on, I'm not going anywhere."

"Okay." I repeated, "Okay."

I was drinking tears as I approached the crowd and a white sheet draped over what was clearly a dead body came into view. I started shaking and yelled, "Oh God." I couldn't take another step. "Oh God."

"What happened?" Isaac asked frantically.

"Somebody's dead." I began to hyperventilate. "There's a body covered up by the door."

"Lord have mercy," he mumbled. "Hang up, I'll call Madison and tell her to meet you there."

"Okay."

"I'll pray," he said. "You be strong."

"Okay." I didn't know if he had anything else to say, but when the phone fell from my fingertips I knew I wasn't turning around to pick it up. I burst through the crowd and sprinted toward the police line in search of my mother's face. "Mama!" I shouted above all the other cries. "Mama!" My calls went unanswered. No face was recognizable. "What happened here?" I asked a skinny grief-stricken man staring at the building.

"Bank robbery." A tear rolled down his face.

"When?" I didn't give him a chance to answer. "I just talked to her."

"About thirty minutes ago."

"Who is that?" I pointed at the body.

"I think it's one of the security guards." He turned to me. "Thank God I was in the restroom when everything happened."

I had to know. "Was anyone else hurt?"

"I work here." He was overwhelmed. "They rushed a few people to the hospital already."

"What hospital?" I had a thousand questions. "Who?" My breathing was scattered and I found myself gasping for air but still trying to get the words out. "Do you know Nadia Tyree?"

He didn't understand me. "Everything happened so quickly." He wiped his tears away. "A few people inside died."

"Died inside?" My knees nearly gave out. "Who?"

My heart raced; I wanted to go into cardiac arrest; I didn't want to be around; I couldn't deal with this. "Oh, Lord, help me," I cried as the thought of her with a bullet launched into her head raced through my mind. I couldn't imagine my life without Mama. "I have to find her."

I crawled under the police line and when I saw an officer approaching I tried to run toward the entrance but he caught me. "Ma'am, no one is allowed in the crime scene area."

I fought to get out of his grip. "Please." I was weak and gasping for air again. "Please, let me go." I kicked and screamed as he lifted me up and placed me on the other side of the line. Before he walked away I grabbed his hand. "My mother works here."

His eyes were full of compassion. "I understand how you feel but I can't let you in there." He called another officer over. "Joey, keep her with you while I secure the area. Her mother works here." He put my hand in the hand of the other officer who walked me to a cruiser on the other side of the bank.

I leaned up against the car. "I just want to know if she's all right." He offered me some water and I turned it down. "She's a loan officer." I saw movements in the building. "Is that her?" He grabbed my hand. I looked at him. "She's not out here, just please go in and tell her that I'm here, I have her glasses, she knows that I would be worried."

The officer said, "What is your mother's name?" All of a sudden I didn't want to speak. I didn't really want to know if something was wrong. "What is her name?" he asked again. I didn't say a word. Telling him her name meant I'd have to know the truth, and I found myself not really wanting to know anymore. I continued to look for her in the crowd. If I didn't find her she'd eventually find me . . . I had her glasses, she needed them. "Ma'am, if you want me to help you you'll have to talk to me." He handed me a Kleenex. "What is your mother's name?"

I rocked back and forth before I opened my mouth. "Nadia." My breathing was heavy. "Nadia Tyree."

"Okay. I need you to wait right here for me, okay?" He gave me a serious look. "Don't move. Please wait right here, I'll find out some information on your mother."

As he walked away a lady sauntered over to the car. "You're looking for your mom?" she asked.

"Yes." I was anxious. "Did you see her?"

"Yes, she's fine, the police took her back inside because she saw the entire thing unfold, they wanted her to point some things out for their investigation." Her words were like a glass of cold water to a person in the pits of hell.

"What?" I had to hear her say it again. "She's okay?"

"Yes, she's fine." She reached for my hand and held it.

"Thanks." I was so relieved. "Thank you very much. I was so worried."

She squeezed my hand gently.

"I'll stay here with you until she comes out."

I felt closer to Mama than ever before. I couldn't wait to see her walk out of the building. Those frightening ten minutes made me never want to be away from her ever again. However, I remembered that someone else had lost a mother, father, sister, or brother and I quickly said a prayer for their loss. When I started to relax the policeman returned. "Ma'am, what's your mother's name again?"

"Nadia Tyree, but don't worry, she . . . "

"Beverly Williamson is not your mother?" The strange lady holding my hand looked at me in shock.

"No." The sun went down in my life again. "No, Nadia Tyree is."

"Your mom's inside," the policeman said.

"Good," I said. "Just how much of this whole thing did she see?"

"Loan officer, right?" he asked.

"Yes," I said.

He mumbled something and then said, "We have a grief counselor on site." I wanted time to freeze. I didn't want to hear another word from him.

"Grief counselor for what?" I asked him.

"I'm sorry about your mother." He looked away from me.

"Sorry about what?" I grabbed his hand. "You said that she was inside." My breathing got heavy again. "You said that she was inside, right?"

"Yeah, but . . ." The officer choked up. "Ma'am, she didn't make it."

Now I knew how the families of the Sago miners felt, to fear the worst and then be told that your loved one is alive and then have someone confirm the most horrible truth. The police officer looked down at the asphalt. "I'm very sorry."

"What do you mean? I have her glasses." I pushed the lying woman away. "May I just talk to her?" I asked the officer. "May I go inside?"

"We cannot allow you in there." He never once looked me in the eyes. "You'll be able to see her later. We'll call on you to identify the body."

"The body?" I trembled violently. "The body?" I got hot, my eyes shot out, and my stomach turned into a knot. "What do you mean her body?" I shook my head from side-to-side. "No. Just tell her to come out here," I belted. "Tell her that I'm out here, she asked me to bring her glasses; she didn't wear her contacts today."

"Baby, it's going to be okay," the strange woman who brought the good news said, as she rubbed my back.

"Get your hands off of me!" I yelled at her. "No, it's not gonna be okay." I wanted to strangle her. "You said that she was all right." I pulled away from her. "You said that she was inside." I ran toward the building and the officer grabbed me again. I pounded him with my fists knocking the radio out of his hand. "Ma'am, calm down, give me a number where I can call someone to be with you."

"Mama," I shouted at the building as he talked to me. "Mama." I felt that she'd walk out soon; she would never miss our lunch. She couldn't see. She couldn't go anywhere without her glasses. She'd come out and I'd run to her and say, "Do you know how much I love you?" and she'd smile and say, "You'd die for me," and I would. I would. I'd die for her, that's why she couldn't be dead because I would die *for* her. I'd die just to have her live another day. There is no way she wouldn't be around for me anymore. There was no way she'd die before marrying my father. "Tell her to come out, please," I wailed at the policeman.

"Ma'am, I'm sorry." It seemed like he wanted to cry. "Let me call someone to be with you, do you have a phone number where I can contact someone?"

"Call my Mama." I couldn't stand; I leaned on him for support. "She'll come out." He gained control of my frail body and sat me down on a bench under a tree. His mouth was moving and it didn't matter if he was speaking English, Russian, or French, I couldn't hear him. I held my head in my hands talking to myself. "Mama, you can't just go like this. What about me? Mama, don't leave me like this."

I had already found myself missing her more than I ever did in my life. The pain in my chest was forty-something years too early. She was supposed to die when she was ninety-something, that was the way I had planned it. I was supposed to stand by her bedside and hold her hand when she took her last breath. She wasn't meant to die this type of death.

Each time I blinked I envisioned a man with a gun pointing it at her and squeezing the trigger without caring that she belonged to me. I don't know how long I was pacing with my hands high in the air before I saw Madison running toward me. She wrapped her arms around me. I pointed at the building. "Madi, go get her for me." She didn't move. "Madi, go give these to her." I handed her the glasses.

I pulled away from Madison and looked at her as tears streamed down her face. "Lia, she's gone."

"No, Madi." I got angry. "Why would you say something like that?"

She grabbed my hand. "I'm sorry, Lia."

"Go get her." I shrieked at Madi. "Do you know how much I love that woman?"

"She knew how much you loved her." Hearing her

speak in past tense about the woman that gave birth to me was a bullet to the very core of my soul. I released a loud yelp right before I fell backward onto the pavement. My world turned into the saddest, scariest, most solemn shade of the blackest brown. I never wanted to see the light of day again, not without my mama.

Chapter 22

What Took You So Long?

"Lia." It sounded like Madi was singing. "Lia." Her voice flew over me. "Are you awake?" Her face was just inches from mine when I opened my eyes. I was lying in a hospital bed and I felt an IV in my arm. "Welcome back." She smiled.

"Hey." It was the only word I could get out.

"Lia, I'm here too." I saw Yvette for the first time in over a year. "We're going to get you through this."

I saw a male figure approaching but couldn't make out who he was until he touched my hand and spoke. "What's up big sis?" It was my baby brother, Chance, with bloodshot eyes. His honey brown chiseled facial features where still intact, complimented by his fresh cornrows.

"Hi, Chance." I spoke weakly. "Where is Mama?"

"You look good." Because he refused to answer me I knew that it was true. "How is your head feeling?" he asked as he kissed my forehead.

"I'm fine." I noticed the slight pounding in the back of my head when I first woke up, but I had other things to worry about.

Chance sat on the bed. "So what are we going to do?" This was the first time I'd seen him cry since we were kids. "What are we going to do now?"

I couldn't answer him. "So I guess this isn't a bad dream after all, huh?"

"I thought it was too until I came home last night."

"Chance, I don't know." Tears slid down my cheeks. "I guess we've got to be strong."

"How?" he sobbed.

I was very weak but found the energy to strengthen him. "We have to find the strength that she taught us to have during tough times." It could only be the drugs allowing me to stay as calm as I was. Yvette walked over to console him, and then she followed him back to the window.

"How long have I been here?" I asked Madi. "What happened?"

"You passed out in the parking lot yesterday and hit your head. You were awake last night but heavily sedated." She chuckled. "You were talking some crap that I don't even think was English."

"Really?"

Madi laughed. "Yes and everyone was here."

"Who?"

"Mr. Banks, D.J., Tyann, a bunch of your cousins, your uncle Jessie, and your aunts Ruthie, Pat, and Debbie. Tyann wanted to stay, but I told her to go get some rest and I'd stay the night."

"Thank you." I looked away. "I was hoping to wake up and tell Mama about this bad dream."

"I know how you feel." Her face quickly saddened. "I still can't believe this."

I asked about my sister. "How is Ty?"

"Not good."

"Devon?" I asked.

"He's holding up the best. He got in town last night and he's already making arrangements.

"Dad?"

"Terrible." She paused. "The doctor had to keep checking his blood pressure."

I struggled to sit up and she helped me. "So what happened?"

"You fainted and hit your head pretty hard on the concrete." She added, "You suffered a concussion."

"I don't mean to me." I had to know. "What happened to Mama?"

"Lia." She looked away. "Let's talk about that later."

"Just tell me." I wanted to know.

She stared down at the tile. "Gunshot wounds."

"Wounds?" The scene from the day before came back quickly bringing with it feelings and tears. "Where?" I held my hands up to my head to try to stop the pounding. "Where was she shot?"

"They shot her in the fuckin' chest!" Chance yelled. "Two grown ass fuckin' men killed Mama like a goddamn dog." His breathing labored. "They caught those motherfuckas last night, but wait until I get my hands on 'em."

The fact that she wasn't shot in the head brought a little comfort, at least I'd be able to see her face one more time.

Chance has asthma and after an hour his breathing didn't get any better. Yvette took him back to her place, where he had spent the night and left his asthma pump, for him to get some rest. Madison left to go to the cafeteria to get lunch.

I was left alone with my thoughts. My mama, the woman that brought about my very existence, was no more. I was glad that I moved back when I did. I couldn't imagine flying home after hearing such news. I'd never see her, touch her or hear her laughter again.

I closed my eyes and began asking God for strength and heard the room door open. I kept my eyes closed because I wanted the nurse who promised to be right back to go away. Instead there was a gentle stroke on my cheek. "I said that if you needed me I'd be here."

As much as I thought I wanted everyone to disappear and leave me to bask in my depression alone, there was someone I secretly wanted in my world. "Isaac," I said as he rested a large bouquet of roses on the hospital-serving table. It was an arrangement of two-dozen white roses.

In the midst of all of the hurt, pain, and confusion, seeing him was like taking Tylenol with codeine for a toothache; things could only get better now. He bent down and scooped one arm around my neck, kissing me tenderly on the cheek. My comforter had arrived, I felt safe as the tears reintroduced themselves to my face. "I'm here for you," he said as his hands moved up and down my back.

My frail body went limp in his arms so he laid me back against the bed. "Drink some water." Isaac offered me the same bottle of water his daughter had twice, but this time I accepted it.

"Thank you." I took a few sips and handed it back to him. "When did you get here?"

"Just now," he answered. "I came straight here from the airport."

"It's not Monday is it?" I tried to remember.

"No, it's Saturday."

"I thought you were coming back on Monday?"

"Didn't I tell you that if you needed me here I'd come?" He clutched my hand. "When I learned what had happened I couldn't imagine being anywhere else."

"Thank you." I looked at the flowers. "They're beautiful, thank you."

The hospital room door opened and Madison walked in with a tray of food. "Dad, what are you doing here?" She rested the tray down and hugged him. "When did you get in?"

"My plane landed about two hours ago."

While they talked I escaped to a world where I found myself questioning my sanity. I wished for death so that I wouldn't have to live to feel the present pain or the pain that was ahead.

"Welcome back, Miss Tyree," a man said as he entered the room wearing a white lab coat.

I was weak. "Hi."

He checked my vitals and said, "We're letting you go home today." He spoke while he examined me. "However, being that you suffered a mild concussion, I really need you to get some rest for the next two or three days." He looked down at my chart. "You'll be experiencing headaches off and on, so I'll prescribe you something for pain." He paused. "You'll also feel dizzy from time to time for a while too. I know that you're going through a very stressful time but it's very important that you don't take on too much right now."

Isaac listened attentively as the doctor spoke and asked many questions; he thought of things that I didn't even care about. "What types of fluid do you recommend?" Next he asked, "Does she need to be out of bed at all?" Then he turned to me. "Are you allergic to any medications?" I shook my head side-to-side. He asked at least eight more questions and the doctor answered them all before he exited the room.

Madison laughed. "You see what I've had to go through all my life?" She playfully shook her head. "I guess that's why I love him."

"I wanted to make sure that Thalia knows what she needs to do." He smiled.

"Thank you, Mr. Flack."

He looked at me like I had never called him that before. "You're welcome, Miss Tyree."

"Dad, how did you know what was going on yesterday?" Madi questioned her father.

He didn't flinch. "I was on the phone with someone that happened to be going to the bank and they said that something was wrong."

She turned to me. "You need to rest like the doctor said; we can't have you passing out again." She tried to get me organized. "Are you going to stay at your mother's house?" She had no clue how much her question cut through me until the tears trickled down.

"I can't." I didn't want to be near the house, I couldn't even stand the thought of sitting on the couch where I did her hair or being in the kitchen, and especially not the dining room table where I sat with her as she ate her last dinner. "I can't go there right now."

Isaac touched my head. "You're going to be fine." Everything in his touch told me that he wanted me in his arms.

"I'll stay at my apartment," I said.

He interjected, "I don't think you should be alone in your condition."

"I don't either," Madi chimed in. "You don't even have furniture."

"I know," I said firmly, "but I can't go to her house."

"You can stay with Nekia and me," Madi said.

Her father disagreed. "You two can barely turn around in that place." Isaac had another idea. "What about Tyann and Colin?" he asked.

"No," Madi and I answered in unison.

"You won't be alone at your mom's house. Chance and Devon are there and I think his wife and the kids will be here tomorrow, and I think your dad will be there most of the time too." Madison was trying to convince me.

"No." My mind was made up. "I'll just get a hotel room."

"What?" Isaac sounded offended. "You have too many family members here to be living in some hotel room all alone."

"I don't want to be around people that want to talk about this." I wanted to be as far away from the truth as possible.

"I'll tell you what." Madison had an idea. "Why don't you stay at Dad's house in my old room?"

"You're welcomed to stay." He was already waiting for my answer. "I have a lot of free time right now, so I can escort you around. That's where you can get the rest the doctor ordered."

"I don't want to get in the way." I didn't mean a word I said.

"Dad is there alone and Tyler left for Morehouse last night." Right then Madison's cellular phone rang and she stepped into the washroom and closed the door.

"It looks like you don't have a choice." Isaac smiled.

I pretended like he twisted my arm. "How much is room and board?"

"Just having you there will be a gift to me," he said with a smile. "I should be asking what it is that I owe you."

I thought. "Just a shoulder, a few hugs, and some Kleenexes." He bent and kissed me quickly on my forehead.

A minute later Madison returned and I informed her of the decision to stay in her old room. Isaac left to prepare the place, but she stayed by my side until I was released later in the evening. As Madi drove out of the parking lot she asked if I wanted to at least stop by my mother's house to quickly see my family. I said yes. However, deep inside I was terrified of seeing all of the things and people that reminded me so much of her.

Mama's street was lined with cars. I immediately regretted my decision to visit. Madi parked on the grass in the back of one of the many cars on the lawn. As I walked past my mother's car I remembered the smile on her face just a few days before when she first showed it off to me. I touched the car; it was one of the last things that she touched.

I kept my head down as I entered the house. I said quick greetings to the many strange faces and hugged the necks of the familiar ones. I knew that they meant well but it wasn't them that I wanted. They couldn't do anything for me. What I really needed was to rewind the tape of my life.

I found my father, Devon, Chance, and Tyann sitting at the dining room table talking to Mr. Bowes, the funeral director. Chance had his head down on the table and Yvette was still at his side. Colin was in the kitchen on the phone.

My eldest brother, Devon, greeted me and took me into his arms. "I have everything under control here. You guys don't worry, okay?" He was more handsome each time I saw him, just like our father.

Tyann stood up and asked, "How are you feeling?" In lieu of words I threw my arms around her. While we embraced I heard Chance wailing and we both moved to comfort him. When Chance was stable I looked for my father who was no longer at the table. Devon told me that he went into Mama's room. Then I asked, "Did Dad tell you?"

"About their engagement?" Devon asked.

"Yes."

He smiled. "He told us all last night."

"He finally wanted to do right by her," I sobbed. "She was so happy about it. The three of us had dinner on Thursday." I looked at Tyann. "He really *has* changed."

"I know," Devon said.

Tyann reached for me. "I told you so."

Chance walked up on us. "Well, y'all can believe his ass if y'all want to, but that motherfucka better not have nothing to say to me."

"First of all," I snapped at him, "you watch your mouth in this house." I almost sounded like Mama. "Second, you need to stop trying to play Mr. Tough Guy everywhere you go." I paused. "And you *will* respect our mother by showing our father some respect," I huffed. "He's a part of this family and we will all stick together so you need to build a bridge and get over it right now." He just stared and had nothing to say.

We all sat at the table and listened to what Mr. Bowes had to say in regards to the funeral arrangements. When he discussed the order of service I just didn't want to be a part of it any longer, so I strolled down the hall to Mama's room and found my father there in darkness. I turned on the light and saw him sitting on the bed holding the white dress she was to wear to the reception.

"Hi," I said softly.

He didn't look my way. "Hi, baby girl." He didn't say it with the same vigor he normally did and I didn't expect him to.

I sat next to him. "She showed me that dress right after you left that night."

He cried. "I should've married her a long time ago."

"Dad," I rubbed his back, "she knew that you loved her, even when you weren't around. That's why she always took you back because she knew that someday you'd find it in your heart, and you did."

"I was too late." He clutched the dress tighter. "I wanted to see her in this dress so badly."

I said, "You still can." I grabbed his hand. "Let's go tell Mr. Bowes."

He seemed shocked at my suggestion. "No, I can't interfere with what Devon is doing."

"What?" I asked.

He was humble. "I was trying not to get too involved in the planning."

"Why?"

"I just didn't know how you kids would feel about me," he paused, "stepping in like that."

Before he went any further I said, "You're just as important as she was to us. You're our father. We want you to be a part of whatever is going to happen." We left the room together and headed for the dining room. As we approached the table my father began to speak. "Junior, I'll give you a few blank checks for whatever you think is best." He handed the dress over to Mr.

Bowes. "This is the dress she was supposed to wear at our wedding reception; I'd like her to be buried in it."

When he said the word 'buried' I started to feel dizzy and leaned against the wall to avoid falling to the ground. Madison saw me. "Are you okay?"

"No." I couldn't lie; I was ready to drop.

"You need to lie down," she said. "Let me get you to Dad's house." Madison pulled Tyann aside and told her what the doctor ordered, she also explained that I'd be at Isaac's house staying in her old room for a few days and gave her the phone number.

Chance walked us to the car. "Lia, I'm sorry. I'm just angry at everything and everybody," he said.

"I know, but we've been angry at *him* too long." I looked at Chance and said, "Try to forgive him, she'd want you to." Then I added, "Plus, he's all that we have now." I kissed him on the cheek and got in the car. Yvette followed Madi in my car so that if I needed a way around town my car would be there.

It was shortly after nine P.M. when we arrived. Isaac acknowledged his daughter with a smile but walked toward me. He still had the power to make my soul jump with a simple word. "Hello."

"Hi," I said and felt my heart flutter. I couldn't believe that in the middle of the crisis I was in, my body was still reacting to him.

Before Madi and Vette left, they saw that I took a shower and my medication and the last thing I remembered was sitting on the couch leaning on Madi.

I woke up and expected to still be leaning on Madi, but I wasn't . . . I jumped up in a panic in Madison's old bedroom. The moonlight was shining enough for me to see that no one else was in the room with me. The clock showed 3:28 A.M. I didn't want to be alone. Actually, I was scared to be alone. I eased out of bed and made my way to the dark corridor. I had been in Madison's house enough to know that her father's room was to the right and all the way down.

I walked carefully in the darkness with my hands out so that I wouldn't bump into anything. I felt the door and then reached for the knob. I turned it; it wasn't locked. I walked in and felt my way around until I bumped into the bed. I carefully pulled down the sheets and slid under the covers.

Isaac rustled then turned my way. "What took you so long?" He didn't wait for an answer. "Come here." I scooted next to him in the middle of the king-sized bed. "Are you okay?" he asked.

"No," I pouted. "But I'm glad that you came back from Chicago."

"I thought of you being all by yourself until Monday." He paused. "I couldn't have that."

Tears slipped from my weak eyes. "Thank you."

I was afraid to touch him, and he didn't touch me, but we were as close as two people could be in bed without physical contact. He asked, "Are you in any pain?"

"Slightly, I think that's what woke me up." Before I was completely through with my statement he was out of bed and turning on the lamp on his dresser.

"Let me get you a pill." He was wearing only a pair of black silk boxers and for the first time I saw him without a shirt. His chest was peanut butter brown and bulky, arms thickly built, stomach flat and not an inch of fat anywhere. Within two minutes he was back with one of the pills prescribed for pain and a glass of water. I tried not to look at his thighs as he walked back around to the other side of the bed.

"If that doesn't work then I'll be the remedy." He

dimmed the light and got back under the covers. My head fell on his shoulder, and he cradled me, pulling me close to him with his other hand. "So I'm the best thing since slice bread, huh?" He chuckled.

"Are you?" I asked, remembering telling him that was what Mama thought of him. "Are you really all of that?"

"Personally, I think that I'm the best thing since the invention of the wheel," he joked. "By the way, that pill I gave you was to make you crazy about me."

"Another one?" I played along. "I think I took one of those in Chicago." My head was already starting to ease, but I felt drowsy. I asked, "Are you sure that wasn't X?"

"You'll know when I'm giving you ecstasy." He looked me in the eyes and smiled. "And the ecstasy I'll give you won't wear off after ten hours."

I laughed out loud for the first time in two days. "Thank you."

"Don't thank me just yet," he said. "Remember the other night when I told you that it wasn't my night to tickle you?"

"Yeah."

"Well tonight is the night." He began tickling me until I begged him to stop, but it was a front . . . there was nothing I wanted more than his hands on me.

Chapter 23

C-A-U-G-H-T . . . Caught!

It was after eleven the next morning when I found Isaac in his den on the computer. I snuck up behind him and covered his eyes with my hands. "Guess who?" I asked playfully.

"Oh my goodness, I have an intruder?" He pretended to be afraid.

I giggled. "Would you allow an intruder in your bed?"

He grabbed my hands and slid them down to his chest. "It depends on what she's trying to steal."

"Well, I'm not here for anything you're not going to give me willingly."

He swiveled in the chair to face me. "I'm willing to give you so much." He stood and wrapped his hands around my waist, staring deeply into my eyes. He moved closer until his lips touched mine. They collided softly over and over again in a series of supple, slow, sensual pecks. He stopped and I searched his eyes for more, and just like a boomerang, he came back.

The house phone rang and he pulled away from me to answer it. "Hello?" He paused. "I'm fine." He was still a little worked up and had to control his breathing. "Oh, she's fine." He sat in his chair. "Wednesday?" He grabbed a pen and jotted something down. "Man, I'll do anything for you guys." He smiled. "Do you need me to do anything else?" He wrote down a few more things. "Consider it done." He looked at me. "Yes, she's right here, hold on."

I took the phone. "Hello?"

"How are you?" Devon asked.

"I've had a few dizzy spells, but I'll be okay." I walked out of the office and headed toward the kitchen.

"Don't overexert yourself." He showed concern. "Do you need me to bring you anything?"

I remembered Mama. Then I was crying again. "The thing I want most I'll never have again." I never made it to the kitchen. I stopped and sat in the corridor. I felt like screaming. "I knew that she'd go one day."

"Me too," Devon wept in my ear and said the same words I had planned on saying, "but I never thought that anything like this could happen to her." He put me on hold to get himself together and came back a bit stronger. "I called to go over the funeral arrangements with you."

"Funeral." I said the word in hopes of taking away some of its strength. "Funeral," I said again and took a deep breath. We were planning Mama's funeral.

Of course the funeral would be held at Mount Pleasant. We agreed not to prolong things by waiting until Saturday. We'd do it on Wednesday at eleven A.M.

Devon asked me about singing a song at the service and as soon as I said yes I let out a loud scream.

"Thalia, are you okay?" Devon asked.

I was stunned that Isaac was already standing over me. He took the phone out of my hand and finished the conversation. He then stood me up and walked me to the sofa. He sat next to me and positioned my head on his chest. He rubbed his fingers through my hair. I tried to forget the reason for my tears by getting lost in him, but right then a car pulled into the driveway. I jumped up like a teenager who wasn't supposed to have company over. "Who's that?"

"It sounds like Madison." He kissed my hand. "I'll give you girls your time together." He stood up. "I'll be in the study." I threw myself on the couch and turned the television on. Less than a minute later Madison walked in.

"Hey, girl." She smiled. "How are you feeling?"

"I'm fine." I stood up and as we hugged the door opened again and a woman came through with a vase full of beautiful flowers. She had a pretty round face and was about Madi's height. She was dark brown, and her jet-black hair fell to just below her shoulders. "Hi." She approached with a smile. "These are for you." She handed the flowers to me.

"Thalia, this is Nekia." She pointed. "Nekia, this is Thalia."

"Thank you so very much." I rested the flowers on the table and hugged her. "I've heard so much about you."

Madison handed me my purse, which I had left in my car at the bank. "Thank you." I looked in it. "I had forgotten all about even having a cell phone."

They also came bearing Chinese food and as we talked and ate my cell phone started ringing. "Hello?"

"I'm very sorry to hear about your mother." It was Andre.

My plan was to hit him with one word answers. "Thanks," I said under my breath.

Suddenly he was half-human. "How are you doing?"

"Better." I walked to Madison's old room and sat on the bed.

"How is Ty?"

"Sad."

"Chance?" he asked.

I said, "Sad."

"Devon?"

"Sad," I replied.

He wasn't getting it. "And your dad?"

"Sad."

"What's with the one-word answers?" He sighed. "Look, I know that you don't want to talk to me or hear from me, but I figured I could at least be there for you."

"At least?" I said. "Andre, you don't have to do anything for me."

"She was important to me as well." He continued. "I'm flying in tomorrow." Was I supposed to find accommodations and transportation for him? "My parents will be there on Tuesday."

"Don't come here, Andre."

"What do you mean?" he asked.

"I mean, don't come here," I lashed out. "I don't need your drama on top of what's going on with my family."

"I'm not coming there with or for any drama. I'm coming there because she was like a mother to me too."

I wanted to laugh at his comment. "Plus, she'd want us back together."

I snapped, "She wanted you the hell away from me."

"She wanted you to be happy," he fought back.

"Exactly, and that's why I'm back in Miami."

"Thalia," Andre whispered, "I love you."

"What?" I looked at the phone; it had been months since he said those words to me. "I can't deal with this right now."

"After the funeral why don't you come back to Philly with me?" he asked. "I'll take some time off and we can start things over again."

"Even though it hasn't even been a week, my life has changed so much that I can't see wasting anymore time on you."

"C'mon, don't be like that."

"Don't be like what?" I was about to freak out. "I thought you called with sympathy."

"I'm sorry, okay!" He went on. "But whether you like it or not I'm coming to Miami for the funeral." Was I supposed to be moved?

"I need to go, Andre."

"See you on tomorrow." Before his sentence was complete I hung up.

Back in the living room my entire immediate family had shown up to make sure that I was all right. Everyone talked about funny things to avoid the matter at hand. It was eight o'clock when everyone left and Isaac and I were alone again. I was cold, sitting on the sofa with my arms tucked into my shirt. Isaac brought me a blanket. "Do you want to make it a Blockbuster night?" he asked while pointing at his DVD collection.

"Sure." I named a title I had noticed earlier. "Let's

watch *Rush Hour.*" He slipped in the DVD and turned off all the unnecessary lights. Lying on the sofa with my back against his chest, I spread the blanket over us. During the entire movie there were no phone calls, no visitors, and most importantly, no crying. We barely talked during the movie, but I was reminded of his presence by his laughter and with soft kisses on the back of my neck.

After the movie he stood up and pulled me to my feet and over to the sliding door. As he drew back the curtains and hit the light switch, I saw a screened in pool and Jacuzzi. It was news to me. When I moved away Madison's backyard was nothing but green grass.

"Let's get in," he raved.

"I don't know about that." I wasn't as enthusiastic. "I don't even have a swimsuit with me."

He thought. "Well, Madison comes here every so often to get in. She keeps her things here, check her room."

I looked through Madison's drawers and found three bikinis; one was brand new. I ripped the tags off and put it on. The top was a little small; it slammed my breasts together and gave off the illusion that I had more cleavage than I actually did. I wasn't complaining about that.

Isaac was already in the pool swimming toward the far end. As I walked to the pool his head popped up. "Very nice," he said as I stepped into the cold water.

He stood up and I felt faint while walking toward him. "You're looking very nice yourself." His upper body glistened. Beads of water ran down his chest and I wanted to trace them with my fingertips. His pecks looked like two mounds of melted chocolate. Suddenly reality set in, I was trembling. "This water is freezing."

"Put your whole body in quickly and you'll adjust," he advised.

"I can't," I said, still shivering.

"Yes, you can. On the count of three." He stepped closer and wrapped his hands around me. "One, two, three."

Before I knew it I was up to my forehead in water. I panicked and sprung up coughing. "What was that?" I playfully punched him. "I hadn't planned on getting my hair wet."

"That's how you have to do it," he said, then pulled me closer.

I was sure I looked like a wet long-haired German Shepherd. "Can I tell you a secret?" I asked while holding him around the neck.

"What's up?"

"All of these years," I confessed, "I've always thought you were the most handsome man I knew."

My breasts were now pressed up against his chest. "Really?"

"Really," I confirmed.

He slowly pulled me back down into the water until only our heads were out. I held onto him and we drifted into the five-foot area, coming to a stop with his back against the wall.

"I hope that I don't scare you by saying this," he looked serious, "but I want you in my life for the long haul."

"That didn't scare me at all." I smiled. "I want you in my life too."

"I don't want this to be a passing thing." He struggled with his next set of words. "I want you here all the time." If possible our bodies got even closer as he made a move for my lips. "May I?" he asked and I knew that I didn't have to answer. I just closed my eyes.

I ran my tongue over his mouth then took his lower lip in and gently sucked him in. He followed my lead, taking my bottom lip and tenderly pulling on it again and again; I was at his mercy. Our breathing was heavy and the kiss grew more passionate than any we had shared. The waters around our hot bodies boiled. The more our tongues intertwined I tangled my legs around his waist. Doing so I felt his hardness against me below. His hands rubbed my back and then moved to my waist.

"What in the hell is going on here?" I looked up and saw Madison approaching us with tears pouring down her face. "How could you two do this?"

C-A-U-G-H-T . . . caught! I pushed away from Isaac as he calmly asked, "How long have you been here?"

"Long enough." She made it to where we were, but by that time I was already in the middle of the pool. "Long enough to see my best friend screwing my father." She threw a shoe at me.

"Madi, it's not like that." I was crying.

Isaac pushed himself up and got out of the pool and tried to reason with her. "Listen to me, Madison."

"There is absolutely nothing that I want to hear from either of you!" she yelled at him. "You're supposed to be a pastor. Yet you bring her here to fuck her in your backyard?"

"Watch your mouth." He got in her face. "I am your father and you will not disrespect me." I had never heard him speak in such an angry tone. "I don't owe you an explanation and I don't owe you my life." He patted his chest. "Yes, I'm a pastor, but I'm human as well and for all these years I've lived too concerned about your happiness to even dream of my own." He shook his head. "No more, Madison, no more." He looked over at me. "I want to be with her and I *will* be with her, and if that's a problem with you then that's exactly what it'll be, your problem."

"Is this why you came back to Miami?" she asked me. "Is that why you showed back up wanting to know all of my business?"

"No." It was all I could say.

Isaac spoke for me. "We ran into each other in Chicago."

Madison spun around like a crazed maniac with a psychotic look on her face. "It was you?" she shouted. "You answered his cell phone." She jumped into the pool but Isaac jumped in after her. I nervously made my way to the edge and jumped out.

"How could you use your mother's death to come into my mother's house and do this?" She looked up at me.

"This was your suggestion, Madison," I yelled. "You wanted me to stay here." All the drama triggered a headache. "It's not like you think it is." Isaac had a hold of her as I wrapped the towel around me. "It's not what you think."

"What is it then?" She freed herself of Isaac's grip and made her way to the edge of the pool. He tried to catch her but couldn't, and I wasn't going to run, I wasn't backing down; I hadn't done anything wrong. She stood two feet away. "What is it then?" Before I could answer she slapped my taste buds from one side of my mouth to the other. "What is it, bitch?"

I thought of the way Isaac made me feel, the way he respected me, and the way my heart fluttered when he was around. I remembered the way I felt in his arms that first night in Chicago, the tickle wars, thumb wrestling, and the dinner cruise. The pure fact that he came all the way from Chicago just to be at my side said enough. I only knew one word to describe what I felt. "Love," I told Madi.

She wasn't expecting that. "Love?" she asked. "How?" Madi backed away. "How, Lia?" She was shaking. "Love?"

"Remember how you said you felt about Nekia?" It was the only way I could explain myself. "It's the same feeling, the same emotional longing, it's no different. It's the spirit within the person." I didn't realize what I was saying. "He just happens to be your father, the same way Nekia just happens to be a woman."

"You bitch." She looked at me. "Are you happy now?"

I truthfully didn't realize what I had done. "What do you mean?" I asked.

"The cat is out of the bag." She turned to Isaac. "Nekia is my girlfriend, I'm gay."

"That's no secret," Isaac said. "I knew that before you met Nekia and I didn't love you any less." He walked over to her. "It's your life, Madison, and I've respected you. Please respect me and the way I've decided to live mine."

She sounded like the little girl she was when I first met her. "What about Mom?"

"Madi, your mother is gone," I spoke before Isaac, "she's gone, just like my mom is . . . gone. Your father has been alone for a long time, and he has been nothing but dedicated to you and your brothers." I finished with, "I'm not trying to fill her spot, but I am trying to fill the void."

Isaac sat in one of the lawn chairs and asked Madi to do the same. When she did I walked into the house, scuttled through the room, threw on a pair of pants and a shirt, grabbed my tote bag, and before another tear could fall, I was out the front door and in my car down the street.

Chapter 24

Sister Thompson Heard Everything

My face was still stinging. I wasn't mad at Madi though. If I walked in on her kissing my dad I would've slapped her too. What bothered me most in this situation was that I was supposed to be mourning my mother's death. And though I could find no time to do much, I found the time to carry on like she never existed . . . in Isaac's arms. I felt selfish.

My drive ended at the Biscayne Bay Marriott, downtown Miami. The lady at the front desk couldn't stop staring at my hot-damn-mess hair. I was crying, barely found my credit card, and didn't know how many nights I would stay. I'm sure I was the epitome of the 'red flag guest' she learned of in training.

I made it to my room on the eleventh floor. It was two in the morning when I called Tyann knowing full well that I would get her voicemail. "Ty, let everyone know that I'm okay and that I'll be back on Wednesday in time for the service. Please don't worry about me." I powered off my cell phone.

The next day I didn't leave the room. My only contact was with the room service staff. On Tuesday, however, I went out in search of a black dress and shoes for the dreaded next day. When I returned to the room around five in the evening, I felt horrible, the viewing at the funeral home was set to start at six. I wanted to drive south, but that would mean facing reality. I'm sure my family thought that I had lost my mind, but seeing the shell of Mama's body would mean no turning back, no more hoping that this was a dream, it would mean she was really gone. I was comfortable living a lie . . . at least for one more day.

I decided to check my messages; I had fifteen of them, which was the max amount. Message number one: "Thalia." It was Isaac. "I'm sorry about what happened. Please call me as soon as you hear this." He sounded concerned. "You shouldn't be driving on those medications. I hope that you're okay. Madison and I had a long talk. She's still angry, but a little more understanding. Call me," he paused, "or just come back to the house."

Message number two: "Thalia, where are you?" Tyann was frantic. "How in the hell are you going to disappear now in the middle of everything that's going on? Leave it up to you to be selfish!" she shouted. "Madison called here early this morning looking for you. You need to call *somebody* . . . anybody. We're all dealing with the same thing. Call me or get your behind to Mama's house."

Message number three was from Madison: "I'm sorry about hitting you, but understand how I'm feeling."

She paused. "You were dealing with my dad behind my back." She snickered. "I'm hurting and I do not like you a lot right now, but I've had some time to sit and think," she said. "I don't know what kind of friends we'll be after this, but we do need to talk." She hung up.

Message number four: "Ah jes, dis message is for-rrrr Stacy." It was a Spanish man. "Ah, how you say, Imma de guy frrrrom the club las nie." The automated voice spoke my actions. "Message deleted."

Message number five: "Lia, this is Vette, what in the hell happened last night?" She was concerned. "Madison just called me. I don't mean to get all up in your business, but I want to hear your side of the story." She continued. "What is going on between you and Mr. Flack? Please call me when you get this message, I'm not here to judge you, blame you, or tell you how to live your life. Call me, I'm here to listen." I should've known that Madi would talk.

Message number six: "Thalia, I thought sure that you would've come back or I would've heard from you by now." It was Isaac again. He sighed. "I stayed up all night. Where are you? Your family is calling and I don't know how to answer their questions." He continued. "I know that this is a lot to deal with, especially during this time, but please just call me to let me know that you're okay."

Message number seven: "I hope that you have room for another message from me." Isaac was smiling; I could hear it. "I guess you think I'm crazy for calling so much, but I can't stop thinking about you. Please call me. There is something I'd like to give to you."

Message number eight: "Thalia, this is Andre. I'm in Miami, at the airport. I don't see you anywhere so I guess Tyann didn't find you to give you my flight information. I know that you probably have a million things to do so I'll just get a cab. I'll be at your mother's house in about an hour and a half. I was wondering if you made hotel arrangements, if you didn't, don't worry about it because I'd like to be wherever you are. See you in a few."

Message number eight: "Okay, now everyone is freaking out. We're worried to death about you." Tyann sounded upset again. "Not to mention Heather called me saying something that she heard from Tyler's friend Avery who is all the way in Austin, Texas!" she yelled. "What is going on between you and Reverend Flack? Oh and don't lie, it's such a coincidence that he was in Chicago last week too. You better let somebody know where in the hell you are and what the hell is going on." She slammed the phone down.

Message number nine: "Yo, this is Chance! There is mad shit, I'm sorry there is mad stuff in the air about you and the Rev. yo. Apparently, you, Madison and the Rev. were having some sort of argument or scuffle and her cell phone somehow dialed Avery's house, so nosy Sister Thompson heard everything that was said and told everybody." He was trying to whisper. "Yo, we wanted to hear from you 'bout this, but since you ain't callin' nobody we called Madi and she came over and told us some powerful shit, I mean stuff. Where are you, ma? Holla!"

Message number ten: "Well, well, well," Andre said. "One of your cousins filled me in, Sister Tyree." His sinister chuckle almost melted my ear. "Damn, you give new meaning to being saved. I guess this is how you give your ten percent to the church."

Message number eleven: "It's me again." Isaac sounded tired. "It's Tuesday morning, even if you just call and hang up, please call me." He was angry. "Everyone has been leaving you messages and you haven't called anyone back, so I am minutes away from calling the police," he said. "As you may know, the word about us is around town. I don't want to deal with it alone, and neither do you." He paused. "Please call me."

Message number twelve: "Thalia, this is Devon, please call us."

Message number thirteen: "Ms. Tyree this is Mary from Cultured Furniture. We've been trying to contact you since Friday. Please give us a call."

Message number fourteen: "Baby girl," it was my father. "Out of everyone in the world I know that running away from family when things get tough is not the way to handle it." He continued. "Give me a call at the house. Let's deal with this, and let's get over it."

Message number fifteen: "I miss you." They were the only three words Isaac had to say.

I thought about all of the messages and said, "I've created a monster." I still had to walk into a crowded church in eighteen hours. The bereaved family always had a scandal going on behind the scenes, but this was the end all be all. The last thing I wanted was for Mama's funeral to turn into the Jerry Springer Show. I needed to grow up.

I packed my things and headed south. I still didn't want to attend the viewing or see her house, so I went to where I knew I was welcomed and the very arms my mama told me were meant to hold me. I left my car at a park down the street and walked to his house to find it in darkness. I sat on the steps and knew that soon my prince would come . . . who knew it would be two hours later.

* * *

"Thalia?" He walked toward the door and grew more anxious with each step. "Is that you?"

"Hi."

"Where have you been?" He knelt down and embraced me.

"A hotel downtown." I felt terrible. "I didn't mean to make you worry, but things happened so quickly that night." I held him tighter. "I'm sorry about all of the problems I've caused."

"You are not a problem to me." He kissed my forehead. "In one week you've managed to erase things that I never thought would go away."

"I don't want to be alone anymore, Isaac," I cried. "But it's only been a week and things are happening so quickly between us, I don't know what's real."

"I'll tell you what's real." He picked me up. "Look at me." My head was still buried in his chest. "Look at me," I looked up at him and he spoke, "what's real is my love for you."

"What?" I had to hear that again.

He repeated himself. "I love you."

My lips trembled. "I love you too."

Though I was wearing a black dress the reality of where I was going still didn't hit me until I passed the mirror. I stood still and studied my reflection in my black crepe two-piece suit. I was the spitting image of Mama and instantly felt dizzy. Isaac braced my weak body as I pointed at the mirror. "I look just like her." I was surprised that I wasn't crying.

"You do, she was beautiful." He smiled. "I'll be in the

pulpit today." He pushed up my sleeve and placed his index and middle fingers on my wrist like he was checking my pulse. "Though I won't be at your side I still want to be the closest thing to your heartbeat." He slipped a gold bracelet around my wrist. "I got this for you two days ago."

I stared up at him. "Today is going to be the hardest day of my life." I tried to stay strong. "Will you pray for me?"

"Certainly, let's pray." He held both of my hands and closed his eyes; I followed suit. I felt the power of his words before he even spoke. "Lord, I come before you, first and foremost, to give You thanks. I thank You, oh God, for life, health, and strength. I thank You for being a way-maker and for being just a prayer away." He continued. "But most of all, Lord, I thank You for being omniscience. Father, I ask that You would look upon Thalia right now. You are El-Shaddai, the God who is more than enough. You are Elohim, an almighty and immortal God. You are Jehovah Shalom. God, you are her peace. You are Jehovah Shammah, the God who is always there. You, Lord, are Jehovah Rophe, our healer. Heal her heart today, God. Heal the very wound in her heart. Send Your angels, God, to bind up her broken heart. For it was for this purpose, God, that You sent Your son Jesus to heal those who are hurting." His hands continued to clutch mine. "Look down upon her now, God, and see the need. Most of all, Lord, give her understanding. God, she doesn't understand why this had to happen. She doesn't understand, Lord, why this had to be. She doesn't understand, Lord, why she's hurting so badly. You are God, and there's none like You. You're in control of all things. God, You have to do it. For her sake, God, do it. We know, Lord, that all things work together for our good, if we love You, according to Your purpose for our lives." He touched my face. "Wipe away every tear from her eyes. We know that the joy of the Lord is our strength. Give her back the joy that she once knew. Help her to remember that her life isn't over, Lord. Remind her that You love her, most of all. Father, these, and all blessings we ask in the precious and holy name of Your son, Jesus Christ, of Nazareth, and it is in His name that we pray this prayer." Together we said, "Amen."

"Thank you," I cried. "Thank you so much."

He kissed my forehead. "You're going to be just fine."

"Eventually." I tried smiling.

In his car we headed for my mother's house. Once again cars were lined up and down the street. Long lost cousins and friends were crowding the front lawn, all wearing black, white, or shades of gray. I still hadn't called anyone so when we parked I saw shocked and surprised faces; it was as though they didn't expect to see me.

As I walked up the driveway people asked, "How are you?" I heard someone else, "Where have you been, girl?" Another voice, "Everything is all right, baby." A high-pitched voice said, "Don't worry, you're in my prayers." When Isaac and I entered the house everything and everyone went silent like there was a show about to begin.

"Hello," I said to everyone in the living room. Devon, his wife, and their children, Chance was with Yvette . . . again (hmmm), Tyann and Colin, along with his parents and also my aunts, uncles, and cousins from all across the country.

"Oh my God." Tyann jumped up and pulled me into

my old room and slammed the door behind her. "Where have you been? Do you know what you've put us through? We didn't know if you were dead or alive," she yelled at me. "And how could you just walk in here with him?"

"Whoa." I guess the show had begun. "To question one, I was at a hotel downtown. Number two, sorry for what I've put you through. Three, I'm alive. And four, I will not be discussing my personal relationship with you or anyone, not today." I paused. "I am here to celebrate our mother, who by the way gave our relationship her blessings."

"Mama knew?" She tried to contain herself. "Fine, but there have been a lot of rumors flying around here."

"Well, they talked about Jesus . . . so I'm no exception." I giggled off her comment.

She smiled. "Yeah, you're no Jesus, you're not even Mary Magdalene." She thought, "You ain't even Judas." She laughed.

We left the room. I had an hour before the limousines would arrive so I properly greeted my family. In the process of doing so a cousin that I only saw at funerals and weddings had the nerve to look at me and giggle as she said, "Girl, I went off on your no good daddy last night when he tried to tell the funeral director what he wanted and what he didn't want."

"What did you say?" I asked and that heifer repeated it with the same enjoyment. *Somebody check my blood pressure please!*

"Excuse me," I yelled above all the conversations. "There is something that I need to say before we leave for the church." In three seconds flat the room fell silent. "I'd like to share with you the last few moments I spent with Mama." I cleared my throat. "Mama was sitting on the very top of the world. I had never seen her as happy as she was the day before . . . she died." I paused and looked at my eldest brother. "She was proud of you, Devon. You are an officer in the United States Navy, you have a beautiful wife, and the only grandchildren that Mama had, she bragged about you to everyone."

I scoped out Ty. "Mama wanted a grandbaby from you so badly, and she nagged you about it every day from what I've heard." I laughed. "She appreciated and loved you and I think she thought that Colin was really her son instead of a son-in-law." She did.

I brought my attention to Chance. "Mama wanted to knock you upside your head plenty-a-days, but you were her baby. She gave you your name because you were born in the middle of one of the most difficult times of her life. The Lord had given her life another chance. She loved your strength and your headstrong attitude. She was looking forward to you graduating college next year. We all know that you'll get that record deal you want so badly, but just in case she wanted to be sure that you'd use your bachelor's degree in business to be the next Sean Combs of the music industry."

I looked at the cousin that made the remark about my father and continued. "But the highlight of Mama's life was her fiancé." Everyone looked around in shock. "Mr. Devon Banks Senior, our father, asked my mother for her hand in marriage. Though they had many ups and some extreme downs, she forgave him, she loved him, and he made her happy. He gave her something that no one else could: Devon Junior, Tyann, Chance, and me. He gave her love and happiness, and though it took him a while, he gave her his heart. If she has forgiven him along with my sister, brothers, and I . . . then I think that you all can." I added, "If you cannot find it within to forgive him the least you can do, on our behalf, is respect him. I will tolerate nothing else." I felt like I had preached a sermon. "The past is the past and I can't change it, but so help me God my future with him will be unforgettable." I eyed my rude cousin once more. "If there is another negative word spoken of him in my presence today, you will be asked to leave."

When my father and his brothers walked through the front door the family flocked around him like he was a new puppy. Isaac had to leave to prepare for the service. I said goodbye to him, walked into the kitchen, and saw Andre. "Good morning," he said.

"Hi." I opened a cabinet, got a glass, and poured out some apple juice.

"You look very nice."

"Thanks," I said, half opening my mouth.

"I know that you don't want me here," he said, "but I couldn't leave you alone."

"I'm not alone." I remembered his sarcastic voicemail. "Thanks for the message you left; that really consoled me."

"I'm sorry." He moved closer to me. "Jealousy does that to a man." Andre looked as good as the day we met, sporting a navy Ralph Lauren single breasted two button suit, with a white shirt and a navy, black, and beige tie. He took his hands from his pockets and wrapped them around me. He seemed sincere for the first time in a long time. "Sorry about the message. I should've thought before I spoke." He pulled away and looked into my face. "Is there anything that I can do to make this easier?"

Actually there was something that he could do. I

grabbed his hand and led him to Chance's old room and sat him in front of the Yamaha keyboard. Right after I moved to Philly, Andre bought a Roland RD-150 portable piano and found a new hobby. After a few lessons you couldn't tell him that he wasn't Duke Ellington. "I have a solo today and I need you to play for me."

"That's the least I can do for you." He turned on the keyboard. "So we're even now?"

"No, we'll be even after you play this song for me." I smiled back. "It's called *Farewell*, by Beverly Crawford." His expression said he hadn't heard of her. "She's a gospel singer. Just follow me." And he did. For the next thirty minutes Andre and I made music . . . together.

"The limos are here," Mama's pudgy neighbor screamed throughout the house.

"This is it." Andre looked at me.

"Thank you." I couldn't help but ask, "Do you still want the ring back?"

"I was trying to get you back when I asked for it," he admitted.

"I'll give it back," I surprised myself by saying. "I know that you paid good money for it and all."

"Just like I told you when I first met you," he smiled down at me, "economical isn't my style."

I gathered my things and made my way to the front lawn. There were five black limousines waiting in the middle of the street. The very first car was for my father, Tyann, Colin, Devon and his family, Chance and me. The rest of the family members filed into the limousines behind us and whoever was walking too slowly had to drive their own car.

Chapter 25

I Am the Resurrection, and the Life

The church parking lot was filled to capacity. The driver opened the door but I hesitated. I knew that the longer I avoided the situation the less real it would be. Finally I stepped out and when both feet were on the asphalt I said, "It feels like my heart isn't beating fast enough."

"I used to feel the same way." It was Madison. My first response was to jump back. "I'm sorry," she said as she took off her shades.

"There is nothing to be sorry about." I was happy to see her. "Just know that after this is all over I have a slap with your name on it."

"By the way," she looked at me, "if this thing goes

anywhere, I'm not referring to your kids as my sisters and brothers." She continued. "I want to be god-mother."

We held hands as the rest of my family lined up two by two to enter the church. Chance almost made me shout hallelujah when he paired up with my father at the front of the line to enter the church first.

Minister Blackwell stepped outside. "Is the family ready?" he asked the assembling crowd.

"Give us five minutes," the funeral home worker shouted from behind me. "We need everyone to pair up."

With Madison still at my side, when Isaac walked out everybody's eyes seemed to focus on the three of us to see if what Sister Thompson was spreading was the gospel truth. Isaac spoke. "Hi, Madison."

"Hi, Dad."

He grabbed my hand, the one which he had adorned with gold, touched the bracelet as a hidden message to me, and said, "Everything is going to be all right." His other hand slid down my cheek. "Take good care of her." He winked at Madi and walked away.

Shortly after, Isaac and the other members of the clergy led the procession into the church. As we stood in the lobby area I heard a man's voice come across the speakers. "Please stand as the family enters the sanctu-ary."

The organ began to play a slow beat and the drums sadly joined in. "*Oh they tell me of a home,*" a soft distin-guished alto voice cut through the speakers. The choir softly joined the woman and then the double doors of the church opened up toward my family and me.

Isaac looked back, but as quickly as he turned to me, he turned away and began to speak, his voice flowing through the speakers of the church. "Jesus said . . . I am the resurrection, and the life, he that believeth in Me, though he were dead, yet shall he live, and whosoever liveth and believeth in Me shall never die. Believest thou this?" My family and I took baby steps into the church; it was like leading cows into the slaughter-house, we had no idea what would come of us.

Isaac's voice filled the air again. "Let not your heart be troubled, ye believe in God, believe also in Me. In My Father's house are many mansions, if it were not so, I would have told you. I go to prepare a place for you. And if I go and prepare a place for you, I will come again and receive you unto myself, that where I am, there ye may be also. And wither I go ye know, and the way ye know." My family and I continued to march to-ward the unknown.

I leaned over and looked in front of the pulpit and my eyes caught a glimpse of the closed white stainless steel casket decorated with four-dozen white roses and I didn't want to take another step. Madison felt my hesi-tation and put her hand around my waist. "Step-by-step, Lia," she whispered in my ear. Beautiful flowers sur-rounded the casket, but she'd never smell their sweet aroma. Since I was a child I believed that God wasn't a cruel God, I believed that he allowed people to see their funerals, so I looked around the large building and asked weakly, "Mama, where are you?" By the time we were in the front of the church I was hot, I felt sweaty, but I wasn't. Mama was only ten feet away, the closest we've been since the night I greased her scalp. I felt myself sit down and couldn't believe that I made it without falling.

I stared at the casket and couldn't tell if what I was feeling was my blood boiling or wanting to throw up. "Mama, Mama, Mama, Mama, Mama," I repeated over and over while rocking back and forth hoping that somehow she'd come to my rescue. "Oh Mama, please." Tears kept hitting my hand. "Mama, please don't go." Madi cradled me.

I came to my senses as the choir was singing another song, but I never looked up. I closed my eyes and shortly after I heard Minister Blackwell say, "Now we'll be blessed with a solo by Thalia Tyree, the daughter of Sister Tyree." Madison nudged me. I stood and saw Andre approaching from the back of the church. I slowly walked over to the casket, placed one hand on it and whispered, "Help me, Mama." I turned to face the crowd and was given a microphone by one of the ushers.

"Good afternoon." I don't know where the words came from, but they came. "If Mama would've passed away five months ago I would've been mad. I would've been mad because at that present time she would've thought that we'd never meet again." Tears fell. "But I'm glad that before she died she knew that I changed my way of living." I remembered Mama telling me not to be ashamed, to acknowledge the Lord so I corrected myself. "I'm saved! It was always her prayer that I give the Lord a try. It was her prayer that I'd have a testimony, it was her prayer that I wouldn't die and go to hell. She wanted to know that she'd see me on the other side." My spirits were lifted. "So today I stand before you and I know that I'll see her face again, I'll hold her hands, and I'll tell her that I love her." I placed my right hand on the casket again. "Mama, someday we'll meet again and farewell will be no more." With that said, Andre played a soft prelude. I closed my eyes and for the next five minutes Beverly Crawford's song belonged to me. *"Farewell I'll miss you, never forget you."*

When I was done the spirit of God was in the house. Most of my family was on their feet and even Andre was crying. People were really moved. All I could hear was, "Hallelujah!" "Glory!" "We worship your name, Jesus!" and "Oh, thank you, Lord." I walked back to my seat and looked up into the pulpit. Isaac managed to give me the biggest brightest smile I had seen in days. I lifted my hand so that my sleeve would fall back and expose the bracelet, and when it did I ran my hand over it and smiled right back at him.

Now I don't know what happens in the rest of the world but in the dirty south we have church at funerals. Pastors don't try to give a cute, polite, or politically correct eulogy . . . they preach. Isaac stood up and started out with vigor. "Looks like we having church up in here, and that's what we should be having. This is the day that the Lord has made. This isn't a time for sadness; this is a time for worship. This is a time to tell the Lord thanks, this is a time to get right if you're still allowing the devil to lead you around by a noose. We don't have to cry for Sister Tyree, this is a celebration for her. She is where I long to be. Oh, don't you wanna go?"

"Yeah," the crowd yelled, and like in any southern Baptist church, the tambourines were already shaking and the organ playing was backing up the pastor's every word.

Isaac continued. "The songwriter says: When peace like a river, attendeth my way. When sorrows like sea billows, roll. Whatever my lot, thou hast taught me to say. It is well, it is well with my soul." He took a deep breath.

"Though Satan should buffet, though trials should come, let *this* blest assurance control. That Christ hath regarded my helpless estate, and hath shed His own blood for my soul. It is well . . . with my soul . . . It is well, it is well, with my soul." He shouted, "Is it well with your souls today?"

"Yeah." The congregation was moved.

"I don't think ya heard me." He went on. "Is it well with your soul?"

"Yeah!" most people yelled.

"Some of y'all can't get to heaven doing some of the things ya doing. Some of y'all can't get to heaven keeping the company ya keepin'. Some of y'all can't get to heaven living in sin like ya do. I said is it well, is it well with your soul?"

"Yeah." The crowd was jumping.

Isaac shouted, "I don't know about you, but I came to praise the Lord. I don't know about you, but I came to jump for joy. I don't know about you, but I came to worship. If you came to worship lemme see ya stand to ya feet." It didn't take much for him to stir up the crowd; half the audience was standing way before he asked them to. "To be absent from this body is to be present with the Lord." Isaac was already on fire. "If you wanna go to heaven let me hear you say yeah."

"Yeah."

"Say yeeeeeeeeeeeeeah."

"Yeah."

"If you plan on making heaven your home, there is no better example to follow than the lady laid before us today." He spoke with strength. "Our dear sister is resting in the bosom of my God. She is walking around Heaven with the angels. She's asking Moses about the Red Sea. She's listening to Shadrack, Meshack, and

Abednego talk about how they walked out of the blazing furnace and didn't need treatment for any burns. She's sitting at the table with Jesus." He continued. "We're gonna have church in here, 'cause she wouldn't want it any other way." He let the congregation get their praise on while he flipped through the pages of his Bible. "Let the church say Amen."

"Amen," we all said.

He spoke a little more calmly. "If you would've told me last Sunday that I would be giving a eulogy for Sister Tyree, I would've told you that you were..." He stopped and looked down for a second before he continued. "I would've told you that you were out of your mind." Isaac then began his thirty-five minute sermon. It was phenomenal and resulted in more than ten people turning their lives over to the Lord. After the prayer for the new saints, the choir sang Kirk Franklin and the family's *Can You Hold Me Now*.

The funeral home staff made their way to the front of the church, and when they opened the casket, pain was unleashed throughout the church. Immediately I heard moans and throaty groans. People on the opposite side of the church stood and made what seemed to be almost an eternal line to get their last glimpse of Mama.

"We're going to get through this," I heard my father telling Chance. "Just take a deep breath." Chance used his asthma pump as my dad spoke. Madison's strength was gone; she was now leaning on me. I was scared. Who would be there for me? My tears overflowed as the thought of seeing my mother's lifeless body came closer. I wanted to run out of the church. In just a few minutes the reality of what I still hadn't come to grips with would hit me in the face and then they'd take her away, and bury her. "No," I yelled and within seconds Isaac was at my side.

He knelt in front of me and I wrapped my arms around his neck. "I can't do this." I'm sure it was my paranoia that made me feel like the funeral stopped so that everyone could look at us. Forget what people would say, I needed him. "Look at me," he said, but I didn't. "Look at me," he said again and finally I looked up. "You don't have to do anything alone." He touched my chin. "We'll do it together." I couldn't hear anything but his voice. I saw people crying and throwing their hands up, a few people even passed out, but I couldn't hear anything. He kept saying, "We'll get through this."

Soon the spooky tall men dressed in all black began pushing the coffin in my direction. My body began to shake and my breath became shallow. "I'm right here." He pulled my body up from the seat.

It was time! I looked into my mama's face and she looked so peaceful that I think I remember smiling as I said, "Open your eyes, Mama." I bent to her ear. "Do you know how much I love you?" She didn't answer me so I asked again. "Mama, do you know how much I love you?" Her lips didn't move. "I'd die for you, Mama." She looked five years younger. "Mama?" She had a smile on her face. "Mama, I have your glasses." She was wearing her white dress proudly, as though she had put it on herself. "Mama." I touched her hand. "Mama, answer me." I couldn't deny it any longer; she was gone. At this very moment death proved that it really was big and bad. It could take Mama away. I kissed her on the cheek and felt Isaac's hand move up and down my back. My tears dropped on her dress. "I'll be good to him, I promise." I touched her hair. "I'll always love you."

I sat back and tried to block out Tyann's screaming.

The choir began singing and I joined them. *"I am free, praise the Lord I'm free."*

My dad was the last person to look into her face. He kissed her gently then slipped a piece of paper by her side. He unhurriedly placed the satin material over her face, and with the assistance of the funeral home staff, he sealed the top of the casket closed, and barely made it to his seat before he yelled, "Sleep on, baby, sleep on." Mama was back with her Father, who loved her best.

Chapter 26

How to Get a Minister 101

Five months after the funeral I still had major issues. One, I couldn't find a permanent elementary teaching job anywhere in Miami. I was forced to drive from school to school working as a substitute. I subbed for a high school English teacher, Ms. Paige Patrick, for a week after she resigned, admitting to carrying on a sexual relationship with an eighteen-year-old student. I pretended not to be interested in the details of the story when the teachers whispered about it in the break room, but the truth was that after learning from Ms. Patrick's former students what the boy, Theo, looked like, I went on Amazon.com and ordered and read the tell all book, *Fly On The Wall.* You think Isaac and I have a story. Man . . . they had it bad for each other. I read the book in two days.

Anyway, my second issue was missing Mama. There were still days where I picked up the phone to tell her to watch a certain television program, find out what she was cooking, or to ask her—on one of the five chilly days we get a year in Miami—if she had her heater on. Yep, my heart couldn't let go of the person it held closest for twenty-five birthdays, Christmases, Mother's Days, New Year's Eves, and twenty-five Thanksgivings. I had had too much of her, and just like anything the body is addicted to, I craved her . . . but my supply had run short.

The last issue was falling in love with Isaac. He helped to balance the scale that seemed to weigh high with insanity on the opposite side. I thanked God every single day for him. Isaac and I made no secret about our relationship. He has brought me ten giant steps closer to God and one small step closer to choking Sister Stride, who looks at me out of the corner of her eyes during church services as if I was about to steal her Wal-Mart clearance rack purse.

Sex is the best thing about our relationship. Why? Because there is no sexual relationship between Isaac and me. Yet he satisfies me in ways a brotha with eleven inches and two vibrators couldn't. We're not abstaining from sex because we fear that it could ruin our bond, or because we fear HIV, or because I'm no longer on birth control. We haven't had sex because we connect on a level so spiritually intense that the Lord just won't allow it. Don't get it twisted, he has been stimulated by my touch, kiss, or words, and God knows that I have experienced extreme arousal, but he means so much more to me than a half a cup of sweat and two tablespoons of sperm. I was willing to wait.

It was Friday night and Isaac and I had made plans to go to a park and have a picnic, but due to rain we called it off. Instead he arrived at my apartment with DVD's and Chinese food. I spread a blanket on the floor, and played Will Downing's *Invitation Only* CD, which I had planned to rock at the park.

"Come here, baby." He beckoned to me as the prelude to Will's *Angel* played. Isaac held me around the waist and glided slowly with me in his arms, and though he wasn't much of a singer, sung the words to me. *"I hold you near in my arms."* He smiled. "You're my angel."

Later as I enjoyed my honey chicken, egg roll, and pork fried rice. I bit into something and almost cracked my teeth. "Ouch." There was something in my rice. I brought a napkin up to my mouth and I spat everything into it. When I looked into the napkin and saw something gold and shiny, too many Meg Ryan movies had me believing that this could be my magic moment.

With Isaac watching the entire thing unfold I was blushing, my adrenaline was pumping, and I was two nanoseconds away from yelling "yes," when it turned out to be the latch from a watch. The thought of it slipping from the wrist of a big greasy cook almost made me vomit. Issac took the piece of metal as I laughed at my naivety before confessing to him what I had assumed.

"So you thought it was a ring?" he asked with a chuckle.

"Yeah," I was embarrassed, "but only for a split second."

Isaac raised his right hand above the table, shook it, and a gold watch fell from his wrist. He reached over and picked up the latch and said, "Though it seemed like I was fully functional I wasn't, I was very much broken." He clicked the latch into place and my heart jumped. "But then you came along and gathered my wounded spirit, my weaknesses, and my broken pieces and made me whole again."

He got on one knee and I was trembling; this couldn't be real. "You complete me." He reached into his pocket, pulled out a ring, and slipped it onto my ring finger. He smiled. "Thalia, will you marry me?"

"Yes, yes." I was crying just like Meg Ryan always did. "Yes."

We decided right there in my mini-living room that our engagement wouldn't be a year long, not even six months. We wanted a breakfast wedding in two months.

Three Sunday's later Sister Miller read our wedding invitation during the morning announcements. "You are cordially invited to attend the joining together of Reverend Doctor Isaac Michael Flack to Miss Thalia Michelle Tyree . . ." The members were quite joyful as they pretended to be surprised. They didn't want us to think that it could've possibly been them who had been a part of the ongoing gossip.

From bench to bench hearts broke in Mount Pleasant that day. The older sisters cried out of what seemed like joy, but I was certain that it was because of the lost hope of their unmarried daughters that they were grooming for Isaac. And all of the single women ages twenty to forty-five in expensive pastel suits, big hats, five-inch heels, and three hundred dollar purses with degrees in Pastors Wifeology and studying How To Get a Minister 101, stared at me the way a runner who placed seventy-third in a marathon would at the gold medal winner.

I was marrying Isaac! Because he had been such a positive leader in the community, businesses were lined up to offer their services to the man who had done so much for them. I had florists, caterers, and banquet establishments calling me for weeks. The only money I spent was the $2,300 I collected from the sale of Andre's ring, and with that I bought my dress and everything else needed to make me the most beautiful bride in the state of Florida on that particular day.

Bishop Ducreay was marrying us and was footing the bill for our honeymoon. The only information I was told was to pack tropical for two weeks. I didn't care where we were going but I did go insane in Victoria Secrets thinking of my first nights in bed with Isaac. My only worry was that I could possibly be on my period on my wedding day. That would suck!

Two weeks before the wedding Isaac was in Atlanta speaking at The Southeastern Regional Pastor's Fellowship Meeting. Madison and I were leaving David's Bridal with the bridesmaid's dresses when Tyann phoned out about her kitchen catching on fire. I walked into her house frantically expecting the smell and look of smoke, but all I got was, "Surprise!" Tyann and Madi teamed up to throw me a bridal shower to top all others. It was also a time for Tyann to announce too that she was a month and a half into her first pregnancy.

I had a ball! In fact, I laughed so much that I giggled up a headache right before the night was done. "Madi, you got any Advil, Excedrin, or anything for a headache?"

"No." She frowned like she felt my pain. "You should probably get some rest. We've been going all day."

"Colin," Tyann yelled upstairs, "bring something down for Lia's headache, please." Madi and I started loading her car with the many gifts, but thanks to so many generous friends we needed another vehicle.

"Colin," Tyann whined again as she washed the last of the glasses, "when you come down please put the rest of the gifts in the Jag, I'm going to follow Lia home."

"Yes, dear, yes, dear, yes, dear," Colin said sarcastically. "Is there anything else, dear?" He dropped the pills in my hand. "Can I bite your toenails for ya?" he joked as he kissed her neck.

"Ty, you can bring them in the morning if you want." I popped the pills and drank the rest of my juice. "When I get home I'm going to crash." I looked at the clock; it was fifteen minutes until midnight.

"No, I'll be right behind you guys," Tyann promised as Madi and I left.

Madi helped me rush the boxes and bags into my place and then was out of sight. My headache was gone but suddenly I felt pretty darn dizzy. My vision was blurring in and out and suddenly making it up the five steps to my bedroom door was unattainable. I stumbled onto the couch and just laid there with my eyes closed.

I woke up after one in the afternoon and rolled over in bed to answer the phone. "Hello?" my voice cracked.

Tyann complained. "You can't still be in bed."

"Well, I am." As I pulled the covers over my nude body I felt like I needed to drink a gallon of water.

"I'll let you get back to bed," Tyann said, "but when you get up see if Colin dropped his phone over there last night when he brought your gifts. Bye."

I straightened up to call her back to tell her that Colin never made it to me last night and if he wasn't there and not answering his phone she needed to dial 911. But when I sat up it felt like my period was on. I checked my sheets for blood but I found grayish stains instead. Out of my opened room door I saw boxes that Madi and I didn't bring in. And in my haste to get out of bed my feet knocked from beneath the covers a BlackBerry 8700c, Colin's phone.

"What in the hell?" I searched myself for answers and kept coming up with falling asleep on the sofa. "Wait a minute," I thought. "Nah, that couldn't happen." But if anybody knew the scent of sex . . . a twenty-five-year-old woman who hadn't done it in five months would. Sex was the smell I came up with after rubbing my fingers between my thighs. In tears I stared at that Blackberry and couldn't believe that Colin, my ex, and now my sister's husband, had drugged and had sex—no, raped me two weeks before I married the man I had been saving myself for.

For hours I rehearsed how I would tell someone . . . but whom? Telling Isaac would mean telling him everything since college, if I was trying to be truthful. Plus, Isaac would want to 'lay hands' on Colin and it wouldn't be to pray, although Colin might need prayer when it's all said and done. If I confided in Madi she would tell her father. And Tyann, my pregnant sister and matron of honor, was the last person I wanted to talk to. Telling anyone would cast a shadow on my wedding day.

If I wasn't going to the police with this then something as evil as this was better off unsaid. That was my decision. Since I had nothing other than a bad feeling about what occurred I would pretend that it never did. Before I could change my mind I did the one thing they asked rape victims not to do . . . I took a shower, washing away all evidence. Then I filled the sink with water and drowned that stupid phone. Then in the midst of my hysterical tears I pounded that thing with a stapler like it was attached to the devil himself.

A few days later I couldn't take anymore, I had to know. I walked right past Colin's secretary and into his office. "What did you do to me?" I asked.

"Mistress Kirkpatrick," he held a finger up toward me while leaning back in his custom-made leather executive chair. "Let me get right back to you after I check those facts, okay?" he said into the speakerphone and pressed a button. "Hey, Lia, I'm glad to see that you're feeling better."

"Cut the B.S." I wanted to spit on him. "I'm not stupid, Colin, I know that something happened on Saturday night."

"Yeah, your bridal shower at my house." He loosened his tie.

"What did you do to me?" I asked.

"What?" He had a blank look on his face. "Thalia, what are you talking about?"

"What were those pills that you gave me?" I approached him. "You drugged me didn't you?"

He laughed and put both of his hands out to imply that I was going too far. "*That* is a serious accusation." Spoken like a true lawyer. "Let's start over." He spoke calmly. "What exactly is the problem?"

"What happened on Saturday night when you came to my apartment?" I tried to keep my voice down.

"Okay." He scratched his head as if struggling to remember. "The apartment door was unlocked and you were passed out on the sofa. I figured you were tired so I just brought the gifts in and left." He added, "Oh, do you know what the crime rate is like in that neighborhood? You should never leave your door unlocked."

"So how does that explain your phone under my sheets?" I crossed my arms over my chest and waited.

"Damn, is that where I dropped it?" he asked. "I carried you to bed. I figured you didn't normally sleep on the couch." He chuckled. "Girl, you've gained some weight since college. I couldn't put you over my shoulders like I used to do."

"Shut up." Tears streamed my face. "I know what you did, Colin."

"Lia," he stepped toward me, "what in the hell is going on with you?"

I looked into his eyes. "You raped me."

"Oh, what the fuck?" He threw his hands up. "I mean . . . are you serious?"

"You know that I'm serious!" I yelled. "The pills that you gave me were . . ."

". . . from Tyann's cabinet for Christ's sake," he finished my sentence and snatched up the phone's receiver. "Call her and ask her. Call her and tell her all of this crazy bullshit you're in my office with." He paused. "I will even tell her about college to get you to believe that I am telling you the truth about what happened on Saturday night."

I didn't know what to think, feel or do. Was he lying? I put the phone back into its cradle. "I don't want to tell anyone, I just want to know for myself what happened."

"Think about it, Lia." He stepped closer. "Why would I go through all of that for a pussy I know that I can still have . . ." he whispered, "*if* I wanted it?"

"Yeah?" His comment angered me so I came back with a lie. "Well, when the police come around be sure to tell them just how much you *don't* want it." I moved to walk away but he grabbed my arm.

"You didn't complain about it that night in college, you knew what you were doing, you wanted it," he said in an almost inaudible whisper. "If the police were looking for me they would've found me at home right after your *examination* on Saturday." Then Colin loudly reminded me, "Sweet thang, you're standing in a law firm, talking to a lawyer, with no proof and no evidence because I'll bet my next lawsuit that you trashed my phone and your sheets." He was right, and he smiled, winked, and cleared his throat. "So, if I were the kind of guy to do such a thing, it sounds like you're the type that would've enjoyed it." He let go of me and walked back to his desk and pressed a button. "Mira, will you get Mistress Kirkpatrick back on the line for me, please." He turned to me. "Tell yourself that it was Tylenol, and the world will be a better place."

I walked out of his office feeling worse than I did when I arrived. I didn't know if I had proven a point or pointed out the fact that I was losing it.

Chapter 27

Trumpet Voluntary

It was for the best that I didn't have any recollection of the incident. It made it easier to forget. And with the wedding just a day away it wasn't hard to forget much. Rehearsal started at noon and was done by three. The decorators arrived at the church and I trusted them to do what we discussed. The reception was being held at the country club where Isaac golfed and that was already squared away.

After the rehearsal Isaac walked me out of the church. "So this is it, huh?" We wouldn't see each other again until the final hour. "I'll be seeing you at ten sharp, right?"

"I'll be here at nine forty-five if I can." I giggled.

He touched my cheek. "What if we hadn't stopped in the same Starbucks at the same time in the same airport?"

"I ask myself that question every day." I paused. "And I'm thankful that there isn't an answer."

Madi was honking her horn, so he gave me a quick peck. "I'll see you at ten in the morning."

"Nine fifty-nine." I blushed and said goodbye.

My friends and I had a four-car caravan and a full day ahead of us to get pedicures, manicures, waxes, and facials. Vette parted with us at the nail shop to get her house ready for the six women that would be spending the night, but we didn't get there until well after nine. As we entered the house balloons were everywhere and Vette handed each of us gift bags that read "Thalia's Last Night." Big fluffy pillows covered the living room floor so we all gathered there.

After most people had champagne, Vette yelled, "Okay, we're going to play the ABC game."

"What?" Madison asked.

She passed around already filled champagne glasses. "In order to play everyone has to down their glass right now." She handed me a large glass of water. "Well, everyone except the bride." She smiled at me. "She doesn't drink anymore." They clapped their hands as if I used to be a lush. Well, maybe I was. "Thalia will have to drink a champagne glass of tomato juice, which she hates, to make up for it. And Tyann, you too. I heard it's good for pregnant people."

"How do we play?" Ty asked.

Vette continued. "We're going to go around the room and in ABC order, you'll have to say the name of a person you've been sexual with that at least one person in the room knows. For instance," she pointed at Victoria, "if you got the letter H, you'd say Henry. If you take longer than five seconds or refuse to call a name you have to drink the entire glass."

"How did you know about Henry?" Victoria asked.

"I got it," Tiffany smiled and started the game herself. "A, ah let's see, Allen," she said quickly.

"B," Victoria said nervously. "Gosh, I can't call his name here." She downed her second glass of Veuve Clicquot champagne.

Vette called Vicky out. "You might as well call Brandon's name, I know he gave you that Rock of Gibraltar." It was now her turn. "C." She pretended to think. "Chance."

"What!" Tyann and I asked in unison. "Chance?"

"C'mon, y'all know that your baby brother is fine," she said. "We've been together since the funeral."

Madi laughed. "You want me to slap her for you?"

"You're always trying to slap somebody," I joked. "Don't worry I haven't forgotten that one that I owe you." I turned to Vette. "Take good care of my baby." I smiled.

"Okay, the letter D." Patty, a former co-worker yelled, "Damion."

"Oh, now the truth comes out," Krystal said to Patty.

"E is for Eduardo Espinosa, baby." Krystal was representin' her son's father who was now in jail.

"F." Tara hid her face in her hands with a smile, and then she swallowed the champagne in two seconds.

It was Sandra's turn. "Gabriel." She giggled. "It was so damn good."

Yvette shocked us all by saying, "Hans."

"Oh my God, you mean your old boss?" Krystal asked.

"Yes, ma'am." Yvette had to be feeling a buzz to let that out of the bag.

"You mean the Arab guy?" Madison asked.

Vette said, "Yeah."

"Oh my word," Madi said. "Wasn't he from Afghanistan or Uzbekistan?"

Vette corrected her. "Hans is from Pakistan."

"One of those Stans." Madi sucked her teeth. "How could you trust those suicide bombing motherf . . . "

"Madi, you got the letter I." Tyann tried to move on with the game.

"I?" Madi was in deep thought. "Irene." Most people in the room were in shock, but we moved right along as though Madison had said Ivan.

"J! Oh no," Tiffany blushed. "I can't put myself out there, fill my glass."

Vette brought out a platter of Buffalo wings, club sandwiches, and chips and we ate like pigs. The Name Game went around the alphabet four times and they all had at least five more glasses of champagne each, and I had three glasses of tomato juice. The Name Game came back around to Tyann with the letter W. Tyann refused to call a name and opted for the thick glass of juice instead.

"Damn! No W, Ty?" Madi, the drunkest, said. "Everybody has fucked a Willy."

"Not me," Tyann said.

Madi continued. "You act like you were a virgin before you married Colin."

"How do you know that I wasn't?" Tyann asked, not knowing what Madi knew.

"A man that likes his dick sucked that much," Madi smiled, "would never marry a virgin."

"Shut up." Ty had to regret sharing her sexual secrets with Madi at the bridal shower, but continued jokingly about Madi's growing closet of women. "Well, from the sound of your inventory at least I won't have to worry about him asking you to do it."

Why did I mess around and get stuck with the letter C?

"Put that bastard on front street, Lia," Madi slurred. "If you don't I will."

"What?" I asked and hope that Madi's alcoholic banter was meaningless. "David." I said trying to slide by.

"No not D, you have the letter C." Madi stood up. "Put that muthafucka on blast."

"Who?" Tyann asked. "Spill it."

"No more drinks for this chick." I laughed Madi's antics off. "I don't know who you're talking about."

"Oh no?" She smiled. "I'm sick of hiding this, Lia, people need to know." She cleared her throat. "When she was a sopho . . . "

Vette cut in, "Sophomore in high school she had sex with Craig," Vette finished Madi's sentence. "Big deal." She glared at Madi. "You need to lay your drunken ass down somewhere and stop talkin' people's business." Vette had just saved my behind from a secret I didn't even know she knew.

"Oh my God!" Tyann was in shock. "Sister Goodman's son Craig?"

"Yeah." I never thought I would ever be so glad to tell a lie. "No questions please, that was a long time ago."

I woke up at five in the morning puking up all the tomato juice that Vette forced me to drink during her stupid game. I was too nervous to go back to bed; the hairstylist was scheduled to arrive at five thirty and the photographer was due in by seven.

The beautician arrived, and in no time I had a soft and beautiful pin up. My tiara and veil made me feel like all I needed was a throne. My friend Tara, a makeup artist, did my face. So by the time the photographer showed up I was already bride beautiful, and it seemed as though in just minutes I had to put on my dress.

Jeremiah Clarke's *Trumpet Voluntary* filled the air and everyone stood to their feet as the doors of the cathedral opened to my father and me. The church looked like a wine and platinum colored heaven. The arch, the candelabras, the silk fabric draping the pews, the huge floral arrangements, everything was a dream. And in my platinum, strapless, satin, A-line gown with beaded lace at the neckline and split overskirt I felt like Cinderella's bigger more beautiful sista walking into the ball. And straight ahead was my Prince Charming. Isaac stood in front of the arch smiling at me.

I tried to hold back tears but only death could keep me from it. My father and I slowly marched to the front of the church. Isaac was truly the most handsome groom I had seen in all of my days.

"Dearly beloved, we're gathered here today to join this man and this woman in holy matrimony . . . " I stared blankly at Bishop; I was too excited to understand what he was saying. Minutes later we exchanged vows and then rings and by that time I wanted to yell, "Honeymoon!"

Bishop Ducreay said, "Well, here comes the part most of you have been waiting for, so get out your cameras and be certain that your flash is on," he joked. "Isaac, you may now," he paused, "kiss your bride." Isaac reached for the bottom of my veil and lifted it above my head. He slowly wrapped his hands around my waist and I moved closer to his smile. Our lips locked and we were now completely blessed to do so.

After our kiss he stared down at me. "The words I love you suddenly don't seem like enough to say anymore," he said.

"Jinx." I put my arms around his neck and closed in for our second kiss as husband and wife.

There was a Rolls Royce waiting with our names "bride and groom" on it outside of the church. As the driver closed the door I jumped in Isaac's lap and tried getting him to tell me about the honeymoon. "So where are we resting our heads tonight?"

"On pillows," he joked.

"Come on," I begged. "Please tell me."

"I'll tell you on the plane."

"Oh, so that rules out the cruise I thought we were going on." I was in deep thought. "How long is the flight?"

"Pretty long." He wasn't going to tell me.

Thirty minutes later we arrived at the banquet hall and the mistress of ceremonies named everyone in the bridal party as they entered. She then asked everyone to stand for the entrance of the bride and groom as Musiq Soulchild's *Love* played. When we started walking across the dance floor Isaac stopped me. "May I have this dance, Mrs. Flack?"

The crowd clapped as I nodded yes. He held me in his arms as though I was a long lost toy he'd never part with again. We sung the words into each other's ears and floated around the dance floor. I knew that I would fall even deeper in love with him as the days and years went by.

We sat down at our special table and as breakfast was served I saw Sister Stride being ushered in by her grandson. When she sat down and looked over at us I gave her my biggest Christian smile and wondered if she called Sister Deborah Baker with the good news. In the midst of my gloating Isaac leaned over to me and whispered, "This dress looks like it might be hard to get you out of."

I flirted, "All you have to do is pull one string, brotha."

"Whoa." He smiled. "How about skipping breakfast then?" he joked.

"No way, honey." I blushed. "You'll need all of your nutrients tonight."

Finally, the reception was almost over. My brides-maids ushered me to the ladies room to help me out of my dress and all of the other things holding me to-gether. Vette helped me into a beige two-piece linen skirt set and Madi slipped on my new sandals while Tyann touched up my hair. I finished up by touching up my makeup.

They followed me with my bags, but when I caught a glimpse of my husband standing next to the limousine my legs couldn't move fast enough. I was ready for the day to be over and our life to begin. The driver took my four pieces of luggage, we said goodbye to our family and friends, and then crawled inside.

"Alone at last." I crashed onto the backseat.

"You're not tired already are you?" He pulled my head to his chest.

I smiled. "Tired of sharing you."

"Be careful what you wish for," he said.

"What do you mean?"

"From here on out it's just you and me, kid." He squeezed me and kissed my forehead.

Chapter 28

You Don't Have to Beg

Anxiety was killing me as we approached the ticketing counter. The American Airline clerk passed Isaac our boarding passes and said, "American Airline's flight number one five four seven to Los Angeles is scheduled to board through gate D thirty-three."

"We're going to Los Angeles?" I was thrilled but not as excited as I would've been had we been going to Tahiti.

"Yep," he smiled.

Halfway into the flight my head fell onto Isaac's shoulder and I was out like a light. When I woke up the pilot was briefing the passengers on the current weather conditions in Los Angeles. Within twenty minutes the plane was on the ground and Isaac looked at his watch and said we needed to hurry.

"What's the rush?" I was disoriented and needed to stand still for a minute but Isaac insisted that we keep moving. "What's the rush?"

He stopped and smiled. "Don't you want to get to Hawaii?"

"Hawaii?"

"Yep, our plane to Honolulu leaves in forty-five minutes." He pulled out the tickets.

I yelled, "No way."

"Come on." He grabbed my hand. We ran all the way to the gate, and thank God we did because the plane was already being boarded.

For the first hour of the trip Isaac and I read an article together about the top one hundred romantic things a couple can do together for under $20. We laughed at about seventy of them but promised to give the rest a try.

Soon Isaac laid his head against the back of his seat, reclined his chair, and closed his eyes. An hour later I heard the pilot's voice over the speakers. "Ladies and Gentlemen, we have been warned of some turbulence up ahead so I'm turning the fasten seat belt sign back on." He sighed. "Once we've passed the weather and all is well we'll turn it off and you'll be free to roam the cabin once more. For now, and for your safety, we'd like for everyone to remain seated. Thank you."

I always hated those announcements. I always felt like the pilot was saying, Look people, I don't know if we're going to make it through, so just sit down, shut up, and buckle up so that if we crash all of your remains will be found in one general area and your family will be able to give you the proper burial. My heartbeat accelerated and my palms got sweaty. I purposely bumped into Isaac to wake him up. "Are you okay?" he asked.

"Not really."

He sat straight up. "What's wrong?"

"They're expecting bad weather ahead," I said nervously.

"God is in control." Isaac wasn't worried at all. He reached for my hand and held it. "God would never take me out of this world without allowing me to make love to you." I was about to grin but at that very moment the plane was pushed to the left and then it dropped about twenty feet. He kissed my hand and after a while the bumps and dips went away.

After a total of ten hours in the air, landing anywhere would've been all right with me. We made it to the Honolulu Airport and the local time was nine P.M. It was the start of our first night together as husband and wife. He informed me, "Now, from here on out I seriously don't know what's going to happen," he said. "Bishop Ducreay just told me to get to the Honolulu Airport baggage claim area."

We rushed through the airport to find the baggage claim section like we were contestants on the Amazing Race. We looked around and saw a man dressed in a black suit holding up a sign that read: Mr. and Mrs. Isaac Flack. Isaac pulled out his ID and approached the man who loaded all of our bags onto a trolley and asked us to follow him. Outside the door was a white town car. As the driver loaded our bags in the trunk I tried to find out our destination. "How long will it take us to get there?"

"Where?" the man asked.

"Where you're taking us," I said.

"About twenty minutes," he answered with a smile.

"What exactly is the name of the hotel?" I thought I had him.

The man looked confused. "Hotel?"

"The resort?" I tried another approach.

"Resort?" The man smiled. "I was told that you'd try to get it out of me, so I was given a few extra dollars to keep my mouth shut." We all laughed.

Once inside the car Isaac teased me with soft kisses all over my neck and hands and offered me a look that told me that he was anxious to finally fulfill my desires. We didn't have to talk, our bodies did, the heat took control, and passion almost consumed me as my tongue wildly examined his mouth.

The car stopped, the driver opened the door, and we found ourselves at a marina. Large boats bobbed up and down all around us. "Are we taking a boat to somewhere else?" I asked. The driver didn't answer, but continued to lead us down a dark path and then onto a wooden pier that extended at least twenty yards into the water. At the end of the pier was a one hundred foot yacht that was simply called "Majesty." A crew dressed in all white was standing at the entrance of the vessel.

The driver turned to us. "Mr. and Mistress Flack, this is the Captain Donell Michaels and the crew of the Majesty."

Isaac and I shook the captain's hand. "Welcome aboard the Majesty, she will be your home for the next two weeks while we cruise along and visit the Hawaiian Islands. My crew and I are here to serve you; your wish is our command."

Isaac and I boarded the boat and I was in awe. There was a large black sectional sofa along the wall with black and gold pillows aligned perfectly. On both ends of the couch were black end tables with elegant gold lamps. The shiny wooden floor reflected the romantic glow of the lamps, and in the distance I saw a glass table set for two with a small bouquet of live flowers as a centerpiece.

Isaac stood beside me with an expression that equaled mine. The yacht was amazing and this was just one part of it. Captain Michaels led us downstairs and showed us the kitchen where everything was black marble or sparkly silver. He also showed us the three small rooms where the crew lived and the bigger room that he called home. We walked back through the dining room and saw the crew taking our luggage to the other side of the ship. Captain Michael insisted that we visit the top deck to see the captain's dominion, which was a large spacious room filled with nautical devices and a helm to steer the vessel.

Once we were back on the second level he led us to the master suite. As my hand touched the doorknob I playfully looked back at Isaac. "Are you sure you want to do this?"

"I've never wanted anything more." His hand covered mine, pushed down on the knob, and the door sprung open. There were six lit candles scattered throughout the room, lighting it dimly.

The first thing I saw was a Jacuzzi with warm water already gathering in it along with three dozen rose pedals dancing wildly with each splash. Encased in mahogany and set in the middle of the room was a California king-sized bed with a fluffy beige comforter. It was built into the wall of the ship with a large mirror as a backboard. Mahogany drawers with golden handles lined the walls on both sides of the mirror. There was also a matching entertainment center ten feet away directly in front of the bed. To the right of it was a beige loveseat, and behind a door next to it was the master bathroom.

"Can you believe this?" I spun around and gave the room another look while making my way to Isaac. But I stopped. Suddenly I was afraid of what would happen next. After all of the flirting, wanting, and playing, the time was finally here and I was scared to touch him. "I'll be right back." I had gotten used to men that lost interest right after sex. We were married, so what happened if he lost interest? What happened if he changed? What happened if I changed? I busted a 180 degree turn into the bathroom and freaked out behind closed doors for five minutes before I got myself together. This was *my* husband!

I opened the door and walked into the soft romantic jazz of Miles Davis and now there were just two candles sparkling. The water ceased and Isaac's wet body slowly emerged from the Jacuzzi. "Come here," he commanded.

I walked toward him and when I was on the top stair of the whirlpool my hands reached for the bottom of my blouse. As it fell to the ground the cool air rushed to my chest and my nipples hardened beneath my lacy bra. To the slow melody floating through the speakers I removed my skirt. I zipped it down and slid it slowly down my thighs to my ankles and stepped out of it, kicking it to the side. I was now standing before him in nothing but a brand new burgundy bra and matching low cut panties.

"Mrs. Flack." He smiled his approval to my body. "Mine to have and to hold from this day forward."

I was still standing on the top stair and when he stood, in the water, he was eye level with my chest. "You are stunning."

I suddenly remembered the special wedding night lingerie I spent two hundred dollars on. "I . . ." I stuttered, "I was actually supposed to change into an outfit . . ."

"Let me help you change, baby," he said, interrupting me with his wet fingertips as he enclosed my upper body and removed my bra while branding my stomach with tender kisses. He kept me silent as his hands then trailed down to my waist and so did his mouth. He kissed me softly through my panties and brought them down slowly until I was completely naked. "There," he reached for my hand and guided me into the tub, "you're all changed."

Our lips met as my nipples raked against his wet chest. My hands were draped around his neck, as his hands moved from my waist slowly down to my juicy brown butt.

His lips planted seeds of pleasure down my neck, then onto my chest. He found my nipples and licked and sucked them to the jazz saxophonist's teasing tone. I thought I would pass out in the water and drown. With one hand bracing my back and the other holding my supple breast steady, he moaned gently and my imagination ran away.

My hands dove underwater like a submarine. When I made my way to his lonely treasure his body quivered and his lips went dead on my sensitive peak, but as he eased into the feeling, his mouth came alive again. My hands clung to and stroked his thickness, not too hard, but not too gently either. The soft jazz moved our bodies, yet we were making a song of our own.

Slowly his hand slipped beneath me and his thumb pressed against my swollen pressure point. He stepped backward taking my body with him. He sat down in the Jacuzzi and as I stood before him he purposefully stared into my face to view the pleasure he was inflicting.

He rubbed my lower lips rigorously; I couldn't contain the ecstasy that he stirred. "Oh please!" I tried to whisper, but there was nothing soft about it. Loving what he felt, his finger began traveling inside, deeper and deeper every time. "Oh, Isaac," I moaned. "Please." I didn't know what I was begging for but I said it over and over again. "Please," I whimpered. "Please," I groaned. "Please," I begged him once again as I climbed onto him with both hands on his shoulders.

"You don't have to beg," he said, kissing my lips. "There's nothing I want more than to give this to you." He held his black stallion steady, so that it wouldn't buck, prance, or throw me off. "Make love to me, Thalia," he said and when his eight inch stranger knocked on my door, I didn't look through the peephole, or ask, "Who is it?" I just opened up and allowed him in . . . it must've been cold out . . . he was trembling. He filled me to capacity in depth and width.

The jazz tune had a strong drummer and my body rose and fell to the slow but entrancing beat. I opened my eyes to find Isaac sweating and as his sweat beads dripped to the water they seemed to sizzle. Without blinking or looking away he stared at me as I rode him. His look challenged me so I rolled my hips, wiggled, and shook my body until all of him was mine.

The Jacuzzi jets silenced and so did the song. We became the music as our lips met and we moaned, grunted, and grinded until our bodily oils became one with the water around us and I collapsed on his chest. *That was off the chain!* I thought to myself.

He traced my mouth with his damp fingers and I playfully pulled two of them between my lips and sucked them. "Umph, umph, umph." He bit his bottom lip and smiled. His *oral* curiosity was peaked and when he stood up I satisfied it for him.

Chapter 29

Aisle Seven

Isaac should've come with an eleven year warning. Before our first night together was over Isaac had me screaming his name and digging my nails into his back. There were a few times when I was scrambling up the bed trying to catch my breath. He put me to sleep in the fetal position, and I was sore in joints I only thought horses had. On top of that, my body's time clock was out of whack. I was up at six A.M. Hawaii time, which was noon in Miami. The boat rocked and my stomach ran up to my mouth. I bolted to the bathroom and whenever I thought I was finished vomiting the boat did something dumb again and left me worse than I was before. My stomach was up and down for ten minutes.

"Are you okay?" Isaac asked through the door.

"A little seasick." I didn't want him to worry. "I'll be okay."

"Are you sure?" he asked.

"I'm positive." I started brushing my teeth, and then

I looked in the mirror and was surprised to see that my hairstyle survived the night. "Just give me a second."

I exited the bathroom and saw two trays full of breakfast foods, fruits, and fresh flowers on the bed. "Awh, thank you, honey," I greeted him with a smile.

"Thank *you*." He hugged me.

"What did I do to deserve this?" I asked playing innocent.

"What didn't you do?" He chuckled.

When we were done eating I rested our trays on the floor and lay back on bed. He sprung up. "There is something I didn't get to taste."

I looked down on his tray. "Baby, you ate everything."

"Shh." His hands reached down and untied my robe, spreading it open beside me like wings. He trailed my stomach with kisses, and once he reached my pleasure patch he opened my legs wider. "Here it is." His fingers parted my gates and his tongue playfully plucked my knob like it was a string on a guitar. I reached for his head and then felt his nose up against me and couldn't help grinding into it. I moaned deeply when his tongue dipped into me repeatedly.

He was so gratifying that I couldn't handle it. "Stop," I groaned. Either he didn't hear me or he knew that I secretly meant that no one had ever brought me to that level with just their mouth. He pulled on me hard and my hands crashed onto the bed as my love came down and landed on his lips.

His mouth glistened and as he climbed my feeble body I pulled his pants down and he was ready. I guided his body down into mine and watched his eyes roll back into his head as I folded around him. His strokes were long and deep. "You feel like a dream," he whispered while filling my body up over and over again. Soon he flipped me onto my stomach and from this angle I had to bury my face in a pillow to mute my cries, or the crew might call the Coast Guard to rescue me. From the back his movements were fast and rough. Before long he crashed into me, sending both of our bodies into wild convulsions.

After our shower we retired in the living room area, sat on the couch, and watched the tropical glory slowly drift by from a mile away. While drinking a virgin strawberry daquiri my husband sat between my legs and rubbed my feet.

The next morning I woke up to see Isaac next to the bed doing sit-ups, side bends, and squats. The popular saying 'stand by your man' couldn't mean *that* early in the morning. "Good morning, Mr. Fitness," I joked.

He was stunned to hear my voice. "Did I wake you?"

"No, I've been watching you for a few minutes."

"We're docked in Maui, I went for a jog on the beach." His eyes opened wide. "It's beautiful out there."

"Why didn't you wake me?" I was a little disappointed that he saw a bit of the island without me. "What time is it?"

"A little after eight," he said. "You want breakfast?"

The word breakfast took my mind straight to eggs and the thought of eggs brought on the smell and left me nauseous. "No, thank you."

We spent our first day in Maui bike riding, walking on the beach, and swimming in the crystal clear water. The island was breathtaking; the word tropical doesn't even begin to describe it. There was something about the combination of palm trees and mountains that set my soul on fire.

While on the beach Isaac befriended a sand crab and chased me up and down the beach with it. I screamed, shrieked, and almost cried trying to get away from him; we looked like two big kids. Later we spent an hour making the world's most ugly sand castle, and to end our day we watched the sunset while lying together in a hammock hung between two trees.

"Where do you see us in about five years?" Isaac asked.

I thought for a moment. "I see us together in the living room snuggled up watching a movie and sneaking a kiss before we hear five-year-old footsteps dashing around the corner saying, 'Mommy I can't sleep'."

He tightened his grip on me. "If the kid is five, that means we need to be starting on that right now." He kissed my neck.

"Oh, that's right." I changed my mind. "Actually we can wait a few years before we start."

"Well," he frowned, "I don't want to be seventy-five years old at a high school graduation," he said. "Let's face it; I'm old enough to be *your* father." He tried to smile. "I don't want to be too old to help you out, I want to raise them with you."

"Me, a mother? Now?" The last time I came close to changing a soiled diaper was when I experimented on Chance and I got a whooping for emptying the whole bottle of powder on him. That boy was coughing for days.

"I'm not pressuring you about this," he said. "You let me know when you're ready."

I thought hard, but not for very long. "It doesn't hurt to try." He was right, he wasn't getting any younger, and neither was I. "Let's go."

"Where?" He was confused.

"Let's go half on a baby." I guided him to the water where we didn't find Nemo, but we put on quite a show for his fish friends. We did all we could in Maui over the allotted two-day period. On the third day we were in Kauai. We were scheduled to arrive in Kauai early the fourth morning.

When the boat docked in Kauai, Isaac invited me to go jogging. I washed my face, combed my hair into a lazy ponytail, and I brushed my teeth, but the toothbrush must've went back too far into my mouth because I started throwing up in the sink. What a morning!

After putting on my socks and sneakers I met Isaac in the living room where he was doing stretches. "The last time I went running was in high school," I let him know.

"Were you on the track team?"

"Track team?" I laughed. "I was running behind the school bus when it pulled off without me."

"Did you at least catch it?" he asked.

I pouted. "No."

We jogged on the gorgeous beach for about twenty-five minutes. As the sun began coming up Isaac changed directions and ran toward a thatched hut further inland. "Let's watch the sunrise over there," he said. "I'll race you." I felt like I was on a conveyor belt, I was working but I wasn't getting anywhere.

He made it to the hut a full minute before I did. "Welcome to Kauai," he said as I saw a table for two draped in fresh white linen with three hibiscuses in a vase. There was toast, scrambled eggs, bacon, pancakes, milk, orange juice, coffee, and muffins.

I was in awe, again. "Thank you." I sat down at the table.

"Thank the crew." He laughed. "I got them up at five to get this ready."

Breakfast on the beach was amazing. When the sun was completely in the sky Isaac wanted to finish his run, and I wanted to lie back down. So we parted ways. However, on my way back to the boat I noticed a store in the distance and walked there instead.

I took a basket at the door and hit the candy aisle first, and then I picked up some deodorant, lotion, fingernail polish, polish remover, hairpins, bubble bath, and eyeliner. I also gathered a few items that Isaac needed, but my search for his brand of shaving cream took me down the wrong aisle, aisle number seven. There were all sizes and colors of condoms, KY jelly, massage oils, and at the very end of the aisle they were staring at me, calling my name and asking me 'how could I forget?' It was the devil himself disguised as a pregnancy test. My forgotten night with Colin suddenly came back to mind, along with all of the throwing up I was doing. "My last period?" I asked myself and tried to force myself to remember. "The next one should already be here."

I counted the days and thought harder and harder. "Colin," I said under my breath, "you bastard."

I rolled my eyes at the test. "I can't be," but it stared back at me like 'child please, that's what you think.' I didn't know if I was coming or going but the final word was that I was more than a week late.

I snatched the rectangular box and got in line, but just my luck the elderly man at the front of the line had a situation with an item that was supposed to be on sale. The cashier explained it to him over and over, so during her fifth explanation I ripped the barcode off of the bottom of the box and planted it and a twenty-dollar bill on the counter. "Keep the change," I told the girl.

I found the restroom, locked myself inside a stall, and when I felt warm liquid coming down, tears started down my cheeks. I had planned on telling Isaac about the Colin situation in the future. Never had I planned on telling him during our honeymoon that I was pregnant by my sister's husband who I think raped me but I don't remember it or have any proof. "Damn," I whispered to myself.

I waited five minutes before looking at the results. There were two lines. "This can't be right." I pulled up my pants, threw the test into the trash, and made my way back to aisle seven and grabbed two different types of test. I took them both and they confirmed that my life was over. I was pregnant!

Chapter 30

Take All of It

The Majesty slowly bobbed up and down, as though she was shaking her head at me, "Tsk, tsk, tsk." One side of me wanted to run to the boat, but the other side wanted to jump into the water and never resurface. My heart raced and I held back tears as I took baby steps toward the boat. I walked onboard and then into our suite where Isaac was lying down. "I thought you would've gotten here before me."

"I . . . I," I stuttered. "I went to the store."

"If I knew you were going I would've gone with you." He pulled me down on the bed. "What did you get?" I didn't answer him. I just sat there staring at myself in the mirror. "Are you all right?"

"Not really."

"Well, let the doctor get his hands on you," he joked as he sat up. "You feel hot; as a matter-of-fact you're burning up. We better get you out of all of these clothes," he suggested while removing my shirt.

"No," I uttered faintly as he kissed my neck and caressed my breasts. "Isaac, stop." I pushed him away. "Stop." I couldn't allow someone like him to touch my soiled sinful body; I felt guilty. "I can't," I told him. "I can't do this."

"What?" He was confused. "What are you talking about?" he asked. "What happened?"

"I'm sorry." I should've told him from the day it happened, I should've told someone. Maybe Colin was right . . . maybe deep down within I was the kind of girl who liked what he did. "There is something that I have to tell you." My tears were traveling from a different place this time, a place where there was no hope.

"Talk to me," he begged. "What's wrong?" By this time he was holding me.

I started from the beginning. "When I was in Tallahassee in college, I had a boyfriend. Things between us were okay until he upped and moved, and he just so happened to move to Miami and one Christmas my sister brought him to dinner. They got married."

"Colin?" he asked.

"Yeah." I continued. "We never told anyone, and he and I never talked about it, we just pretended to be strangers and over the years he has shown nothing but love and respect for my family."

Isaac thought I was done. "Baby, we all have a past." He smiled. "I'm not holding that against you, it's not like you fooled around with him after they got married. You had no way of knowing and he obviously didn't know that she was your sister."

"Tell me that you love me." I cried harder knowing that I had to continue.

"I love you." He gently pushed me back so that he could look into my face. "Is there something else?"

"Yeah." I looked away from him. "Colin and I did ecstasy once together."

He tried to cheer me. "Baby, we've all done dumb things."

"A few weeks ago, while you were in Atlanta, when Madi and Ty had the shower for me, while at their house I had a headache and Colin gave me some pills." I stopped.

"Go on." He was nervous.

"Well," I tried to catch my breath, "all of the gifts couldn't fit in Madi's car, so Tyann asked Colin to load her car up and she'd follow us. Well, apparently Colin told Tyann, because it was late and she's pregnant, not to worry about the drive, that he would do it." I wiped my eyes with my hands. "I got home and felt very woozy, but I remember passing out on the couch." Here was the dreaded information. "The next afternoon I woke up in my bed feeling as though I had had sex . . . and Colin's cell phone was under my sheets. But I don't remember anything."

"That bastard." Isaac angrily jumped up from the bed. "Please tell me that you went to the police."

I hesitated. "No, I . . ."

"No? Why not? He raped you!" he yelled, not really at me, but through hostility for Colin. "He drugged and raped you. Why didn't you go to the police?" he asked.

"The wedding was just two weeks away, and I didn't want to hurt Tyann," I cried. "I would've had to tell her the truth about knowing him in college, and I didn't want her to turn on me. I lost Mama, I can't lose her too," I wept. "Plus, because she's pregnant I didn't want to shatter the perfect world that she thinks that she has."

"But it's okay for him to shatter your world?" he asked me. "If you couldn't tell Tyann then why didn't you tell me?"

"I didn't want things to change between us. I didn't want you looking at me differently," I sobbed. "I was going to keep this to myself . . . but I just couldn't anymore."

"Fine, it's going to be okay," he comforted me. "I'm going to start making some calls right now, and he'll be in jail by the end of the day, trust me."

"Isaac, I don't want any trouble."

"Thalia, listen to yourself!" He held my head up and spoke loudly. "He raped you!"

"Isaac, there's more." I closed my eyes and in my mind I said this prayer, *Lord, I need you to come through for me one more time. Father, I need You to help to me be truthful. I'm asking You for strength, for mercy, and for understanding. Please touch his heart so that what I am about to say won't make him run away from me. Give him an abundance of patience, love, and understanding, Father. Lord, I need You right now. Amen.* "I'm pregnant," I whispered.

"What?" He froze in place. "What did you just say?"

I broke down. "I'm pregnant, Isaac."

"Pregnant?" he wanted to confirm again.

"Yes."

"I don't understand." He collapsed on the bed with his head in his hands. "How could you know all of this and not tell me?"

"I didn't know," I explained. "I found out today at the store. I went there and then realized that my period should've been on. I took three tests right in there and they all said the same thing."

"Please laugh and tell me that this whole thing is a joke," he pleaded.

When I touched his shoulder I felt his body tense up. He stood and my hand fell to my side. "I need to think." He didn't look at me; he didn't touch me or smile at me. He made a beeline to the door and before I could say anything else he was gone. I fell to the bed as though he had never wakened me and cried myself back to sleep.

When I woke up hours later I was still alone. I showered, put on a sundress, and knew what I had to do. The sun was setting and I found him sitting about a quarter of a mile down the beach staring at the water. "Is there enough room on this beach for the both of us?" I asked as I sat Indian style next to him.

"I'm sorry about walking away." He placed one hand around me. "I shouldn't have left and because of the way that I left I didn't know how to come back."

"I understand." I stared out at the sunset. "You're human, I expected you to be hurt." There was only one thing left to say. "If you don't think that you want to be with me anymore I can understand that too."

"I was hurt, there is no denying that." He paused. "But there is nothing and no one that will ever stop me from loving you." He touched my stomach gently. "This baby simply means that I'll have another part of you to love."

I was astonished. "Well, I hadn't planned on keepi . . ."

"No, I won't allow you to terminate a pregnancy just because the child isn't biologically mine." He spoke firmly. "God doesn't make mistakes. That child has every right to walk this earth and because it's yours, it's also mine."

Isaac then explained to me that I had exactly what Colin told me that I was lacking, proof. DNA testing would certainly name him as the father and for the next hour we discussed the situation and I agreed that I would pursue pressing charges on Colin, but it would be done the minute we were back in Miami. I didn't want us cutting our time in Hawaii short or weighing the remainder of our time down with talk of Colin. Truth is I don't even remember the incident . . . so it was easier to move on than other victims who relive their gruesome episode day after day.

That night we slept close, enjoying the heat our bodies emitted, but were too drained emotionally to dabble into anything else, which was fine with me.

The next morning, we were dressed and off of the boat before seven in the morning. A car was waiting at the end of the deck to take us to a motored yacht for a breakfast cruise and a whale watching excursion. I was excited about it because when I was in eighth grade I had to write a paper on humpback whales for extra credit in marine biology, and ever since I've longed to see the mammals. It was awesome!

That afternoon we took a tour of Kauai on a crowded tour trolley. Then we did some shopping. When we made it back to the boat we were both exhausted. When I got out of the shower Isaac was fast asleep and I was beginning to wonder if my news was already affecting our intimacy. I sighed, pulled the covers over me, and bumped into him on purpose. He moved but it was only to drape his hand across me and kiss my back. "Goodnight, sugar," he whispered.

The next day we went horseback riding with Keoni, our Hawaiian riding instructor and island guide. The island on foot was beautiful already, but on horseback there are no words to express its true beauty. We rode up and down two hundred foot rolling green hills, and took in dazzling views of the ocean. It was my first time on a horse and though at first the thought of sitting on a live animal and having it possibly not listening to me loomed within, I must say that I loved every second of it. We strolled through fresh water streams and alongside a few small waterfalls spilling into crystal clear pools. "This is paradise," I said to my horse.

Once we were close to the ranch Keoni took us to a private area where we found a picnic setting. He left with the horses and told us to follow the fifteen-minute asphalt trail back to the ranch whenever we were done. The rose colored blanket was adorned with a large picnic basket, place settings for two, wineglasses, a bottle of grape cider, and a small radio playing sweet Hawaiian tunes. We gladly rested on the blanket, and in the basket I found sandwiches, cookies, tropical fruit, juice, and other little things to snack on. Isaac picked up the bottle of sparkling cider. "Remember when you had that bottle of wine delivered to my hotel room in Chicago?"

"How could I forget?" I remembered it like it was yesterday. "I was so embarrassed when you knocked on my door with it in your hand."

"Tell the truth." He smiled. "Was that your way of getting me to your room?"

I wish I had been smart enough to mastermind the operation. "No." I added, "But that was your way of asking me to dinner."

He mocked himself. "You shouldn't drink this on an empty stomach." He smiled just as he did back then. "So how about joining me for dinner?"

I batted my eyelashes and spoke in a bad southern accent. "Why Mr. Flack, are you asking me out?"

"Yes," he said. "Rumor has it that you wanted me from that night."

"Rumors were wrong," I said with a smile. "I wanted you a long time before that."

We ate and enjoyed our private picnic area for another hour before we started our walk back to the ranch where the car was waiting. Once back at the yacht, we collapsed in bed exhausted again. As bad as I wanted sex I waited for him to initiate it . . . he didn't.

It was our honeymoon, but we hadn't made love since he learned of what happened between Colin and me. It had only been three nights, but I felt like an addict being forced out of a habit. I wanted to talk to him about it, but I didn't want to make it into a big deal if it really wasn't. Were we not doing it because he didn't think I wanted to, because he didn't want to, or was he truly tired from our every day outings?

The next day, Saturday, Isaac and I celebrated our first week as Mr. and Mrs. Flack. We asked Captain Michaels to take us somewhere where we could go fishing. And after we all caught enough fish we shocked the crew by telling them to take the day off. We cooked and served them our catch. It was our gift to them; they had been so good to us.

Late into the night I left the living room wanting Isaac to follow my lead, but he didn't. He and Captain Michaels were engrossed in fishing stories off of the coast of Bimini, in the Bahamas. I took a shower and before I fell asleep I made up my mind that we had something we needed to talk about the next day.

"Thalia." I felt kisses on my neck. "Baby, get up."

"Huh?" I was confused.

I peeked at the clock and it read 2:15 A.M. "Get up? What do you mean?"

He pulled the covers from my body revealing the laced navy number I had put on especially for him. "Put on your robe."

"Is something wrong with the boat?" My heart went limp.

"No." He kissed my forehead and said, "There's something that I want to show you."

"Now?" I whined.

He helped me put on my robe. "Yes, now."

I put on my slippers and followed him through the dark ship and then down the ramp. "Uh, uh! Where are we going?" I asked.

"Shh." He put his finger over his lips and grabbed my hand. Seconds later we were we strolling down the dark beach.

Away from the ship he stopped me and pointed at the sand in front of our feet. "What's so special about where we're standing?" Isaac questioned me.

I looked around. "I don't know." The moonlight didn't reveal anything out of the ordinary.

"Look again." He started removing my robe.

"What?" The chilly ocean breeze ran through the lace of my teddy and over my body as he threw my robe aside. "What's special about it?"

"Right here on the very sand we're standing on I want to make love to you." He cupped my face and kissed me and then did away with his shirt. "I can't let another night go by."

I tossed my teddy away on the sand and in the darkness his now wet fingertips told him how badly I wanted him. I helped him out of his Dockers, and without words we both fell to the earth. As he stretched out over the sand I got on my knees.

He watched me seductively, knowing that the warm moisture of my mouth would soon soothe him. I teased him with kisses on his chest and stomach, and then moved to taunt his lower region, leaving a saliva trail along the way. Finally I made it to his erect chocolate stick. I stroked it and felt it grow even more solid between my fingers. A trickle of juice slid down his mountainside and I sucked the sweet sap from his skin and worked my way upward to the source of the miniature eruption. I took him in as far as I could physically go, and his body trembled beneath me.

I aggressively licked and applied suction around the top of his dick as waves pulled in and out beneath me. Isaac uttered sounds of enjoyment, fulfillment, and encouragement. He solidified even more with every stroke of my mouth and flick of my tongue. Holding him firmly between my lips I took him on a tour of who I really was: Thaila Flack an upstanding citizen by day, freakishly satisfying by night.

"Let me feel you," he moaned. "Come here." I crawled up his body and as our lips met I slid down his pole like a fireman responding to a four-alarm fire at the White House. I grinded my body into his and he said, "Give me some more of that sweetness, baby," and pushed deeper into me. "Take it," he commanded. "Take all of it."

Later, I was on my knees looking out at the ocean as he entered me from behind. With his hands attached to my waist he pulled me back to meet him a few times until I got his rhythm. With every smack of our skin he fell deeper and deeper into the unknown depths of my love and I began calling his name to the moon and sea. He moaned loudly and kissed my back with his right hand cupped underneath my body. The pressure he applied to every stroke sent my breasts slamming into the sand. "Oh, oh yes, yes," he said and as the time came, he filled me with everything he had. Our bodies trembled and then we collapsed on the beach until hints of the sunlight poked through the sky.

Chapter 31

Lawyers and Doctors and Tears . . . Oh My!

For the next few days the majority of our time was spent rocking the boat with satisfaction. We had to make time to do other things. If the crew wasn't there I think we would've christened every room aboard the Majesty twice, but we kept our magic bottled up inside of the master suite or on the sandy beaches. We even made love in the ocean one afternoon while we were supposed to be shallow water snorkeling. It started with me flashing my breasts underwater, and then of course he flashed me. So instead of looking at the Hawaiian sea life we admired each other and raced to the surface giggling and kissing, but beneath the water my legs were wrapped around his body. He pulled my bikini bottom to the side and let me have it.

It finally came down to our last night on the Hawaiian Islands. Bishop Ducreay made arrangements for us to spend our last night at a five star resort in Coconut Coast. When we arrived the clerk greeted us. "Mr. and Mrs. Flack, I presume?" she asked. "We've been expecting you."

The lobby was large and surprisingly didn't have a tropical theme, but a more elegant and formal look. It was very ritzy and I had to think twice to remember that I was in Hawaii and not at the hotel in Chicago. The ceiling was tall and vaulted, huge paintings with extravagant gold frames lined the walls, and live flowers adorned every table.

"My last night with my husband before Miami takes him away from me," I whispered in his ear.

"What do you mean?"

"Well, I know that you're a busy man with long days." I leaned into his chest. "You'll be pulled in all directions."

"But at the end of every long and busy day there is only one direction I'll be pulled in." He kissed my forehead.

"I'll welcome you with open arms." I tickled him.

"Ahem." The clerk cleared her throat to get our attention and gave us the key to our suite.

When he opened the door to the room I knew that he'd have to tear me away from it the next day. "Wow, this has to be about half the size of your house."

"Our house," he reminded me.

I ran to the balcony and looked out at the ocean. "I can't leave this place."

"Well don't." He gently grabbed my hand and led me back into the room, undressed me, laid my naked body on the bed, and with his body he showed me that long after the end of our honeymoon he'd continue to make love to me as though the wedding was over just hours before. He pressed his flesh into mine and intentionally stared into my eyes without saying a word, his body telling me all I wanted to know.

Afterward I snuggled closer to him. My eyelids struggled, but the power of gravity dragged them down. We woke up right as the sun was going down and in white terry cloth robes we sat on the balcony and watched the orange glow slowly sink behind a mountain far away.

"That was beautiful," he spoke. "But I'd choose to watch you instead of the sunset any day." If those were his last words to me I would be satisfied.

That night the hotel invited all of the guests to a luau and we attended. There were about fifty people all seated on mats in a large circle around a huge fire.

All of the natives were dressed in their traditional Hawaiian style garments, grass skirts, leis around their heads and neck, etc. They danced around and sung Hawaiian songs, and before long they were teaching us Hawaiian words and we were all singing along. Mountains of food were served to each individual in large bowls. The roast pig was served with chicken long rice, Hawaiian sweet potatoes, and poi. We washed it all down with pineapple calabash punch.

Later a native amazed us with his fire magic. He waved two wands of fire high above his head and caught them both between his teeth. Then he began juggling five wands while he danced wildly as another man played a drum and spat out Hawaiian chants. The entertainment became even more interesting as the hula dancers came out and began picking their partners out of the audience.

"You," a young Hawaiian girl pointed at Isaac.

He looked behind him to see who she could be talking to. "Me?"

"Yes, you." She grabbed his hand and pulled him to his feet.

He made his way to the center of the circle, where all of the other victims had been dragged. The drums started and the girls started doing the hula, shaking their waists and hips, showing Isaac and the other men how to do it. The drums stopped and started again and the men tried, but hilariously failed. Isaac had his hands high above his head and moved his waist the way little girls do when they're too skinny for the hula-hoop.

That night as I lay in his big, brown, beautiful arms and with bright mahogany eyes staring at me, he said, "Hey, you."

"Hi." I smiled but was in deep thought.

"Our last night," he reminded me.

My heart got heavy. "I know." I closed my eyes. "Let's stay,"

"okay," he joked.

"I'm serious." I pouted. Returning to Miami meant coming face-to-face with the new and uncomfortable drama in my life. In a few months my stomach would be showing and I'd have to tell people the truth if asked. "Going back is going to be hard." I squeezed my eyes shut so that the tears wouldn't fall. "I wouldn't know how to respond the first time someone walks up to me and says 'You and Reverend Flack didn't waste any time.' Or 'Does the Reverend want a girl or a boy?' What happens when channel seven news learns that a prominent attorney is on trial for rape? Do I tell my baby that his real daddy is his uncle too?"

"C'mon, baby." Isaac held me tighter. "It's going to be all right."

"This is going to be hard and embarrassing for me," I cried.

"But we're in this together." He touched my chin and moved my head upward to look directly into his face. "Remember that day at your mother's funeral when I told you that you don't have to ever do anything alone?" He smiled. "I meant that then and I still mean it today, you don't have to do anything by yourself."

I wanted to know. "What am I supposed to say to people when . . ."

"Nothing," he interrupted me.

"Do you know how embarrassing this is going to be?" I asked.

"Nothing that God blesses you with is anything to be embarrassed about." Moving his hand down my cheek, he said, "Do you know how many women wish they knew what it felt like to have a child grow inside of them?" He continued. "They'd trade anything to be in your shoes." He made sense, again. "Thalia, you have to thank God for all things. You can't be selfish; this goes beyond you and me." He touched my stomach. "This is the beginning of something God saw fit to bless us with."

"I know, but even if they think that it's yours they'll think that before we got married we . . ."

"What people think doesn't matter to me." He stopped me in mid-sentence. "People will always have something to say about you and me." He paused. "As a matter-of-fact they're already talking about how I'm old enough to be your daddy. They're already talking about how you're going to walk into Mount Pleasant and act like you've been saved for twenty years. They always thought that we were having sex." He shrugged his shoulders. "Let them talk."

It was the very beginning of the end of our honeymoon. The audacious mountains and waterfalls would soon be replaced with lawyers and doctors and tears . . . oh my.

Chapter 32

Touch Not My Anointed

We woke up at six the next morning and moved around the room depressed like it was our last day on earth. Shortly after eight we headed to a small private airplane that would take us from Kauai to Honolulu where we would catch our ten o'clock flight to Los Angeles. The small propeller plane took off and trembled, bounced, and rattled all the way to the big island. Thank God it was just a thirty-minute flight.

We made our flight to L.A. and were on our L.A. to Miami flight a little after 7:30 P.M. Pacific Time, and was scheduled to land in Miami at 5:40 A.M. After dinner was served almost all of the lights in the first class cabin were off. With my head rested on Isaac's shoulder, I closed my eyes and entered my comfort zone.

Hours later Isaac shook me. "Wake up baby."

"We're here?" I stretched.

"Yeah." A concerned look stole his face. "But something is wrong."

"Like what?" My eyes widened. "What do you mean?"

"We've been flying in circles for the past forty minutes," he looked at one of the flight attendants, "and the crewmembers seem worried."

I hoped for the best. "Maybe there's a lot of activity at the airport and we have to wait to land."

"Maybe." He tried to smile.

A minute later I reached for his hand as a bad feeling suddenly came over me. "Something *is* wrong."

The pilot came on the speakers. "Ah, ladies and gentlemen this is Captain Brick." He sighed. "You may have noticed we've made our descent into Miami." He paused. "We've had to circle the area three times in hopes of correcting a problem with the aircraft. The landing gear isn't cooperating." There were shouts and gasps throughout the plane as the captain continued. "As you know this is a cross country flight and fuel is limited, staying in the air any longer will only lead to bigger problems. Because an emergency landing seems unavoidable we have burned off enough fuel to avoid a highly combustible situation." He sounded scared. "I will work toward the best possible outcome." His last words were, "This is an emergency situation. Please follow the instructions of the flight attendants."

C'mon . . . you had to know that I was already in tears. I was terrified. Isaac grabbed both my hands and began to pray, and I joined him. We didn't care who was on the plane, it was time to call on the name of Jesus. We knew that Our Father was holding the plane in the palm of his hand and the only way He'd let us fall was if our work here on earth was done. We asked the Lord to cover us and all the passengers and crewmembers in His blood. We told the Lord that not our will, but His will be done, but if it wasn't His will we'd walk away more than conquerors and with testimonies for the rest of our lives. We ended by saying the Our Father Prayer loudly and many people joined in.

The flight attendants gave instructions that I didn't understand. The oxygen masks dropped from overhead and everyone grabbed one. I grabbed one and didn't know what to do with it. Isaac looked at me and said, "Everything is going to be fine."

"But the pilot said . . ."

"I heard what the pilot said, but I also heard what God said," Isaac informed me.

"I'm scared." Even though we had prayed, my flesh still wanted to make it off of the plane with breath in my body. But my soul was telling me that to be absent from this body was to be present with the Lord.

He squeezed my hand. "The Lord said 'touch not my anointed', Thalia." He brought me closer to him. "We're going to be fine." I made sure that our seatbelts were fastened and tried to feel peace but couldn't. Loud cries echoed throughout the plane. Everyone was frantic, but we couldn't do anything but sit and wait for whatever was next. "Why did this have to happen?" I asked.

He looked at me. "Remember when I told you that you never had to do anything alone?"

I said, "Yeah."

"Well, you're not alone." He almost smiled. "Whatever you are is what I'll be too after this is over."

I was confused. "What do you mean?"

"If you're alive then I promise you that I will be too."

"You promise?" I felt that a heart attack would be better than this torture.

"I'll always be right by your side. I won't leave you." He kissed me quickly.

My hands were trembling. "This can't be it," I cried.

Tears fell from his eyes too. "The Bible says that if we have faith the size of a mustard seed, we can move mountains." He stared at me. "So that means that if only two people are alive after this it'll have to be you and me." He touched my face. "Do you believe that?"

Regardless to all the wrong I've done in my life I always escaped unharmed and knew that it had to be God. When I got into situations I thought sure had me locked, I constantly got out of them with time to spare; it had to be Jesus that was the key. The many times I was close to throwing up my hands and begging for my life to be over, it had to be God that stopped me. And today I knew that the man sitting next to me had to be sent by God. "Yes, I believe."

"Flight attendants," the pilot came over the speakers again, "ladies and gentlemen, please brace yourselves; we are preparing for an emergency landing." He paused and sounded full of fright. "May God be with us all."

I wanted to look out of the window but didn't want to know how close we were to the ground. Isaac and I sat with our hands locked in the position the flight attendants urged us to get in earlier. The plane was dropping fast. I looked at Isaac. "I love you."

He smiled but as he opened his mouth time was no longer on our side. The plane rumbled, grinded, and seemed to explode. My world weakened into black and Isaac's hands slipped away from mine. Suddenly living without him wasn't living at all.

I opened my eyes and everything was bright white and I was confused. I took a deep breath of cold air and medicine . . . that hospital smell. I struggled to remember what went wrong. How did I get here? I remembered safely getting off of the whale watching boat. I didn't fall off of the horse and the driver made it safely to our various destinations. How did I get here? My mind wandered off.

"Lia." It sounded like Madi was singing. "Lia." Her voice flew over me? "Are you awake?" Her face was just inches from mine when I opened my eyes. I was lying in a hospital bed and I felt an IV in my arm. "Welcome back." She smiled.

"Hey." It was the only word I could get out.

"Lia, I'm here too." I saw Yvette for the first time in over a year. "We're going to get you through this."

I saw a male figure approaching but couldn't make out who he was until he touched my hand and spoke. "What's up, big sis?" It was my baby brother, Chance, with bloodshot eyes. But his honey brown chiseled facial features were still intact, complimented by his fresh cornrows.

"Hi, Chance," I spoke weakly. "Where is Mama?"

"You look good." Because he refused to answer me I knew that it was true. "How is your head feeling?" he asked as he kissed my forehead.

"I'm fine." I noticed the slight pounding in the back of my head when I first woke up, but I had other things to worry about.

It was like déjà vu. Didn't this happen already? Something wasn't real. Didn't Mama die months ago? Or did I just lay here and dream up an entire relationship, wedding, and honeymoon?

Chance sat on the bed. "So what are we going to do?" This was the first time I'd seen him cry since we were kids. "What are we going to do now?"

I couldn't answer him. "So I guess this isn't a bad dream after all, huh?" *It had to be a bad dream because I thought I had already lived all of this.*

"I thought it was too until I came home last night."

"Chance, I don't know." Tears slid down my cheeks. "I guess we've got to be strong."

"How?" he sobbed.

I was very weak but found the energy to strengthen him. "We have to find the strength that she taught us to have during tough times." It could only be the drugs allowing me to stay as calm as I was. Yvette walked over to console him, and then she followed him back to the window.

I was confused. I could tell everybody what they were going to do or say before they did or said it. Soon the doctor would come in and tell me that I had a concussion and blah, blah, blah.

I went along with the questions I knew I was going to ask next. "How long have I been here?" I asked Madi. "What happened?" I continued to question her. "Isn't the funeral over? Didn't you catch me with your dad and we got married?" I asked her, not caring if she thought I was crazy. I could always blame it on the medication later. "Didn't we go to Hawaii on our honeymoon?"

"Honeymoon?" Madi looked at me and laughed and was then joined by Chance and Yvette. They laughed so long and hard that the melody of their constant, "Ha, ha, ha, ha, ha, ha, ha-ing" rocked me to sleep.

The end . . . if you like your love served raw.
(Medium well lovers . . . read on)

I woke up, again, to find everything bright white cold and medicine smelling. How did I get here? I wanted real answers. Once again I remembered safely getting off of the whale watching boat. I didn't fall off of the horse and the driver made it safely to our various destinations. But I couldn't remember getting off of the plane; I didn't remember collecting my luggage. Suddenly I remembered the torture, agony, and darkness of the plane crash and began to scream.

Immediately the door to the room swung open and a nurse ran to my bedside. "Mrs. Flack, Mrs. Flack, calm down." She tried to hold me back against the bed. "Calm down, honey, everything is all right."

"No," I continued to scream. I remembered being lifeless and bruised. "No." I also felt the heat from a fire just a few feet away. "The plane," I looked around, "what happened?"

"You're okay." She spoke very peacefully. "You're off of the plane. You're fine. You're alive." She held me down. "Wiggle your toes." I did and they moved. "Now your fingers." They were intact. "See, you're in one piece." Her words comforted me, I was alive, and I could move. Now that we had all of that out of the way there was something that was even more important to me. "Where is he? How is my baby?" I asked.

She looked at me disappointedly and walked to the door beckoning someone to enter. A short stubby white man in a white lab coat walked in and she whispered something into his ear.

"Where is he?" That was all I wanted to know. "Where is my baby?"

"Mrs. Flack." The doctor approached the bed. "There was nothing we could do."

"What?" I screamed.

"I'm sorry," the nurse added.

"No," I cried and looked around the room. "He promised me," I pointed to myself, "that if I lived he'd live too." Life? Forget living if I can't live with him. "You can't tell me this," I yelled at the doctor and shook my head from side-to-side.

"Mrs. Flack," he sounded frustrated. "There was absolutely nothing that we could do. The injury sustained when the plane hit the ground was substantial." He added, "It's amazing that *you* made it."

**The end . . . if you like your love dished up
medium well.**
(Well-Done lovers . . . continue)

With my eyes closed and plastered with tears I heard the room door open and the doctor lowered his voice. "Can you please talk to her, she won't listen to me."

"Thalia, honey, they couldn't save the baby." I heard Isaac's voice. "They tried everything but . . ."

"Isaac?" I opened my eyes and saw him approaching me with a small bandage on his forehead. Tears of joy . . . oh my soul. "You said that he was dead." I looked at the doctor.

"No, ma'am. You asked about the baby." He probably wanted to slap me. "I was trying to tell you that we couldn't save the fetus, the impact was too severe, and it resulted in a miscarriage," the doctor said. "We'll leave you two alone for a while." He walked out of the room and the nurse followed.

"How could you think that I was dead?" He reached my bedside and grabbed my hand just as he had on the plane.

I was still crying as he helped me sit up. "I, I, don't . . ." I touched his face to make sure that he was real.

"Didn't I make you a promise?" he asked.

I answered softly. "Yes."

He lowered the rail to my hospital bed and sat facing me. "I'll never leave you." He pulled me into an embrace and I wept like a baby. "Now, before I was rudely interrupted by the plane crash," he chuckled, "I was about to say that I love you too."

"I love you, Isaac." I ran my hand over the small bandage on his head. "Are you all right?"

"Yes. A few stitches, but other than that I'm in one piece." He touched my stomach gently. "I'm sorry, Thalia." It wasn't until then that I realized what everyone was trying to get through to me. "I'm sorry."

I was given an easy way out and felt very guilty. "I didn't want the baby to die." He held me tightly. "I didn't want things to happen like this." The room went quiet for a few moments. Heaven had a new angel that I'm certain my mama was glad to see.

After a while I asked, "So what happened to the other people on the plane?"

"Well, no one died. Everybody got hurt though, some more serious than others, but we all made it out." He added, "It turned out that the back landing gear actually came halfway out right before landing, but that made all of the difference." He smiled. "Prayer changes things."

"Just have faith the size of a mustard seed." I smiled.

"We moved mountains." He kissed me. "We moved mountains."

He kicked off his shoes and crawled into the hospital bed with me. I fell back against his arm and draped the other across me.

The nurse walked in the room, looked at us, and smiled. "You're in bed with her again?" She walked over to the machine and changed the IV. As she walked out she turned to us. "I don't want any hanky panky from you newlyweds."

"You were in bed with me?" I asked.

"Yep, all last night, and a great portion of the morning." He smiled. "I told you I would never leave your side." He paused. "But the minute I run to the cafeteria you wake up screaming and thinking I'm dead." We laughed.

He *was* the best thing since sliced bread. He was the absolutely best thing that could ever happen to me. What would've happened had I not left Andre the day that I did and my path never crossed Isaac's the way that it had? It was all predestined, it was written, and it was sealed, it wasn't a coincidence. But iπt was, as my mama said, the perfect will of God.

I gazed into his eyes and repeated the Hawaiian words we had learned. "Aloha au ia oe."

"Jinx." He pinched my cheek softly. "Aloha au ia oe . . . you too."

The Real End
(Love . . . served just the way you like it!)